"Children need parents invested in their lives, Sheriff Garrett," Allison said.

"They need boundaries. They *ache* for boundaries. They need to be brought up, not just allowed to grow up."

The indictment had the ring of truth that hit Colt like a blow to the solar plexus. "Now, just you hold on a minute! You've gone too far."

"On the contrary," she retorted. "I've not gone far enough. Consider this a warning, Sheriff Garrett. Either you get your children in hand, or I am leaving Wolf Creek. And I expect you to have my spectacles that they destroyed replaced at your earliest convenience." With that, she slammed the door behind her.

Colt watched her stomp down the walk, conflicting emotions darting through him. Anger, guilt and worry for certain. And just a hint of something he couldn't put his finger on. It felt a little like grudging admiration.

Penny Richards
and
Dorothy Clark

Wolf Creek Father
&
Wooing the Schoolmarm

LOVE INSPIRED
INSPIRATIONAL ROMANCE

LOVE INSPIRED®
INSPIRATIONAL ROMANCE

Recycling programs for this product may not exist in your area.

ISBN-13: 978-1-335-47438-4

Wolf Creek Father & Wooing the Schoolmarm

Copyright © 2020 by Harlequin Books S.A.

Wolf Creek Father
First published in 2015. This edition published in 2020.
Copyright © 2015 by Penny Richards

Wooing the Schoolmarm
First published in 2012. This edition published in 2020.
Copyright © 2012 by Dorothy Clark

This edition published by arrangement with Harlequin Books S.A.

For questions and comments about the quality of this book,
please contact us at CustomerService@Harlequin.com.

Love Inspired
22 Adelaide St. West, 40th Floor
Toronto, Ontario M5H 4E3, Canada
www.Harlequin.com

Printed in U.S.A.

CONTENTS

Penny Richards has been publishing since 1983, writing mostly contemporary romances. She now happily pens inspirational historical romance and loves spending her days in the "past" when things were simpler and times were more innocent. She enjoys research, yard sales, flea markets, revamping old stuff and working in her flower gardens. A mother, grandmother and great-grandmother, she tries to spend as much time as possible with her family.

Books by Penny Richards

Love Inspired Historical

Wolf Creek Wedding
Wolf Creek Homecoming
Wolf Creek Father
Wolf Creek Widow
Wolf Creek Wife

Love Inspired

Unanswered Prayers

Visit the Author Profile page
at Harlequin.com for more titles.

WOLF CREEK FATHER

Penny Richards

And be ye kind one to another,
tenderhearted, forgiving one another,
even as God for Christ's sake hath forgiven you.
—*Ephesians* 4:32

This book is for Colt Garrett Cleaves,
my redheaded, never-walk-when-you-can-run
daredevil, two-year-old great-grandson, whose
infectious smile and cheerful disposition light up
everyone's world. Love you bunches, baby boy!

Chapter One

Wolf Creek, Arkansas—1886

Sheriff Colt Garrett sat behind the desk that faced the jail's front door. His chair was cocked back on two legs and his booted feet rested on the desk's scarred top. Hands laced behind his head, he stared in moody contemplation at the rough-sawn wood of the ceiling.

He was in the doldrums and his life was in a rut. Ever since Ellie Carpenter had told him there was no sense in taking their fledgling relationship any further than the friendship they shared, his life had settled into a grating sameness. A few words and *poof!* Another potential wife was gone, a reminder that change could happen fast and without warning, something he'd forgotten in the years since his wife, Patrice, had been taken from him.

Though he'd be the first to admit that he was not suffering from a broken heart over Ellie's rejection, he'd looked forward to the time he spent with her. Now his days had settled into boring predictability. He felt like some of the older folks in town must feel. They had their set routines and heaven help anyone who disrupted them. Except Colt wished something *would* happen to shake up the even tenor of his days. He came to work, ate lunch at home, the café or Hattie's, and then went home, slept and repeated the sequence day after day.

There hadn't even been any major crime lately to take his mind off things—not that he was complaining about that. The robberies he'd dealt with in the spring had seen one of his friends injured and another wrongly incarcerated. No, Wolf Creek didn't need any more crime. It was just that he was lonesome, as lonesome as the rain crow outside his open window sounded.

He hated going home and having no one to share the ups and downs of his day with except a couple of kids. Not that he didn't love them. He did. But he wasn't too proud to admit that he not only wanted a wife, but also needed one. His kids needed a mother. Cilla was growing up, and more and more Colt felt that a woman's influence was essential. What did he know about young girls on the verge of womanhood?

Brady needed a mom to kiss his cuts and scrapes, and he himself…well, he was tired of trying to deal with problems he had no earthly idea how to solve, so he supposed he could add that he was an ineffective father to his general misery.

He wanted to hold hands with a woman as they walked along Wolf Creek. Wanted to have someone listen as he talked about his day, and he wanted to hear about hers. He wanted someone next to him at night. He wanted a wife.

Since taking the sheriff's position more than a year ago, he'd courted a few of the town's single ladies, but the relationships had reached a certain point and fizzled out, and pickings were mighty slim in a town the size of Wolf Creek.

To top it all off, Ellie had flat-out told him that part of his problem was that whenever he showed interest in anyone, his two children launched an all-out campaign to sabotage the courtship. She'd been the recipient of some of their ploys, and that, along with her own reasons for not becoming more involved, had ended that!

He was so caught up in his unhappiness that the turning of the doorknob didn't register. Not until the sound of the door slamming and someone stomping across the room penetrated his reverie did he lower his arms and his gaze to see what was afoot.

He was shocked to see Brady and Cilla's teacher bearing down on him, her bosom heaving as if she'd run for several blocks. Miss Grainger's sassy little chipped-straw hat sat cockeyed on her head, and a lone fabric rose dangled over one eye. Her freckled face was as red as the hair scraped back into a severe bun atop her head. One curling, recalcitrant strand trailed down one cheek and onto her shoulder. She was squinting at him as she neared the desk, but even though her eyes were narrowed to mere slits, there was no mistaking the fury blazing there.

What now? Putting on his most professional mien, Colt swung his feet to the floor and sat up straight, as befitting his station. He offered her a friendly smile, which fled when the usually polite teacher slapped something onto the desk with a gloved hand. He stared down at the mangled item. Hmm. Gold wire and a round piece of glass with a webbing of cracks that looked as if a spider had been plying its skill.

He glanced up at the squinting Miss Grainger and

back at the object. Glasses! He was looking at a pair of beyond-redemption eyewear. The metal frames were crunched, one lens was cracked and the other missing completely.

He was about to ask her what on earth had happened when a familiar feeling sent his stomach into a sickening lurch. His mind whispered that while he might not know *what* had happened, he was pretty sure he knew *who* had done the deed.

"Well?" the teacher snapped. "Aren't you going to say something?" Her usual warm contralto was shrill with outrage.

Resisting the urge to bury his face in his hands, Colt looked up at her with a puzzled expression as fake as the roses adorning her bedraggled headpiece.

"Uh, what happened to your glasses?" he managed to say, after swallowing a lump the size of Texas.

The petite, plump teacher placed her palms flat on the desk and leaned toward him, her crocheted reticule dangling from her wrist. "Your children happened!" she spat out. "They accosted me!"

Colt's heart sank, but he sat even straighter. This young woman—obviously too young and inexperienced to be in charge of a classroom of children—had just accused his two offspring of a disgraceful act. Parental outrage kicked in, erasing the fact that Miss Grainger had only confirmed his own suspicion that Brady and Cilla were responsible for the damage he was looking at. Never mind their guilt or innocence. This woman had verbally *attacked* his children! Flesh of his flesh. Blood of his blood. It would not do. It would not do at all.

"Perhaps you should explain yourself, Miss

Grainger," he suggested through clenched teeth. "Tell me what happened to put you in such a snit."

"Snit? *Snit?*" Her eyes widened and her voice climbed at least two octaves. Then she squeezed her eyes shut, drew herself up to her full height—all of five feet and maybe an inch or two if he had to guess—and took a deep breath, trying to regain control of her emotions and her temper.

When she opened her eyes, it was a toss-up as to whether it worked or not. The heat of battle still smoldered there.

"By all means, Sheriff," she said in a well-modulated, low-pitched voice, taking care to enunciate each word with utmost care. "I am in a *snit,* as you put it, because I was assaulted by your...your hooli—" Her mouth snapped shut and she pressed her lips together to keep from crossing the invisible line of civility. "Your *children* in the mercantile."

Colt bolted to his feet, mimicking her stance. He leaned across the expanse of the desk, his tawny eyes as narrow as hers as they faced each other almost nose to nose. He was a tall man, with more than enough muscle to make most men back down, and he possessed a ruthless expression he could muster in a heartbeat. Many a lawbreaker and bully had been known to tremble before the combination.

Pint-size Miss Grainger didn't budge an inch.

"Now see here!" he growled. "Those are pretty harsh words. How can two kids, age seven and twelve, *assault* a grown woman?"

Still regarding him through narrowed eyes, she spluttered, "Brady...*p-pushed* me."

Was it Colt's imagination or was there a hint of trembling in her voice?

"Your children, sir, are a menace to polite society, and I begin to fear that much of the fault must be laid at your feet."

"My fault?" Colt exploded. He told himself that his thunderous response was a normal reaction to this…this mousy little…*twit* speaking about his precious children in such a derogatory way. Miss Grainger's eyes widened in sudden fright and her face paled, making her freckles stand out against the chalky whiteness. Colt suspected he'd overreacted.

Not very professional, he chided himself silently as they stood glaring at each other. He'd always prided himself on his professionalism, but this woman rubbed him the wrong way. Always had, though he had no reason why.

Okay, Colt. No more yelling. He had a reputation to maintain, after all. But dagnabbit, it was a blow to his image that she stood there so defiant and unafraid. He decided to try "the scowl" once more.

He folded his arms across his chest and fixed her with another intense look. As he let his gaze bore into hers he couldn't help noticing that her eyes, an unusual sherry-hued brown, were set beneath delicately shaped eyebrows a couple of shades darker than her hair and framed by thick, curly lashes. The hazy, almost unfocused softness he saw in them belied her anger, and went a long way toward cooling his.

She licked her lips in a nervous gesture, drawing his gaze to her mouth. Funny. He'd never noticed just what a nice mouth she had, maybe because more often than not her lips were pressed into a prim, no-nonsense line.

Now, all moist and soft-looking, she gave the impression of a woman who had just been well and soundly kissed, though it was hard to imagine any man being interested enough in the fiery-haired, fiery-tempered teacher to do so.

Colt reined in his thoughts. No way did this termagant have any softness. Kissing her would be like kissing a board. No, a wildcat, maybe. He gave his head an imperceptible shake and straightened, breaking the strange spell that seemed for a moment to bind them.

In response, she blinked and squared her shoulders, drawing attention to the rows of ruffles marching down the front of her pale yellow shirtwaist, intended no doubt to disguise her plumpness.

"Yes, um, your fault," she reiterated, but she sounded vague, as if she'd lost her train of thought. Then she raised her chin, mustering her indignation once more. "As I have said on more than one occasion, your children are out of control. I have requested time and again that you do something about it, but this time I demand that you take them in hand."

The words themselves condemned and challenged, but her voice seemed to have lost some of its sharpness. She *had* told him more than once that Brady and Cilla were disruptive in school. Now with Ellie's newest accusations echoing through his mind, he realized it was time he stopped delaying the talk he should have had with them long ago and get to the bottom of things. Just one more thing a woman would be much better at handling.

Still, it didn't sit well that she'd gone from asking to demanding that he take charge of his children, but it was plain to see that there was no getting around this latest transgression with one of his glib apologies and a promise to "take care of it." He sighed and waved a hand toward the chair across from him.

"Have a seat, Miss Grainger," he offered, struggling to make his tone professional and conciliatory. "I need to hear your version of what happened before I decide on a course of action."

Regarding him with more than a little suspicion, she perched on the chair's edge, almost as if she were readying herself to jump up and flee should the need arise. Her back was ramrod-straight, and her rounded chin was lifted to an angle just shy of haughty. Her gloved hands clutched the small drawstring purse resting in her lap.

Colt took his own chair, pressed the tips of his fingers together and, resting his elbows on the wooden arms of the chair, pressed his tented fingers against his lips while he regarded her with an expression of polite inquiry.

"Why don't you start at the beginning, Miss Grainger," he suggested, happy to hear that he sounded more or less like his usual controlled self.

Looking a bit taken aback by the sudden change in his attitude, Miss Grainger blinked again, cleared her throat and began with a bit of hesitation. "I, uh, went into the general store to pick up the Earl Grey tea Mr. Gentry had specially ordered for me."

Tea! What sort of red-blooded American drank tea instead of coffee? Colt wondered. He managed to hold back a disgusted snort—just. Still, he noticed that she, too, sounded more like the concerned schoolteacher he'd dealt with so often the previous school year. He rotated his hand at the wrist, indicating that she should continue.

"I saw Brady and Priscilla at the counter," she told him, leaning forward. "They seemed to be trying to decide what kind of candy they wanted. I smiled at them and asked Brady how his summer reading was going and if he thought it was helping him be better prepared when school took up again."

Colt felt a jolt of guilt. Brady was falling further and further behind in all his subjects, and Miss Grainger seemed to think it was because his reading wasn't up to snuff. She'd called Colt to a meeting before school let out, suggesting that he not only encourage his son to read during the summer, but also that Colt spend time each day working on it with him.

Brady had been furious. So had Colt. When he'd expressed his displeasure to Ellie and suggested that perhaps her sister wasn't the teacher everyone thought she was and that maybe she was picking on Brady, Ellie had told him in no uncertain terms that her youngest sibling was very qualified and pointed out that the suggestion had nothing to do with "picking" on anyone. Instead, it demonstrated her concern over Brady's continued lack of progress.

Put in those terms, Colt had bowed to the teacher's wisdom. Now, faced with the upstanding Miss Grainger and the look of expectancy on her face, he realized that he'd been more than a little lax carrying out her request. His only excuse was that Brady's reading was pure torture for them both, not something he wanted to do at the end of a hard day. It was the sort of thing a wife should contend with.

If he had a wife.

When he made no comment, she continued. "Brady became very…agitated and told me he hated reading, and that it was summertime and he had no intention of doing schoolwork when he was supposed to be having time off from it. I suggested that it was for his good and explained that reading can be very pleasurable. I told him that when a person reads he can go anywhere, be anyone and do anything within the pages of a book."

"And?"

"He told me that if it was so much fun, for me to do it, and he wished that *I* would go somewhere and not give him any more grief."

Colt dragged a palm down his cheek.

"Since it was clear that I was getting nowhere with him, I told him that his attitude was very disappointing, said goodbye to him and Priscilla and walked away. As soon as my back was turned, he raced out from behind a row of shirts, screaming something about always disappointing people, and flung himself at me."

Colt stifled a groan. Though Brady did have a temper when he was riled, it was hard to imagine him actually *attacking* someone. Surely Miss Grainger was exaggerating.

"I wasn't expecting to be assaulted," she said, the look in her eyes suggesting that her temper just might be on the rise again. "I lost my balance and fell to the floor. My head just missed a counter, but I fear my hat was not so lucky. It was knocked off in the fall, and the hatpin almost ripped the hair from my head."

So that was why the strand of hair was hanging loose!

"My spectacles fell off, too."

Her voice rose as she listed her grievances. She held

her palm toward him, showing a tear in her glove. "If I weren't wearing gloves, I'd have splinters in my hands from trying to catch myself. As it is, one of them is ruined."

Colt ignored her ruined glove. His attention was caught by the anger that had returned to her eyes during her recounting of the story. This newest fiasco was worse than he'd imagined, but how could he be sure she wasn't embellishing the tale for her own benefit?

"And where was Cilla while all this was happening?"

"Standing to the side smiling, as if the whole thing were vastly amusing. Then she walked over as if she planned to help me up and deliberately stepped on my glasses *and* my hat. It was new," she added, almost as an afterthought.

Whoa, now! Colt knew his kids could be ornery. They were not the kind of children who were seen and not heard, and they were certainly not the kind adults seemed to find endearing, but these accusations were beyond anything he'd been told before.

Talking back and playing practical jokes on occasion was one thing. Not good habits, to be sure, but still a far cry from the physical harm of which Miss Grainger was accusing them. Colt clenched his teeth, a muscle in his cheek knotting as his own resentment mounted.

"Now see here, Miss Grainger," he said, leaning forward and pinning her with another fierce frown. "Those are pretty severe allegations. How can you be so sure that what Cilla did was deliberate? Did you stop and consider that maybe it was an accident?"

Miss Grainger looked positively incensed. "Not deliberate?" she cried, leaping to her feet. "When a person looks you in the eye and saunters along as if they haven't a care in the world, and makes certain that you can see everything they are doing, I would say it is deliberate. So, severe or not, my accusations are true, Sheriff Garrett. What happened was in no way an accident."

Colt pushed to his feet. Once again, they glared at each other over the expanse of his desk. "Maybe you just don't like my children," he said.

"And maybe you are so busy making excuses for them and being the big bad sheriff and single man about town that you are blind to their faults. Children need parents invested in their lives, Sheriff Garrett. They need boundaries. They *ache* for boundaries. Perhaps you should try being a father instead of a friend. They need to be brought up, not just allowed to grow up."

The indictment had the ring of truth that hit Colt like a blow to the solar plexus. "Now, just you hold on a minute! You've gone too far."

"On the contrary," she retorted. "I've not gone far enough. Consider this a warning, Sheriff Garrett. Either you get your children in hand, or I am leaving Wolf Creek."

"What?"

"L-e-a-v-i-n-g. I'd rather resign my teaching position than deal with your children for another year." She stalked to the door, wrenched it open and turned in the aperture. "I expect you to have my spectacles replaced at your earliest convenience. And a new hat and pair of gloves would not come amiss."

With that, she slammed the door behind her.

Colt watched her stomp down the walk, conflicting emotions darting through him. Anger, guilt and worry for certain. And just a hint of something he couldn't put his finger on. It felt a little like grudging admiration.

* * *

Shoulders back, chin high, Allison stalked down the street and turned the corner. Only when she was confident she could no longer be seen from the sheriff's office did she release the fury, uncertainty and misery that had driven her to a showdown. Waves of self-reproach swept through her.

With a little groan of shame, she ripped off her damaged glove and used it to blot at the tears that slipped down her overheated cheeks. She had acted in the most amateurish way possible. Never in her life had she talked about and accused children the way she just had! The fact that what she'd said was true did not give her license to indulge in such an unladylike, unprofessional and *peevish* manner.

A sound that resembled a strangled laugh escaped her. Dear sweet heaven. Had she really left Colt Garrett with the ultimatum that he gain control of his children or she would quit her teaching position? She'd been fortunate to land her position in Wolf Creek, and she had no idea where she would go or what she would do if the sheriff called her bluff.

Never mind calling your bluff. When he tells the mayor what happened and word gets around town, you won't have to quit—you'll probably be fired. The thought was like a slap in the face. What parent would want a woman with so little control instructing the town's children? She gnawed on her lower lip and dabbed again at her eyes. There was no helping it. She must confess to the mayor what she'd done before he heard it elsewhere.

Her shoulders slumped in dejection. She liked it here. She didn't want to leave, though she'd spent much of the past few years moving from place to place after begin jilted by her lifelong love. Growing up a pleasingly plump redhead with freckles had not been easy, not when her sisters, Belinda and Ellie, were both not only pretty, but also sweet and good. Though everyone said Allison was just as delightful and nice, when compared her to her beautiful sisters, she had always come up short, feeling as if she were somehow a shoddy replica, second-rate and inadequate.

Her sisters were exotic hothouse orchids; she was the spinster, the wallflower—her name for herself— the one who went unnoticed or was asked to do the tedious tasks no one wanted to undertake. She was the one asked to watch the children while others indulged in the entertaining activities. She was the one to pick up the slack wherever or whatever it happened to be.

She found scant consolation in the knowledge that the dictionary said that the upright, woody stems of wallflowers gave them strength, resiliency and tenacity, enabling them to thrive on cliffs, rocks and walls. Though many would consider those wonderful traits, they were hardly the qualities men found attractive.

Ellie and Belinda were beautiful; Allison was robust. Ellie and Belinda were accomplished in many areas; Allison was adequate. Except when it came to her vocation. At teaching, she excelled.

In fairness, her sisters had done their utmost to try to make up for the unfair comparisons, and Allison felt no hard feelings toward either of her siblings...at least not once she gained adulthood and was able to put her feelings of inferiority into proper perspective.

Jesse Castle had been her anchor, her friend, her playmate, her other half since they were children. A bit of a bookworm himself, he'd understood and accepted and loved her for who she was, not for how she looked. They'd been just two months from their wedding day nearly ten years ago, when he'd taken her aside and told her that he was terribly sorry, that he loved her dearly, but that he was not *in love* with her. He had fallen for pretty, vibrant Callie Boxer, who'd come to spend the summer with her grandmother. He wanted to make his life with her.

Allison hadn't been just shocked; she'd been devastated. Shamed. Embarrassed. Since childhood, everyone had taken it for granted that she and Jesse would marry and spend the rest of their lives living out a happily-ever-after fairy tale.

Feeling his rejection as if it were the weight of the world, she had cried the entire summer and shut herself off from everyone but her family. She'd spent her time at the park or a hidden corner of the parlor reading Miss Jane Austen's novels over and over—which infuriated Belinda, who claimed doing so was comparable to wearing a hair shirt.

In many ways, the stories were painful to read, but at the same time a tiny part of her battered heart clung to the nebulous hope that perhaps someday she might find the happy ending she so desired.

Feeling that her only chance at marriage was gone and harboring the outlandish notion that she could run from her heartache and shame if she only ran far enough, Allison mapped out a course for her life that would satisfy her as well as give her something at which she excelled. Something that would enable her to provide for herself and thus to need no man.

She would become a teacher. The best teacher ever.

Through the years she had moved from job to job and town to town in an effort to put distance between herself and her heartache, only to realize that it followed her wherever she went.

She hadn't exactly blamed God for what had happened, but she wasn't on the best of terms with Him, either. Then, a couple of years ago, Belinda had grown weary of Allison's refusal to let go of the past and had taken her to task for continuing to *wallow,* as she so indelicately phrased it, in her unhappiness.

She'd said that yes, Jesse was a nice enough young man, but he had not been perfect, nor had God thrown away the mold after creating him. There were thousands of men out there just as kind, just as understanding, and equally willing and capable of loving her. And, she'd added, there was one special man out there who would sweep her off her feet and make her forget Jesse Castle ever existed. Furthermore, Belinda told her in no uncertain terms, Allie should be thankful that she had not married Jesse and *then* discovered that he didn't love her as he should.

Belinda also lectured at length about how Allison clung to her grief, using it as a shield to protect her from further hurt, and how she refused to allow the Lord to work in her life to ease the pain of her loss and bring her peace.

Belinda believed that Allison had adopted the notion that if she didn't allow joy and happiness into her life, it could not be snatched away from her again. Her sister had finally convinced Allison that she should embrace life and everything it had to offer, even if it did cause occasional hurt. Experiencing down times, sorrow and pain, only made the good times sweeter.

Allison had taken her sister's loving counsel to heart. With much prayer and the Lord's help, she had changed her attitude, not only about embracing life, but also with regard to her own shortcomings. She took inventory of herself and realized that while she was no great beauty, she had nice, though unremarkable, features and was at the very least passably nice-looking. There was not much she could do about the color of her hair or its unmanageable curls, but she could brush and pin it into subjection. She was intelligent. Kind. Patient. And loving.

She'd made peace with the possibility that perhaps it was not her lot to marry and have children of her own, but as a teacher she had the opportunity to mold and influence dozens of young lives. She felt she was on her way to contentment at last.

Then, just over a year ago, her prayers had brought her to Wolf Creek. She was thrilled to be near her middle sister once more, and for the first time in years, she was enjoying life. She loved the rolling hills around her, loved her work, and she felt as if she'd made life-long friends. Abby and Rachel Gentry, Gracie Morrison and Lydia North had become her closest friends. They shared fears, confidences and hopes and dreams. Widowed or spinsters, or like Ellie, uncertain of their status in life, their friendship benefited them all.

And now she might have ruined everything.

Realizing she had arrived at the mayor's office, Allison paused at the door, her heart heavy with remorse and humiliation. Taking a deep breath, she stepped through Homer Talbot's door before she lost her nerve.

The mayor started to rise but stopped halfway out of his chair. Even through the fog of her nearsightedness, she could see the shock on his face. Remembering that she must look as if she'd been dragged through a knothole backward, she lifted a hand to tuck the hair behind her ear and push back the drooping rose. Then she attempted to smile without bursting into tears.

"Hello, Miss Grainger," the mayor said, rising fully and eyeing her from head to toe. The expression in his eyes was wary, but his tone friendly. "What can I do for you this fine summer day?"

Allison drew herself up to her full five feet, one inch. "There was an…incident with the Garrett children at the mercantile earlier, and I wanted to come and tell you the straight of it before you hear something that isn't true."

"I see," he said with a frown. "Have a seat."

Half an hour later, she stepped inside Ellie's open door and let her gaze move around the café. Without her glasses, everything looked soft and fuzzy, as if she were peering through a fog. She squinted in an effort to bring things into focus, but even without her glasses it wasn't hard to spot familiar faces. Mousy Grace, plain and tall and all angles with a smile to rival an angel's, and Ellie, exquisitely proportioned and with a face to match, were engaged in a serious conversation at the back of the dining room. Almost as one, they looked up and saw her in the doorway.

"You've already heard."

"Sarah VanSickle was here," Ellie said, moving toward her with open arms and an expression of sympathy.

Allison's mouth twisted into a wry smile. "So much for Sarah's vow not to indulge in any more hurtful gossip."

"Oh, she wasn't really gossiping," Gracie clarified, her pale blue eyes serious. Gracie never said a harsh word about anyone. "It's just that she saw the whole thing and she said that those children needed a woman to take them in hand and one to take the sheriff to task, since it appears he has little control of them. She said it's a wonder you weren't really hurt."

"*Are* you all right?" Ellie asked, holding Allison at arm's length.

"I'm not sure." Sudden weariness washed over her. The emotion that had carried her through the past hour had drained her and she wanted nothing more than to go back to her little three-room house across the railroad tracks and crawl into bed. Maybe the whole messy ordeal would turn out to be nothing but a bad dream.

Drawing a fortifying breath, she pulled off her other glove and shoved both into her reticule. "I think I just sabotaged my future here."

"What?"

"How?"

Both Ellie and Grace spoke at once. Ellie pushed Allison toward a table and called for her daughter, Bethany, to bring her aunt a cup of coffee.

The fortifying beverage delivered, Ellie said, "Tell us everything."

"I went to speak to the sheriff about what happened."

"What did he say?" Gracie asked, a frown furrowing her high forehead. She was the worrier of the group.

"He said a lot of things, among them that I was in a snit and that maybe I didn't like his children." Recalling the menace he'd radiated as he glared at her across his desk, Allison gave a little shudder. "He'd already accused me of picking on Brady."

"What? When?" Gracie asked.

"At the end of the year when I suggested that he and Brady work on his reading throughout the summer."

"Tell us what happened," Ellie commanded in a gentle tone.

They listened as Allison related her encounter with the sheriff. As she talked, Ellie's smile grew broader.

"It isn't funny," Allison said after she wrapped up the tale. "I've already talked to Homer, who was none too pleased."

"What on earth did you tell him?" Ellie asked.

"Well, he already knew I'd spoken with the school board about the children on numerous occasions. I'd assured him I'd discussed things many times with the sheriff but that nothing changed.

"Then I told him what happened at the store. He seemed shocked, and when I told him I'd confronted the sheriff, and that he and I had…words, Homer was not happy. I may lose my job over this." She groaned and shook her head. "I can't believe I lost control that way. I *never* fly off the handle like that."

"No one is perfect," Gracie said. "And maybe if the mayor talks to Colt, he'll be forced to do something about Cilla and Brady's behavior."

"I pray you're right."

"Well, I'm glad you told Colt just how dreadful his kids can be," Ellie said. "I told him as much, too. And having been a victim myself, I can only imagine what you've been dealing with the past year. I dread the thought of coping with those two all day."

"Surely they can't be that bad," Gracie said. "I mean, I've heard rumors, but…"

Ellie pressed her pretty lips together to keep from

saying something she shouldn't, and gave Allison a pointed look.

"Well, Priscilla disrupts class at least two or three times a day, and must be either stood in the corner or given extra work to do. She is sarcastic, argumentative, and at times her behavior verges on outright defiance."

"Never say it!"

Allison nodded. "In general, Brady is a sweet enough child, but he falls more and more behind every day, since he can't seem to grasp any part of the concept of reading. As you know, if you can't read, you have trouble with other subjects and even some mathematical problems."

"That's true," Gracie said, frowning.

"When I comment on an incorrect answer, he becomes resentful and belligerent and often refuses to do anything I ask of him for the remainder of the day. He'd rather stand in the corner than comply with any request I might make."

"What does the sheriff say?" Gracie asked.

"That he'll take care of things, but he doesn't."

"The thing is," Ellie chimed in, "Colt is smart, dedicated and honorable. He really cares about people and he's very hardworking, but when it comes to those kids, he's a total failure. They rule the Garrett roost."

Allison nodded in agreement. "I told him he needed to take more control." She made a disgusted face. "He didn't appreciate it much."

"Well, if they're as bad as all that, don't you think someone should try to find out why?" Gracie said, looking from one friend to the other.

A little surprised by the logic of the comment, Allison and Ellie stared at each other. Leave it to Gracie to cut to the chase.

"Let's face it, men don't relate to children the way women do. Don't you imagine it's been hard for them growing up without a mother?" Gracie asked, ever the one to see the other side.

"I suppose so," Ellie conceded.

Allison shifted in her seat, as a wave of shame and failure swept through her. "I'm ashamed to say that I've never given it more than passing thought," she said. "I've been more concerned about their behavior and Brady's grades."

"I'm no alienist," Gracie said, "but I would venture to say that the reason they're so mean to the women Colt shows interest in is that they're afraid someone might come between them and their father."

"That doesn't make any sense," Ellie said at last. "They should know that he will love them no matter what."

"Actually, it does, Ellie," Allison said, acknowledging her own oversight and latching on to the levelheaded Gracie's theory.

"Well, why were they so terrible to you?" Ellie asked. "There's nothing going on between you and Colt."

Not that I wouldn't like there to be.

Without warning, the thought flashed through Allison's mind, and she stifled a little gasp of surprise. Now, where did that come from? Not once since Jesse had she felt any serious attraction to a man, and Colt Garrett was not the sort of man who could ever interest her!

"Oh," Gracie said. "You're right. Allison is their teacher, not the sheriff's lady love."

"Who knows what goes through the minds of children?" Allison said, warming to this new viewpoint. "Especially Sheriff Garrett's children. You could be onto something with the notion that they don't want anyone upsetting the status quo. I'm not sure children understand the different kinds of love or that it's possible to love more than one person."

She took a final sip of her cooling coffee and drew her purse closer, ending the conversation. "Homer said he'd think things over and decide on a course of action."

She pulled some coins from her purse to pay for the coffee, but Ellie pushed them aside. "It's on the house."

"Thank you. I'd better start pinching pennies since I may soon be without employment. You don't need a waitress, do you?" The expression in Allison's eyes belied the lightness of her voice.

"Not really," Ellie said with a laugh. She gave Allison's hand a pat. "I know you're worried, sister dear," she said, falling back on the childhood term for Allison. "I can't imagine it coming to that. Homer is one of your most loyal fans."

"Maybe so," Allison said, "but everyone knows that he's very pleased with Colt as our sheriff, too."

Chapter Two

Colt scraped the fingers of both hands through his light brown, sun-bleached hair, rested his elbows on the desktop and clutched his aching head. The minute Allison Grainger was out of his sight, his anger had more or less dissolved. He resented her audacity, but he couldn't deny that what she'd said, combined with what Ellie had told him, brought sharp focus to something he'd known for a while: he had a problem.

He wasn't totally oblivious. He'd heard the whispers that accompanied the kids wherever they went. The people he considered true friends, like the Gentry brothers, had come straight out and told him pretty much what the teacher had—that he'd best get them in check before it was too late. As hard as it was to swallow, he knew they were all right. Something had to give. He didn't want Brady to be illiterate or Cilla to be a shrew. Patrice certainly hadn't been, and Colt didn't think he was too cantankerous…except maybe when he dealt with the oh-so-prim Miss Grainger.

Why was he such a hopeless parent? He loved his kids. Would die for them. He tried to balance his time at home with work and gave them pretty much whatever they wanted, but according to Miss Grainger, they wanted *boundaries*. In other words, rules. Oh, he'd made lots of rules through the years. The problem was that he was much better at enforcing the laws of the land than he was at enforcing his own regulations.

He admitted to being bad about threatening them with dire consequences if they misbehaved but not following through. He knew he was too lenient and should punish them when that happened, but the thought of them being unhappy was more than he could stand, especially since he was their only parent. He supposed that leniency was his way of trying to make up for the loss of their mother.

Patrice had died when Brady was born, forcing Colt to take on the role of both parents. His son had been reasonably easy until he started school, but as Miss Grainger had told him time after time, he had a problem learning, which frustrated Colt and made Brady angry. Too often that anger drove him to disobedience.

Cilla, just five when her mother died, was definitely Daddy's girl. Like her brother, she hadn't been much of a problem until she'd begun to grow up. In a lot of ways, she seemed too old for her twelve years, and in others she was very immature.

In recent months, her moods had begun to fluctuate from childlike joy to pouty moodiness. Colt knew enough about the fairer sex to know that it was because she was fast approaching the time when she'd become a woman in the truest sense of the word. He had no idea how to explain the physical and emotional changes she was going through, so he just ignored them—and her—as best he could until her disposition changed back to something he could deal with. It seemed that women were born knowing how to deal with those emotional things men were not so good at.

There were times, though, like today, when he was forced to face his shortcomings. When that happened, he tried to put himself in their place and imagine what it must be like to grow up without a mother to confide in, talk to or look up to.

Wallowing in self-pity wouldn't get him anywhere. The handwriting was on the wall. Looking the other way wouldn't work this time. He knew Homer Talbot thought Allison Grainger was tops when it came to teachers, so it made sense that he would not want to lose her, which meant Colt would have to take charge of his progeny at last.

How are you going to do that? You haven't been able to do it in seven years.

He had no earthly idea, but he thought he knew where to go to get some no-nonsense advice.

When Dan Mercer, Colt's deputy, returned from running some errands, Colt left the office in his care and went to get Ellie's take on things. Thankfully, the café was all but empty. Ellie was filling saltshakers. The expression on her face when she looked up told him she'd already heard the news.

"You've heard."

She nodded and gestured toward an empty table. "From several folks, actually, including Allison."

"Do you think she's telling the truth?" Colt asked as he pulled out a chair for her.

Ellie glared at him over her shoulder. "Her story matches Sarah VanSickle's."

Colt planted his hands on his hips and tipped his head back to stare at the ceiling.

"Sit," Ellie said.

He sat, and buried his face in his hands.

"Colt, look at me," she commanded, circling his wrists with her fingers and tugging his hands down. His troubled gaze found hers. "You have to know… even I've told you…that the kids are…less than angels."

A bitter laugh sputtered from his lips. "So it seems."

"Well, then, the time has come for you to do something about it."

"What? I don't have a clue about what needs to be done."

"Well, first you should stop letting them take advantage of you."

"How do you figure?" he asked, scowling.

It was Ellie's turn to laugh. "Everyone in town knows you're tough on criminals and soft on your kids."

His eyes widened in disbelief. That was exactly what he'd just been thinking. "So it's a topic of dinner discussions, is it?"

"You know as well as I do that everyone's circumstances are the topic of dinner discussions at one time or another," she said with a little shrug.

"I'm all they have," he said, as if that explained everything. "And they're all I have of Patrice. Priscilla still misses her mom, and I hate to make things tougher on her by—" he spread his hands in a vague gesture "—being too strict. And Brady has never known what it is to have a mom, and as his only parent, I don't want to be an ogre."

"And they instinctively know that and use it to their advantage."

"How could they know?"

"Children are like a wild animal stalking its prey," Ellie said with a wry smile. "They instinctively know the weakest link. Even Beth is a master of it. It's just a part of their makeup. I don't want to make you angry," she said, "but—"

"I have to get them under control," he said.

"Yes."

They sat in silence for several moments, while Colt digested the situation. It didn't sit well. "Your sister said she would give up her teaching position before she spent another year with them."

"She told me," Ellie said in a gentle voice. "She's a good teacher, Colt. A good person."

"If you say so."

Ellie smiled. "I do, and I think I'm in a position to know. Have you ever tried talking to Brady and Cilla about why they're so disruptive?"

"I've had talks about them not misbehaving, but no, I've never tried to get to the root of *why* they do it."

"Gracie has a theory," Ellie told him. "And both Allison and I think she's onto something. She believes they sabotage your associations because they don't want to share you. I think she's right."

"That's crazy," Colt said with a hint of irritation.

"Is it? I started thinking back over the past year, and every time you've shown interest in a woman, they've done something to ruin things."

It was true that something had gone wrong with each attempted relationship. Now, looking back, the kids *were* somehow the culprits in every case. Holly Jefferson. Leticia Farley. Jocelyn Cole. All of them had cried off, citing that they had too little in common and it would be silly to try to take things further. Rachel Stone was the exception. He and the lady doctor had soon realized that while they liked each other a lot, there was no romantic spark between them.

"If you plan to marry at some time in the future—"

"I do," he said.

"Then you'd better make it clear to the kids that marrying again is your intention no matter what they think, how they feel about the woman or if they approve."

"Isn't that being a bit insensitive to their feelings?"

"Do they care about yours?" Ellie retorted. She reached out and gave his hand a friendly pat. "I don't mean to sound cold, Colt. You should tell them that they must trust that you won't fall in love with someone who will mistreat them or you."

"I'd hope I'll be smarter than that."

"Allison made a good point, too."

A muscle in Colt's jaw knotted at the teacher's name. He wasn't sure he wanted to hear anything she had to say about children. "And what profound statement did Saint Allison contribute?"

Ellie gave him a strange look. "She pointed out that children don't always understand that you can love more than one person at a time," Ellie said, "or that there are different kinds of love."

Colt conceded that she had a point.

"The main thing to remember is that you're the adult. You set the rules and the tone from here on out. If they don't follow them, then there are consequences. And stick with those consequences!" she added, giving his hand a light slap. "Don't let them butter you up to get on your good side. Believe me, they might not like it now, but they'll thank you later."

Boundaries, again. He blew out a deep breath and said the word aloud. It tasted like ashes in his mouth.

"What?"

"Your sister claims that children need boundaries, that they ache for boundaries."

Ellie smiled. "She's right. They do."

"It's a tall order, Ellie," he said, rare uncertainty in his eyes.

"Perhaps," she agreed, nodding, "but there's far more to being a parent than doing your part in their conception. It means molding and shaping them into good people and productive citizens, and giving them the necessary skills to cope with whatever comes along. With God's help, you can do this."

God. Colt's relationship with the Almighty was a topic he didn't want to address. He'd once been a devoted Christian, but when God hadn't answered his prayers to spare Patrice, Colt had turned his back on everything spiritual, though he still tried to live a decent, honest life.

"Who would have believed I'd be raising a couple of kids alone when Patrice and I got married?"

Who would have thought that circumstance would force him to cross the boundary into a woman's role? But someone had to.

Colt thought about his conversation with Ellie all the way home. He had to admit that what she said made sense, and so did Gracie's theory about why the kids were so unkind to the ladies he'd courted. Ellie agreed with her sister's claim that children needed limitations, and as much as it galled him, and as uncertain as he was that he could set and maintain those restrictions, his gut told him they were right. He wanted to have children people liked, children whose behavior he could be proud of. It was no fun wondering when he would hear about another of their escapades.

He'd also talked with the young women he'd courted, and when pressed, they'd each acknowledged that Cilla and Brady were the real reasons behind their breaking things off.

The onus was definitely on him. It wouldn't be easy, and it wouldn't happen overnight, but he was nothing if not determined. Or maybe that was hardheadedness, something he'd passed on to his children.

Colt's gaze sought the small white house situated at the edge of town. Smoke billowed from the open parlor windows. A giant fist seemed to grab his heart. *Fire!* Gripped with sudden panic, he broke into a run, sorting impressions as he went. No tongues of flame licked at the curtains, and he didn't hear the pop and crackle of burning wood. The house didn't appear to be on fire, so what was going on?

Breathing heavily, he pulled open the screen door, flinging it against the outer wall and rattling the windows in their frames. A thick fog of smoke and the stench of charred bacon assaulted him. Narrowing his burning eyes and waving his hand in front of his face in a futile attempt to dissipate the acrid air, he made his way to the kitchen. A quick look around the room told him he'd been right. There was no fire. Thank heaven.

Cilla stood at the open back door, an old apron of Patrice's tied around her waist as she fanned the air with it, as if the feeble effort might clear the room faster. Brady stood bent over with his palms on his knees, hacking and coughing. A cast-iron skillet lay in the yard beyond the covered porch, where Cilla must have thrown it, its charred contents scattered about. The neighbor's mutt approached a piece of the bacon, nudged it with his nose, whimpered and backed away. Colt wondered if it was still hot or if even the dog found it unpalatable.

"What happened?" he asked, nearing the two culprits.

They both looked at him, smoke-induced tears streaming down their cheeks. "I was trying to fix you some supper," Cilla said, her blue eyes, so much like her mother's, filled with remorse and trepidation.

Newly aware of how they played on his sympathies, and with the unexpected declaration coming so close on the heels of his talk with Ellie, little warning bells began to sound inside his head. Why was Cilla attempting to cook when she seldom had before? Was this one of those attempts to "butter him up," as Ellie suggested?

"Why?" he asked, taking them each by the arm and ushering them out into the fresher air of the summer day.

Wide-eyed, Brady looked at Cilla, who was dabbing at her watering eyes with the hem of the apron. Colt waited.

Cilla finally looked at him, a limpid expression in her eyes. "I was going to fix you some bacon and pancakes since it's your favorite and you hardly ever have them."

Oh, yes. Definitely buttering him up. Colt hooked his thumbs in the belt loops of his denim pants. "That's mighty nice of you," he said, "but why today of all days? Are we celebrating something?" He looked from one child to the other with feigned nonchalance.

"Uh, no, not really. We just thought it would be a nice thing to do, since you work so hard and everything."

Never one to put off an unpleasant chore—unless it came to his children—Colt decided it was time to get on with it. No more dillydallying. After all, he was turning over a new leaf as a parent. "Then is anything wrong? Did something happen?" he asked with an inquisitive lift of his eyebrows.

Cilla stared into his eyes for long seconds, and turned to her brother with a sigh. "He knows, Brady."

"Who told you?" Brady demanded, whipping up a healthy indignation.

"Miss Grainger."

"That mean old tattletale!" Brady cried, his voice strident with outrage. Cilla gave an unladylike snort.

"Let's go sit under the oak tree," Colt said, gesturing toward the shaded area. "Maybe the house will air out enough to go back inside in a bit."

When they were settled beneath the gnarled limbs of the tree, Colt stretched out his long denim-clad legs and crossed them. Where should he start? He decided to approach the situation the way Patrice would have. The trouble was, he had no notion of how she might have handled things.

"It's way past time the three of us had a talk," he said, deciding to jump in feet first.

"About what?" Cilla regarded him with wide-eyed innocence.

Colt pinned her with a look that said without words that she knew what was coming. She dropped her gaze and plucked at the apron still tied around her waist.

"We need to talk about you and Brady and the fact that the two of you are gaining quite a reputation. And not a good one, I might add."

The children darted glances at each other.

"First let me explain that my position in town is an important one. It makes me look bad when the two of you are mixed up in one unpleasant incident after another."

"What does it mean that you look bad?" Brady asked.

"It means that the whole town thinks that I'm a bad father. They think I don't care about you enough to teach you how to behave, and that I'm allowing you to be hurtful, disrespectful and destructive."

"But you do care!" Brady cried.

"Well, you know it and I know it, but folks in town think I'm letting you grow up with no discipline and no instruction on how to be good people."

"That's silly!"

"Is it?" he challenged. "Actions speak louder than words, son, and all they know is what they see, which doesn't make any of us look good."

"How are we destructive?" Brady asked.

Colt looked directly at Cilla. "Miss Grainger's glasses are ruined. They can't be fixed, so she'll have to have new ones, and I'll have to pay for them."

Cilla's gaze dropped to the hands clasped in her lap.

"And her hat was ruined in the scuffle." He gave his daughter a look that said without words that he knew exactly how the hat had been damaged. "I'll have to repay her for it and a new pair of gloves. The worst thing, though, is that she might have been hurt badly if her head had struck the corner of the counter."

No one spoke for a while. Finally, Colt asked, "Do either of you even know *why* you do what you do?"

Cilla and Brady exchanged hangdog looks.

Cilla finally spoke. "When you come home at night and you're in the same room with us, it doesn't feel as if you're really here," she said, staring at the hands twisting in her lap. She glanced up and met his troubled gaze. "Sometimes it's like you've gone off in your mind somewhere. When you scold me for something, you pay attention to me," she confessed, looking up at last. "For a little while, anyway."

Colt felt a stabbing pain in the vicinity of his heart. This was much worse than he'd thought. He attempted a light tone that fell far short of the mark.

"See? That's what I mean. Everyone in town is right. I *don't* pay enough attention to you. I need to change that." He looked at his son. "Brady, why did you shove Miss Grainger?"

Brady stuck out his lower lip.

"Did she do something to upset you?"

"She said she was disappointed because I haven't been reading this summer."

"And so you pushed her?" Colt asked in an incredulous tone.

Brady nodded.

"Well, she should be disappointed," Colt said, though the admission galled him no end. "I told her that I'd work with you on your reading this summer, and I haven't been very consistent with it. It's something we need to fix."

"Pa! It's summer," the boy wailed.

"I understand that, but Miss Grainger is concerned about you falling behind in school. She wants your reading to improve so all your grades will get better. She told me that you get disrespectful when she tries to explain things to you, and you don't listen. True?"

Brady nodded. "I don't like it when she points out my mistakes in class. Everyone stares at me."

Colt racked his brain for what their mother might have told them. "Behaving badly doesn't change things," he said at last. "You still feel bad and Miss Grainger feels frustrated. She has a job to do, and she's doing her best to help you. If you don't do your part, how can you expect to do better?"

The boy shrugged.

He turned to Cilla. "What's your excuse for jumping into the fray?"

Her shoulders drooped. "I don't know!" she cried. "I just get really angry sometimes, and I don't have anyone to talk to about how I feel."

Colt started to say that she had him, but they'd already established the fact that he wasn't really there for her. "Explain what you mean," he said.

Cilla gave a shake of her head, the loose dark curls, so like her mother's, bouncing with the movement. "The girls at school talk about how they do things with their mothers, and it makes me sad and angry because I don't have a mother to do things with. And Miss Grainger makes me madder than almost anyone, because she's so sweet and happy all the time. She's never sad. She never gets mad. Sometimes I just want to see if I can make her lose her temper."

Colt could attest that the pint-size schoolmarm had a temper to equal anyone's, but had learned to handle it… for the most part. Feeling like a total failure, he found himself wishing he'd never opened this Pandora's box, but he knew he couldn't stop now. There was still a lot to get into the open, a lot to understand.

"One more thing, and then we'll talk about how we're going to change things."

"Sir?" they both said, sitting straighter.

"What about the bad things you've said and done to the ladies I've been squiring around town?"

"Who says we do?" Brady challenged, a belligerent tilt to his chin.

"I've talked to them all, and every last one says the two of you treated them differently when I wasn't around. What about it, Cilla? You say you miss having a mother, so why do you try to come between me and every woman I show interest in? Don't you want me to be happy?"

"We don't want a stepmom!" Brady blurted. "They're mean."

"Who says?" Colt threw his son's words back at him.

"Bobby Petty has a mean stepmother and mean stepsisters," Brady responded, his expression grave.

Out of the mouths of babes, Colt thought. "It's true that some stepparents can be unkind and unloving, but not always."

When Brady didn't answer, Colt continued. "Ben and Daniel Gentry both have new parents. They both seem pretty happy with the situation. Besides, do either of you think that I'd marry someone who didn't care for you, or that I could even love someone like that?"

Brady shrugged. Cilla said, "She'll have babies and you'll like them better."

Colt dragged a work-roughened hand down his face. "It's true that I might have other children, but that doesn't mean I would ever love either of you less. Love is something that grows the more you give." Hadn't Patrice often said as much?

Pinning them with a serious look, he said, "I want the two of you to listen to me. I do plan to marry someday, if I find a woman to love who loves us all, so you'd both better get used to that idea. Squiring a woman around doesn't mean I'll marry her, and doesn't mean I won't. Courting is a time when two people try to find out if they could be happy spending the rest of their lives together. So far, I haven't found that woman, but if I had, and you'd driven her away, I'd be very disappointed in you. I'm onto your tricks now, so no more."

"Yes, Pa," Cilla said, her habitual look of innocence firmly in place.

"Okay," he said. "Right here and now, the three of us are going to make a pact. I'll do my best to be here for the two of you and you're both going to stop behaving like brats. If you don't, there will be consequences. Your bad behavior has to stop, and I mean from this moment on. Got it?"

Cilla opened her mouth to say something, but Colt reached out and tipped her head back, silencing her with a hard, unyielding gaze. "I mean it, Cilla. It ends right now, and I warn you not to try me on this. Now go wash up and comb your hair."

"Why?" they asked in unison.

"We're going to go to Miss Grainger's house, and you're both going to apologize for what you did."

"Aw, Pa!" Brady cried. Cilla looked as if she'd like to argue, but for once, held her tongue.

"This isn't negotiable. Now go."

Cilla and Brady exchanged another stunned look and nodded. What on earth had gotten into their pa?

The first thing Allison did when she stepped through the door of her little house after leaving Ellie's was to change into a faded navy skirt and a simple blue-patterned blouse that had seen better days. She left the top couple of buttons undone and rolled the sleeves up past her elbows. The pins holding her hair were digging into her scalp, so she took it down, ran a brush through it and covered the curly mass with a triangle of fabric to protect it from dust while she cleaned.

Cleaning was her cure-all for working through problems, sorrow or anger. She was out back, beating rugs that didn't need it, when she saw the trio headed in her direction. Even without her glasses she knew who it was. Dismay skittered through her. Knowing it was too late to escape inside and pretend she wasn't at home, she stood there, shoulders back, the rug beater clenched in her hand.

Was it her imagination or did the sheriff's gaze linger on her exposed throat just a bit too long to be proper? Though she was dressed modestly, Allie felt the urge to hide from his piercing look.

"Miss Grainger," he said, as he and the children stopped in front of her back porch.

"Sheriff. What can I do for you?"

Colt shifted his weight to one booted foot and hooked his thumbs in his belt loops. "I can see that you're busy, so we won't take much of your time. Cilla and Brady have something to say to you." He gave the children a pointed look.

"I'm sorry, Miss Grainger," Brady said. "It was wrong for me to push you. I didn't think that you might get hurt."

Allison saw genuine remorse in his eyes. Brady was not really a bad child, just a troubled one. "I accept your apology, Brady. We all act without thinking sometimes."

"Even you?" he asked, looking up at her with a frown.

Allison thought of the way she'd stormed into Colt's

office with no thought but to give him a piece of her mind. "Even me," she told him with a slight smile.

Cilla had yet to raise her gaze from the ground in front of her. Colt gave his daughter's shoulder a nudge, and her chin came up to a haughty angle. "Sorry, Miss Grainger," she quipped with one of her phony smiles.

"Priscilla…" The warning from her father was a low growl.

The girl gave a deep sigh, and the light of battle left her eyes. "I really am sorry, Miss Grainger. It was wrong of me to step on your glasses…and your…hat." She gave a slight shrug. "I guess I was just taking up for Brady."

The simple statement explained so much that Allison hadn't understood before. In that split second, she realized that Cilla's terrible conduct always came on the heels of an incident with Brady. It all made perfect sense. Cilla created a new calamity to take the attention from her little brother. While Allison couldn't condone the girl's actions, she applauded her devotion to Brady.

"I understand," she said with a nod. "My sisters often fought my battles, too."

With apologies made and accepted, she looked at Colt, whose face wore a bewildered expression.

"Well, we'll let you get back to work now," he said, placing a big hand on each child's shoulder. "We'll talk…later."

Allison nodded. She would need to tell him this new insight into the situation. Surely it was something she could use to her advantage with changing Cilla's attitude.

Colt was hardly aware of walking back home. His mind was still trying to come to terms with the picture of Allison Grainger without her prim-and-proper teacher persona in place.

He hoped he hadn't made her uncomfortable with his staring, but wearing a simple skirt with a minimum of petticoats and an unadorned shirt, she looked nothing like her usual self.

He hadn't been prepared for the pale perfection of her throat and shoulders or the soft contours of her bare arms, all spattered with freckles, as if someone had taken a paintbrush laden with gold dust and splashed it with carefree abandon over her creamy skin.

And her hair! Freed from the tight confines of her habitual knot and tied back with a scarf, the curly mass cascaded halfway down her back. Sunshine had given it a fiery, breathtaking radiance. He doubted she was aware how tempting the unassuming disarray was. And then there were the little spiral curls around her face that clung to her damp cheeks and forehead, just begging a man to brush them back....

Whoa! He caught his thoughts up short. What on earth was he doing, looking at the prudish teacher as a woman? Well, of course she was a woman, but she wasn't the kind of woman he was interested in. He'd never been overly fond of redheads, except maybe for Ellie, and her hair was more auburn than red, and she was off bounds, so she didn't count. Miss Grainger was his enemy, his nemesis. Well, maybe nothing so strong as that, but at the very least she'd been a constant irritant since he'd moved to Wolf Creek.

"What are you muttering about, Pa?" Brady asked, as Colt stomped up onto the porch.

"Nothing," he snapped.

Cilla looked at her brother with raised eyebrows and

preceded the men into the house. Colt gave them milk and sandwiches for supper. He helped them clean up the kitchen and told them to go to the store before it closed to see what Gabe might have for them to do to pay off their debt.

"What's wrong with him?" Brady asked as they made their way down Antioch Street.

"I don't know," Cilla said, "but he sure is crabby."

Colt was still crabby when he went to bed. He fell asleep along toward morning and dreamed of pressing his lips to each and every one of the freckles adorning Allison Grainger's straight little nose.

When he woke the next morning, he was crankier than ever.

Chapter Three

Allison didn't fall asleep until late for worrying about her future. She prided herself on being a good person and a good teacher, and in general felt she was. Since she'd reached her teen years and realized she would never be the beauty her sisters were, she had tied her self-esteem to her teaching skills. Now even that was in jeopardy.

Perhaps it was time to give up teaching and find another career. She'd fallen asleep thinking that it was too bad that she couldn't just find a husband to take care of her, but even as she'd thought it, she wondered if she would be happy with that solution.

Allison was barely out of bed the next morning when someone knocked on her door. Tightening the sash of her seersucker wrapper and pushing back a lock of hair that had sprung free from her nightly braid, she opened the door to find Danny Stone—no, Danny Gentry now that his parents had been reunited—standing there, a serious expression on his face.

"Mornin', Miss Grainger," he said in a self-important

tone. "Mayor Talbot sent me to tell you that he wants to see you in his office at nine sharp."

A sick feeling settled in the pit of her stomach. Time for a reckoning. Time to see whether or not she would have a job come the start of the school year.

"Thank you, Danny," she said. "How is your mother?"

"She's fine, Miss Grainger. She and my dad are real happy."

"That's wonderful. Give them my best." Allie meant every word, even though the news left a hollow feeling inside her she was beginning to think might never be filled.

"Yes, ma'am, I will. 'Bye."

"Goodbye, Danny."

She closed the door and leaned against it, tears of self-pity burning beneath her eyelids. She reconsidered her thoughts about finding a husband from the night before. Even if she did consider that as a solution, the major drawback about living in a town the size of Wolf Creek was that unattached men were scarce, and of those who were eligible, few were considered decent husband material. Even fewer wanted a near-sighted, middle-aged spinster with freckles and a few too many pounds. She saw no husband or children of her own on her horizon.

Finding another career was not possible, either—not at this point in her life. What else could a single woman do to support herself besides, perhaps, nursing? She gave a little shudder. God bless the people who could take care of the sick. That was not for her. Though she did not faint at the sight of blood, she did tend to panic in emergencies.

She sighed. There was nothing for her but years of

teaching other people's children, wiping their runny noses, cleaning up after them when they got sick and kissing their bumps and bruises. The best she could hope for was contentment, a pleasant place to live and a job that gave her satisfaction.

Job. She glanced at the mantel clock and saw that it was already 8:00 a.m. Muttering beneath her breath about Colt Garrett and his unruly children, she shoved away from the door and headed for the bedroom to get ready. She only hoped that after the meeting with Homer, she had a job.

When Allison stepped through the mayor's door, she saw that Colt was already seated in one of the chairs in front of the desk. Even without her glasses, there was no hiding the scowl on his attractive face. As she neared the empty chair beside him, she noticed that his cheeks still bore yesterday's stubble, as if he, too, had been given short notice of the meeting and hadn't had time to shave. Combined with the unyielding expression in his unusual tawny eyes, he looked a tad dangerous and 100 percent handsome male. Somehow, she was not in the least surprised that he was already angry, or at the very least irritated.

Her heart fluttered in a sudden burst of awareness that sent her heart racing beneath the wide flounce that made a V from her waistband up and over her shoulders.

Knowing it was futile to have any physical response to him, no matter how attractive he might be, and desperate to control her runaway emotions, she forced her gaze to Homer, smiled and murmured a polite "Good morning, gentlemen."

The mayor and the sheriff muttered their replies almost in tandem.

"Have a seat, Miss Grainger," Homer said, indicating the empty chair. "This shouldn't take long."

As Allison stepped between the two chairs, she drew her skirts aside to keep them from brushing against the sheriff's long denim-clad legs. Unnerved by his nearness—indeed, by everything about him—and wondering what had happened to make him so surly since they'd talked the previous day, she dropped into the chair next to his with a decidedly ungraceful and unladylike plop.

Her cheeks burned with mortification. What was it about the man that caused her to lose her professional demeanor and behave with uncharacteristic gaucheness? Sinking her teeth into her lower lip, she kept her gaze on the mayor.

"I was up half the night considering the situation," Homer began, "and after consulting with the members of the town council, two of whom are on the school board, I think I have a clear picture of the situation."

He turned toward Colt. "It's a well-known fact that your children get out of hand on occasion. Would you agree with that?"

"I would." Colt's response was curt.

"And it's a matter of record that Miss Grainger has had several meetings with you and the board, not only about their conduct at school, but about the need to supply Brady with extra tutoring at home."

Colt shot a dark look at Allison from beneath golden-tipped eyebrows. "She has, yes."

"And have you complied with her requests?"

"Not to the degree she would like, I suppose," he admitted with a slight shrug of his wide shoulders. Only the whitening knuckles of his hands as they tightened on the arms of the chair said that he was not as indifferent as he appeared.

"Well, it's obvious to everyone that the situation must change, if it is to ever be resolved," the mayor declared.

"I realize that, sir, and I promise to try to do better, but what she asks is no easy task."

"Parenting is never easy, son," Homer said, his impatience clear. "You should know that by now. I expect you to do better. Brady will thank you for it in the long run."

Dull red color crept up the sheriff's cheeks. "I'm sure you're right."

Satisfied that Colt would do as he was told, Homer barreled ahead. "What do you plan to do about the property damage the children inflicted on Miss Grainger's personal belongings?"

"I've spoken to the children and made arrangements to have the eyeglasses replaced, and I've also talked to Gabe about replacing Miss Grainger's hat and gloves at my expense. He's agreed to let the children work off the debt by helping out at the store every day."

"Well done, Colt, well done! Your willingness to do the right thing somewhat restores my faith in my choice of you as our sheriff."

Satisfied that Colt had been put into his proper place, Homer switched his attention to Allison. "And you, Miss Grainger. Everyone knows that I have always thought we were fortunate to hire you, and with your sister living here, it seemed a mutually beneficial arrangement. However, I was under the impression that you were made of sterner stuff. I never thought two misbehaving children would cause you to threaten to cut bait and run. It grieves me to tell you that I'm re-thinking my initial response to your qualifications."

It took a moment for Allison's pleasure at his praise to catch up to the fact that he had condemned her actions with his next breath. It was one thing to announce she'd rather move on than teach the sheriff's children another year, and quite another to be faced with termination.

Homer leaned forward and rested his arms on the gleaming desktop, his frowning gaze moving from her to Colt and back.

"I must say that I'm shocked by the way you two have handled things. The people of Wolf Creek will not be pleased with either of you when word gets around about your conduct. Both of you should be more mindful of your station in town and be the best examples you can be in all situations. And as for you, Miss Grainger, I must say that I am quite disappointed in your inability to preserve your temper and your composure. As the town's educator, you're held to a higher standard than a regular citizen."

Allison swallowed her pride and decided to take full responsibility for the fiasco. "You're certainly justified in your feelings, Mayor Talbot, and I know you're right. Perhaps Sheriff Garrett would have been more amenable if I hadn't let my anger get the best of me. I have no excuse except to say that the incident far surpassed the bounds of reasonable behavior, and I overreacted."

Even as she said the words, she was dreading another year with Cilla and Brady—if she were lucky enough to be offered another year. "I do, however, think the sheriff should get to the bottom of whatever is causing their conduct, and he should also be more conscientious about keeping his promises."

"On those things, Miss Grainger, we are agreed. So it seems to me that the solution to this whole debacle is very simple."

"It is?" she said, somewhat in shock since she'd lain awake many a night the past year trying to come up with a way to solve the problem.

"I believe so, but it will require a high degree of cooperation between the two of you if there's to be any significant change in the situation. Wouldn't you both agree?"

"Of course," Allie hastened to say while part of her mind was wondering just what "cooperation" Homer was talking about.

Colt nodded but his eyes held a wary expression.

"Well, then, here's what's going to happen. School takes up in little more than six weeks. If the two of you don't have this worked out by the beginning of the school year, you'll both be looking for jobs come September. Understood?"

Homer rose, and rounded the desk, heading for the coatrack near the door. "I'm due for a few rounds of checkers with Lew, Artie and Pete over at the store," he said, reaching for his hat. "You two feel free to use the office as long as you like."

"For what?" Colt asked, speaking up for the first time since Allison had begun her apology.

"Why, for working out the details of just what and how the two of you will work together to solve the issues with Brady and Cilla. Y'all have a good day now."

Stunned at the sudden, unexpected dismissal, Colt watched the mayor leave the office. He felt as if he'd just taken a punch in the gut. He'd escaped being fired. Barely. Maybe. Of all the scenarios that had crossed his mind since Danny Gentry had knocked on his door to tell him the mayor wanted to see him at once, this particular conclusion had never entered his mind.

He loved his job. Loved the people of Wolf Creek. Moving the kids again would be hard on them, and Brady might never catch up if he kept moving from school to school. Children needed roots. Lifelong friends. They all did. Thank goodness they had another chance.

He glanced over at the schoolmarm, whose lips were still parted in shock. At least she had her hair pulled back in some sort of bun again, he thought with ill-tempered satisfaction. The no-nonsense style made it easier to think of her as his adversary instead of a real person he was forced to work with closely.

"I suppose you got a lot of pleasure telling Homer every word I said," she snapped. "You probably ran to see him right after I left your office yesterday."

"I wasn't tattling."

"No?" she said, her shock giving way to annoyance.

"No. I was just trying to tell him what happened during our…discussion to the best of my recollection." Minus losing his own temper, of course. "I certainly never intended to put our jobs in jeopardy."

"Hmpf!"

Though she sounded disgruntled, Miss Grainger was looking at him with an expression that hovered between dismay and apprehension. No doubt she was regretting a few of her actions, too. After all, she was not just any woman, he reminded himself crossly. She was *Miss Grainger,* the town's shining example of virtue, deportment and intelligence. Cosseted and corseted with no idea what children were like since she'd never had any. Laced so tight and so caught up in her expectations for learning there was no room for womanly tenderness or sensitivity to his children's needs in her tiny little heart.

"So what do you propose we do?"

Her prim voice grated on his already raw nerves. Did the woman ever loosen up?

"How should I know?" he said, getting to his feet and glaring down at her. "Aren't you the one with all the answers?"

Her brown eyes narrowed in a way that was fast becoming familiar. "Please sit down, Sheriff," she commanded. "After yesterday, you must have learned that I am not so easy to intimidate."

Feeling as if he were a schoolboy who'd been scolded, he sat.

Miss Grainger frowned. "I'll be the first to say that I don't have all the answers. However, even though you may not like it, I feel that it is important that we continue working with Brady until we can figure out some way to help him. I'll write some letters to my former professors. Perhaps there have been some new discoveries in the area of learning disabilities since I began teaching."

"Disabilities!" Colt barked. "My son is not *disabled* in any way."

"That's not what I—"

"There's nothing wrong with Brady," he snarled. "Did you ever stop and think that maybe the reason he isn't doing well is because you aren't a good enough teacher?"

"Every day."

The soft confession robbed him of his anger. It wasn't the answer he'd expected. There was uncertainty and misery in her sherry-brown eyes, and maybe just a hint of dampness. He turned away from her, hoping she wouldn't resort to tears, that handy-dandy feminine standby that women the world over used to manipulate the opposite sex.

After several long seconds, Colt calmed himself and searched his mind for something to say. Miss Grainger, too, appeared to gather her emotions. Her chest rose in a deep sigh and she seemed to shake off her melancholy, looking up at him with renewed determination. "I daresay if we both work hard at it, together we can help him."

Colt doubted it, but it wouldn't hurt to try to appease her, since she did seem upset by the whole affair. Besides, Homer had given them an ultimatum. "Maybe you're right."

"Thank you for Cilla and Brady's apologies. I believe that was the right thing to do."

"You're welcome."

Silence reigned in the small room until she said, "Have you tried to find out what's at the root of their behavior?"

"In fact, I did," he told her. "I was a little surprised at what they had to say."

She raised her eyebrows in question.

"Brady told me he was tired of disappointing everyone all the time. He also said that it's embarrassing when you make mention of him having the wrong answer in front of the class."

Miss Grainger looked shocked. "It was never my intent to humiliate anyone. I just try to point out the error and offer to help them after class. I'll try to figure out another way to…soften things."

"I'm sure he'll appreciate that," Colt said. He looked straight into her eyes. "And I promise I'll work with him for thirty minutes or so every evening. I'm not sure I can do more than that. It's frustrating and stressful for us both."

A tight smile played at the corners of her mouth. "Believe me, Sheriff Garrett, I understand only too well, and I can assure you that my frustration equals, if not surpasses, yours.

"For my part I promise to investigate every new teaching technique available. There is always some educator coming up with new and different methods of instruction. Some are better than others, but it won't hurt to try a few of them." The sound of her stomach growling punctuated the statement. Her freckled face flushed deep red.

"Look, I was up half the night," he told her, not offering any reason why. She'd never know he hadn't slept for thinking of their argument and…her. Frowning, he scrubbed a palm over his bristly cheek. "When Danny came to get me, I didn't even have time to shave much less have a cup of coffee. Would you mind if we continued this conversation at Ellie's?"

An expression of pure panic flitted over her face.

"Please," he coaxed. "Let me treat you to breakfast. I'll be able to think much better once I have some coffee, and I think your stomach will agree that a plate of ham and eggs wouldn't come amiss."

He accompanied the request with a stiff smile. If possible, she looked even more flustered. He could see in her eyes that she was about to refuse.

"Look, Miss Grainger, I'm doing my best to make up for yesterday," he said in his most persuasive tone. "How about meeting me halfway?"

After regarding him with a solemn expression for long moments, she rose. "Well, then, since you put it that way, I accept. We really *must* reach some agreement about the children."

The instant she and the sheriff walked through the door of the café, all eyes turned their way. Allison heard the murmurs of conjecture sweep through the crowd. Grasping her elbow, he ushered her to a table and pulled out her chair, the epitome of a Southern gentleman.

Ellie approached carrying two mugs of steaming coffee. "Straight from the pot for Allison," she said, setting the cup down in front of her and pressing a sisterly kiss to her cheek. "The usual, Colt?" Ellie asked.

"Yep. And thanks for bringing the coffee right over. I needed it."

"I could tell," Ellie said with a slight smile.

Allison watched wide-eyed as he added a generous amount of cream and two heaping spoonfuls of sugar. If she used cream and sugar in every cup of coffee or tea she drank, she would soon be waddling, but the sheriff's lean, muscled body didn't appear to have an extra ounce of fat anywhere.

"Allison? What for you?"

"Just a piece of toasted bread and an egg, please."

"That's it?" Colt asked.

"No sense arguing with her," Ellie said. "It's what she usually has."

Allison felt decidedly uncomfortable at being the

topic of conversation. Heaven knew—everyone knew—that she didn't need a full breakfast.

His shoulders lifted in a shrug of disbelief. "Bring the lady some toast and an egg."

"Got it," Ellie said, and walked away, her slim hips swaying.

Colt sighed.

"She's lovely, isn't she?" Allison's tone was wistful.

"She is."

His agreement brought a lump to her throat. Well, she had asked, and there was no denying the obvious. "And just as beautiful on the inside."

It was the sheriff's turn to look uncomfortable with the turn in the conversation. He took a hearty swig of the steaming coffee without flinching.

"She deserves a good man."

He scowled. "You've probably heard the scuttlebutt that it won't be me."

Allison *had* heard from Ellie that she'd told Colt they had no future since she had no idea if the husband who'd deserted her when Bethany was born was alive or dead. Besides, as nice a man as he was, she didn't love him.

"I'm sorry."

"So am I. She's a sweet person and wonderful company, but I think we both always knew we were never going to be more than friends."

The knot in Allison's chest loosened.

"Back to the children," she said, deciding that she should return the conversation to their mutual problem. "What did Cilla have to say about her behavior?"

Colt cleared his throat but met her curious gaze head-on. "It seems that as a father, I've fallen far short in the attention and support areas of their lives."

"I'm not certain I understand."

Colt placed his elbows on the table and leaned toward her. Allison listened as he explained what Cilla had told him about the reason she misbehaved.

When he finished, Allison said, "She misbehaves to get your attention?"

"So it seems. She says that even when I'm at home with them, my thoughts are far away." He leaned back in his chair and lifted his coffee mug. "As bad as I hate to admit it, she's right. It took me a long while to get past losing Patty. Maybe I still dwell on it too much sometimes."

He met Allison's troubled gaze. "When Patty was alive, she took care of most of the child rearing, and I made the living. When she died, it all fell to me. I didn't know what to do besides feed and clothe them, and that's more or less all I've been doing. It seemed to work okay when they were small, but now that they're growing up, they need more."

Allison looked at him, wondering what it would be like to be loved by a man who still missed you after so many years. "That makes sense. Most men would probably handle things the same way. And Cilla's comment fits with something she said yesterday."

"What's that?" He took another swallow of coffee.

"She said that she stepped on my glasses because she was standing up for Brady. After I thought about that awhile, I realized that almost every time she gets into trouble, it's *after* Brady and I have had some sort of exchange about his schoolwork. I believe one reason she acts out is to take my attention away from her brother."

Colt looked dumbfounded. "She's always been protective of him, so that makes a strange sort of sense," he said after a moment. "Sometimes I think she's trying to take the place of her mother."

While Allison tucked that bit of information into a corner of her mind to ponder later, he explained how Cilla was feeling sorry for herself over not having a mother to instruct her in the ladylike pursuits her schoolmates enjoyed.

"She also told me they tried to wreck my relationships because they're afraid a stepmother might take me away from them, and a new wife will have children that I will love more than I do them."

"You can't be serious!"

"I assure you I'm quite serious," he said. "Where do they come up with all these strange notions?"

"Never having had children, I couldn't say."

"I may as well tell you that she has a problem with you, too."

"Me?" Allison's shock was apparent. "What sort of problem can she possibly have with me? It isn't as if you're looking at me as a candidate to become their stepmother." A rush of color flooded her cheeks the instant the words left her lips.

"No, no, nothing like that," he replied, his agreement blunt and crisp. "Uh, Cilla says you're too…happy all the time."

Allison's jaw dropped. Amused despite the confession, she shook her head and a totally unexpected and unprofessional giggle escaped her. "Well, that's one for the books."

"Here you go!" Ellie said, setting a plate piled high with a mouthwatering array of breakfast goodies in front of Colt and a piece of dry toast and a single soft fried egg in front of Allison.

She eyed his plate of eggs, ham, grits, biscuits and a small bowl of gravy with an expression of pure envy. How long had it been since she'd enjoyed a real breakfast? She glanced at Colt and saw that in complete contrast to his earlier grim seriousness, there was the barest hint of a smile in his eyes.

"I tried to tell you."

A yearning sigh escaped her, but not for the food this time. No doubt about it, the man could be potentially fatal to a lady's heart!

Get hold of yourself, Allison Grainger. Every single woman in town would agree that he's attractive. Most of those same women have been dated by him and nixed by his children, so just stop drooling over him like a dog over a ham bone and get back to the business at hand.

Gathering the remnants of her scattered wits, Allison forced a prim smile and picked up her knife and fork.

"I'd be glad to share."

"No, thank you." She gave a quick mental thank-you for her food, took a small bite of the egg and chewed slowly. She wasn't sure why, but she hated eating in front of people she didn't know, especially men.

"I'm not sure what I can do about my…irritating happiness," she said after washing down the bite of egg with another sip of coffee. "Except for a few years after losing someone I loved very much, I've more or less always tried to have a positive outlook, no matter what came my way. I believe with all my heart that God bestows so many blessings on us that we ought not whine and sulk or be angry when difficulties do crop up."

"And what about your behavior when you came into my office yesterday?"

Her guilty gaze flew to his. Oh, dear! She hoped this

conversation would not decline into another shouting match. To her eternal thankfulness, she saw that he was not provoking her at all. In fact, the expression in his eyes held more curiosity than challenge.

"I was afraid you'd bring that up," she said with a shake of her head. "I can't apologize enough. It was not at all like me."

"I believe you." The simple acknowledgment made, he asked, "Perhaps I'm prying, but who was it that you loved and lost?"

"My fiancé."

The shock on his face might have been comical if it hadn't hurt so much to realize that he seemed surprised that she had caught the attention of any man.

"Believe it or not, Sheriff, some men look beyond the exterior of a woman."

Once more, discomfiture flushed his rugged features.

"I'm well aware of that, Miss Grainger. All men should do the same. It's just that Ellie never mentioned anything about you having had a man in your life. Do you mind if I ask what happened?"

She regarded him for several seconds. The last thing she wanted was for Colt Garrett to feel sorry for her.

"I do, actually," she told him. "It's something I seldom talk about."

He nodded in understanding and returned his attention to his breakfast, ending that line of conversation.

Allison spoke up, her voice once again professional. "At least what you've told me has given me some ideas. I think we should work on involving Cilla in activities that will make her feel as if she has more in common with girls her age. Of course, it will be up to her to decide which pursuits she'd like to try." Her forehead wrinkled in thought. "I can check to see if Hattie has room for any new piano students."

"She might like that," Colt said with a nod.

"As for sewing and such, it so happens that I am quite an accomplished seamstress. In fact, I make all my clothes. But I fear my other handwork is passable at best. My sister Belinda does beautiful embroidery and petit point, and Ellie is quite good herself. I tend to attack it," she added, almost as an afterthought.

"Attack it?"

A memory surfaced, and, their earlier tiff forgotten, her lips curved and her smiling gaze met his. "My mother used to tell me that I wasn't supposed to go at it like I was killing snakes, that it was designed to be a pleasurable ladies' pursuit, but once I start a piece, all I can think of is how soon I can finish."

Colt's gaze clung to hers a moment longer before he began to saw at a piece of ham with unusual fervor. Like her earlier giggle, the smile did amazing things to her appearance. They ate in silence for several moments…an awkward silence, to be sure.

Allison used her last bite of toast to mop up the rich yellow yolk on her plate. Colt forked up a bite of biscuit, swirled it through some milk gravy and popped it into his mouth, leaving a tiny smudge clinging to the corner of his upper lip. Before she realized what she was going to do, she reached out, leaned across the table and wiped at the smear with her napkin.

Warm, calloused fingers circled her wrist.

She gasped, mortified by her spontaneous action, excited by the feel of his fingers against her skin.

"I… I'm so sorry," she apologized in a whisper, aware that the pulse in her wrist was throbbing wildly beneath his thumb. "It's just such a...natural thing for me to wipe tears and runny noses and..." Her voice trailed away and her gaze fell from his to the sugar bowl sitting in the center of the table. "I'm sorry."

"No apology necessary," he said, releasing his hold on her as if she'd become hot to touch. Changing the topic, he said, "I appreciate your time and your input, Miss Grainger. When do you suggest that we put our plans into motion?"

She squared her shoulders. "Well, July is more than half gone, and Labor Day will be here before we know it, so the sooner the better if we hope to make enough progress before then to keep our positions. I'll try to get some letters off today and I'll speak to Hattie, as well."

A thoughtful expression filled her eyes. "Cilla is at a precarious age—no longer a little girl and not yet a young lady. Her emotions are all a jumble."

Colt blew out a breath. "You're right about that. Some days it's like she's all grown up and others, she bursts into tears over nothing."

"I recall those years as being quite vexing, as I believe most young girls do, but now that we both have a better grasp of the problem, I believe we'll work through this."

Though he wasn't happy at the prospect, he said, "I'll do my best, but you may have to spell things out for me." He stood, reaching into his pocket for some money. "I'll catch up with you later today or tomorrow," he said. "Or feel free to stop by the jail to talk over any ideas or suggestions if you're over that way."

"Thank you. I will. And thank you for the breakfast."

After Allison hugged her sister and niece goodbye, she and Colt parted ways. He watched her cross the street and head toward the mercantile, her back ramrod-straight. Unlike her sister, there was not one bit of sway to *her* hips.

Grunting in frustration, he headed toward the jail, thinking about the time he'd just spent with the spinster teacher. After talking to her, he was convinced that she *was* concerned about the children, and with her optimistic attitude, he even felt a seed of optimism himself that they might be able to bring about a much-needed change. He hoped so.

As a lawman, he was pretty good at reading between the lines and piecing together things that might seem unrelated but often led him in the right direction when it came to capturing the bad guys, like Elton Thomerson and his buddy. Unfortunately, that talent seemed absent when it came to his kids.

During the time spent with Miss Grainger, he had noticed some very interesting things. For instance, her outward composure was a front that hid a lot of insecurities. He'd seen it in her eyes when she'd talked about her beautiful sister, and he'd heard it in her voice when she'd made the offhand comment that he wasn't interested in her as a wife, and again when she'd said that some men were interested in more than looks. That lack of confidence had been obvious from the droop of her shoulders and the sorrow in her eyes when she'd talked about understanding what Cilla was going through.

Clearly, she was sensitive to the fact that she was not as attractive as her sister. Ellie was tall and curvaceous; Allison was short and plump, thus her skimpy breakfast. Her hair wasn't the pretty auburn of her sister's. Allison was a carrottop, and she kept her unruly hair scraped back into a severe knot, as if she were afraid that one loose tendril would mar her image of respectability. Like Ellie's, her face was oval and her skin was just as creamy and smooth and flawless, except for the overabundance of freckles, which were nothing but a light dusting across her nose.

Her eyes, perhaps her best feature, were a warm brown, framed with long, curling eyelashes that were shades darker than her hair. Her nose was nice, too—one of the few features she and her sister had in common. And the little indentation in her left cheek when she smiled was very eye-catching.

He stopped in the middle of the street. Why was he even thinking about Allison Grainger's physical appearance? Was he so desperate to find a wife that he was even looking at the town's spinster teacher as a prospect? No way! It was just a natural thing for a man to look a woman over and catalog her good and bad qualities. He did it all the time. Not that Allison's flame-red hair and freckles were *bad* qualities, or even unattractive when taken one by one. There was actually a cuteness about her that some men might find appealing. Just not him.

Then what was that little twinge you felt when she made the offhand comment about you not being interested in making her a stepmother?

Colt gave a grunt of consternation. She'd actually sounded appalled by the idea of being his prospective wife. He didn't think he was conceited, but neither was he accustomed to ladies looking dismayed at the notion of being linked to him. It was downright demoralizing. He wondered what kind of man she'd loved and what she'd been like before he'd broken her heart.

Forget it! he thought, stomping up onto the wooden

sidewalk. He wasn't in the market for a woman like her. No doubt in time she would find another man who would care for her, someone who wouldn't be intimidated by her intelligence, as many would be—himself included. Someone who didn't mind that his woman was…well, *dowdy*.

While it was admirable that she made her own clothes, her sense of style left much to be desired. He was no expert, but even someone as unschooled in fashion as he was knew that the styles she favored were not at all flattering. Flounces and ruffles and gathers! He supposed she was trying to hide her plumpness, but all she was doing was enhancing it. She'd looked much slimmer in her cleaning clothes the day before.

Oh, well, he thought, pulling open the door to his office and stepping inside. Her style or lack of it was no concern of his.

He found Big Dan Mercer, his deputy, sitting at the desk, reading the latest St. Louis paper.

"Did you and Miss Grainger get things figured out?"

"We came up with a plan of sorts," Colt told him. "It remains to be seen if it works or not."

Chapter Four

A̶llison left her sister's café, well aware that the sheriff was watching every step she took as she crossed the street. The knowledge made her even more uncomfortable. Only when she rounded the corner to Hattie's and was certain she was no longer being watched did she relax.

What a worrisome couple of days! she thought, her mind wandering from one meeting with Colt Garrett to the next. She wasn't certain which was more troubling—the sheriff's children or the sheriff himself. She couldn't deny that she was very aware of him as a man. What woman this side of the grave wouldn't be? What puzzled her was that he was nothing like Jesse, who had been the yardstick for every man she'd met since he'd said he loved someone else.

So why was she experiencing this sudden, unexpected awareness? She'd met men just as handsome and with *much* more amiable personalities. Men who had more money than the peace officer of a small Arkansas town. Smarter, better-educated men. But not since her relationship with Jesse had changed from a lifelong friendship to love at the age of sixteen had she met a man whose touch could make her heart race. Truth to tell, even Jesse's touch had never affected her the way the sheriff's did.

Remembering the way she'd reacted when he'd circled her wrist with his fingers, she gave a little frustrated groan and fanned at the heat in her cheeks. This could not be happening! It simply would not do! Not with a man like Colt, who could never love a woman like her. She didn't think she could withstand another broken heart.

Pushing her troubling thoughts of him to the back of her mind, she went to the boardinghouse and asked Hattie about an opening for a new piano student. Hattie said there was a spot available, but when she heard who the prospective beginner was, she shook her head.

"Are you daft, woman? That child is a menace and her brother, too! I heard what they did to you over at the store. Why, I might not have a building standing when she leaves."

"I understand how you feel, Hattie," Allison pleaded, "but this is important. I've spoken with her father, and I believe he finally understands the seriousness of the situation. We've decided to work together to see if we can find ways to help the children."

Arms crossed over her narrow chest, foot tapping an impatient tattoo, Hattie snorted in contempt of the whole notion. Allison poured on the pitiful details and saw Hattie weakening.

"O' course, the sheriff is happy to pay for the lessons and we would both really, really appreciate your help with this," she persisted, knowing that Hattie had a soft spot for Colt.

"'We,' is it?" the boardinghouse proprietor asked. The impatience in her faded blue eyes had been replaced with a twinkle.

"Don't start, Hattie," Allison warned, feeling her face flush hotly. "We're just working together to help his children."

"Of course, dear," Hattie said with a knowing smile and an innocent lifting of her eyebrows. The effect was ruined by her next sentence and wide smile. "This is an excellent thing, Allison. You need a good man like the sheriff in your life."

"He isn't in my life," Allison argued. "Except in a marginal way. The children are sort of like a project we're working on together."

"Project?" Hattie snorted again. "That sounds pretty unfeeling, if you ask me."

"What do you mean?"

"What I mean is that it sounds like even though your hearts might be in the right place, you and the sheriff are looking at this all wrong. Ornery as they are, those children aren't an assignment given to you by the mayor...." After seeing the shock on Allison's face, Hattie offered a shrewd smile. "Surely you didn't expect *that* to stay a secret, did you?"

The idea that everyone in town knew that she and Colt were not only trying to help the children, but that they were also fighting for their jobs, was disturbing to say the least.

"Anyway," Hattie continued, "Cilla and Brady aren't an assignment or a project that needs to be done by a certain day. If you and Sheriff Garrett go into it with that attitude, all you can hope for is failure. It will take having the right mind-set to make any meaningful changes."

Hattie was right, Allison thought. She had been looking at it like a tiresome chore, a necessary duty to be dealt with by the beginning of the school year.

"So," Hattie said, her voice scattering Allison's uneasy thoughts, "I'll agree to help you, at least a time or two, but if that child doesn't work hard or if she won't listen or if she talks back, the deal is off."

"I understand."

Allison hugged the older woman and left, her heart much lighter. Wearing a broad smile, she practically skipped across the street back toward the café. Now she just had to try to talk Ellie into helping teach Cilla embroidery. She'd thought about asking her when she was there earlier, before she and Colt left, but hadn't wanted him around, in case her sister declined. Of course, Allison doubted she would. Ellie was such a softy that it shouldn't be too hard to convince her to help.

"Oh, Allison!" her sister wailed when Allison explained what she and Colt hoped to do. "You know I'm stretched pretty thin."

"I realize that, but I also know that you're much better at needlework than I am, and I know that you're teaching Beth in the evenings. I wouldn't expect you to take her every night, just an hour or so once or twice a week to show her the different stitches and watch her progress."

"Well…it sounds like a good plan," Ellie conceded.

"I think it will be," Allison said, knowing that she'd won. "I feel fairly confident that in time I can make some inroads with Cilla, but Brady's another thing altogether. I hope I can find the key to help him learn."

"You're a good person, sister dear," Ellie said with a fond smile. "Some man should snatch you up, love the living daylights out of you and give you a house full of babies of your own."

The image that flashed through Allison's mind robbed her of breath. Colt loving the daylights out of her. Two little boys with sun-streaked hair who looked just like him, running and flinging themselves into her arms.

"Allie?"

Allison's head jerked around, a faraway expression in her eyes. "Hmm?"

"Are you okay?"

"Fine." A sigh whispered through her lips. Pipe dreams. Hadn't she already acknowledged that a man like Colt would never be interested in someone like her?

"How was Colt about all this?"

"Hmm?" Allison said again.

"Allie…what is it that you aren't telling me?"

Rats! She'd better get control of herself and her errant daydreams. Ellie was as sharp as a tack. "Nothing. It's just been an eventful morning and I still have a lot to do."

Still wearing a look of skepticism, Ellie let the comment pass.

"I think I'll go over to the mercantile and see what Gabe has in the way of embroidery notions. It would make a nice gift for Cilla, don't you think?"

"It would," Ellie agreed. "When you get finished, stop back by and have a bite of lunch. I'm making a big kettle of chicken and noodles."

"I don't need noodles," Allison said. "They'll go straight to my hips."

"Silly girl. When will you ever get over the fact that you are not overweight? Well, not *much,* anyway. You're built more or less like me."

"Am not!" Allison said, her gaze roaming her sister's tall voluptuousness.

"Are so!" Ellie responded, one of their favorite means of arguing as kids. "You're just me in miniature, but the thing is that you're… Well, there's no way to say it but to tell the truth. You're much…uh, bustier than I am."

Allison's mouth fell open in shock. "Bustier?" she squeaked in a horrified whisper and glanced around the café to see if anyone had overheard.

"Yes. And the clothes you insist on wearing to *hide* the problem only add insult to injury," Ellie added, disregarding her sibling's warning look.

"I appreciate your loyalty and your love," Allison said, "but I am what I am. Plump."

Ellie's eyes sparkled with mischief. "Are not."

In spite of her irritation with her sister, Allison couldn't help laughing. "You're impossible," she said, giving Ellie an impulsive hug.

As she passed through the doorway, she thought she heard her sister murmur, "Am not."

Allison spent more than an hour at the general store, looking at table scarves and pillowcases already stamped with floral designs, ready to be filled in with colorful threads and fancy stitches. Finally settling on a table runner with bachelor's buttons and butterflies, she spent more time deciding just which thread colors would make the prettiest combination, adding her choices to the embroidery hoop and needles already stacked on the counter. A small pair of scissors rounded out her purchases.

"Taking up handwork, are you?" Gabe Gentry asked, as he tallied up her purchases.

"These are for Cilla," she told him, eyeing a bit of blue satin ribbon on a spool across the aisle. "Ellie is going to teach her to embroider."

"Brave soul, Ellie," Gabe said with the roguish smile that had set many feminine hearts aflutter during his single years. Probably still did, she mused, even though he was now happily married. Not even the scar on his left cheek, the reminder of an attack by a couple of hooligans a few months ago, detracted from his looks.

"Shall I put this on Colt's bill, then?" he asked, stacking the items and setting them in the middle of a square of brown paper he'd ripped from a large roll.

"Oh, no. I'm buying it for her," Allison said. "Sort of a peace offering."

"That's awfully nice of you after what those two did to you."

"Well, let's just say I'm trying a new strategy, and at this point I'm not above bribery to get cooperation. Before you wrap it up, will you add a half yard of that blue satin ribbon? It will be perfect with Cilla's dark hair and blue eyes. Oh! And some of that maple candy for Brady."

"Sure thing."

Gabe measured the ribbon and added it to the package as she'd requested. "You didn't look for replacements for your gloves and hat."

"I'll do that another day. I'd like to have my glasses back first."

"Good idea. They should be here soon, and I should

have some new hats in at the end of the week." Finished tying up the package, he slid it across the counter. "Who knows where this might lead for you and Colt."

Allison raised her eyebrows in question. "I beg your pardon."

"I mean you're single and he's single…" Gabe shrugged, leaving the sentence unfinished.

Once again, Allison experienced a sudden loss of composure. Why on earth was everyone insisting on making more of this arrangement than there was?

"And neither of us is looking to change that," she said in her most prudish tone. "This is about the children. Nothing more."

Gabe held his hands up, palms outward. "Sorry. I didn't mean to offend. It just seems like it would—" he shrugged "—be a good thing for you both. Rachel and I have even talked about it once or twice."

Allison resisted the urge to stomp her foot and scream in frustration. So now she was the topic of dinnertime conversations! Forcing civility to her voice, she said, "I appreciate that, Gabe, really, but just because you and Rachel are ridiculously in love doesn't mean that the whole world wants the same thing."

"You're right," he said, nodding. "But I can't imagine why they wouldn't."

"I'm perfectly happy with my life. I do not need a man to feel fulfilled."

She imagined she saw a hint of impudence lurking in his blue eyes. "You should have quit while you were ahead," he said, the cheeky grin reappearing.

"I beg your pardon," she said again.

"Methinks you're protesting too much, as Shakespeare would say."

He was right, of course. Rachel claimed that Gabe had always known how a woman's mind worked better than any man she'd ever met. Allie took refuge in irritation. "I don't know how Rachel tolerates you," she said, snatching up her package.

Still smiling, he shrugged, recognizing her response for what it was. "It's a mystery to me, too."

She was all the way to the door when his voice stopped her.

"You gonna pay for that?"

Turning with a huff, she said, "Put it on my bill."

"You don't have a bill," he reminded her gently.

"Well, then, start one!" she snapped, and whirled to leave. She turned back in the next instant, full of contrition. "I'm sorry, Gabe. I don't know why I'm so irritable."

"Don't worry about it," he said in a soothing tone. "I understand perfectly." And he did.

Allison spent a good part of the remainder of the morning writing letters to two of her favorite, most helpful professors, and then headed to the post office to see that they went out on the next train. Back home, she ate a light lunch, freshened up, snatched up the package, squared her shoulders and walked to Colt's house at the edge of town, hoping Cilla and Brady would be there when she arrived.

To her relief, Brady answered the door on her first knock. Allison smiled. "Good morning, Brady."

"What are you doing here?" he countered.

Not a good beginning, she thought, smiling wider. "I've come to see you and Cilla and talk to you about the things your father and I discussed."

"He's already told us a buncha stuff."

Allison suppressed the urge to sigh. "May I come in? I've brought you and Cilla some things from the general store."

"Why would you do something like that?"

The question came from Cilla, who was crossing the parlor from the back of the small house. She paused behind her brother, a wary expression in her eyes.

"Well," Allie said in a reasonable tone, holding out the gift, "because you'll need these things if you're going to learn needlework, and I didn't suppose you had them." She handed Brady a small brown bag. "This is for you."

"Come on in," he said, grabbing the sack with one hand and her hand in the other. Well, one of them could be bribed, anyway. Holding back from Brady, she looked at Cilla for permission.

"Come on in."

"Thank you."

The sheriff's house looked much as she would expect a house inhabited by a single man and two children to look. The brown sofa was worn, and the plain blue curtains were faded. All in all, it looked clean enough, just…tired. Neglected. It needed pictures on the whitewashed walls and flowers in vases, and rag rugs and crochet doilies, and a man's boots by the door and—

Stop it, Allison! Just because that's what you like doesn't mean that Colt and the kids aren't fine with the way things are.

Gathering herself, she asked, "May I sit down?"

"Sure," Brady said, his hand already deep in the paper bag. "There's a broke spring in the divan. If you're not careful, it'll poke you in the behind. The rocking chair is comfortable, though." He popped a piece of the candy into his mouth and chewed.

"Thank you, Brady," Allison said, settling into the chair.

"Ugh!" he said. Allison watched wide-eyed as he ran out onto the porch and spit the candy onto the grass. He came back inside wearing a look of reproach and shoved the bag at her. "It's *maple.* I hate maple."

"I'm sorry," Allison said, appalled by his actions. She felt as if she'd taken one step forward and two back. "It was always a favorite of mine, and most children like pancakes with maple syrup, so I just thought— Well, never mind what I thought. What do you like? I'll bring it next time, even though it was rude of you to reject my gift the way you did."

"Sorry," he quipped. "Next time? Are you gonna make a habit of coming over?"

It was clear that he had no notion what to think about the recent changes in the status quo. That made two of them, she thought, curbing a sigh. "I'll come sometimes. You and Cilla are welcome at my house, too."

The plan must have been acceptable because he nodded his shaggy brown head. "Butterscotch."

"Butterscotch next time, then," she said, summoning a slight smile. She turned her attention to Cilla, who had untied the twine around the package and spread the paper wide. "I saw the ribbon and remembered that you have a blue gingham dress. I thought the color would be pretty with your eyes and your dark hair."

Surprised, Cilla looked from the contents of the package to Allison, disbelief in her eyes. "It's thread and embroidery stuff."

"Your father mentioned that you might like to learn,

and my sister does fine needlework. She's agreed to teach you the stitches."

"You don't embroider?"

"Actually, I do, just not very well. I always make a mess of something and have to pick it out. I can sew, though, if you'd like to learn. I have a new treadle sewing machine."

Afraid to give away too much of the excitement Allison saw in her eyes, Cilla said, "That might be nice. When can I start the embroidery?"

"Ellie said for you to come over tomorrow after she closes the café."

"Will Bethany be there?"

"Of course. She lives there." For convenience sake, Ellie and Bethany lived in rooms above the eating establishment.

"Cilla says Bethany's a dummy," Brady offered.

A sharp pang of sorrow pricked Allison's heart.

Cilla's face flamed red. "I did not!"

"You said she was dumb. Same thing."

"Don't quarrel," Allison said in her best teacher voice. "Bethany is not dumb."

"What's wrong with her, then?" Brady asked.

"She was born with a learning disability."

"Why?"

"No one knows why, Brady. She can learn, but what she can learn is limited, and some things will always be beyond her comprehension. But she cooks, and sews and plays the pianoforte rather well. She's also a fairly accomplished artist."

"She plays the piano?" Cilla asked.

Allison nodded. "She takes lessons from Hattie— Mrs. Carson. I think that if you got to know Bethany, you'd like her. She's very sweet and she loves doing all the usual things young girls like."

Cilla looked thoughtful.

"Your father said you might be interested in learning to play the piano," Allison said.

"I might," she said with studied nonchalance.

"Well, I spoke to Mrs. Carson and she has room for another student, but you must understand that if you agree to study under her, you must work hard. She doesn't care much for slackers who just take up her time."

The sound of boots on the porch snagged everyone's attention. The screen door swung open, and Colt filled the aperture. The sunlight at his back glinted gold on his streaky hair, creating a portrait of masculine planes and shadows of his face. Standing there with his feet spread apart as if he were bracing for a storm, his broad shoulders filling the doorway and an unreadable expression in his eyes, he looked more than a little dangerous and very exciting.

His posture relaxed when he saw there were no fireworks going off in the room.

"Hello, Miss Grainger."

The sound of his deep voice speaking her name sent her surging to her feet, her reticule in one hand and the sack of maple candy in the other.

"H-hello," she said. "I, uh, brought some things over for the children. I was just about to go." Was her voice as breathless as it sounded?

"Don't let me run you off. We'd be glad to share our lunch with you."

"No, thank you. I ate before I came, and I didn't intend to stay long." She turned to Brady. "Brady, I'm sorry I made you angry when I said I was disappointed in you. The fact that you can't read as well as I would like *is* disappointing, but only because I know that school will be much easier if we can figure out what the problem is and fix it. I get disappointed in myself, too, because I can't seem to help you. What makes me disappointed in *you* is when you don't give me your best effort. Do you understand?"

"I think so," he told her after a moment's thought.

"I know you don't like doing schoolwork while you're supposed to be out of school, but I'm going to work hard the rest of the summer, too, to try to find a way to make things easier for you. Is that fair? That we both work even though it's break time?"

He shot a glance at his father. "I suppose so."

"Good." Allison looked at Cilla, who had been watching the exchange and weighing every word.

"Would you like for me to come and walk you to Ellie's tomorrow evening?" Allison asked.

"No, ma'am. I'll go by myself. Brady and I are helping out at the mercantile." She shot her father a dark look. "I'll walk over from there."

"Fine, then." She gave the child an encouraging smile, hoping she didn't look *too* cheerful. "Good luck. When you decide about the piano lessons, let me know and I'll set things up with Mrs. Carson."

"I don't think I'll be doing the lessons," Cilla said, "since I don't have a piano to practice on."

"You're welcome to come to my house whenever you like."

Cilla considered that. "I'll think about it," she said with an indifferent shrug.

"Well, goodbye," Allison said. "I'll see you soon."

She headed for the door and paused when it became obvious that she would have to step very close to Colt to make her exit.

"I'll walk out with you," he said, stepping aside and pushing the screen door open for her to precede him.

"Cilla, will you go warm up those peas while I walk Miss Grainger out?"

"I already did."

"Then set the table, please. Brady, help your sister."

"Yes, sir," they said in unison.

Colt followed Allison onto the porch. "Let me repay you for whatever you bought for Cilla."

"Oh, no. That's not necessary. Let's call it a peace offering."

"How did things go before I got here?"

"Better than I expected."

A frown drew his eyebrows together. "When I saw you headed this direction, I got here as fast as I could. I was almost afraid of what I might walk in on."

"That was pretty obvious," she said, recalling his face when he stood in the doorway.

He wrinkled his straight nose in embarrassment and rubbed at it in an awkward gesture, shooting an amused glance her way. "Downright shameful, isn't it?" he said. "The town's lawman scared of two little kids."

For an instant, there was no awkwardness between them, just two people sharing a little joke.

"Nothing I'd want getting around town," she agreed. The seriousness of her tone belied the smile on her lips. She sketched an *X* over her heart. "I won't tell if you don't."

"Thanks," he said, growing serious. "And thanks for

what you said to Brady. Taking part of the blame your-self was brilliant."

"I didn't just say it to appease him," she clarified, surprised that he would think she'd do something like that. "I do disappoint myself when I feel I've failed a student in some way. I meant it when I told Brady that I would work hard this summer. I got the letters off ear-lier, so maybe I'll soon have some fresh insight."

"Thank you."

"As for Cilla, Hattie says she'll take her as a student if she doesn't give her any trouble and works hard."

"So you offered to let her practice at your house."

"Well, I do have a piano that's sitting there gather-ing dust."

"Do you play?" He hooked his thumbs in his belt loops in a familiar gesture.

"In my family, all young ladies learned to play the pianoforte, but not necessarily well," she said, looking at a spot somewhere beyond his shoulder.

"I'll wager you did it well. In fact, it's almost impos-sible to imagine that there's anything you don't do well."

Was it a compliment? Just a statement of how he per-ceived her? What? She flashed a quick, uncomfortable smile. "Let's just say that I play the piano better than I embroider, and that I do a lot of things adequately, if not well."

"Like what?"

The question caught her off guard. What was going on? Why was he talking about her and not the children? "Why do you ask?"

He lifted one shoulder and a sandy eyebrow. "You intrigue me, Miss Grainger. After watching you one-on-

one with my kids, I'm curious about the woman beneath that prim-and-proper exterior you show the world."

"Why?" she asked again, even more perplexed.

He shook his head, looking as confounded as she felt. "Just trying to get to know the woman who teaches my children a little better, I guess. The woman who buys a young girl a gift after that girl ruined her glasses and hat."

Allison longed to ask one more "Why?" but figured she should stop while she was ahead. She wasn't sure she wanted to know what was behind his questioning. In fact, she wasn't sure why the sheriff was engaging her in personal conversation.

"I'd better be going," she said, turning toward the steps.

"What's in the sack?"

She whirled back around. "What?"

He gestured toward the small brown bag crushed in her right hand. "What's in the sack?"

"Oh. Maple candy I brought to Brady. He didn't like it."

Colt's eyes brightened. "Maple? That's my favorite."

"Mine, too," she confessed, a bit surprised. Then before she realized what she was doing, she thrust the brown paper bag at him. "Here. Enjoy."

"Thanks."

He reached out and took the candy from her, his fingers, warm and strong and rough to the touch, closing around hers for the briefest of seconds before she snatched her hand back.

"I'm sorry I lost my temper over the children," she said in a rush. "It isn't like me to be so…poorly behaved. I really was brought up to know better."

"I didn't exactly put my best foot forward, either," he admitted. "So now that we're working together and have mended fences, don't you think we should call each other by our first names? I mean, we'll be spending a lot of time together, and it seems silly to be so formal under the circumstances."

"I… I suppose it would be all right. I'm Allison."

"Not Allie?"

"Only to my family," she told him. "I don't know what my mother was thinking. With Ellie and Allie in the same room it can become confusing, so I usually go by my full name."

He smiled and her heart leaped. "Colt."

"Colton?"

"Nope. Just Colt." He smiled again. "I'm glad we got that settled. I'll see you soon."

For some reason, the innocuous words threw her into a tizzy. She nodded and turned, hurrying toward the street. She'd taken no more than half a dozen steps when she whirled back around to face him. "I was thinking about a couple of things. Cilla has told us about things she'd like to do, but I was wondering about Brady. What does he like to do with his spare time?"

"I don't know," he said, clearly embarrassed that he didn't.

Allison was both surprised and not surprised. She was careful not to let her disappointment show. "Well, I was thinking that it might be a good idea to find out and encourage him to pursue something he likes. It seems to me that since he struggles so with his schoolwork, it would do him a lot of good to find something he can excel at. I think it would give him a lot of confidence."

Colt mulled over the idea a minute and nodded. "That makes sense."

She flashed him a quick, nervous smile. "And when you read with him, try not to let him see how frustrated you get. It seems to me that sometimes he puts the wrong sound with a letter. You might try to reinforce the sounds each letter makes. If he's slow, that's okay.

"Oh, and he loves hearing stories in class, so I was wondering if you could take a little time each day to read to him since it's such a chore for him. He's missing a whole wonderful world of books."

She saw color rise in Colt's lean cheeks. "I don't have any books except Patrice's family Bible."

Allison was certain her shock was reflected in her eyes. To her, the notion that any home would be devoid of books was inexcusable, if not downright sinful. "I'm not a reader."

"But you can read?" she asked, wanting to make certain she was dealing with an even more difficult situation.

"Of course I can read. I just don't like to."

Allison released a deep sigh of disbelief. Unimaginable. Still, it was not her duty, nor was it proper, for her to criticize Colt Garrett's habits, unless those habits were detrimental to his children.

"I have a few books I think he'd enjoy. You, too," she mused. "*Adventures of Huckleberry Finn* and *The Story of a Bad Boy.* I'll have to look and see what else is on my shelves. It's a shame Wolf Creek has no library."

"I'm not sure we should give him any more ideas about being a bad boy," Colt said. "Seems like he's a natural at that."

Allison couldn't stifle a sudden burst of laughter.

"Not to worry. He'll love it. It's a humorous story about a little boy with bad manners."

"Sure. Why not?" he said with a shrug. "Actually, it's a great idea since Cilla claims I don't show them enough attention. We'll all read together."

Allison turned again to leave, figuring she'd said enough for the moment.

"Allison?"

The sound of him calling her name brought her to a stop. She turned slowly.

"I really appreciate what you did for Cilla and Brady today."

"It's nothing."

"It means a lot to me."

The expression in his eyes said he was sincere. Her heart throbbed with a sudden ache.

"Thank you," she said, then turned toward town and hurried down the street. She walked home, her heart lighter than at any time the past couple of days. She wasn't so naive as to believe that just because she and Colt had apologized for their deplorable behavior and were working together for his children's sake that everything would come up roses, but she *was* encouraged by their tentative truce.

For the first time, she felt he understood that the situation and her concerns were real, and to his credit, he had taken her suggestions for helping Brady far better than she'd expected. His concern seemed genuine, but like her, he was at a loss as to what to do. At this point, he seemed willing to try almost anything to better the situation, including reading to the kids.

The first thing she did when she got home was look through her book collection to see what might be interesting for a boy Brady's age. Besides the two books she'd mentioned, she found two other Twain books as well as a copy of *Moby-Dick* and a much-read edition of *Little Women* that she and her sisters had almost worn out. Cilla was at an age that she should enjoy the tale of the four sisters.

Then, needing some company, she unhooked her purse from a branch of the hall tree and headed to the café. She thought of taking the books over to the sheriff's, but after a moment's hesitation, she decided that she would wait until the following day. She didn't want him thinking she was too eager, or that she was interested in him. Heaven forbid!

"Here we go again," Cilla whispered to Brady after Miss Grainger left and she'd scurried from her hiding place near the front door, where she'd been stealing peeks at the two grown-ups on the porch.

"What do you mean?" Brady asked, putting down a glass next to his plate.

"Pa wants to call her *Allison* instead of Miss Grainger, and he wants her to call him Colt instead of Sheriff Garrett."

"So?" Brady's forehead was furrowed in puzzlement.

"When grown-ups start calling each other by their first names, it means things are getting more serious."

"You mean like he might start squiring Miss Grainger around like he did those other women?" Brady asked with wide-eyed shock.

"That's exactly what I mean."

"I think they're just working together to try to get us to act better."

"Maybe," Cilla said with a sigh.

"And even if there is more to it, we can't do anything. You heard Pa. If we try to scare her off, it'll be bad for us, so if you cook up one of your schemes, you can count me out."

That evening, after Colt got home from work, whipped up the pancakes Cilla's disastrous trial had given him a hankering for, he sat the children down and tried to get a feel for what they thought about Allison's ideas to make things better. Neither child said much, but in the end they both agreed that they would try to think before they acted, and they would do their best to cooperate without behaving like brats.

Then he spent the miserable, promised time reading with Brady, but felt little was accomplished except that he had done what he'd said he would. He vowed to keep his end of the bargain if it killed him, and while reading with Brady might not actually kill him, it just might drive him nuts.

Later, stretched out in his lonely bed, his arm across his face, the scenes from the past couple of days played through Colt's mind as they had throughout the day. When he slept, he dreamed of the prissy teacher who reached out and wiped his mouth with her napkin. In his dream, as he had that morning, he caught her wrist in his fingers, an automatic reaction to her unexpected, disturbing touch. Her skin felt soft and warm against his fingers. This time, he didn't let go. Instead, he pulled her closer and pressed his mouth to hers. Her pulse thudded beneath his fingertips, and his heart echoed the crazy rhythm as he sank deeper into the kiss....

Chapter Five

Colt had no recollection of his dream when he awakened the next morning. He was shaving when a rogue memory of thoroughly kissed lips flitted unexpectedly into his thoughts, causing the razor to slip. Muttering, he pressed a clean cloth to his chin and glared at his grumpy reflection, searching his mind for any other bits and pieces of the fantasy to give him some hint whom he'd been kissing. Nothing concrete came to mind, but there *was* a nagging suspicion that kept cropping up.

He did know a couple of things. First, he'd accepted the fact that the problem with his children had passed the nuisance stage. Second, he recognized that they needed guidance, love and more attention than he was giving them. He could do that, too, but what they needed was a mother. And as much as it galled him to admit it, he needed someone, too.

It was becoming increasingly clear that he wasn't going to find the kind of love he and Patrice had shared this second time around, but that didn't negate the fact that it was time to find a wife. This time he'd approach it in a different way. He would give serious consideration to every female in Wolf Creek, not just those who struck his fancy, as he'd done in the past. Surely there was someone in town who would be suitable. When he got to work and took care of his morning duties, he'd give it some serious thought.

PROSPECTIVE BRIDES

Colt wrote the title at the top of the tablet on his desk, using bold capital letters and underlining it. He wrote numbers down the left-hand side of the page and spent the next ten minutes staring at the front door, racking his mind for the names of eligible young ladies who might make a decent wife.

Finally he wrote *Holly Jefferson* and *Letitia Farley* in positions one and two, even though it was doubtful that these two young women whom he'd wooed before would give him another chance, even if he explained to them that he'd laid down the law to the kids and promised there would be no more trouble. As his mama always said, a person had only one chance to make a first impression.

Besides, Holly had been seen around town with James Turner the past few weeks, and after some observation, he'd realized that Letitia, who was mighty easy on the eyes, had to be the most helpless female in town, hardly the kind to be much of a helpmeet. He just couldn't picture her standing up to Brady and Cilla without dissolving into a puddle of helplessness.

He drew lines through their names and stared some more, softly whistling the evocatively beautiful "Lorena" while he tapped the pencil on the table. Ellie and Doc Rachel were out since Ellie had made it clear she could not marry anyone, and Gabe had won Rachel's hand. *Think, Colt. Think!* Young unmarried women.

Finally, he wrote *Jocelyn Cole.* Another of Cilla and Brady's victims. Jocelyn was younger and more likely to be forgiving of the kids' trespasses than the other two. Beside her name, he added *Young. Pretty. Likes kids. Sweet.* He thought of the irritating way she often burst into giggles at the most immature things and scratched through her name…twice. *Too* young. He needed a wife and a mother for his kids; he didn't need another one to bring up.

He needed someone older, settled. Ellie's friend Gracie Morrison came to mind. He sighed and determinedly wrote *Gracie Morrison* next to the number four, then added *Twenty-five or twenty-six. Smart. Very nice.* He couldn't put that she was homely and ungainly, though it was true. Besides, her genuine goodness made up for her lack of beauty and grace, giving her her own brand of prettiness. What else? He knew for a fact that she'd been trained from childhood in all the wifely pursuits. Gracie was also very perceptive and fair-minded. She would be a good wife.

He leaned back in his chair and tapped the pencil against his lips. The problem was, he felt not the slightest bit of attraction to her, and desperate or not, if he was going to have to settle for less than love, he at least needed to feel some sort of desirability.

4. Gracie Morrison. Twenty-five or twenty-six. Smart. Very nice.

With a single bold line through her list of attributes, Gracie was out of the running.

Single women, Garrett! Think.

Ah! Widows! He needed to consider widows, not just

women who'd never been married. Let's see—there was Lydia North, but she'd made it pretty clear that after losing her husband, Jake, she would never marry again. Besides, she was so shy, he doubted she could even hold up her end of a conversation. He didn't even bother writing down her name.

How about sweet-as-apple-pie Sophie Forrester? Sophie's husband had been killed more than two years ago in a logging accident. She was a sweet woman and pretty enough in a tired way, and she was only a couple of years older than he. On the negative side, she had three ornery boys of her own. Nope. Sophie was definitely out. He didn't want to add to his misery. Not intentionally, anyway. He drew a heavy line through her name.

He was staring at the scratched-out names on his list when Dan spoke up from behind him. "What's wrong with Gracie?"

Colt flinched in surprise and glared at his second-in-command, who was peering over his shoulder. Big Dan Mercer, his fortysomething, never-been-married deputy, had taken their solitary prisoner's dirty breakfast dishes back to Ellie's. Colt hadn't heard him come in the back door. Blast it all! He hadn't intended for anyone to know about the list. Now Dan would no doubt blab it all over town.

"Not a word about this, Dan," Colt growled.

"What's to say?" the burly older man demanded, a cross expression on his craggy face. "It ain't like everybody in town don't already know you're huntin' for a wife. I'm just curious about why you crossed out Gracie. She's a fine woman, if you ask me."

"I agree," Colt said. "She's one of the finest. She's just not the right one for me."

"Oh." Big Dan cleared his throat and shuffled his weight from one foot to the other. "Well, since you marked her off your list, you won't mind if I ask to call on her, will you?" Dull color crept into his lean cheeks, which bore several scars from his years spent boxing for a living back East.

Colt grinned at his assistant. So that was the way it was. "Not at all."

"Well, all right, then." Big Dan started to walk away.

"I had no idea you were interested in Gracie," Colt said, stopping him.

"I don't tell you everything, you know," Dan said. "The fact is, I've liked her a good long while, but everybody knows she won't tolerate anyone squiring her around who's in the habit of tyin' one on now and then."

He shrugged and continued. "I thought about it, and decided that she's a good woman and deserves the best. Not that I am, of course. Far from it. But you have to admire a woman with principles like that. So I been workin' on things for several months now. I'm even readin' my Bible and such, since I know that's important to her."

Colt stared at the man, impressed, as he often was, by just how far a smitten man would go to win a lady's hand. Pretty potent stuff, love.

"That's great, Dan," Colt said, and meant it.

"So you gonna be here a spell? If you are, I think I'll go talk to Gracie."

Colt smiled again. "What's the hurry?"

"If other guys are considerin' her for matrimony,

maybe I'd better not let any more grass grow under my feet."

"I'll be here," Colt said with a laugh. "Go do your sparking."

"Thanks, boss. I'll be back in an hour or so."

"No rush."

Big Dan turned at the door and held up a rough finger. "Don't forget Ellie and her sister," he said, and then, with another foolish smile, he almost danced out the door.

Ellie and her sister. He'd already established that Ellie was out of the question, and her sister... Colt frowned. Sighed. He'd said he'd consider every eligible female he could think of, and Miss Grainger certainly fit the bill. After another moment's hesitation, he wrote *Allison Grainger*.

Thought a moment and wrote *Smart. Educated.*

It had been very kind of her to buy the things Cilla would need to begin her embroidery.

Thoughtful. Caring. Likes kids.

She'd proved that by writing to her professors and making arrangements for Cilla to learn some feminine pursuits.

What about the attraction, Colt?

Well, he certainly didn't find her unattractive. In fact, she was more than all right, he supposed. Frowning, he kicked back, swung his feet to the desktop and laced his fingers together behind his head, his habitual thinking position.

He stared up at the ceiling and recalled how different she'd looked when he'd taken the children to apologize. There was no doubt that her hair made a tempting sight hanging free down her back. It made a man's hands fairly itch to test the springy curls to see if they were as soft as they looked.

He sat bolt upright, the front legs of his chair hitting the floor with a thud. *Tempting? Soft?* A humorless chuckle escaped him. A man would have to be crazy to use those two words in the same breath as *Allison Grainger.* He picked up the pencil, determined to add her other good features to the list. She might be a tad plump, but she had nice skin, a nice nose, really unusual eyes and incredible eyelashes. Not to mention a pretty mouth.

He wrote everything down and scanned the list. There was no denying that it was impressive. If he were just looking at positives, Miss Allison Grainger had several. Of course, she had quite the temper when she was riled, but then, it was his experience that most women did. Still, he wrote that down, too—*high-tempered. Stubborn.*

Definitely stubborn and...*opinionated.*

He heard the door open and looked up. To his surprise, it was none other than the object of his thoughts, carrying an armload of books.

The list!

Allison watched as Colt stood, dragged open his middle desk drawer and shoved a tablet inside, almost in one motion. "Am I interrupting anything?"

"No, ma'am," he said, a bit nervously. "Just, uh, making a list."

"Oh." She offered him a tentative smile and crossed to the desk, placing the books on the scarred top. "I found some books I thought you and Brady might enjoy," she said. "And one I think Cilla might like."

She hoped he could see that she was taking their problem seriously. He gestured toward the chair across from him, and she sat, smoothing her simple gray skirt and lacing her fingers together in her lap, hoping her own tension didn't show. There was something about being in the same room with the sheriff that taxed her nerves. Next to her he was so big and tough-looking, not to mention so very good-looking that it was a wonder the ladies didn't swoon when he passed them on the street. Her fingers tightened.

"That's very thoughtful of you," he told her, taking his seat again.

"I'm just doing my job, Sheriff," she said, the tension she was feeling causing her to resort to her previous stiff demeanor.

"Colt," he reminded her. "And it isn't your job to lend us books, or buy Cilla sewing notions or offer her your piano to practice on."

She granted him another jumpy, fleeting smile. "Well, since we have no lending library, it seemed like the thing to do. I'm hoping the children will see me as someone who really does have their best interests at heart."

"I need to work on my fathering skills, too," he said. "I'm planning on spending more time with them in the evenings." He gave his head a shake. "I can't believe they doubt that I love them."

"Growing up is hard," she said. "Children need to be shown love as well as being told they're loved." She gave a sad little sigh. "In fact, everyone does. Wouldn't you agree?"

As soon as she said the words, she dropped her gaze to her lap, longing to call them back, lest he think she was getting too personal. Or he might think she was pining for love herself. Which, of course, she was. Even worse, he might think she was hinting that she wanted love from him! She pressed her lips together. Oh, why was she so inept when it came to conversing with the opposite sex?

She looked up, her gaze meeting his. The intensity in his eyes almost robbed her of breath. Why was he looking at her like that?

"I would definitely agree."

Surely it was her imagination, but his voice sounded husky. Allison's eyelids drifted downward, and just for an instant, she allowed herself the luxury of imagining that throaty voice whispering into her ear.

Desperate to change the subject, she raised her head and said, "I'm sure you'll figure it out. Has Brady said what it is that interests him?"

Colt looked taken aback by the sudden change in the conversational topic. "Actually, he said he wants Lew Jessup to teach him how to play the harmonica, and he wants to learn to shoot a bow and arrow."

Colt rubbed his cheek in a familiar gesture. "Thing is, the only person I know who can show him that is Ace, and I'm not sure where he is at the moment."

"Ace Allen?" Allison couldn't hide her shock. Ace, an improbable combination of Irish and Cherokee, had been sent to prison earlier in the year, along with Meg Thomerson's husband, Elton, for a series of thefts and an attack on Sarah VanSickle. Fortunately for her, Gabe Gentry had come along to help on his way home from Antoine.

"But he's in prison!"

Colt shook his head. "Not anymore. Actually, he's

been in prison twice. The first time was a manslaughter charge a few years ago."

"Manslaughter! What happened?"

"I'm sure you can imagine that it's tough being a half breed. He's spent a lot of time defending himself to all the people who look down on him. He got into a fistfight taking up for his mama. The guy hit his head on a rock and died. It was an accident, but because of who he was, Ace spent two years at hard labor. When he got out, he went to Oklahoma for a while then came back here to help Nita out when Yancy died."

"I had no idea," Allison breathed.

Colt shrugged. "Word got around that Elton's partner was Indian. Ace may be half Irish, but everyone considers him Indian, and they knew he'd done time. To top things off, Elton corroborated that Ace was his partner even though Sarah and Gabe said otherwise."

"Why would Elton lie about something like that?"

"I don't have a clue. He must have something against Ace we don't know about. Maybe he just likes to cause grief. I had no choice but to arrest him. Like I said, he got a raw deal, but thanks to a pardon from the governor, he was out pretty quick. We've kept it quiet on purpose, and there aren't too many people who know. When he got out he took off like he did before, and no one knows where he is—not even his mother."

"And you're certain he's innocent?" Allison asked, horrified that a criminal might be walking among them.

"I'm positive. Ace gave me a couple of names and I started digging around. It didn't take long to link Thomerson to Joseph Jones from over around Murfreesboro. I also verified Ace's whereabouts on the days of the other robberies, and there's no way he could have been involved. A lot of folks in town will be eating crow when the truth comes out."

Allison was impressed with Colt's determination to seek justice for his friend. He was a good lawman, and despite his ambivalence toward God and his haphazard parenting skills, she believed he was a good man.

She remembered seeing Nita Allen's son in town a time or two, and recalled his dignified bearing and the unrestrained beauty in the noble bone structure of his angular face. Both attributes said he'd walked through the fires of his own personal hell, come out on the other side and was somehow better for it.

"And you're all right with him spending time with Brady even though he's a convicted felon," she stated.

Colt's mouth twisted into a grim smile. "Why wouldn't I be? I've proved that he wasn't the one with Elton, and the death of that other guy was an accident. Young men fight. I know I did. There but for the grace of God, what happened to Ace could have happened to me or a dozen of my buddies."

"I had no idea the two of you were friends. How did that happen?"

Colt smiled, and Allison's heart did a little flip. "Like I said, after he got out of prison the first time, he went to Oklahoma to be with his family there until his wounds healed."

"Wounds?"

"Prison isn't a very nice place, and his wounds weren't just physical. He needed to sort of cleanse his mind of the things done to him. He was up there a couple of years or so. He came back about the time I moved here, though he didn't hang around town much. When we did meet, we hit it off. I reckon we're as close as two people with such different backgrounds can be. All I know is that he's always around when I need him, and he's never let me down or turned me down, no matter what I ask of him."

"He's lucky to have a friend like you."

"That goes both ways."

"So you have no idea where he is?"

"Not exactly. He's in the woods somewhere. He spends as much time there as he can and still provide for Nita. He says he needs time alone with God to help keep things in perspective."

Though he hadn't been around since before his latest arrest, Allison knew Ace had been to church services a few times, but he always came in after everyone was seated and sat on the floor near the door. His knack for slipping out during the closing prayer was a favorite topic of the church members.

She also knew that cleaned game and garden bounty sometimes showed up at some needy person's house. The general consensus was that the gifts were left by Ace. Meg had mentioned it happening several times when Elton was gone on one of his extended absences.

"After lunch I thought I'd go put out the word that I'm looking for him, but even if I don't find him, he'll turn up sooner or later."

"I'm sure he will." Allison picked up the small watch she wore on a chain around her neck. "Speaking of lunch, I'd best get home and start something."

"What are your plans for supper?"

Her startled gaze found his. What on earth did he have in mind? "N-nothing special," she managed to say.

"Since I'm making a real effort to spend more time with the kids, I decided to have Ellie fix us some sandwiches and get some cold sarsaparillas from Gabe for our supper. He said I could borrow his croquet game and set it up out back. We're having a backyard picnic. Would you like to join us?"

"I don't—"

"Don't say no," he said with a persuasive smile. "I may need your help."

The magic word. Help was what she did best. Allison hesitated only a moment. "Well, all right. I'd be glad to join you. Shall I bring a dessert?"

"Do you by any chance make chocolate pie?"

"My chocolate pie is far better than my piano playing or embroidery," she said with a smile.

"I'll look forward to trying it, then," he said, smiling back. "About six?"

"Fine." With her heart almost beating out of her chest, she made her way to the door.

"Allie?"

She sucked in a sharp little breath at his use of her family nickname. "Yes?" she said, turning.

"How does your croquet game stack up against your embroidery and piano playing?"

She looked at him with raised eyebrows and a taunting expression in her eyes. "It ranks right up there with my chocolate pie, so beware. What about you?"

"I'm new to it, but picking it up pretty fast," he told her with a cocky smile.

"Well, you might have a fighting chance since I'm not seeing as well as I might if I had my glasses."

"Oh, my!" he said with a grin. "Is that a challenge? I've never been one to turn down a dare."

She gave a slight lift of her shoulders. Then, without

another word, she opened the door, leaving Colt standing there with a bemused look on his face.

"You've been a great help," Mr. Gentry said, handing both Cilla and Brady a handful of penny candy when they finished their chores at the mercantile.

"Thank you, Mr. Gentry," they said in unison, thrilled to receive something tangible for their efforts when they'd been expecting nothing but the reduction of their debt. Mr. Gentry was really nice and a lot of fun, even though he expected the work to get done.

He smiled. "You're very welcome. I'll see you tomorrow about the same time."

They said their goodbyes, left the store and headed to the jail. Cilla wanted to tell her father that she was going by the boardinghouse to talk to Mrs. Carson about starting her piano lessons, and her dad was a real stickler when it came to letting him know where you were and what you were doing.

Cilla sucked on a piece of taffy as they made their way to the jail. She was surprised to realize that working off their debt wasn't going to be as onerous a chore as she'd imagined. She was used to doing most of the housework, and she had a natural tendency toward tidiness, so it was no hard task to straighten and dust shelves and arrange items in a neat way.

Mr. Gentry had even trusted her to unpack and display the new shipment of hats, and she found herself examining each one as she set it on its form, considering which one might look best as Miss Grainger's replacement. There were six in all, but Cilla's favorites were a small hat with an upturned brim and lace edging that sat toward the back of the head; a chipped straw with a wide brim and a cluster of blue and purple flowers in front; and a tall one that Mr. Gentry called a "flowerpot" hat, adorned with both flowers and feathers. That was Cilla's favorite.

Brady helped Gabe and his son Danny in the back, though from the way they were laughing, it hadn't sounded as if much work was getting done.

It had been an interesting afternoon in many ways, and she had a lot of thinking to do. She'd caught Danny alone and asked how their friend Ben Carter liked having Caleb Gentry as a stepfather. Danny said Ben loved Caleb, even though he hadn't liked the notion of his mom marrying at first. Then Cilla asked how Danny liked having a new father. He told her it was swell having his parents together and being part of a real family.

Still unconvinced, Cilla figured that maybe Ben was just thankful his stepfather had found him when he'd fallen down that steep embankment and broken his leg. And Danny *would* like Mr. Gentry, because he was his *real* father, after all.

At the moment, she was no nearer accepting the notion that her pa would take a wife. Contrarily, she'd more or less reconciled herself to the fact that it was bound to happen whether she liked it or not.

Leaving her troubled thoughts behind, she pushed through the front door of the jail. There was no one behind the desk.

"He's not here," Brady said when they stepped through the door.

"I can see that," she said crossly.

"What are you gonna do?"

"I'm sure Dan is around here somewhere," she said, heading through the door that led to the cell area. Sure enough, the deputy was there, taking a nap on one of the narrow cots, flat on his back, his hands folded across his middle and his mouth hanging open. He was snoring softly. Brady put a hand over his own mouth to stifle a giggle, but his eyes were alight with laughter. Grinning, Cilla dragged him back to the office and eased the door shut.

"I'll leave Pa a note," she said, pulling open the desk's top right-hand drawer. Nothing but a couple of pairs of handcuffs, a bandanna and some shotgun shells. The lower one was empty. She drew open the middle drawer and spied the tablet on top.

Pulling it out, she plopped it onto the desk and was about to tear out a sheet of paper when she saw the list of names. She read it slowly. Then read it again. There was no way she could misunderstand what she was seeing, since it was labeled at the top of the page, and unlike her brother, her reading skills were excellent.

"Oh. My. Goodness."

"What?" Brady asked, rounding the desk and trying to see the pages.

"Pa wasn't kidding," she said, turning a wild-eyed look toward her brother. "He really does mean to get married again. Maybe sooner than we think."

"How do you know? What does it say?" Brady asked, craning his neck to get a better look.

"It's a list of single ladies in town."

"Who's on there?" Brady yanked the pad from her grasp and studied it for a moment. Then he handed it back. "Wow."

"Let's go," Cilla said, pushing the tablet back into the drawer.

"What about your note?"

"I'll go see Mrs. Carson tomorrow. I need to go home and think."

"Doesn't seem to me there's any sense in that," Brady said as he and his sister headed outside. "You heard what Pa said, and it looked to me like he's made up his mind."

Cilla paused in front of the barbershop and pinned him with a sharp look. "How do you figure that? There's no way you could have read that list so fast."

"I didn't have to," he grumbled. "All the names were crossed out but one, so it was the only one that mattered. And it was Miss Grainger."

It was nearing supper time when Colt rode back into town. Antioch Street was all but deserted, with most folks headed home for their evening meal. He hadn't found Ace, but Nita said she was expecting him to stop by anytime. Colt knew that she would tell her son Colt was looking for him when he decided to rejoin civilization.

He dismounted in front of Ellie's and tied his gelding to the hitching post. She and Bethany were both bustling around, serving plates of delicious-smelling food to a packed house.

"Hi, Colt!" she said as she passed him with a plate of roast beef and all the trimmings. "I'll have your sandwiches ready in a jiffy."

"No hurry. Will you add another one to the order, please?"

"Sure," Ellie said, giving him a curious look. When she'd delivered another half-dozen plates, she preceded him to the back counter. "Is someone joining you?" she asked, casting a curious look over her shoulder.

"Yep."

"Anyone I know?" She kept her tone casual.

"Yep."

"Male or female?"

"Female."

"Well," she huffed. "Aren't you going to tell me who she is?"

Feigning nonchalance, he shifted his weight to one leg and hooked his thumbs in his belt loops. "Nope."

"Colt Garrett, if I didn't like you so much, I'd bash you over the head with an iron skillet."

"It's your sister."

"What?" Ellie screeched. Every head in the café turned their way. "Allie?" she said in a loud whisper.

Colt relented of his teasing. "It's not what you think."

"It's not?" She sounded almost disappointed at his denial.

"You know Homer laid down the law about getting the kids straightened out by the time school starts. Allison is doing everything she can on her end. Since I need to spend more time with them, I've borrowed Gabe's croquet set for this evening, and thought we'd have a picnic out back. I asked your sister to join us. Sort of as a buffer, you know?"

"Oh." Looking let down by the news, Ellie slipped through the swinging doors to the kitchen.

Colt watched her go, pondering her disappointment. Was she hoping some sort of spark would ignite between him and her sister? Surely Ellie knew him well enough to realize that Allison wasn't his type. But as he took his wax-paper-wrapped sandwiches, he couldn't help noticing Ellie's downturned mouth and thinking it looked exactly like Allison's.

Chapter Six

He was nervous! Imagine that. A game of croquet and sandwiches with the kids and their teacher and he was as jumpy as a new student on the first day of school.

"Hurry up, Pa!" Brady said. "We've gotta get the game set up."

"Right." Colt took a final glance in the mottled shaving mirror, ran a hand through his damp hair and frowned, wondering why he'd bothered, since he'd be hot and sweaty by the game's end. Instructing Brady and Cilla to help, he paced off a rough rectangle fifty feet long and twenty-five feet wide, marking it with a little sprinkle of flour. Then he estimated the approximate center and told Brady to place the first wicket there. Then it was a matter of stepping off the general spots for the remaining eight. No need for perfection. It was only a backyard game, after all.

Brady was just pounding in the last stake when a feminine voice said, "Looks like I'm just in time."

The whole Garrett family turned to see Miss Grainger standing there, a cloth bag dangling from her wrist, a pie topped with golden-brown meringue in her hands. It looked delicious, Colt thought. Actually, so did she. He frowned at the inappropriate thought. Like the "cleaning lady" Allison, this was an Allison he'd never seen before.

She must have seen the look on his face because she tucked a wayward spiral behind her ear in a gesture that betrayed her own nervousness.

She was hatless and gloveless, and dressed in a simple pale green skirt that fell smooth and straight from the waistband, flared toward the hem from about her knees and brushed the grass with each step she took. Her white blouse was sewn of some soft-looking, lightweight fabric with narrow pin tucks marching down the front. As she had on cleaning day, she looked much slimmer. Her watch hung around her neck on a plain green ribbon, and her hair was tied at her nape with another, the shimmering curls flowing down her back in riotous rebellion.

"Hi, Miss Grainger!" Brady said at last.

"Hello, Brady," she said, giving him one of the full-blown smiles Colt had heard about and never seen. A strangled breath of wonder whistled through his parted lips. What could Cilla possibly see in that smile to complain about? It was nothing short of astonishing, lighting Allison's eyes and creating the merest hint of a dimple in her left cheek.

Feeling a bit off balance, he started toward her. "I'm glad you could come."

"I've been looking forward to it." She held out the pie. "For you."

"What kind is it, Pa?" Brady asked, running toward them.

Colt took the pie and regarded her with raised eyebrows. "Chocolate?"

"As per your request." She held up the fabric bag. "I stopped by Gabe's and picked up some bread-and-butter pickles and Saratoga Chips. I haven't tried them, but I understand from Mrs. VanSickle that they're quite tasty."

"So I hear. Let me take this inside, and we'll start the game. Or would you rather eat first and let it cool off a bit?"

"I get lazy after I eat," she confessed, placing her hands on her shapely hips. "And I'm sure the children would rather play."

They agreed, and Colt carried Allison's contributions to their meal inside. When he came back out, she was sitting on the edge of the porch. It looked as if she was taking off a shoe. When she heard the door slam, she made a quick, deft movement, peeling off her stocking and uncrossing her legs all in one smooth motion before wadding the sheer silk into a ball and stuffing it inside one of the white shoes whose needle toes were adorned with black patent leather. She looked up, clearly embarrassed.

"What are you doing?" he asked, his gaze moving from her scandalously bare ankle to the small feet and toes that were curled into the clover beneath her feet.

She jumped up and robbed him of the socially disapproved-of view, giving him a mischievous grin to cover the awkward moment. "I always play barefoot."

"Why?"

She shrugged. "So I can curl my toes around the ball when I need to whack it and send someone else's ball far, far away. Besides, the grass feels good on my feet."

"Aren't you afraid you'll wallop your foot?" he asked, shocked by the announcement.

"I suppose it's a possibility," she called over her shoulder as she headed toward the children, who were arguing over who would go first. "But I never have.

"Okay, you two, stop arguing," she told them with her schoolteacher's voice and a sharp clap of her hands. To Colt's amazement, they did. "There's a proper way to determine who goes first."

"Tell us!" Brady cried.

"No," she said with a shake of her head. "We'll all choose colors and then I'll tell you. The colors you choose determine who your partner will be. Brady, you pick first, since you're the youngest, then Cilla and then your dad." She glanced over at Colt, who was still marveling at how easily the children obeyed her. "I'll take what's left, since I know the rules."

"Blue," Brady said without hesitation. "For boys." He grinned. "Too bad there's no pink for girls."

Cilla glared at him. "Red."

"I'll take black," Colt said before another argument could break out. "I don't think I'm a yellow sort of guy."

"That means I'm yellow," Allison said. "Blue and black are paired up, and red and yellow. Brady, you and your dad are a team."

Brady crowed with happiness and ran over to Colt, who ruffled his dark hair. Colt was a little surprised by how little it took to bring a smile to the kids' faces.

"Blue goes first," Allison said. "Then the order of play is red, black and yellow, which means that you and your opponents alternate play." She looked from one to the other. "Does everyone understand?"

Colt and the kids said they did, and she explained how Brady was to start the game and what the objective was. As each turn came up, she gave them their options of play and let them decide what to do. Of course, Colt and Brady knocked Cilla's and Allison's balls as far from each other as possible.

For the next half hour or so, they romped and played, bandying about threats and warnings and laughing as their balls either made it through the wickets or were knocked off course.

With the game more than half over and Brady and Colt almost certain to win, Allison's ball wound up touching Colt's. He cut a startled glance in her direction. She was in perfect position to knock his ball away and deal him and Brady some serious damage. It hadn't taken him long to learn that she was as competitive as he was, something most women would never admit to a man. He liked that she was willing to pit her wits and skill against his, whether or not it was acceptable ladies' comportment.

She glanced over at him, her eyes sparkling with mischief, a playful half smile on her lips. "Cilla, what do you think about me putting your father's ball over by the oak tree?" she asked her partner.

Cilla jumped up and down, chortling her approval. Brady stomped his foot. They both knew she could probably do it.

"Don't do it, Allie," Colt warned with a look of mock ferocity.

"You know what they say about croquet," she told him, sauntering toward the balls, her intention clear. "It may look like an easygoing game, but it's really very, very wicket."

Colt was laughing at the pun and the children were looking at him and each other, trying to figure out what they'd missed, when Allison gave a little yelp of pain and began hopping around on one foot.

Colt was at her side in an instant, and the kids weren't far behind, all asking some variation of "What's the matter?"

Slipping his arm around her waist to steady her seemed like the natural thing to do. The sweet aroma of honeysuckle radiated from her body, soft and warm against his side. She sucked in a sharp breath, stiffened and tipped back her head, her pain-filled eyes finding his.

A wave of concern swept over him, and he tightened his hold on her waist so she wouldn't pull away. "What's wrong?"

"I—I s-stepped on s-something," she stammered.

Allison gave another little gasp when he scooped her into his arms and headed toward the house. Since she couldn't figure out what else to do with them, she looped her arms around his neck, fighting the urge to close her eyes and lean her forehead against his cheek. Instead, she gave the children, who trailed behind, a wavering smile of encouragement.

When he reached the back porch and leaned over to set her down, his temple brushed the crest of her cheekbone. Wondering why he jerked back, she looked up at him. He was looking at her as if he'd never seen her before. She wasn't aware that her arms still circled his neck until he closed his hands around her wrists and tugged them free.

Suddenly all business, he knelt on one knee in the grass and rested the heel of her bare foot on his other knee, giving it a close examination. Allison tried to ignore the way the lighter streaks in his hair trapped the sunlight and turned them into gleaming strands of gold. She leaned back on her elbows to keep from reaching up and threading her fingers through the soft thickness, and closed her eyes to block the image of his warm, calloused fingers circling her foot. His thumbs rested in her arch as he tilted her foot to see better. She was unable to stop the little catch in her breathing when one thumb moved ever-so-softly up to the ball of her foot.

"I'm sorry," he apologized, misunderstanding the reason for her shortness of breath. "I didn't mean to hurt you."

Afraid to trust her voice, Allison only nodded.

"Looks like a honeybee stung you. The stinger is still in there, and it's already getting red and puffy."

"Are you all right, Miss Grainger?" Brady said, plopping down beside her.

"I'm fine, Brady," she told him with a weak smile.

Colt lowered her foot to the ground and stood, then reached into his pocket and pulled out his knife. "Cilla, will you please go in and mix up some baking soda and water for Allison's foot? And bring a clean hankie from my drawer."

"Yes, sir."

He opened the bone-handled knife, glanced at her and smiled. "Trust me, I'm not going to cut it out. I just need to get the stinger between my thumb and the knife blade to make sure I get a tight hold on it."

"Oh."

By the time he got the stinger out, Cilla had reappeared with the things he'd asked for. He applied a generous amount of the soda paste to her foot and tied the

handkerchief around it. The pain eased almost immediately.

"I'm sorry," she said, "but I don't think I can finish
the game right now."

"Aw, me and Pa were winning!" Brady said, clearly
disappointed.

"Pa and I were winning." Allison's correction of his
speech was as natural as breathing.

"Pa and I," Brady repeated with a disgusted down-
turn of his mouth.

"That's all right, Miss Grainger," Cilla said. "We can
play another day, right, Pa?"

Colt gave his daughter a look that said he wasn't sure
he believed what he was hearing. "Sure."

"Well, I should probably go home now that I've ruined the evening."

"It isn't your fault," Cilla said. "It's that stupid old
bee's."

"But you're supposed to stay to eat with us," Brady
wailed.

"That was part of the deal," Colt reminded her. "A
game of croquet and supper. If," he added, "your foot
doesn't hurt too much."

"No, it's just a dull throb. Just let me put my shoes
on, and I'll stay. I just hate that I've ruined the evening."

"Not a problem," Colt assured her. "You sit tight
while the kids and I get things ready."

"I can help."

"Nope. You're company," Colt told her. "Come on,
kids. Let's set the food out."

To her surprise, putting on her shoe was a bigger
ordeal than she'd expected, since her foot was already
swelling.

"Are you okay?" Cilla asked, stepping out onto the porch. "Pa said you were taking a long time."

"I'm sorry," Allison told her, "but I'm having a hard time getting my shoe on."

Cilla watched a moment as Allison tried to wriggle her heel into the soft leather slipper. She was surprised to see Cilla trying to bite back a smile.

"I'll have you know, it isn't funny, young lady," Allison said with mock annoyance, which was accompanied by a smile of her own.

"But it is!" Cilla said with a giggle. "You look like Mrs. VanSickle trying to stuff her foot into some shoes that were way too small the other day!"

The mental image was so vivid that Allison burst out laughing. "I think I'll just leave it off," she said after a moment. "These stockings are old. I can go home with one shoe off and one shoe on."

"Then you'll be like Diddle Diddle Dumpling!" Cilla cried, her eyes alight with laughter. Allison began to laugh, too, and when Brady and Colt came to the door to see what was going on, they found both females wearing wide smiles.

"What's so funny?" Brady asked.

"Miss Grainger can't get her shoe on," Cilla said. While Allison hobbled onto the porch, Cilla told her dad and brother what had been said. Colt laughed, but Brady only frowned, as if he didn't understand what was so funny.

"You won't have to walk home," he said when things quieted down. "Pa can take you home in the wagon."

"That's a good idea," Cilla added.

"That isn't necessary," Allison told him. "It isn't that far, and I'm perfectly able to walk."

"How about we discuss it after we eat?" Colt said, opening the screen door for the ladies to precede him.

"Let's," Cilla said. She smiled at Allison as if there had never been any animosity between them.

Considering their past, Allison was a trifle wary of Cilla's sudden friendliness. History had taught her that if Colt's children were behaving, it was because they had something up their sleeves. Their actions had been exemplary thus far, and she was happy that things were going so well, but she was still expecting the other shoe to drop. She followed them inside, suppressing a shudder at what it might be.

Like the rest of his house, Colt's kitchen was worn, but cleaner than she'd dared to expect. She'd heard from Gabe that most of the cleaning was done by Cilla, and complimented the child on a job well done. Cilla glowed under the praise.

The meal went well. As usual, Ellie had outdone herself with the ham sandwiches, slathering the soft crusty bread with her special mayonnaise and adding thick slices of cheese, fresh tomato and lettuce. Colt declared that the addition of the pickles Allison had brought made the sandwiches perfect. As predicted by both Gabe and Mrs. VanSickle, the crispy fried potato chips were a hit with everyone, and with the cold sarsaparilla to wash it all down, the casual meal was fit for a king.

Allison couldn't say when she'd enjoyed a supper more, but was struck by the bittersweet realization that it had as much to do with the people she shared it with as it did with the simple, filling fare. She must take care not to allow her emotions to become too involved with the Garretts, since the arrangement was only temporary.

When they'd finished eating and her hosts had cleared the table, Colt told Allison that she should probably soak her foot in some Epsom salts.

"That's a good idea," she said, rising.

"I didn't mean right now," he said. "I'm not trying to run you off. It was just a suggestion."

"Oh. Well, I should be going anyway. It'll take me a while to hobble home."

"I'm taking you home," he told her. "No arguments. I should have come and picked you up."

"Brady and I will pick up all the balls and wickets and stuff while you're gone," Cilla offered.

Colt regarded his firstborn with a look that could only be described as "stunned." Wearing a frown of bewilderment, he mumbled something about appreciating the help.

Allison visited with the children while he hooked up the wagon. She was standing there, wondering how on earth she was supposed to get up into it with the skirt she was wearing and a sore foot, when Colt climbed down, rounded the rig, picked her up and set her on the seat. It was done so fast that she was seated before she could do more than open her mouth to object. Climbing in beside her, he clucked to the horse, and they were off down the street.

Neither spoke much along the way. Allison sneaked a peek at his profile, and thought for perhaps the hundredth time what an attractive man he was. As she was staring at him, he turned to look at her and smiled that lazy half smile. Her heart melted and she felt a tremulous smile curve her own lips.

"Thanks for joining us," he told her.

"I enjoyed it."

"The pie was delicious. You've been holding out on everyone."

She gave him a questioning look.

"Everyone thinks Ellie's the cook of the family. They don't know you're as good as she is."

"Well, we *were* brought up by the same mother," she said. "And really, she's much better with a lot of things than I am."

"Time will tell."

"What does that mean?"

She wasn't aware she'd spoken the question aloud until he said, "We only have a certain amount of time to work miracles with my kids, so it only stands to reason that we'll be spending a good deal of it with each other, don't you think?"

"Oh. Of course." A heady thought, to be sure.

"And I think it's fair to say that some of that time will be spent eating together."

"Oh," she said again and could have died of mortification that she was unable to come up with some sort of teasing, scintillating answer. No wonder she couldn't hold a man's interest.

They reached her house far too soon, yet not soon enough. Once again, Colt got down from the rig to help her alight. This time, he slipped his arm around her to steady her as she limped toward the house.

"You don't have to hold on to me."

"I think I do."

Something in the tone of his voice sent her gaze winging to his. There was a look in his eyes she couldn't name, but it sent a shivery feeling tripping down her spine. Suddenly edgy and a little irritated with herself for her reaction to his nearness, she hurried toward the porch. This time he let her go.

At the door, Allison turned, her hand resting on the doorknob. He was standing in a familiar pose—thumbs hooked through his belt loops, his weight shifted to one leg. From where she stood, his shoulders looked impossibly broad.

"I enjoyed the evening. Thank you for asking me to join you." Her tone of voice told her that the prim-and-proper teacher was back. Thank goodness. There was no sense wishing for impossible dreams.

"While you were hitching up the wagon, I was talking with Cilla and Brady about church. I was wondering if it would be all right if I take them with me on Sunday. They seemed a bit skeptical, but when I told them Danny and Ben and some of their other friends would be there, they said they might like to go, if you have no objections."

"No," he told her, looking at her strangely. "No objections."

"Thank you. I really think it will be good for them, and it's another way for them to be included in some activities. You're welcome to join us."

"No, thanks." He turned and headed toward the wagon. Settled on the seat, he said, "Either the kids or I will bring the pie tin by when we finish with it."

Even though she knew they would be seeing a lot of each other, the moment felt oddly like goodbye. "That's fine. And I'll be sure and let you know as soon as I hear from my professors. Oh! And remind Cilla that she's welcome to come and practice her piano anytime."

"I will. Don't forget to doctor your foot."

"I won't. Good night."

"'Night, Allie."

She watched as he turned around in the middle of the deserted street. When he was nothing but a speck in the distance, she went inside and straight to the bedroom mirror.

She hardly recognized the stranger staring back at her. This was not the tidy, genteel Miss Grainger. The ribbon holding her hair in place was gone, stuffed into the pocket of her skirt. This woman's hair was an untidy jumble of red curls. Allison threaded her fingers through the heavy tresses and lifted it away from her hot neck, noticing that her face was flushed. From playing croquet in the late-afternoon sun, or from knowing that her actions at Colt's bordered on improper?

She let the hair fall and pressed her hands to her cheeks. Good heavens! Had she really taken off her shoes? Never mind that she'd always played the game shoeless. This was different. She wasn't playing with family. She'd been playing with a single male and his children, a man who was little more than a stranger. And she'd allowed him to handle her bare foot! What a scandal that would be if word got out!

With a little cry of distress, Allison turned from the mirror. No more! It was silly of her to let her emotions run amok just because she'd spent a couple of pleasant hours with the Garretts. Today was just an unusual contradiction to the status quo. Everyone was being nice, putting their best foot forward. Why, even the children had been as close to angels as they were ever likely to be.

Usually, she and Colt were at each other's throats. Natural enemies, so to speak. She might find him attractive, but he was the single man about town who could have anyone he wanted. And he would never want her. Even if by some miracle he did, he was not the kind of man she was looking for. Why, he was still blaming God for Patrice's death! Allison was looking for a man willing to lead his family to Heaven. She was afraid to settle for less, even if it meant she went to the grave a spinster schoolteacher.

Satisfied that she had things in proper perspective, she began to unbutton her blouse, praying her thoughts would not keep her awake.

While Colt was driving Allison home, Cilla and Brady gathered the croquet pieces. Her dad had seemed surprised but pleased that she'd offered to put the game away, and she liked that she'd pleased him for a change.

"She's really not so bad, is she?" Cilla asked, putting the last mallet into the holder.

"Who? Miss Grainger?"

"Of course I mean Miss Grainger. I think we've misjudged her."

"What do you mean?"

"You know how Mr. Gentry puts up a new scripture every day or so? Well, today it said that we would be judged by the way we judge other people, and after seeing how nice she's been since we were so terrible to her, I think we may have been wrong about her. I think she does care about her students and that it really does bother her when she feels like she hasn't done a good job."

Brady frowned, thinking hard. "She has been pretty nice to us," he agreed. "Well, to you, anyway. Not many people would have bought you those embroidery things, or talked to Mrs. Carson about piano lessons and stuff."

"She brought you books," Cilla reminded him.

Brady's mouth turned down at the corners. "I hate to read. Do you think I'll ever be able to read like you?"

"I don't know," she told him, "but it seems to me that Miss Grainger really is trying to help."

"I guess so," Brady acknowledged with a nod. "And Pa is gonna have Ace teach me to shoot a bow and arrow and he's buying me a harmonica, so I can learn to play."

"The idea of finding something you'd like to do was Miss Grainger's idea," Cilla remarked. When he didn't reply, she said, "I think she's the one, Brady."

He scowled again. "The one what?"

"The one to be our stepmother."

"Are you crazy?" Brady stormed.

"Think about it. That list we saw in Pa's desk drawer was a list of women he was considering. So far, we've stopped him from marrying any of them, but he's told us he's going to marry someone someday whether we like it or not, and that list proves he's getting serious."

"Yeah," Brady said. "It's only a matter of time." He darted a glance at his sister as they went back inside and into the kitchen. "I think you're right about her being the best one in town, but what if Pa doesn't?"

"She was on the list, wasn't she?"

"Yeah, but so were a lot of others."

"Yes, but Miss Grainger's name wasn't scratched out like the others, so she must be the one he likes the best."

"Do you really think so?"

"Yes. And didn't you see the way she looked at him while we were playing croquet? She likes him."

"How do you know?"

"Her eyes got all soft and dreamy."

"She looks like that all the time without her glasses," Brady scoffed.

"This is different. Pa was really having a good time, too. I haven't heard him laugh so much in…in I can't remember when, but it's been a long time. I'm *sure* he likes her, too."

"So you think she would be a good stepmother."

"Yes." Cilla ticked off reasons on her fingers. "First, she's the best he's come up with so far. A lot better than any of those other ladies on his list. Second, it would be really handy to have a teacher in the family, when our lessons get too hard. Third, I think she likes children, so I don't think she'd be mean to us. Fourth…" Cilla paused, thinking.

"She makes really good chocolate pie," Brady offered.

"Yes, she does, so—"

"But she's a teacher, not a mother."

"Ben's mother was a teacher before she got married. A lot of women are," Cilla explained with the wisdom of a twelve-year-old.

"Okay," Brady said, nodding. "So we're going to leave Pa alone while he courts Miss Grainger. We're not going to try to drive them apart. Is that what you're saying?"

"Not exactly." Cilla looked thoughtful. "Pa told us that courting is a time that two people see if they have things in common and if they like each other enough to get married. We need to try to do everything we can to get them together, because if he doesn't marry her, no telling who else might come into the picture. Mrs. Forrester's name was on the list, and she's got a house full of kids. I'd wind up being a babysitter for the bunch," she said in disgust.

Brady's eyes grew wide. "Yeah, and Johnny Forrester is a really mean kid. I'd rather have a new baby brother than Johnny."

They stared at each other for long seconds.

"Right," Cilla said, but she didn't look convinced.

Brady hung the dish towel on the edge of the kitchen cabinet. "Do you think we should tell him?"

Colt was about to step onto the back porch when he heard Brady's question. The uneasiness in his son's voice told Colt that something was up. Taking a deep breath, he stepped onto the porch and pulled open the door.

"Tell me what?"

Chapter Seven

Cilla cast her brother a troubled look. Colt could almost see the gears in her mind turning.

Before she could formulate an answer, Brady piped up. "We've decided that we really like Miss Grainger's ideas for us, and we thought she was a lot of fun this evening. Cilla and I were thinking that we should tell her that we're glad we'll be spending more time with her."

"Yeah," Cilla said, relief mirrored in her eyes. "Yeah. That's it."

Something wasn't right. On the surface, Brady's answer made sense, but the way he wouldn't quite meet Colt's eyes made him doubt the boy's sincerity. In fact, they both looked too guilty for it to be the whole truth. Just days ago, they were attacking the woman in public, and now they wanted to spend more time with her? He'd had a good time with Allison, too, but was one evening of fun enough to make this much difference in how they felt? It made no sense, unless the two little culprits had something up their sleeves they weren't sharing.

"Family powwow or can anyone join?"

The words were spoken in a familiar, deep voice. Colt turned to see Ace standing on the other side of the screen. A slight, rare smile and the amusement in the ice-blue eyes he'd inherited from his Irish father softened the harsh angles of his face. Those eyes looked out of place with the swarthy skin, jet-black hair and Indian features passed down from his mother.

Colt knew firsthand that those eyes were usually devoid of emotion, a skill Ace had perfected through the years to hide his feelings. Usually, but not now.

"Ace!" Colt said, shoving Brady's statement to the back of his mind and motioning for his friend to enter.

Once he was inside, the two men shook hands and Colt pulled Ace into one of those awkward, back-slapping man hugs that lasted no more than a second.

"I heard you were looking for me."

"Yeah. Brady has decided that he wants to learn to shoot a bow, and I figured there was no one around more qualified to teach him than you."

Ace shook his head. "I hardly ever shoot a bow anymore. I'm a modern man, you know. I like my rifle."

Colt chuckled. "Maybe so, but you've forgotten more than anyone in these parts ever knew. I'd be much obliged if you'd tutor him."

"I'd be glad to. It will do me good to brush up on my own bow skills." He looked at the boy. "When do you want to start?"

Brady's smile was a mile wide. "Whenever you want to."

"How about tomorrow morning? About seven? We'll get some time in before it gets too hot."

"Great!" Brady said.

"I think my mother still has the bow I used as a kid stuck back somewhere. It should be a good fit."

"Yes, sir. Thank you."

That settled, Colt told the kids to carry the croquet set inside. When they'd disappeared through the back door, Ace took a chair at the kitchen table, then fixed a considering look on his friend. "So what's this about you all spending time with Allison Grainger?"

Colt joined his friend and angled his head toward the door the children had just passed through.

He caught up his friend on his argument with Allie, the mayor's ultimatum and Allie's suggestions about how to fix the problem. "Now, since she offered to let Cilla practice the piano at her house and suggested some things to help Brady come out of his shell, and came over for a game of croquet, all of a sudden she's their best friend," Colt muttered. "Something's up."

"She's a fantastic woman. You could do a lot worse than spend time with her."

"Why do I sense there's more behind that statement than what I hear? You wouldn't be suggesting that I... court her, would you?"

"Why not? The kids like her and that's half the battle, isn't it?"

"She's not my type."

"Oh. I see," Ace said with a sage nod. "You're looking for something besides a woman who's good to the bone, sweet as honey, smart as a whip and pretty as a picture."

"Got any other old chestnuts for me?" Colt mocked.

"I'm sure there are some, but they escape me at the moment. The thing is, my friend, they're all true. She'd be a good catch for any man with enough sense to look hard enough."

"I always thought Ellie was the pretty one."

"And since when did you become the kind of man who's swayed by a pretty face?"

"Every man likes to think his woman is attractive, don't you think?"

"What one man finds attractive, another might not," Ace said cryptically, "and we both know that a pretty face can hide an ugly soul. As for Ellie, she's definitely a lovely woman, but Allison is, too. It's just that her unusual coloring makes her stand out. Redheads are few and far between. Have you ever seen her smile?"

"As a matter of fact, I have," Colt told him, recalling how the brightness of that smile gave the sun a run for its money. He cleared his throat. Time to change the subject before his friend thought of another argument for him to woo the teacher.

"Enough about that," he said. "How about some of the chocolate pie she brought over? I'd like to be selfish and not share, but since you're going to help with Brady, I guess I should offer you a piece."

"Allison made a pie for you?"

"Don't start trying to make something of it," Colt growled. "I invited her for supper and a game of croquet, and she offered to bring dessert, that's all."

Ace crossed his arms over his chest. "Hmm."

All eyes turned toward Allison when she walked into the Sunday service with the two Garrett children by her side. Even though she'd talked nonstop about what they could expect, they still looked uncomfortable when heads turned their way. Allison gave them an encouraging smile, and the next thing she knew they were being bombarded by schoolmates. Ben and Danny were the first to rush up to Brady, asking if he could sit with them. Past experience had taught her that that would be a recipe for disaster, so she told them, "Perhaps another time."

Regina Dance's daughter, who was maybe a year older than Cilla, approached her with a shy smile, and Bethany, wearing a wide grin, told Cilla she was glad she had come.

The adults eyed the trio with out-and-out curiosity, no doubt wondering what on earth the children were doing attending church with her and speculating as to whether or not there was anything going on between her and Colt. Well, let everyone think what they would. The truth would be all over town soon enough. That would stop the wagging tongues.

She and the children sat next to Bethany and Ellie, who warned her daughter not to be whispering to Cilla during the sermon. Gracie and Big Dan Mercer came in and sat on the other side. Allison couldn't help but notice the solicitous way Dan treated her, or the happiness that shone from her friend's eyes.

The minister spoke on I Corinthians 13, the importance of love. He talked about how easy it was to love our family and those who were good to us, yet the Bible commanded Christians to love everyone—the poor, those who were different, even our enemies and those who treated us badly, emphasizing that all the good works in the world were worthless if performed out of a sense of duty and not motivated by love.

Much to Allison's surprise, Cilla and Brady were so intent on listening they barely moved a muscle, soaking up the words like thirsty sponges. Or maybe they were just scared to act out with Allison sitting there.

When the service was over, the preacher reminded everyone about the ice-cream social the following Saturday at Jackson's Grove, then dismissed the assembly. Cilla and Brady exchanged excited smiles. Accompanied by their friends, they headed for the door.

Allison was prepared for an onslaught of questions once she'd exited the building with the children, but even though a few asked why she'd brought them, the real topic of conversation was the imminent return of Caleb and Gabe's mother, Libby Gentry Granville.

After making her peace with her sons from her first marriage, Libby had decided to spend several months of the year in Wolf Creek so that she could get to know her older sons better and enjoy her grandchildren. She would be arriving from Boston with her stepson, Win, and her daughter by her second husband on the Wednesday morning train.

As Allison walked the children home, Cilla said her dad would be at the jail working since Dan had the morning off to attend services with Gracie. They asked if they could stop by and tell Colt they were headed home to eat. Allison had no choice but to accompany them. It was the responsible thing to do, after all. To her dismay, her heart began to race at the thought of seeing him again.

Colt was trying to read the latest copy of the *St. Louis Post-Dispatch,* but he couldn't concentrate on the big-city news for thinking about Brady's stunning announcement that they were on board with Allison's suggestions. Ace's not-so-subtle hints that Colt would be smart if he actually tried to woo Allison kept slipping into his mind, too.

He couldn't deny that he'd entertained a few wayward thoughts from time to time since they'd embarked on their joint mission to try to tame his children's behavior. He supposed they were triggered by the fact that he was seeing different aspects of her and her personality than he'd observed before. Even so, he'd never once considered her as a serious candidate for marriage until, in fairness to his quest, he'd added her name to that stupid list.

With Big Dan's stamp of approval and unable to forget Ace's praise of Allie, Colt pulled the list from his desk drawer. He had promised to give thoughtful deliberation to every eligible woman in town, whether she was unmarried, widowed or a spinster. Doggedly, he studied the names he'd crossed out, reconsidering once more the pluses and minuses of each one and trying to visualize each of them in his house performing the various duties as a wife and mother.

He couldn't see any of them in the role.

Clutching his head in his hands, he tried to think of other names to add and came up with nothing. No one.

Every woman, Colt, remember?

Feeling a bit cornered but determined to finish the task, he went through the same procedure with Allison. He imagined her bustling around in his kitchen in a frilly white apron, whipping up some of the same meals he enjoyed so much at Ellie's.

Fine. Okay. He could see that.

He conjured up a scenario of her with him and the kids in the evenings, reading or playing games and helping with their lessons.

He could definitely picture that!

He visualized her in his kitchen with Cilla, sharing cooking duties and even coaxing Brady into setting the table with a bit of cajoling and that amazing smile of hers.

All right, he admitted with a sigh. Maybe it wasn't so hard picturing her in his house and his life after all, but that didn't prove anything except that she was accomplished in many areas and well suited to becoming some man's wife.

What on earth was he doing? He wasn't going to sit here and concoct pleasant scenarios about a woman to try to convince himself that everything would be hunky-dory just because he and the kids wanted and needed a wife and mother. It wasn't just unfair to everyone involved—it was downright wrong!

Wrong or not, he couldn't help thinking that Allison was a good candidate to be a mother, too. Even though she would be strict, she would also be fair. She'd already proved that. And the way things had been going the past few days, Colt believed that even though Cilla and Brady weren't thrilled about him marrying again, if it *did* happen, they would grow to accept and care for Allison in record time.

What about you?

Yeah, what about what was best for him? Maybe he was being idealistic, but having tasted love once, he wanted to find it again. Was that possible with Allison? He believed in the sanctity of marriage. If he felt compelled to enter one that did not have love, he would insist on at least mutual respect and a certain level of attraction…something other than convenience!

A new image stole through his mind: waking up beside Allison every morning, rolling over and seeing her face close to his, her eyes soft and dreamy. Before he could do more than register that the image was more than a little appealing, he realized he was doing it again. He needed to step back and get some perspective on things. But how, when the two of them were more or less forced to spend time together?

At this point, there was nothing he could do about that, but that was as far as it would go. It was as far as he would *let* it go. He would keep things between them just as they were now. Friendly. Casual. Professional.

He was patting himself on the back for his rational decision when he heard voices outside. He covered the tablet with the newspaper and looked up just as the door opened.

When the trio stepped into the office, Allison and the children all decked out in their Sunday finery, he couldn't stop the random thought that raced through his mind. Despite his brand-new resolution, they made a pleasing family portrait.

Brady had been horrified that his father wanted to buy him a new suit for the occasion, so they'd compromised on a pair of long gray trousers with leather braces and a new collarless shirt. Cilla was wearing her blue-and-white gingham dress and her new hair bow. Allison was decked out in another of those wretched frilly frocks!

The sight almost, but not quite, banished the memories of the homey images still clinging to his thoughts. He feared his welcoming smile was more than a bit stiff. "How did it go?"

"I liked it," Brady said with a smile. "The singing sounded like angels."

"That's nice."

"I liked it okay." As usual lately, Cilla pretended a disinterest that the sparkle in her eyes belied. Though he'd had no desire to join them, he was glad they'd enjoyed the experience and knew that Patrice would be happy, too.

"Did they behave?" Colt asked Allison, who, it seemed, had picked up on his intentional coolness.

She offered him a taut smile of her own. "They couldn't have behaved any better. I think their friends were happy to see them there, too."

"Yeah, Danny and Ben were there, and some of Cilla's friends," Brady offered, warming to the subject. "There's gonna be an ice-cream social at Jackson's Grove next Saturday," Brady said. "Can we go?"

"Don't we always?"

"Yeah, but I thought maybe you'd forgotten since you hadn't mentioned it."

"If you recall, we've had an unusual few days," Colt said.

Brady suddenly found the toes of his shoes extremely interesting.

"Are you going, Miss Grainger?" Cilla asked.

"I wouldn't miss it. In fact, I plan to bring peach ice cream."

Peach just happened to be Colt's favorite. Wasn't that a coincidence?

Cilla's eyes brightened. "Why don't we stop by and pick you up? We could do that, couldn't we, Pa?" she said, turning to her father.

Allison looked as dismayed as Colt felt by the innocent request. He pinned his daughter with a look that wiped the happiness from her eyes, but he paused only the slightest bit before saying, "Of course we can."

"That isn't necessary," Allison said. "I'll just see you all there." She smiled at Cilla. "You and Brady feel free to come over tomorrow. Brady can help me weed the front flower bed while you practice on the piano. Mrs. Carson says you're picking it up very quickly."

"Really?" Cilla breathed in awe. "How can she tell? I've only had one lesson."

"Well, she says you're paying close attention to everything she says, and your memory is excellent." Allison offered her a gentle smile. "Sometimes, it isn't reaching the goal that matters, Cilla. It's what we observe and learn along the way, things we can take and use in other areas of our lives. Like paying attention and obeying instructions. Your piano playing may never be exceptional, just as my embroidery skills will never be as good as either of my sisters', but if we learn and get pleasure from doing it, that's all that matters."

Colt was amazed at the wisdom of her comment. Cilla seemed to mull it over before she gave a cheeky smile and said, "Well, along the way to playing the piano really well, I'd like to learn to make sugar cookies."

Allison laughed, the unrestrained delight of the sound filling the room. A bittersweet longing for something he couldn't put a name to pricked Colt's heart.

"All right, then. If you come a little early, I'll show you how to make cookies." With a jaunty little wave toward the children, Allison turned and left the office.

Colt couldn't believe how sad they looked when she left, but was more amazed at how empty the room felt. It seemed she'd taken all the joy along with her.

* * *

To her surprise, Allison received replies from both of her professors in Thursday's mail. Both letters mentioned a learning problem that had been recognized just that year. Dyslexia. She devoured the contents of both dispatches, trying to grasp the nuances of the condition and pulling suggestions from both missives about the methods being used to treat those suffering from it.

She made notes as she read, and hoped she could explain things in a way that would not upset Colt. They had come a long way since their initial bout of headbutting, but she hadn't seen him since Sunday, even though the children came by for an hour or two daily. Something had happened to their easy camaraderie between the time she and the kids had left for church on Sunday and the time she dropped them off at the jail afterward.

Allison had searched her mind for some clue as to what she might have done, but even after four days, she had no idea what that might be. She did know that she didn't want to say or do anything that might add fuel to the fire.

She missed seeing him. It was pure foolishness on her part, but there it was. Like an inexperienced schoolgirl, she'd allowed his solicitousness, gentleness and the intense way he'd looked at her plant the seed that he might be starting to like her a little. Unable to help herself, she'd nurtured that absurd hope, allowing herself a few daydreams, forgetting for a time that the most eligible man in Wolf Creek would have no interest in her other than her ability to help his children.

She heaved a deep sigh of dismay. Colt blowing hot and then cold had triggered her old insecurities and reminded her that it would be the height of foolishness to care about someone again—especially someone like Colt Garrett. Caring too much would only cause the kind of pain she never again wanted to experience. Maybe Colt's standoffishness was a good thing. It had opened her eyes to the futility of wishing for something she knew in her heart could never be.

There was much in her life for which she should be thankful. She was healthy and able to support herself in a comfortable lifestyle if she spent her money wisely. She was a good teacher despite her inability—so far—to help Brady. She was liked and respected in the community. She had dear friends, attended a wonderful church and had a sister and precious niece living nearby whom she loved and who loved her.

She was blessed far beyond many, and yet she wanted more. She wanted a husband and children of her own. She felt the trickle of tears down her cheeks and buried her face in her hands, crying for lost love and shattered dreams. And then she prayed for the strength and common sense she'd need to withstand Colt's charm the next few weeks and for wisdom to know how best to help his children.

She prayed for contentment with her lot.

And peace.

Dreading the conversation she knew she needed to have with Colt, Allison waited until the sun began its descent and she'd run out of excuses before making her way to the Garrett house. Her steps dragged and her stomach churned at the thought of seeing him again and what his reaction would be to her news.

She found them all in the backyard. Cilla sat on the

porch next to her father, an embroidery hoop in her lap, while Ace instructed Brady in the skill of shooting a bow. She paused, wondering if she was catching them at a bad time, looking for any reason to postpone the face-to-face meeting.

The masculine picture Colt made in his dungarees and blue chambray shirt caused her stomach to flutter. His shirtsleeves were rolled above his elbows, revealing tanned, muscular forearms dusted with golden-brown hair. Recalling the strength of those arms when he'd carried her, and forgetting that she was determined to keep their relationship on a strictly business level, she suppressed a little sigh of longing.

Brady noticed her and shouted, "Hi, Miss Grainger! I'm practicing."

"So I see," she called, returning Cilla's wave. "Don't let me stop you."

To her dismay, Colt leaped to his feet and headed toward her.

Sticking with his plan, Colt had avoided Allison since Sunday, which had landed him in the doghouse with both Cilla and Brady. Yet the moment Brady called Allie's name and Colt looked up to see her coming around the corner of the house, he'd experienced an incredible surge of pleasure that swept aside his vows to keep things formal.

He'd missed her.

The realization caught him off guard, depriving him of breath for a split second. Taken aback by the unexpected feeling, he called her name.

From that moment until she found his gaze, his mind registered one impression after another. Her hair, in a variation of her customary topknot, was parted in the center, pulled severely back and coiled at the nape of her neck. Somehow the slight change in the style looked more appealing than it did twisted atop her head.

The second thing to register was that something was wrong. Her eyes looked haunted behind the lenses of the new glasses perched on the freckled bridge of her straight little nose. Not since the early days of their dubious association had she looked so aloof. Not since the morning they'd breakfasted at Ellie's and she'd mentioned her weight had she looked so miserable.

"I hope I'm not disturbing your evening."

The sound of her voice, soft and low-pitched, dragged his thoughts back to the moment. "Not at all. Cilla and I were just watching Brady and giving the kitchen a chance to cool off before we tackle the dishes. Have you had supper?"

"I did, thank you."

"Have a seat." He gestured toward the spot between where he'd been sitting with Cilla.

He saw her lips press together as she realized she would be sandwiched between the two of them. An uncomfortable spot…for her and him. Literally squaring her shoulders, she mustered her courage and sat.

"Do you mind if I look at your work, Cilla?"

"No, ma'am," she said, passing the hoop to Allison, who scrutinized it with care, even turning it over to look at the back. She had no idea that her eyes gleamed with pride and pleasure. "Oh, Cilla, you're doing a wonderful job. And the underneath is just as well done as the top."

She smoothed a gentle hand over the table scarf and smiled. "According to my mama, that was one of the things that makes handwork exceptional. The back should be as pretty as the front."

Colt wasn't sure he'd ever seen his daughter smile so widely. She looked proud enough to pop. For just a second he thought she might fling her arms around Allison's neck and give her a hug. In that moment his own pride swelled within him, along with it a rush of gratitude for the woman who'd made it all possible.

"I haven't seen you in a few days," he told her, as if it were all her doing instead of his. "Is everything okay?"

"Everything's fine."

Her answer was short and to the point.

"What brings you our way, then?"

Idiot! he chided himself. It sounded as if he didn't want her there, and nothing could be further from the truth.

She pulled two envelopes from her skirt pocket. "In today's mail I received replies to the letters I sent to my professors, and I wanted to talk to you as a family so I can try to answer any questions you may have."

"I'll get him." Colt started to rise, only to stop when she placed her hand on his arm. The heat of her fingers sent a jolt of awareness through him. His gaze flew to hers. The reciprocal warmth that flamed in her eyes was proof that she shared his reaction. But there was more than awareness. There was vulnerability. Indecision. A question for which he had no answer. He was as confused as she looked. One thing was certain, though. At that moment he wanted nothing more than to kiss her.

"I'm sorry," she said, snatching her hand away.

"Nothing to be sorry for," he assured her. He heard the huskiness in his voice. Did she? He fought the urge to rub the place that still tingled from her touch.

"Ace said I did real good!" Brady cried as he raced toward them. "He's coming back tomorrow evening."

The sound of his eager voice shattered the intensity of the moment. Colt stood and shook his friend's hand. Flicking a considering look from Colt to Allison and back, Ace said his goodbyes to them all, and they watched him slip silently into the gathering woodland shadows.

"What are you doing here, Miss Grainger?" Brady asked, never one to dither.

"I wanted to let you know that I've received replies from my professors."

Brady looked almost fearful, Colt thought. He needed to make sure his reactions to whatever Allie told them were positive. As if sensing the tension binding them, she gave them all an encouraging smile.

"First, they both mention something that has been recognized as—" Colt could almost see the wheels turning as she tried to phrase the problem "—making learning hard for a certain number of people." She looked at him. "It's called 'dyslexia,' and while I can't say with any certainty at this point that this is Brady's problem, he seems to fit the standards that define it."

"Dyslexia?" Colt echoed. It sounded horrible.

Allison nodded.

"What is it?" Brady asked.

"It's a condition detailed by Dr. Pringle Morgan. The simplest way to describe it is that for some unknown reason, letters look switched around to some people. For example, a person with dyslexia might see 'I am' as 'aim.'"

She shrugged as if lost for words. "It's like a mix-up between the eye and the brain and vice versa. The way things are…processed, for lack of a better word. It makes reading and comprehension difficult, which in turn makes other subjects that require reading hard, as well. It can also affect spelling and mathematics."

Brady seemed to be processing what she'd said. Colt wondered if he looked as flabbergasted as he felt. "What causes it?"

"No one knows, but it is certainly no one's fault." She directed her next comments to Brady. "Some people are just born with it. The important thing, Brady, is to understand that it has nothing to do with how smart a person is.

"There does seem to be some variation in severity of the problem, from mild to acute. Brady has some difficulty with spelling, but I haven't noticed any overly troubling problems with his arithmetic skills, so at this point I'm guessing that he is only mildly affected. However," she added, "today is the first time I've ever heard of the condition, so I'm far from knowledgeable."

"Is there anything that can be done for him?" Colt asked.

She smiled. "The good news is that it seems we're on the right track without knowing it. He needs to be read to and should work on his reading. Of course, he'll need more time to accomplish his assignments than some of the children, but I don't foresee that as a major hurdle.

"I'll try to figure out what letter combinations trouble him most, though I don't even know if some arrangements might be more troublesome than others. I'm afraid a lot of what we do will be trial and error, but we'll just keep working on it."

"And it's okay if you don't ever read as well or as fast as some of the other kids, Brady," Cilla said. "It's like what Miss Grainger said about me and the piano. Even if I'm never as good as Mrs. Carson. The main thing is that you're learning other lessons, too, like not giving up and pushing yourself further than you think you can go. And you'll be able to read about things that interest you and that's all that matters, isn't that right, Miss Grainger?"

Colt saw Allison blink fast to hold back the tears that filled her eyes at hearing Cilla repeat the lesson she'd just heard. Any doubt that she truly cared about his children was laid to rest.

It was gratifying that Cilla had been listening and even more satisfying that she was using her newfound lesson to give her brother a pep talk. Colt didn't know if the changes in the kids had come about because of him laying down the law about their behavior, or if Allison's caring had worked some sort of miracle. Whichever it was, he was grateful.

"Good point, Cilla," Colt said as Allison nodded.

She smiled at Brady. "We're doing something else right, too, by finding things you like to do and can learn to do well, like your bow-and-arrow shooting and learning to play the harmonica."

Brady turned to him. "I forgot to tell you, Pa, but Mr. Jessup says I'm doing good with the harmonica, too. He says I'll be ready to play with the other guys by the time we have the harvest festival."

Though Colt thought Brady might be stretching it a bit, since he'd had only two or three lessons, the pride on his face was something to behold. Colt felt a sudden surge of love so poignant he wasn't certain when he'd last experienced it. "I'm sure you will be."

"Does anyone have any more questions?" Allison

asked. When no one spoke, she said, "I'd best be going, then."

"I'll walk with you," Colt said, reluctant to see her go despite his determination to keep her at arm's length. Before he realized what he was doing, he offered her his hand.

She looked from his hand to his face, decidedly uncomfortable. "That won't be necessary."

"I insist. It'll be dark soon."

They both knew she would reach her little house long before darkness fell. They both also knew she was too much of a lady to protest any further. He thought he heard a little breath escape her, but she placed her hand in his, and he drew her to her feet.

Her hand was small and warm and soft. When he held it a second or two longer than propriety permitted, Allison tugged it free with a sharp look from beneath her eyelashes.

"I'll be back in a little bit. You two start the dishes, please."

"Sure, Pa," Brady said.

"Thanks." Colt stepped back for Allie to precede him. Instead of offering her his arm, he chose to keep a couple of feet between them. They'd gone no more than a step or two when he surprised himself by saying, "Do you need anything for your ice cream?"

"As it turns out, I won't be taking ice cream. I'll be taking apple pie instead." Her chin was high; her voice was cool.

"No peach ice cream? Why?"

"It seems that in my eagerness to contribute I forgot one small thing."

"What's that?"

"That I am a single woman with no husband to bring and crush the ice or help haul the freezer to Jackson's Grove."

The mental image of the pint-size redhead toting a block of ice in a tow sack and using the flat side of an ax to crush it into smaller pieces brought a reluctant smile to his lips. "I'd be glad to help."

"No, thank you," she told him in her prissy school-teacher voice.

Before he could stop himself, Colt took her shoulders in his hands and propelled her gently against the side of the house. Her palms were flat against his chest, as if to keep him back.

"What got your bloomers in a twist?" he asked, narrowing his gaze in question.

Allison's eyes widened and her lips parted in shock at hearing the socially objectionable word bandied about with such ease. "My…my *what?*" she all but screeched.

"You heard me." She was angry. So was he, though he wasn't sure who he was mad at—or why.

"Indeed I did! How dare you speak to me with such disrespect!" she told him in a low, furious tone. "I'm doing everything I can to help you with your children, and it seems you're determined to drive me mad. One minute you're friendly and cooperative—the next you ignore me for days! And how dare you question the way I'm behaving when you've made no move to—"

"Why, Miss Grainger," he said in a silky voice. "I do believe you're trying to tell me you've missed me."

Her eyes widened. "I… I most certainly have no—"

"You talk too much," he interrupted. With that, he pulled her close and pressed his lips to hers in a kiss that was born of irritation, frustration and maybe just a little bit of curiosity.

He didn't know what he expected, but he was pretty sure it wasn't for his heart rate to double or for her to struggle in his arms. Women usually didn't do that. But then, he'd never kissed an unwilling woman, and he'd never known a woman like Allison.

Just when he was about to release her, she sagged against him, all resistance gone. In response to her surrender, he slanted his mouth for a deeper kiss and tightened his arms around her. At that moment he knew it was Allie he'd been kissing in his dream.

Despite the pleasure spiraling through him, his addled brain registered a couple of things. Her hands were fisted between them, her fingers tangled in his shirt. She was kissing him back. With unexpected enthusiasm. A soft sound, something that might have been a whimper, escaped her, bringing Colt to his senses.

Good grief! What was he doing?

It was a bit of a surprise to realize that he didn't want to stop kissing her, but he knew he should, for more reasons than he could comprehend at the moment. Sliding his hands to her shoulders, he put an arm's length between them and stared down into her flushed face. Her eyes were wide with disbelief, and her pretty mouth looked as he'd imagined it would after being thoroughly kissed.

"Why did you do that?" she asked in a quavering whisper.

His wide shoulders lifted in a shrug. "It seemed like a good way to shut you up."

Her eyes filled with tears. "Do you ever take anything seriously?" she choked out and, with a little shove, she pushed him aside and headed toward the road.

"Allie, wait!" he said, his long legs soon overtaking her. He clamped a hand onto her shoulder to stop her headlong escape.

"Let me go, Colt," she said, struggling against his hold.

"I wanted to."

"Wanted to what?" she muttered, trying to pry his hand from her shoulder.

"I wanted to kiss you."

She stilled beneath his touch, her gaze clinging to his, disbelief warring with a question in her eyes. "Why, Colt? Why me? Why now? I'm so beautiful and exciting you couldn't help yourself?" she taunted. "Or are you working your way through all the available women in town and my turn came up?"

The offhand question was so near the truth that Colt felt a surge of panic. He couldn't tell her that after a lot of waffling, he'd decided to use the time he spent with her and the kids as a sort of testing ground to see if they were compatible without actually courting her. That was certain disaster!

There *were* other reasons behind the kiss. He could tell her that her lips had tempted him with their softness ever since the day of their big confrontation. Or maybe because he was curious as to whether she ever shook free of her prim persona or had buried all her feminine dreams with the man she'd loved and lost, just as he'd buried his relationship with God with Patrice. If so, what a pair they made. What a shame.

He chose the course closest to the truth and promised the fewest repercussions. "Curiosity, maybe."

"Curiosity?"

He nodded. "I'm learning that you're much more than you choose to let people see. Maybe I wanted to see what else is hiding behind that wall you put up between you and the world."

He released her and, reaching out a single finger, lifted a wayward wisp of hair from her flushed cheek and tucked it behind her ear.

Allie sucked in a sharp breath. "L-like what?"

"You're not nearly as self-possessed as you'd like everyone to think, which your outburst in my office proved."

"Everyone has a breaking point," she told him, the fire of her defiance burning the moisture from her eyes. "Actually, I found my *outburst* quite liberating."

He regarded her intently. "Good."

"Good?"

"Mmm-hmm. Holding things in is bad, Doc Rachel says. And you're insecure."

He noted her surprise and realized she thought she'd kept that hidden. "But I can't imagine why," he added. "You're a very talented person, and you're smart and kind and caring and good at what you do."

"Ah, yes," she said dramatically. "Saint Allison, living right here in Wolf Creek."

He smiled a lopsided smile. "And you have a wicked sense of humor…when you let it out."

He could tell his comment had caught her off guard. She plunged her hands into the pockets of her skirt and snapped, "Whatever your reasons, I suggest that we put the…um, unfortunate incident behind us. It would make things far too awkward when we spend time with the children."

Uncertain whether to laugh or go nurse his bruised ego, Colt stepped back, putting another foot between them. "You certainly have a way of putting a man in his place."

"I beg your pardon."

"I'm not sure I've ever had a woman call a kiss an 'unfortunate incident.' I must admit that it smarts a bit, Miss Grainger. Still, I suppose you're right. As usual."

"Don't be patronizing," she said, but the animosity had left her voice and she looked as bewildered as he felt.

"I didn't mean to be. I'm just saying that you may be right, but all I can promise is that I'll try."

"Meaning what?"

"Meaning I don't know about you, but I'll be a long time forgetting that kiss."

He turned and walked toward the woods, leaving her to walk home alone, certain in his heart that he'd spoken the truth. His last image of Allison was her mouth hanging open in surprise. Let her sleep on that.

"How do you feel about what Miss Grainger said about why you can't read?" Cilla asked Brady as they washed and dried the dishes.

"I'm glad I'm not a dummy like Bethany."

"Don't call her that!"

"You do."

"Maybe I did, but it was wrong. Bethany was just born different, the way you were."

"I'm nothing like Bethany!" Brady cried, flinging the dish towel down.

"Of course you're not exactly like her," Cilla told him, trying to get her thoughts together.

"I've just been thinking a lot about Mr. Gentry's scripture about judging people and how it goes right along with what Pa always says about not judging a book by its cover. They're both the same thing, really."

"Yeah. So?"

"So that's what I did with Bethany, and it's what the kids at school do to you when you make mistakes in reading. They're judging you by that one thing and not the other things that make you Brady Garrett."

"What do you mean?"

"That there's a lot more to you than how well you read."

"Why are you so nicey-nice all of a sudden?" Brady asked, stacking another dry plate on the shelf.

"I guess Pa laying down the law the day I stomped on Miss Grainger's glasses got me to thinking about things. And I've been thinking about Ma a lot, too." She gave Brady a sad little smile. "Sometimes I really miss her. I'm sorry you never knew her, but do you know what I remember the most?"

Brady shook his head.

"She was always kind, and she smiled and laughed a lot like Miss Grainger does, and I don't think she'd be happy with the way we've been acting."

"I wish I'd known her," Brady said. He lifted his gaze to his sister's. "Is it my fault she died, Cilla?"

"Of course not!" she said. "Things like that just happen sometimes, and no one knows why. Just like Bethany's problem and your dyslexia. It's no one's fault."

"I'm glad about that."

Cilla smiled at him and handed him another plate to dry.

"Another thing. I can see that Pa's really bothered

by the way we've been acting. I don't want him to lose his job and move us somewhere else, and I don't think you do, either."

Brady shook his head. "I like it here, and another teacher might not be as nice as Miss Grainger."

"That's true," Cilla said. "We've been selfish, not wanting to share Pa with anyone. It's really not so bad having Miss Grainger around, and I really do want Pa to be happy. I don't like him being mad at me, and I'd rather see him smile than have him give me a blessing out any day."

"Me, too," Brady admitted.

"Besides," she said thoughtfully, "if we want Miss Grainger to be our ma, we have to be good so she'll like us."

Chapter Eight

What on earth had he been thinking when he'd kissed Allie? Colt berated himself the following morning as he headed toward Ellie's, where he was meeting Gabe for an early breakfast. It was just light, and already the heat of the morning sun promised another scorcher.

Like the kiss.

Why couldn't he get the kiss—and Allie—out of his mind? There was another problem, too. Would that one moment of madness ruin everything? Would she want to keep helping him with the kids now that he'd stepped over that imaginary boundary of propriety? She'd implied that nothing would change as long as they forgot what had occurred between them. As if that was going to happen anytime this side of the grave!

What would he say to her when he saw her later in the day? How would she react? He'd toyed with the idea of surprising her with some ice the following day, and even considered making the ice cream for her as a little surprise, but now he was questioning the wisdom of the idea. The last thing he needed was her thinking he was trying to butter her up for the sake of her help with the kids.

Charlie Pickens, who was unlocking the door of the newspaper office, called out to him from across the street, thankfully delaying his decision a little longer.

The light of Ellie's beckoned. He'd been so wrapped up in the problem with the kids lately, it seemed as if he talked and thought of little else. Maybe some male conversation with Gabe would take his mind off things, at least for a while.

Gabe was already seated, and to Colt's chagrin, Win Granville sat across from him. As usual, the wealthy Bostonian was decked out in the latest style. His double-breasted, dove-gray suit boasted a wing collar and covered buttons, and had no doubt been chosen to make him look more casual. It didn't work. The only purpose it served was to make Colt, in his denim pants and plaid shirt, feel like a poor country relation. Even Gabe, in his tan trousers and plaid, square-cut waistcoat, outdid him in the style department, but then, their jobs were vastly different. As was Win's.

The first—and last—time Win Granville was in town had been in the spring, when he'd taken perverse pleasure in running up the bids at the box-lunch benefit. Colt had been forced to pay far more than he'd expected for Ellie's basket, and Gabe had been none too pleased at the price his stepbrother had forced him to pay for Rachel's.

It looked as if they'd put that behind them, though, if the smiles on their faces were anything to go by. Despite the fiasco at the box lunch and his fancy way of dressing, Colt had yet to make up his mind about Win, unsure if he were just a smooth city slicker or if he possessed a contrary sense of amusement. Colt suspected that, like Allie, there was a lot more beneath the facade he presented to the world than most people suspected. Law enforcement had broken Colt of the habit of underestimating people based on their outward appearance.

Ellie had already delivered steaming mugs of coffee, and when she saw Colt step through the door, she headed toward the table with a plate of biscuits and the coffeepot, another mug dangling from one finger.

Both men stood. Hands were shaken all around. Ellie asked Colt if he wanted the usual, poured his coffee and then topped off the other cups while Colt settled into a chair.

"Thanks, lovely lady," Win said with a lazy smile.

In reply, she plunked the biscuits onto the table, gave him a smile sweet enough to cause a toothache and murmured an equally syrupy "You're welcome." Then she stalked back to the kitchen.

Undaunted, Win grinned and reached for a flaky biscuit and knife.

"What was that all about?" Gabe asked.

"I do believe the lady is smitten," Win said, using the knife to slice the biscuit in half and then spreading it with fresh-churned butter.

Gabe shook his head, chuckling at the sheer audacity of the statement.

"Looked to me like she wanted to put that butter knife in your back," Colt told him.

"Oh, she just hasn't come to terms with it yet," Win said, winking as he added a spoonful of muscadine jelly to the featherlight creation. He took a bite and rolled his eyes in ecstasy. "To say I've missed Ellie's cooking would be an understatement."

He directed a challenging look at Colt. "Just so you know, I plan to marry that woman one of these days."

Colt pondered the preposterous statement for a moment then smiled. "You may try, but so have a lot of men, and she leaves them in the dust with broken hearts."

"Yours?"

Colt shook his head. "No broken heart—just bruised pride."

"Good."

"You may as well hang it up, Granville," Colt told him. "Ellie can't marry anyone."

"I've told him her story," Gabe said. "Didn't faze him in the least."

"I've always loved a challenge," Win said. "Besides, I have a brother who's a whiz of an attorney. While I'm winning the lady's heart, Philip will be looking for the husband. He has a close friend who works for Pinkerton's."

Then, as if he hadn't made the preposterous comment, he looked from Gabe to Colt and hit them with another. "So what's the latest Wolf Creek gossip besides Ellie giving you the boot, Garrett?"

"You're not much for beating around the bush, are you?" Colt said.

The Granville heir shrugged his elegantly clad shoulders. "There may be a time and place for it, but not much sense in it. When you see something you want, you go after it."

He'd said more or less the same thing to Gabe about Rachel last spring, and from what he'd just said about locating Ellie's wayward husband, it must be Win's philosophy. It might be a good one, but Colt's problem was identifying what he wanted. Did he want to give serious consideration to Allison as a prospective wife? Marriage was far too serious a commitment to enter on the strength of a single kiss. Would they suit in other ways? Would he grow to love her wild hair, and could she ever care for a man with a lesser education?

Most important of all, could he learn to love her?

You already do.

The words drifted through his mind softly, as if someone had whispered them, and at that instant he recognized them for the truth they were. He sat stone-still, his cup poised halfway to his lips. How could something so momentous slip up on a person so easily? How had it happened? When? The uncertainty he'd felt since the kiss had vanished. How it happened wasn't really important. It had happened. He'd fallen in love with Allison Grainger, spinster schoolteacher. He set his cup onto the table so hard that the coffee splashed onto the pristine white cloth.

"What's the matter?" Gabe asked, his forehead furrowed in concern. "You look like you just heard your best friend died or something."

"I'm fine." He tried to smile. He wanted to leave, to go somewhere he could be alone to get used to the idea and think about what it would—could—mean. He needed to figure out the best way to handle it.

When you see what you want, you go after it.

He couldn't take Win's advice. Unlike Win, Colt wasn't the kind to rush into things. He liked to think through all the angles and have a plan. Besides, if he told Allie he loved her, she would never believe him. Love didn't happen in a couple of weeks, did it? Especially when the person you thought you loved had been under your nose for more than a year.

He would have to take things slowly, for both their sakes. He would stay with their original plan to spend time together with the kids, but... The kids! How could he tell them his decision without them blabbing it all over town? What would they think? Despite their recent good behavior and his laying down the law about sabotaging his relationships, if he told them he planned to court Allison, would they start their subtle attacks on her?

Questions tumbled through his mind, but he had no answers.

"I wish Ellie would hurry with that breakfast," he muttered. "I'm starving."

He noticed that both Gabe and Win were looking at him as if they weren't quite sure what was going on with him. Not so strange since he wasn't sure himself. All he knew was that the sooner he ate, the sooner he could get to the jail and do some serious thinking. As if in answer to his request, Ellie emerged from the kitchen with two plates. Bethany was right behind her with the third.

Thank goodness.

I'll be a long time forgetting that kiss.

The sound of Colt's voice played through Allison's mind. Even though she'd told him they should forget their brief stolen moment, she was finding it impossible to do. Regardless of his reasons for kissing her, for a few precious seconds she had felt beautiful and desirable, something she couldn't recall ever experiencing before.

Forget it, Allison.

Using the back of her hand, she pushed her spectacles up where they belonged. Drat the heat still radiating from the stove that was causing them to slide down her nose! And drat Colt Garrett for kissing her and causing the sleepless night that left her cranky and with dark circles beneath her eyes.

She'd tossed and turned for hours, thinking about him, wondering why he'd kissed her and what it might do to their unusual, somewhat volatile arrangement. When she'd fallen into a fitful sleep at last, she still had no answers. Even now, wide-awake, she was wondering what would happen next.

She pressed the iron against one corner of Colt's freshly laundered handkerchief—the one he'd tied around her foot—and pulled it taut to minimize the puckering as she ran the hot iron along the edge.

How on earth could they continue to spend time together for the children's sake, when being around him turned her into a mindless ninny? Or a lovesick schoolgirl.

Lovesick.

The thought held her motionless. Was she? Was it possible that after almost ten years of guarding her heart from the possibility of pain she had allowed Colt to slip beneath that guard and overcome her hard-found control with a single kiss? *Was* she falling in love with him—or worse—was she already *in* love with him?

The smell of scorched fabric assaulted her nostrils, and she looked down to see that she had stood with the iron in one spot for so long she had burned a hole clear through his handkerchief. She tossed the ruined piece of fabric to the tabletop and sighed, focusing on Cilla's increasingly nimble fingers as she practiced her scales.

It was just her and Cilla this morning since Brady was with Ace, practicing his archery. Allison had to admit Colt's young daughter was far more engaged in her piano lessons than she'd expected.

Cilla launched into a hesitant, faltering rendition of "Camptown Races," and Allison smiled. She expected no less than the rousing tune from Hattie, who claimed there was plenty of time to learn the classical pieces. The main thing was to make learning enjoyable at first so students wouldn't lose interest as soon as they started.

Adults might think "Moonlight Sonata" was a haunting, beautiful melody, but Hattie claimed that most kids found it dreary. Allison thought it was an interesting insight. Hadn't she often improvised and modified her teaching methods in an effort to reach certain students?

Casting another look at the ruined handkerchief, she decided she might as well take a break. Cilla probably needed one, too. Setting the iron on the back of the stove, she went to the door of the tiny parlor, which was dominated by the upright piano, and poked in her head.

"Cilla?"

Cilla looked up. "Ma'am?"

"Are you ready for a cookie and some lemonade?"

"That sounds good," Cilla said, rising from the round stool to join her.

In the kitchen, Allison poured two glasses of tangy lemonade that was nice and cold from the deep well out back. Then she gave Cilla a couple of raisin-dotted sugar cookies they'd made earlier.

"Thank you, Miss Grainger."

"You're very welcome."

Allison was beginning to believe that the changes

in Cilla were real, that she was not plotting to cause someone harm or pain. Allison truly enjoyed the time she spent with the child. It wasn't her fault her father was…well, the way he was.

Aggravatingly attractive.

"For someone who hasn't been taking lessons that long, you're making great strides," Allison said, determined to rout thoughts of Colt from her mind.

"Thank you. Aren't you going to have any cookies?"

Allison shook her head. "Oh, no. I had two as they came out of the oven. I can't possibly eat everything I bake."

"What do you do with all of it?"

"Give it to the shut-ins and the sick people in town, mostly," she said, sitting down at the oak table across from her guest. She smiled. "And I've been sending an awful lot of it home with you and Brady lately."

Cilla smiled. "Pa really likes that. He has a terrible sweet tooth."

Colt again. The child positively doted on the man! But then, everyone in town did. Yet despite her annoyance at him for kissing her and her own response to that kiss, Allison couldn't deny the thrill of pleasure that shot through her at hearing Cilla's admission.

"He does?" Allison asked with studied nonchalance. "Which ones are his favorites?"

"His absolute favorite is your chocolate pie, but his favorite cookies are the oatmeal." Cilla gave a slight shake of her head. "When you send those over, he has them for breakfast with a glass of milk and tells me and Brady that's all right because he's eating his oats."

"I guess that's one way of looking at it." Allison took another sip of her cool drink.

"Are your new glasses okay?" Cilla asked out of the blue. "Can you see all right?"

"They're very much okay. I can see very well, thank you."

"I'm really sorry for breaking them, Miss Grainger. I don't know what got into me."

Her contrition seemed real. Allison reached out and touched Cilla's hand, which was curled around the glass. "We all do and say things we shouldn't from time to time."

Cilla seemed surprised by the gesture. "Even you?"

Feeling the threat of tears, Allison nodded. She was thankful her relationship with Cilla was progressing so well and pleased that she'd realized what she'd done was wrong.

"Even me. Someday I'll tell you how poorly I behaved when I went to tell your father what happened. My conduct was not very grown-up or appropriate."

Cilla looked fascinated by the admission. "What did Pa do?"

"Let's just say that his behavior was on par with mine."

"I'd like to have seen that," Cilla said with a saucy grin.

Hoping to steer the conversation in a new direction, Allison asked, "Are you looking forward to the ice-cream social tomorrow?"

The smile disappeared. "Yes and no. I want to go, but I wish I had something new to wear. The only really nice dress I have is my blue-and-white gingham, and I'll have to wear that to church the next morning." A flicker of sorrow darted through her eyes. "Some of the other girls have new things."

Allison remembered being where Cilla was. Changing physically and emotionally. Knowing she wasn't as pretty as some of her friends. Knowing she was smarter than most of the boys. Uncertain how to handle either situation. Inherently happy, she was joyful one moment, sad the next. Flying off the handle for little reason.

Poor Cilla! As much as she loved her father and he loved her, Colt was no substitute for the mother she'd lost. She needed a mother, and for the moment, Allison was the closest thing she had. She searched her mind for something to say to make her feel better without putting the father she adored in a bad light. As she often did, Allison mentally framed a short prayer before speaking.

"Well, no doubt they have mothers who sew," she offered when she'd finished and gathered her thoughts. "When I was growing up, dresses got passed down from Belinda to Ellie and then to me. My mother would let out the hem or take it up and add a different style of collar and maybe some cuffs or new sleeves. Sometimes she just changed the old buttons for new and added some lace, just something to make it look new to us."

"You wore hand-me-downs?"

"Oh, yes, and was glad to have them," Allison said. "My family wasn't wealthy, but we did well enough until my father got ill, and then there was no money for store-bought fripperies. We were taught that it wasn't what we had, but how we used what we had that was important. My mama always said that we were very blessed because we had a roof over our heads, food to eat, a bed to sleep in and we were healthy. She told us that there were plenty of people who would be thrilled to have what we did and that we should always be thankful God had given us so much."

Cilla seemed to think about that.

"Here's the problem as I see it," Allison continued. "You don't have any sisters to pass things down, you don't have a mother to sew for you, and I doubt it ever enters your father's head to get you anything new until you outgrow your dresses."

Cilla's eyes widened. "How did you know?"

Allison leaned toward her young friend and lowered her voice to a conspiratorial whisper. "It's men," she confided, her eyes twinkling behind the lenses of her spectacles. "They don't understand that we women need an occasional pretty dress and gewgaws and such. As long as they have a clean pair of pants and a shirt when they need them, they're pretty happy. Why, most of them don't even notice when their collars and cuffs need turning."

"You're right," Cilla said with a nod of wonder. "Pa never notices how worn-out his shirts are looking. I have to tell him to go to the mercantile and pick out some new ones."

"It must be hard to have so many responsibilities at your age." Allison was truly amazed at how well Cilla did with the responsibilities life had handed her.

Cilla's shrug seemed to say that it was nothing; that was just the way things were.

"I admire you for taking such good care of your brother and your father."

"You do?"

Allison nodded. "Very much. I wasn't very domestic growing up, and according to my mother, I always had my nose in a book. I'm not certain I could have done as well as you do."

Cilla clasped her hands in her lap and stared at them

for a moment, then looked up, a solemn expression on her face. "Miss Grainger," she said. "May I ask you something?"

Uh-oh. What now? "You may," she said with a bit of trepidation.

"Did you have a beau when you were my age?" Cilla asked, looking at Allison from beneath her eyelashes.

Oh, dear! She hoped they were not about to get into a discussion about the birds and bees. She drew in a steadying breath and said, "Well, I believe I was a little older than you when I developed my first crush on a boy. Tommy Hartwell."

"Did he like you back?"

Allison laughed. "He had no idea I was even alive." Her smile was self-deprecating. "In my very limited experience, it seems to me that young boys prefer blondes and brunettes, not girls with red hair and freckles. Why? Have you set your sights on some boy?"

"Maybe," she said.

Allison prayed for inspiration and a change of topic.

God must have been listening, because a thought popped into her mind almost instantly. She clapped her hands together and offered Cilla a bright smile. "I have an idea."

"What?"

"It won't help for tomorrow, but I know how to sew, and I can teach you. What if I ask your father if he'll buy some material, and you and I can work together to make you some new things? I can show you how to cut out the patterns and how to use the sewing machine. Would you like that?"

"Oh, Miss Grainger, would you?" Cilla breathed, her eyes alight with excitement.

"I'd love to. Oh!" she cried, as another idea flashed into her mind. "Mrs. Granville just came back to town. What if I ask her and her daughter about the newest styles back in Boston? They're sure to know. In fact, I think Blythe spent a few weeks in Paris last year."

Cilla's pretty face glowed. "That would be wonderful, Miss Grainger! They always look so stylish."

"Indeed they do," Allison agreed. "I'm sure they'll be at the ice-cream social tomorrow. I'll make an effort to speak with them then. I'm sure they'd be thrilled to help us. They're both very nice, though it seems Blythe is a tad shy and a little uncomfortable with our small-town ways."

"Well, I'd be uncomfortable in a big city," Cilla confessed.

"Me, too. Wolf Creek is perfect for me."

That settled, they sipped at their lemonade and Cilla started her last cookie. She seemed deep in thought. After a moment, she sat up straighter, as if she were gathering her courage.

"I was wondering why you never got married."

Allison stared at Cilla. She was so taken aback by the question that it never crossed her mind that it was not one a child should be asking.

"I was going to get married several years ago, but… as it turns out, the man I planned to marry decided that he, uh, didn't love me enough and called it off. He soon married another girl."

"He threw you over for someone else?" Cilla asked with her customary bluntness. "That was shameful of him." Somehow she managed to look both indignant and regretful for asking the question. "I'll bet it really made you sad."

"At the time, yes," Allison quipped, as if the whole ordeal had not been the worst thing that ever happened to her.

A memory of Colt's kiss skittered through her mind. That kiss and the way she'd felt during those few heart-pounding seconds his mouth was pressed against hers had put her past into perspective far better than time and maturity had. Jesse Castle had never come close to making her feel the way Colt did.

"Even though it felt very real, when I look back I see that we were very young and that what I thought was love was perhaps just two people with a strong foundation of friendship and mutual interests."

"And you've never found anyone else you think you could love?"

"I've only just reached a point where I've begun to think about that possibility again," she confessed. "But who knows what life has in store? And I'm very particular."

"I imagine you want someone really handsome."

Colt's face flashed into Allison's mind. She thrust aside the image. "Of course, any woman would be proud to have a handsome man for a husband, but I've always believed that pretty is as pretty does," she said. "For men and women. Outer beauty fades, but inner beauty only grows with time and wisdom. To me, honesty and kindness and a man who loves the Lord are more important."

"Oh." Looking thoughtful, Cilla drained her glass and carried it to the dishpan. "Thank you for the cookies and lemonade, Miss Grainger," she said. "If it's all the same to you, I think I'll stop for the day. I remembered something I need to do at home."

"Certainly," Allison said, wondering at the child's abrupt departure. "I'll see you tomorrow evening at the ice-cream social."

"Yes, ma'am. We'll be there."

The excitement and eagerness she'd displayed just moments ago seemed to have fled. "Is everything all right, Cilla?"

"Fine," she said with a nod. "See you tomorrow."

Chapter Nine

When Cilla left, Allison finished her ironing, changed into a skirt and blouse that were presentable and headed across town to Ellie's. It was still a little early for the noon rush, and she found Bethany refilling the salt and pepper shakers and her sister bustling around in the kitchen, taking care of the last-minute preparations.

"Hello, sister dear," Ellie said, pouring a steady stream of thickening into a large pot of fragrant beef broth. "Grab the potato masher and mash those spuds, will you? I've already drained the water off for the gravy, which I'm trying to finish."

Though Ellie sometimes had help in the kitchen, Allison was used to giving a hand when she was needed.

"Of course." She rolled her sleeves above her elbows, washed her hands and tied the extra apron hanging near the doorway around her waist.

"What brings you here?" Ellie said. "You haven't been in much the past week or so."

"I don't have as much free time," Allison said, dumping some salt into her palm and then, deciding it was the right amount, into the steaming potatoes.

"Brady and Cilla come almost every day to work on their lessons." She added pepper in proportion, and then a large chunk of butter. Taking up the twisted wire potato masher, she began working on the starchy vegetable.

"How's that going?"

"Fine. Cilla is doing very well with her piano lessons, and I hope to see improvement in Brady soon, since I think I've discovered what his problem is."

She told Ellie what she'd heard from her professors and the ideas she'd already put into place or planned to in the near future.

"How did Colt take the news? He was so sure it was you at fault and not Brady."

"Better than I expected," Allison said. "So did Brady."

"Are things still going okay between you and Colt?" Grinning, Ellie looked up from the gravy she was stirring. "I wasn't too sure you'd be able to work together after your, uh, rocky beginning."

Allison blew a wayward strand of damp hair out of her eyes and tossed a wry glance toward her sister. "Well, there's nothing like the threat of losing your job to make a person cooperative."

"You or him?" Ellie teased.

"Both of us."

"Whatever you're doing must be working. The change in those kids is amazing. Even Gabe says they're on their best behavior when they help out at the store."

"It's too soon to say they're really changing," Allison said on a sigh, "but I'll admit that they have been wonderful. I'm almost afraid to hope it might last."

She went to the icebox, took out a crockery pitcher

of milk and poured the rich cream that had risen to the top into the potatoes.

Ellie shot Allison a sideways look. "Have you spent any more…family time together since you played croquet last Friday evening?"

"No," Allison snapped.

"No need to bite off my head," Ellie said, looking taken aback by her sister's reply. "Will you be meeting up with Colt and the kids at the ice-cream party tomorrow?"

"Why all the interest in what I'm doing with the Garretts?"

Ellie shrugged. "Just trying to catch up on what's been happening with you. Why are you so snappy when I mention him?"

"I'm not."

"Are, too."

Allison couldn't help laughing, but the sound seemed hollow even to her own ears. The uncertainty she'd tried to ignore rose inside her. She was in over her head when it came to dealing with men. Far out of her depth when it came to knowing what to do about the situation with Colt.

She looked up at her sister through a glaze of tears. "I just…"

"What is it?"

"He…um, yesterday, he—he kissed me."

Ellie stood very still. "And…?" she prompted.

"I…kissed him back."

"Oh, Allison!" Ellie breathed, rushing to her sister's side and pulling her into a loose embrace. "That's wonderful! I was hoping this would happen."

"It's a disaster!" Allison wailed, wiping at her eyes with the tail of her apron.

"Why would you say that? If he kissed you it means he's interested in you. He likes you."

"According to Miss Austen," she said, referencing her favorite author, "a lady is not justified for falling in love before the gentleman declares his feelings."

Ellie took her by the shoulders and gave her a gentle shake. "Forget Jane Austen. This is real life, and while we all agree that he's a good man, Colt might not meet all of her qualifications for gentlemen."

Allison pulled free of Ellie's hold. "That doesn't alter the fact that he said he kissed me to shut me up."

"Did it work?" Ellie asked with a saucy grin.

"For a few seconds. Oh, Ellie, I'm so confused. Why is it that the first man to interest me since Jesse is someone who could never love me?"

"Why do you say that? You'd be perfect for him and those kids of his."

"This isn't about the kids!" Allison stormed. "It's about me! I want someone to love me for me. I'd rather be an old maid the rest of my life than settle for someone because he and his kids *need* me. You know as well as I do that I'm not the kind of woman who would ever interest a man like Colt Garrett."

"Why?"

"Because he's so handsome and…" She made another swipe at her damp eyes, and her voice trailed away. Making a little pirouette, she said, "Look at me."

Once again, Ellie took Allison's shoulders in a hard grip. "You. Are. Beautiful. You just need to stop dressing like some eighteen-year-old schoolgirl and update your style. With a bit of a fashion change, you'd knock him for a loop." She frowned at Allison. "Didn't we have this discussion a week or so ago?"

Allison gave her a watery smile. "We did. Can we change the subject?"

"In a minute. Did you like it?"

"What? The kiss? That's a really stupid question, Ellie Carpenter. I actually thought I might faint. Didn't you like it when he kissed you?"

"He only kissed me once," Ellie said. "And I didn't hear any bells and the earth didn't stand still or anything. I certainly didn't feel as if I might swoon."

Allison looked at her sister as if she'd grown two heads. Her heart still started racing whenever she even *thought* of Colt's lips touching hers.

"What I did feel was that he might be looking for something more than friendship, so I told him why we needed to break things off." Ellie's past wasn't something she talked about freely or often.

"See? That was only a short time ago," Allison said. "He couldn't be over you already."

"Silly goose! There was nothing to *get* over. It was just a little peck to see what would happen, and it was nothing meaningful for either of us. How did you leave things?"

"I told him we should forget that it happened. As if I could. I hardly shut an eye last night."

"The plot thickens!" Ellie said in a melodramatic voice, rubbing the palms of her hands together in glee. "Well, if it makes you feel any better, I'd say our handsome sheriff didn't sleep very well last night, either."

"Why do you say that?"

"He was in earlier with Gabe and Win." Ellie turned

back to her bubbling gravy. "He looked like death warmed over."

"He did?" Allison felt a rush of pleasure at the notion the kiss had kept Colt awake, too. Common sense reasserted itself, whispering that most likely he felt guilty, or worse, was afraid he might have messed up their bizarre working relationship.

"I don't want to talk about it anymore," she said.

"What shall we talk about, then?" Ellie had gone back to the stove and was stirring a big pot of green beans seasoned with salt pork.

"The Granvilles. With all the excitement, I'd forgotten that they've come back. Have you seen any of them besides Win?"

"Blythe and Libby were in yesterday for supper and Win was in this morning having breakfast with Gabe and Colt."

"I suppose Win is as sinfully handsome as ever."

"If you like fops."

Allison burst out laughing. "Fops? I believe you're in the wrong century. Or at least the wrong country. Win Granville may very well be the best-dressed man I've ever seen, but I don't believe for a moment that he's vain about it."

"It's a free country. Think what you will. Doesn't make it true."

The shortness in her sister's voice stunned Allison to silence. It wasn't like Ellie to take such an instant dislike to someone the way she had to Win. Allison studied her sister, who refused to meet her eyes.

"Oh, El!" she cried after a moment, covering her cheeks with her hands. "You're smitten with Win Granville."

"I most certainly am not, Allison Elizabeth Grainger!"

"It *is* a free country. You can say what you want." She tossed her sister's words back at her. "Doesn't make it true."

A brief but severe thunderstorm moved through Wolf Creek in the early morning hours Saturday, dumping so much rain that it was impossible for the ice-cream social to take place. Homer spread the word that it would be held the following Saturday instead.

Of course every child in Wolf Creek whined and cried with disappointment, but Allison viewed the weeklong delay as an opportunity to speak with Libby and Blythe about some new things for Cilla that she might possibly whip together by the following weekend.

Allison approached the Granville women after services Sunday. After explaining the situation and making certain they had time to speak with her the following day, she met with them in Hattie's parlor as early as was socially acceptable on Monday morning.

"It's very sweet of you to take such an interest in Sheriff Garrett's children, Allison," Libby said, adding a splash of cream to her coffee. "I've heard they can be quite a handful."

"Well, they have been known to create a ruckus from time to time," Allison admitted. "But Colt is spending more time with them, which seems to be helping, and we've identified some of their problems and concerns, and they seem to be turning around a bit."

"You said something yesterday about Priscilla needing some new things," Blythe said.

Allison nodded. "Unfortunately, like most men, her father doesn't understand that the older girls get, the more they want to look pretty and stylish. She's grown so the past few months that she hasn't very many things that still fit. I told her that I knew the two of you could help us with that, since you're up on all the latest fashion trends."

"We're glad to help," Libby told her. "The mayor is having the old newspaper office cleaned out so that I can put my books there. Until he finishes, Blythe and I are sitting around eating too many of Hattie's cookies and twiddling our thumbs. This will make a nice change of pace."

"You're going to store your books there until you find a place of your own, then?" Allison asked.

Libby smiled and gave a little laugh. "Actually, no. Since I have hundreds of books, I've decided to open a lending library. It will give me a purpose while I'm here, and I think it would be a valuable contribution to the town, don't you?"

"Oh, Mrs. Granville! That's wonderful." Allison's smile encompassed both Granville women. "I was saying not long ago that it's a shame Wolf Creek doesn't have a library, and now to think we will. It's the answer to this teacher's prayers!"

"I'm glad you're so pleased," Libby said. She clasped her hands together. "Now, about Cilla. Do you think she can come over so we can get some measurements?"

"I can go after her right now if you like, but I'm not asking you to make the dresses. I can do that. I just need some guidance on what young girls are wearing in Boston, though we have to keep in mind that this is a country town, and they should be appropriate for the area and the events she'll be attending."

"We know just what you mean," Blythe said with a

little laugh. "Mama and I were saying just last night that we feel overdressed with our bustles and such. We're going to need to make some plain skirts and things so we won't stick out like sore thumbs."

"You're staying, too, then?" Allison asked. There had been a lot of discussion as to whether Caleb and Gabe's half sister would make the move with her mother or return to Boston when her brother left.

"Only until Win goes back. I don't see me here."

Libby cupped a hand around her mouth and whispered loudly, "The truth is that there's a young man back in Boston who seems quite taken with her."

"Mama!" Blythe cried, her face turning red. She rose from her chair and said, "I forgot to bring the magazines and catalogs down. I'll run and fetch them."

Allison laughed with Libby, thinking what a nice woman she was and wondering how she would like living in Wolf Creek after spending so many years in a big city. Of course, her situation would be much different this time.

When Blythe returned with the periodicals, they pored over them and discussed fabric and styles for a good thirty minutes. They decided not to make any decisions before consulting with Cilla.

Allison was just about to leave to get Cilla when Libby said, "What about you, Allison? As we were looking through the book, I saw a dress I think would be lovely on you." She proceeded to flip through the pages until she found the one she was talking about and pointed it out to Allison.

She stared down at the drawing. The dress was like nothing she'd ever worn before. The bodice was simple. Fitted. Unadorned. "It's awfully...plain, don't you think?"

"Oh, no!" Blythe said, peeking over Allison's shoulder. "The simplicity is what makes it so perfect for you."

Frowning, Allison turned to look at her. "You don't think it's too...close-fitting? I'm a little, um...plump and Ellie says I'm, uh, busty."

"In Paris they would call it 'voluptuous,'" Blythe said with a daring twinkle in her eyes.

"Don't tease, Blythe!" Libby said.

Blushing, Allison said, "I've always tried to wear dresses that hide my flaws." She grimaced. "Ellie keeps telling me that those styles are what make me look so overweight."

Libby slid an arm around Allison's shoulders. "I don't want to hurt your feelings, my dear, but your sister is right. All that extra fabric just adds extra pounds."

She looked from one tastefully dressed woman to the other. "Do you think so?"

They both nodded in agreement. "All right, then," Allison said, nodding in acquiescence. "I'll try it. Maybe I can have them both finished by next Saturday."

"I'll make you a deal," Blythe said. "You concentrate on Cilla's dress, and I'll do yours. I love clothing design. That's one reason I went to Paris. I'm thinking of opening my own boutique."

"That's wonderful, Blythe! I believe you'll be excellent at it." She considered the offer for a moment then said, "All right. I accept. Do you think we can find some suitable material at Gabe's?"

"If not, I brought along a couple of lengths that might work," Libby offered. She hugged Allison, wrapping her in a lilac scent. "This is so exciting! I predict that you and Cilla Garrett will be the most sought-after girls at the ice-cream social."

* * *

The following Saturday dawned hot and humid. After a week of hard work on their new hobbies, Brady and Cilla could hardly wait for evening and a chance to have some fun with their friends. Colt was less enthusiastic. He'd planned on surprising Allison with everything necessary for her to make the peach ice cream, but the kiss had changed everything. He was confused and grouchy. And Cilla was really getting on his nerves with her wheedling.

He tried—without success—to blank out his mind as he cooked breakfast. It seemed he'd done little else but ponder on the question of what to do with the knowledge that he'd fallen in love with the last person in town he'd ever expected to. And he needed to try to figure out where their friendship stood in light of this new development.

"Please, Pa, please!" Cilla cried again as she set the plates on the table.

Colt, who wore a large flour sack dish towel tied around his middle in lieu of an apron, gritted his teeth to keep from saying something he shouldn't before taking three thick slices of ham from the skillet.

"Why the sudden insistence that I go to church?" he asked, breaking some eggs into the hot fat that sputtered and popped in protest. Muttering, he dragged the skillet to a cooler spot on the stove and began to baste the eggs with the grease.

"We really like it, and you'll learn a lot about the Bible," Brady explained. His sister had coached him about Miss Grainger's requirements for a husband and thus the importance of their father attending church. "And a lot of your friends will be there," he added, using the same argument that had been used on him and his sister.

Frowning, Colt turned and looked from one child to the other. They were the picture of innocence, but even though their behavior had been exceptional of late—doing their chores without complaining, being respectful to others and working hard for Gabe at the mercantile—he couldn't help being wary.

"Ben's and Danny's dads both go. So do most of the other kids' fathers. It's real nice to see them all sitting together as a family," Cilla told him.

The little rascals were really pouring it on. And thick. They were doing their best to make him feel guilty. He'd already heard from Cilla about Miss Grainger showing her how to bake cookies and offering to teach Cilla to sew and consulting with the Granville ladies about a new dress or two in some fashionable, updated style.

Cilla had even acted as a go-between between him and Allison in charging some sewing items to his account at the mercantile. It had chafed that she wouldn't meet him face-to-face, but the truth was, he hadn't found the courage to face her, either. Something had to give—and soon. Time was passing, and if they hoped to make any real progress with Brady before school started, they needed to get a shake on it. Besides, he missed her.

In truth, it seemed that the kids were doing just fine without him and Allie spending time together. In fact, he was still marveling how she had gone from ogre to angel in such a short span of time. Colt realized that the time his kids were spending with her had triggered the inherent need of every human: a family and all it represented.

A twinge of guilt pricked him. It shouldn't have taken a virtual stranger to point out that Cilla was growing up and that she would want and need some new things. He tried to convince himself that it was because he was a man, and for the most part, men were blind to that sort of thing. Which just went to prove he needed a wife. The sooner the better. The question was, would that wife be Allie?

All his reasons for not giving serious consideration to courting her were falling by the wayside one by one. Even though he maintained that she was not his type, he couldn't find any real fault with her. Despite her flame-red hair, which was breathtaking when it hung loose and free, her frumpy dresses and a few extra pounds, there was no denying that she was still a pretty woman. More important, she was pretty on the inside, as his mama would have said.

He'd always maintained that he could not marry a woman he felt no attraction toward, but the kiss the week before had proved beyond a doubt that there was plenty of attraction there—on both sides, if her reaction was anything to go by.

"Well? Will you come with us tomorrow?"

"Did Miss Grainger put you up to this?" he asked, scooping up the last egg and putting it onto a platter next to the ham.

The horror on Cilla's face was real. "Of course not! She'd be furious if she thought we were pushing you to go. She says it has to be something you feel in your heart."

Ah, the saintly Miss Grainger, Colt thought with a wry twist of his lips. *Saintly.* He worried the word around in his mind. Was *that* the real problem? That he felt inferior to her in so many ways?

"Do you think Miss Grainger is pretty?"

Irritated by their obsession with Allie, he put his hands on his hips and stared across the room. How to answer that?

"Pa?" Cilla persisted. "Do you?"

"Yes, I think she's pretty," he told his daughter in a reluctant growl. "Can we have breakfast now?"

"Sure," Cilla said. They pulled out their chairs and sat. Colt reached for his fork and she said, "Brady, will you ask the blessing, please?"

He nodded eagerly.

While Colt bowed his head, Brady said a brief but heartfelt prayer thanking God for their food. Touched, Colt felt the sting of tears beneath his closed eyelids.

The "Amen" said, Brady picked up the conversation where they'd left it. "She's real smart, too."

Allie again, Colt thought. His kids had made a complete turnaround in the way they felt about her, and there was no doubt that her concern and influence was having a marked influence on every aspect of their lives.

"Yes," he agreed as he cut a bite of ham. "She certainly is."

Unlike him, who had gone no further than his second year in high school, Allie was smart and educated, and even though she'd kissed him back with more than a little enthusiasm, he was skeptical of her being agreeable to a prospective husband with a lesser education.

"I think she likes you," Brady offered.

Really? Colt thought with a start. Brady thought Allie liked him? "I like her, too." And he did, despite their on-again, off-again sparring the past year.

"Are you taking her some ice for her ice cream?" Cilla asked.

"I don't know. It depends." On the one hand, after not seeing her all week, he was anxious to see her; on the other, he wasn't certain what he would say or do when he did.

"On what?"

"A lot of things."

"But we will see her at the ice-cream social, won't we?"

Fed up with the game of Twenty Questions, Colt, fork in one hand, knife in the other, rested his forearms on the edge of the table and looked from one of his children to the other. The innocence on their faces didn't fool him for a minute. What was this all about, anyway?

The answer came out of nowhere, slamming into him with the force of Ed Rawlings's angry bull when he'd pinned Colt against a fence. He knew exactly what was up.

"The two of you wouldn't be trying to push me and Allison into spending more time together, would you?"

Brady looked at Cilla, the expression in his eyes begging her to spit it out. "Well, actually," she said, "Brady and I have talked about it, and we think it would be swell if you started courting her."

Glowering at his sister, and swinging that frowning gaze to Colt, Brady said, "What she really means is that since we have to have a stepmother, we'd like her."

"What did you say?" Colt asked, uncertain that he'd heard correctly.

"Cilla and I want Miss Grainger to be our ma."

Chapter Ten

Colt wondered if he looked as stunned as he felt. The kids had bypassed the courting stage and propelled him and Allison straight to the altar. Very carefully, he put down his fork and knife.

"Is that true, Cilla?"

At least she had the grace to blush, though the expression in her eyes was determined. "Yes, it is." She raised her chin to a stubborn angle. "We started thinking about what you said about marrying again one day, and we thought it would be a good thing if we helped you pick out a wife, since we'll be stuck with her, too. We like Miss Grainger a whole lot more than the other ladies you've squired around."

Colt rubbed at the sudden throbbing in his temples. "That isn't the way it works, Cilla."

"Why not?"

"I may not like the same person you and Brady do."

"But you already said you like Miss Grainger," Brady reminded him. "And you think she's pretty."

"Yes, but those things aren't all it takes to make a

good match. There's a lot to consider when the lives of so many people will be affected."

"Well, I can't imagine why she wouldn't be a good match," Cilla said in an exasperated tone, "since you already like her and everything. Brady and I think she has a lot of good qualities." She recounted all the reasons for believing Allison was a prime candidate for marriage and motherhood.

Colt couldn't help being impressed with her thought process. Or agreeing with her.

"And," Brady said, ticking off his own observations on his fingers, "Cilla and I think she's nice, and she was a lot of fun when we played croquet. She isn't silly like Miss Cole, and she's smart, so she could help me with my studies and you wouldn't have to do it." He offered an impish grin. "You'd like that, wouldn't you, Pa? And she makes *really* good pie," he added, almost as an afterthought.

It was hard to argue with that kind of logic, Colt thought with a derisive smile. Simple. Straightforward. No-nonsense.

If only it were that easy.

"Well, there's the small problem that Miss Grainger may not want me for a husband. Did the two of you stop to think about that?"

Brady and Cilla looked at each other. "That's why we want you to go to church," Brady said. "That's important to her."

Ah. So that was what was behind their insistence that he go to church with them. He looked from one to the other. "I appreciate your concern for me and Allison, and it's nice to know you approve of her, but you two need to mind your own business and leave the grown-up stuff to me. Whether or not it's Allie or someone else, I'll find my own wife in my own good time."

He pointed a finger at them. "And don't go telling her what you told me. She's likely to run all the way back to Springfield. Do I make myself clear?"

"Yes, sir," they said, but they looked decidedly crestfallen.

Colt picked up his fork. "Now let's finish our breakfast and go on about our day. We'll see Allison this evening, and I imagine we'll all have a good time."

By evening, the late July day had cooled off enough, at least in the shade, that it was bearable—just. Bingo, checkers and other game tables had been set up under the trees. Some of the older boys had created a rough diamond in the adjacent field and a rousing game of baseball was in progress.

Wagons were backed along the edge of the tree line. Ice-cream paddles had been removed, freezers re-salted and repacked with ice, and covered with several layers of burlap or old quilts to harden.

It was customary to have a cakewalk before dishing up the ice cream. Besides a tempting array of cakes, pies and cobblers were also up for grabs. When all the goodies had been claimed, the desserts would be sliced or scooped and topped with frozen deliciousness that cost five cents a bowl. Then the eating would begin.

Colt scanned the area, waving at friends, trying not to be too obvious that he was on the lookout for Allison. After realizing the day before that he loved her and hearing the kids' stunning proclamation about wanting her for a mother, he hadn't been able to muster up the courage to seek her out, confident he would see her tonight. He knew he should have been pleased by their announcement, but it only added to the anxiety already coiled in his gut.

He saw Ellie talking to Rachel and Abby Gentry and noted the surprise on her face and her wide smile at something Rachel said. While he watched, Caleb and Gabe joined the ladies, accompanied by Win, who stood across from Ellie, with his hands plunged in the pockets of his tailored pin-striped trousers, as if he hadn't a care in the world. His concession to the casual event was to leave his jacket at home. Colt noticed that even though the elder Granville didn't appear to have any special interest in Ellie, he didn't miss a move she made.

Interesting. The Boston native's apparent disinterest was an excellent smoke screen for his attraction to the woman who'd rebuffed the attentions of every eligible man in Wolf Creek. Maybe it was time to swallow his pride and ask the smooth city boy for some tips, since he was far more adept at the game of love than Colt ever hoped to be.

His not-really-a-plan plan was to see what Allison's reaction was to him after more than a week to put things into perspective. He'd also keep quiet for a while about the change in his feelings, and see what else happened.

His gaze scanned the crowd again, sweeping past a red-haired woman making room for a golden-brown creation among the other baked goodies. He whipped his head back to her so fast he heard his neck crack.

Was that stylish-looking woman Allie? Her habitual ruffles and flounces were gone. She was wearing a dress of sage-green, trimmed in flat matching braid around the white cuffs and stand-up collar. Unlike the usual loose style she wore, the bodice was fitted to her with exquisite care. The skirt was not gathered, or bustled or pleated. Instead, it was the same style she'd worn the evening they played croquet, fitting smoothly over her hips with a gentle flaring toward the ground. A section of the front was pleated from the knees down.

She no longer looked overweight and frumpy. If she were a tiny bit plump—and that was debatable—he found no fault with it. She was all womanly curves and shapeliness, exuding style and understated femininity. Her hair was pulled to the nape of her neck in a loose coil.

Wolf Creek's resident wallflower had emerged from her chrysalis like an exotic butterfly came out of its cocoon in the spring. She looked stunning. There was no other word to describe her.

While Colt was standing across the way staring at her, a smiling Nate Willett sauntered over and struck up a conversation. The innocent gesture of interest roused Colt from his shock. He pushed away from the tree he was leaning against and headed in her direction. Before he could reach her, Lawrence Tilley had joined Nate.

Colt clenched his hands at his sides. He'd like nothing more than to plant his fist in both their smiling faces. Allie was smiling, too, though he thought she looked as flustered by the sudden and unexpected attention as he felt about his sudden and unexpected surge of jealousy that had taken control of him.

He approached the threesome with what he hoped was a casual smile, but his "sheriff's scowl" as he looked over the two potential suitors could surely only be described as "intimidating."

"Hi, there," he said, stopping a few feet behind Allison.

Startled, she jumped, then took a breath and turned

to look up at him, a hand pressed against her chest. Her brown eyes looked guarded behind the spectacles perched on her nose.

"I didn't mean to scare you," he told her.

"You didn't." A quick smile flashed. "Well, maybe a little."

They stared at each other a few seconds. She seemed to be trying to gauge his feelings while he spent the brief moment examining the honey-colored freckles scattered over her face. He'd count them one day, he vowed. Count them and kiss every last one. They were adorable, as were the glasses.

Suddenly anxious to be alone with her, he dragged his gaze from her face to her two young admirers, who were shifting from foot to foot. "I hope you gentlemen will forgive me for taking Miss Grainger away, but she promised me a walk."

The young men made hasty retreats with promises to see her soon. Colt wasn't sure what he expected from her after the way they'd parted the last time they were together, but to his surprise, she said, "You fibbed. I didn't promise you a walk."

"I most certainly did," he said, offering her his arm. "Forgive me?"

Still holding his gaze, she wrapped her fingers around his biceps, and he guided her away from the cluster of people milling around the tables to a place near the creek. He stopped beneath the shade of an ancient oak, and they both spoke at once.

"Colt, I'm not—"

"Allie, you look—"

They both stopped and Colt hooked his thumbs through his belt loops. "Ladies first."

She dropped her gaze to the ground for a moment, and then, as if she'd somehow fortified herself, she looked up at him and said, "I just wanted to tell you that I…am not in the habit of allowing men to kiss me."

It occurred to him that even though she was on the downhill side of twenty, a spinster in anyone's book, she was very innocent.

"I never supposed that you were."

"You, uh…took me by surprise."

A soft laugh rumbled from him. "It took me by surprise, too."

"It did?" she asked, wide-eyed.

"Well, I certainly didn't plan to kiss you, and I definitely never expected either of us to like it as much as we did. And you did like it, Allie, so don't try to deny it."

"No," she said with a shake of her head, "I won't." She looked none too happy about the admission. "As I said before, I don't think we should allow it to happen again."

Colt knew she'd been bolstered by indignation the day of the kiss, but now it seemed to him that her crossness had dissolved, leaving her feeling uncertain, with maybe a little guilt thrown in for good measure. He knew she was dealing with embarrassment, too, which any decent, inexperienced woman no doubt would. Still, he felt compelled to probe deeper into her feelings.

"Why not?"

"Because…well, because I'm not that kind of woman, and…and it could create a great deal of awkwardness while we're trying to help the children."

He nodded. He was right on the money about her

mind-set. "And what kind of woman might that be?" he asked, eager to understand more of how she thought.

She looked up at him. Every freckle stood out against the paleness of her cheek. It was all he could do to keep from reaching out and trailing his finger along the delicate line of her jaw. He didn't want her distressed. Ever. By anything.

"Well," she said, appearing to give it serious thought, "I'm not the kind of woman who gives away her kisses willy-nilly to men who want nothing more than to toy with her affections."

"And you think that's what I'm doing?" he queried. "Toying with your affections?"

"I can't imagine it being anything else," she told him, looking bewildered by his question.

He did touch her then. He reached out and gave the tip of her nose a light tap, a rueful half smile hiking a corner of his mouth. "I admit that I'm as confused as you are, Allie, but you can be sure of one thing. I'm not playing with your affections, and I'm not the kind of man who leads women on."

"You don't really even like me very much."

"Not true." He raised his eyebrows and grinned at her. "I admit that I've been pretty mad at you from time to time," he corrected. "As you have me."

"I'm not stupid, Colt," she said, doing her best to whip up a little indignation. "I look in the mirror every day. I know I'm not the kind of woman who would interest a man like you."

He frowned. "You keep talking about the kind of man I am. What kind of man is that, Allie?"

"You're well thought of in the community…"

"That's nice to know. So are you."

"…and excellent at your job," she continued, as if he hadn't interrupted.

"I try," he said with a lift of his shoulders. "So do you."

"You're honest and decent and moral…."

"Hmm. I'm thinking that I sound like a pretty good guy. Not the kind to toy with a woman's feelings," he told her. "And by the way, you're all of those things, too. Anything else?"

She gave a little huff and lowered her gaze. "If you must know, you're very…handsome."

"Really?" he said, pleased. "You think so?"

"You must know I do." Her voice was the merest thread of sound.

"Must I?" Colt reached out and lifted her chin, forcing her to face him. "How would I know that?" he asked in a gentle voice.

Her eyelashes fluttered down to hide her eyes. "Well, because I… I kissed you."

"Yes, you did."

Not wanting to tease her anymore, he released her and said, "So that's how you see me and the kind of man you think I am—your opinion of me."

"And I daresay it's everyone else's, too."

"Do you know how I see myself?"

Allison shook her head.

"I see a man who, for too many years, has let grief and anger rob him of a lot of the good things life has to offer. A man who's put his heartache and his job before his children, who hasn't been a very good father in the ways that really matter.

"But I'm a man who thinks things through, and I like

to think I can weigh the gold from the dross. I believe I know the real thing when I see it."

"I don't understand."

He offered her a wry smile. "I'm not a man with a silver tongue, Allie. What I'm trying to say is that I've been thinking for a while that I'm ready to try love and marriage again." He sucked in a deep lungful of air and plunged, his tentative plan going out the window. "What I'm trying to say is that I want to try it with you."

Chapter Eleven

"I beg your pardon."

Allison's head whirled in shock and disbelief. Was Colt Garrett, one of the most eligible men in town, saying that he wanted to marry *her?* Needing to make certain she'd heard him right, she asked, "You want to… try it with me? Marriage?"

"Yes. I know this is coming out of the blue and that we haven't known each other very long. Not in any way that matters. For right now, let's just say that I'd like to court you."

Allison twined her fingers together. Her stomach churned in panic and distress, though she couldn't imagine why. Wasn't this every young woman's dream? Her dream? Images of making a life with Colt and the children swirled through her mind with dizzying speed. The children! Sudden understanding slammed into her.

Tears shimmered in her eyes as she looked up at him. "Why did you have to go and ruin everything?" she cried in a soft voice.

Colt looked as if she'd slapped him, yet his mouth

curved in a bitter parody of a smile. "Does that mean no?" he said with a miserable attempt at levity.

Allison squared her shoulders and said in a prim tone, "It means that while I'm very flattered by your proposal, as any woman in Wolf Creek would be, it isn't necessary to offer courtship or marriage to assure that I'll continue to help you with the children. I've grown to care for them very much. I would never abandon them—or you—that way."

"Is that what you think this is about?" he said in a low, hard voice. "Cilla and Brady?"

"Isn't it?"

Colt planted his hands on his hips and stared at the ground. When he lifted his head to look at her, all of his uncertainty and confusion was mirrored in his eyes. He reached out and took her cold hands in his.

"I'd be lying if I said that their feelings and well-being weren't a part of my decision. Of course they are. I owe it to them to bring a woman into our home that will care for them in all the ways their real mother would. You've already proved that you're that woman. In fact, they've already given us their blessing. What you've managed to do for them in such a short time is nothing short of a miracle, and I'll always be grateful to you, but it's far more than that, Allie.

"You present a portrait of upstanding refinement to the world, which you definitely are," he hastened to clarify, "but I've seen glimpses of a side of you I feel few people have seen, maybe even a side you feel you have to keep hidden beneath that straitlaced facade."

Allison listened, a bit taken aback that she'd revealed so much of herself to him in such a short time, and more surprised that he'd been able to look beyond the image she presented and recognize the person she was and, more important, the person she longed to be.

"I have great admiration for you," he continued. "I like that you're levelheaded and unwavering when you set your mind to something." He smiled, and Allison's heart skipped a beat. "I like that you take off your shoes to play croquet. And I like your kisses a lot."

She pressed her lips together, and hot color stained her cheeks. "Those are certainly good things, but I want more from marriage, Colt," she said, her voice husky and her heart in her eyes. "I don't want liking and admiration. I want love and…and passion," she said, daring to toss out a word few women would admit to want… or feel, much less express to a man.

"I can give you that."

Her brief mocking laugh wasn't far from a sob. "Oh, so you've fallen in love with me in a couple of weeks, is that it?"

"It's incredible, maybe, but yes." He let go of her hands and stuck his thumbs in his belt loops in an achingly familiar gesture. "I'm not sure when or how it happened, but it has."

Allison had no ready comeback for that. She wanted to believe him, wanted to embrace everything he was offering, but her fearful heart whispered that there was no way a man like Colt could have fallen for someone like her. It insisted that when he tired of the novelty of her naïveté—which she told herself must have been the cause of his proclaimed infatuation—he would leave her for someone prettier and not so dull.

Just as Jesse had.

"You feel something for me, too, Allie," Colt said,

taking a step closer. "I know you do. You feel that spark when I kiss you."

"Yes," she admitted, rubbing at the sudden ache in her temples. It was senseless to deny it. "So you're asking me to believe that in a very short time, you've come to love me and you're convinced that I'm everything you want in a wife?" she asked.

"Yes."

His answer was quick, his conviction unmistakable. She should have shouted with joy. Wished she could have. She tried to swallow, and it felt as if her throat were closing. "Well, as saddened as I am to say it, you aren't everything I'm looking for."

Colt actually reeled back a step. All the color drained from his face, and the earnest entreaty in his eyes changed to bitter disappointment. Then, in typical male fashion, he hid his pain behind a cold implacable mask.

The ache in Allison's heart grew to unbearable proportions. She actually pressed a hand to her chest to try to contain the hurt.

"Forgive me for troubling you," he said. Without another word, he turned to walk away.

She took a tentative step toward him, reached out and caught his sleeve.

"Colt, wait!"

"For what, Allison?" he retorted, tossing her an angry look over his shoulder. "For you to stomp on my heart with those pretty little shoes of yours?"

"I'd like to ask you a question."

His wide shoulders lifted in a shrug that granted compliance while giving the impression that he couldn't care less. "Ask away."

"If I were to agree to become your wife, would you

make your peace with God and try to live for Him?"
She held her breath as he stared down at her. The muscle in his cheek knotted; the hands at his sides fisted.

"Conditions, Allison? Or is it an ultimatum?"

He was the same furious stranger she'd confronted in his office that fateful day she'd told him about his children's abominable behavior.

She hadn't thought of it in that way, but she supposed he was right. "Marriage is a goal of most women, Colt. I want to get married someday, and I believe I will. But my ultimate goal is Heaven, so yes, I guess you can say I have conditions."

She held her breath, waiting for his answer. He gave a single harsh nod. "Fine. Yes. If going to church with you and the kids will make you all happy, I'll go."

She saw how much it cost him to agree. "I don't want you to go to church."

"But you just said—"

"No," she interrupted. "I said I wanted you to make your peace with God and be our example."

"What's the difference?" he asked.

"If you have to ask, then you don't understand at all. My answer is no, Colt. I won't marry you, and I don't want you to call on me. The children are still welcome anytime."

She was trembling like a leaf as she spoke the words that would send him away forever. Instead of responding, he turned and walked away. Allison watched him go, her indrawn breath whooshing from her in a surge of regret and soul-deep pain. The mockingbird on the limb high above her sang a cheerful song, scoffing at her misery.

Brady and Cilla asked Allison to join them in the cakewalk. She made the effort for their sakes, but it was plain that both children knew something was up. Though she scanned the boisterous happy crowd at regular intervals, Colt seemed to have disappeared.

After more than an hour of suffering, Allison declared she had a headache and told Ellie that she was going home. She must have looked terrible because Win, who was standing nearby, surprised her by offering to drive her in his rented buggy. Even more surprising, he asked Ellie to accompany them, and she accepted. He looked pleased, but Allison knew Ellie only agreed out of sisterly concern.

"What on earth is wrong with you?" Ellie asked, as soon as they were seated and Win pulled out onto the road. "This should be a wonderful evening for you. You look astonishing. You're the topic of several conversations."

Ellie was right. This should have been a remarkable time, for many reasons. Thanks to Blythe and Libby Granville, Allison looked her best and she knew it— freckles, glasses and all. Compliments had flown all evening. She had received a proposal of marriage from a man she loved....

The sob she'd been fighting to keep back worked its way up from the depths of her heart, and she buried her face in her hands to try to hide the ugliness of the grief that welled up inside her and spilled down her cheeks.

She didn't notice the worried glance Ellie and Win exchanged, but she did feel her sister's arm go around her and pull her close. Without a word, she pressed a handkerchief into Allison's hand. It smelled of some spicy scent that hinted of faraway exotic places. Win's handkerchief. The part of Allison's brain that wasn't consumed by her misery was aware that Win was no doubt regretting that he'd offered his services.

"What's wrong?" Ellie asked.

"Colt said he wants to marry me."

Ellie's body stilled. For a moment she didn't even breathe. "So why are you crying?"

"I told him no."

"Why would you do something like that?" Ellie chided. "I know you care for him and his children. I can see it on your face every time you talk about them."

"I do love him, Ellie, but I don't believe for a moment that he really loves me."

"Why would he lie about something like that?"

"Oh, I don't know," Allison said in a jaunty tone that reeked of sarcasm. "Because he wants a wife, and he needs someone who can manage his kids. That would be me. In fact, he said they'd already given their blessing."

"And they say miracles don't happen anymore," Ellie teased. "Everyone's noticed the changes in Brady and Cilla. You've been good for the whole family. Did Colt say how he feels about you?"

"He claims he's fallen in love with me."

"Why is that so hard for you to believe?" Ellie asked in exasperation.

"Jesse."

"Well, that's just plain silly," Ellie scoffed. "I thought you'd gotten beyond judging all men by the way Jesse Castle treated you. He was young and easily taken in. Colt is a grown man with grown-up feelings, not some untried boy easily swayed by flirty girls with no more sense than God gave a goose. He's not looking for a girl. He's looking for a woman, and I daresay he knows what he wants."

"But he's s-so good-looking," she stuttered. "What can he possibly see in me?" She mopped at her tearstained face with Win's monogrammed handkerchief.

"Maybe a smart, caring, charming woman who is as cute as a bug."

The statement came from Win, who both women had forgotten was listening to every word they said. He met their stunned looks with a slight shrug. "Sorry. I know no one asked my opinion, but there it is."

"Cute as a bug?" Ellie said.

"Mmm," Win said. "There's something about Allison that makes you want to just pick her up and cuddle her close, keep her safe."

Wouldn't that be nice? Allison thought.

He gave his attention back to the road, but a cocky grin lifted the corners of his mouth. "I might be tempted to give the sheriff a run for his money if my feelings were not otherwise engaged."

"You don't have to say things like that to make me feel better," Allison said.

"Oh, I'm plenty serious, Miss Allison Grainger," he said, his devilish grin growing wider. "I don't say things as a balm for hurt feelings or jest about important matters. Life's too short. It's best to just say what you mean."

"Even if he did love me, I wouldn't marry him."

"And why not?" Ellie demanded.

Certain that Win was not the kind of person to spread what he heard all over town, Allison recounted her conversation with Colt about the importance of God to her ideal of marriage and how he'd chosen to walk away.

Win pulled to a stop in front of Allison's little house before Ellie could comment. He handed Ellie the reins, climbed down, rounded the buggy and lifted Allison down after she'd hugged her sister. Then he escorted her to the door, ever the perfect gentleman.

Smiling down into her eyes, he said, "If it's any consolation, I think any man who walks away from you has taken leave of his senses."

"Thank you, Win," Allison said with a watery smile.

He gave her hand a brotherly pat and strode to the edge of the porch before turning. "I also believe he will come around sooner or later. If not, I may take it upon myself to knock some into him. I was boxing champ at Yale, you know."

"You've ruined everything!"

"So I've been told," Colt said, resigned to his children's scorn. He *had* ruined everything, it seemed.

They'd just returned from the ice-cream social, and Cilla had demanded to know what Colt had done to make Miss Grainger so miserable. He was miserable, and try though he might, there'd been no hiding it. After several people told him he must be coming down with something, he'd gathered the kids and left. Figuring he owed his offspring some sort of explanation, especially since he had no idea what their future with Allie might be, given that he'd "ruined everything," he'd offered them a condensed version of his conversation with her, including a little of their talk about his relationship with God.

By the time they reached the house, the anger he'd whipped up to hide his wounded pride had died a pitiful death. The ache he carried inside was as hurtful as what he'd felt when he lost Patrice. Wasn't that interesting?

Now, thinking back to what Allison had said, a sharp

pain shot through his heart. It had been naive and un-realistic of him to not at least consider the possibility that she would have her own list of what she wanted in a husband.

"She told me the same thing," Cilla said, breaking into his thoughts. "She said that handsomeness and kindness were nice, but that she could never marry a man who didn't love God. We told you—that's why we wanted you to go to church with us."

"She said she doesn't want me to just go to church."

"Well, of course not!" Cilla's acerbic tone suggested that she had reservations about her father's intelligence.

"She says it has to come from your heart," Brady chimed in.

Cilla glared at her brother. "That's right, but I think going to Sunday morning services is a good place to start."

"Go to bed," Colt said in a weary voice. He didn't want to talk about it anymore. He wanted to go outside, sit on the back porch and listen to the lonesome howl of the coyotes and the mournful *whoo-whoo* of the barn owl. At least they had something in common with him.

"It's not too late to fix things," Cilla told him. Her hands were planted on her hips and she was looking at him as if she'd like to put him in the corner.

"I don't need advice from a twelve-year-old about how to handle my love life."

"Well, you need some help from someone."

Colt glared at them. "Go. To. Bed," he growled. "Both of you."

Without another word, they stomped out of the room. Cilla sent him a look over her shoulder that he'd occa-sionally seen on Patty's face when he'd done something she thought was beyond foolish. It was a look he was convinced God distributed to the fairer sex at the instant of conception. Even coming from his young daughter, it packed quite a punch. Despite his bad humor, Colt found a cynical smile. His little girl was growing up.

She needed a mother to help her navigate the upcoming troubling years. She needed Allison.

They all did.

A subdued Colt ambled into the kitchen the following morning after a night of tossing and turning and trying to figure out how things had gone so wrong so fast, and how one curvy, pint-size woman could tie a man in knots with nothing but words.

He found Cilla and Brady sitting at the pine table, dressed in their Sunday best and eating scrambled eggs and buttered bread. Cilla regarded him with all the disdain of royalty regarding a lowly peasant. Brady started to smile a good-morning, but after taking an elbow in the ribs, he caught himself and glowered instead. Colt ignored their rebellious looks and went to the stove to pour a cup of coffee.

The blue-speckled graniteware coffeepot sitting at the back of the stove was cold. Cilla hadn't made the coffee, something she'd been doing every morning since she was big enough to climb up on a stool and pump the water herself.

He sighed. *Ah, mutiny in the ranks.* Without a word, he filled the pot with water, and ground and added the required amount of coffee. Then, moving like an old man, he went to the table and sat, resting his chin in his hands and looking from one of his offspring to the other, careful to let no emotions show.

Brady spoke first. "Did you sleep okay?"

"Do I look like I slept okay?"

"Not really. You look like you been rowed up Salt River," Brady said, never one to be overly concerned with hurting someone's feelings.

"Hmm. I feel that way."

"Cilla didn't make enough eggs," Brady said, and shoveled in another mouthful.

Cilla shifted a little in her chair but refused to meet his eyes.

"I see that."

Though he knew the egg shortage was Cilla's way of inflicting her own brand of punishment on him, Colt was careful to keep his tone bland and non-accusatory. The last thing he wanted was to start the day with another row. "And please take smaller bites."

"Yes, sir."

"Brady and I are going to church." The defiant announcement was Cilla's first words to him.

"What time should I expect you for lunch?"

"Noon." She waited a minute and asked, "You're not working today?"

Colt covered a massive yawn and scrubbed a hand back and forth through his hair. "It's Dan's Sunday."

"Oh."

"I hope Miss Grainger will let us sit with her."

"Why wouldn't she?" Colt asked.

"Because you…you…upset her."

Colt offered Brady an apologetic smile. "She isn't upset with you, Brady. She told me that things between her and you and your sister wouldn't change. She really cares for you."

"She cares for you, too!" Cilla cried, slamming her

fork onto the tabletop. Tears shimmered in her blue eyes. "I know she does."

"We covered this last night, pretty girl," Colt said. "She made it clear that I'm not what she wants in a husband."

Saying the words aloud brought another sharp stab of pain. "The best thing a man can do in a case like this is step aside for someone who *can* be what she wants."

"If you love her enough, couldn't you try to change for her?" Cilla pleaded. "Like Big Dan has done for Miss Gracie?"

"Let it be, Cilla," Colt told her, thinking that this was just one more way he'd failed the three most important people in his life. "Just let it be."

Just then he heard the angry spit and sputter as the coffee boiled over. He bolted to his feet, grabbed the handle and dropped it just as fast, splashing even more over the stovetop. Looking worried about his reaction, Cilla and Brady excused themselves and left the kitchen while Colt looked from the mess to the angry red welt on his palm.

He figured his day would only go downhill from there.

He was hardly aware when the kids left the house. He fried himself some eggs and stared at them until the soft yellow yolks congealed on the plate, then drank some coffee and allowed himself to wallow in his sorrow and the chain of events that had led him to this place in his life. He wouldn't try to sweet-talk Allison into compromising her convictions and accept him as he was. He doubted he could. You didn't change people's minds about love. It happened or it didn't.

It was a time like this, when he felt so alone, that he missed Patrice the most.

Patrice. What would she think of where he and the kids were now? Which, if any, of the women in town would she feel would make the best wife for him and mother for their children? He knew she wanted him to marry again; she'd told him as much as she lay so still and pale, her life's blood seeping from her, and he'd been unable to do anything to stop it. Even then, she'd assured him that she was fine. Just before she'd drawn her last breath, she'd sat up as if nothing were wrong and smiled, a smile that nearly blinded him with its radiance.

And in that memory lay part of his answer. Whomever he chose, Patrice would just want him to be happy with that choice. She would say that if he were happy, the children would be happy. And then she would add the caveat that he would never be truly content until he let go of his anger and made his peace with the Lord. He knew she was right, that Allison was right, but so far, he hadn't been able to do that.

So where did that leave him?

Deep down, he'd always known that God wasn't really to blame for what had happened to Patty. The world was what it was. Things happened to everyone, good and bad. Some people found gold; others were killed for it. Crops thrived; drought killed. It was no one's fault; it was life.

When Patty died, he'd sunk into a deep depression that lasted for a long time. He'd always been the kind of man who solved problems, and he'd run into a situation he couldn't fix. He wasn't used to letting down the people he loved. In an effort to alleviate his pain, he had transferred his feelings of failure onto God, blaming Him for the grief consuming him and deliberately walking away from His comfort and care. In doing so, he had let down his kids.

Without warning, a passage of scripture flitted through his mind, something about fathers bringing up their children in the nurture and admonition of the Lord. Immediately, a rush of guilt and sorrow washed over him.

Patrice had left him with their most precious possessions—the children created from their love. He had not brought them up the way the Lord wanted. He hadn't even brought them up the way she would have wanted. Shame joined the aching regret filling his heart. All he'd thought about after she died was himself. His grief. His needs. His selfishness and stubbornness had deprived his kids of the thing that was most important to their growing up—a life grounded in God. And look what had happened. He didn't want Cilla growing up to be a quarrelsome nag or Brady becoming an angry young man with a chip on his shoulder.

Colt felt tears trickling down his cheeks. Coming face-to-face with his failure wasn't pleasant. Inevitably, conversations with the kids and Allie drifted through his mind. He recalled Cilla's comment about Dan changing his life so that he would have a chance with Grace Morrison. Dan didn't seem to regret giving up his wild ways at all. In fact, Colt couldn't remember his deputy ever being happier. He'd even confessed that he was paying out an engagement ring at the mercantile, and hoped to propose to Gracie soon.

Cilla maintained that attending church services was a good place to start his journey back to God, and he knew she was right. How had she become so wise at the ripe old age of twelve? If he wanted to win Allie's love and her hand in marriage, if he wanted to feel the love for God he knew was essential to his soul, he had to start afresh. Attending church *was* a good starting place, but after thinking about it, Colt decided that a prayer wouldn't come amiss.

Hesitantly, he asked for forgiveness for his many transgressions since Brady's birth, thanked Him for the time with Patrice and that Brady had survived the arduous birth. He expressed his gratitude for both of his children, for bringing him and Allison together. Then, with tears wetting his hands, he prayed for another chance with Allie. When he whispered "Amen" he felt a lightness of spirit that he hadn't known in years.

He wouldn't push. He would take a page from Dan's successful book on courting, and do his best to live the life both Allison and God wanted. With a heart as light as a dandelion puff he headed to the bedroom to get ready for church.

Chapter Twelve

Allison cried most of the night. Knowing that she'd made the right decision did not make living with it any easier. Had it not been for Jesse, she might have chanced accepting Colt as he was, but after Jesse had betrayed her with a flashy girl he'd met while carousing in the city with some of his rough friends, she was too afraid to risk her heart a second time.

She wasn't so unsophisticated as to believe that Christians never made mistakes and never sinned or let others down, but she did feel that having that common bond could go a long way toward fixing many of the problems that cropped up in a marriage.

Deep in her heart, she knew her decision was for the best, but oh, how it hurt. This time, though, she would accept this as God's will, and she would not become cynical and distrusting of all males as she had before. She would just keep looking for that right man.

The early August day promised to be another scorcher. The midmorning sun blazed down, sucking the moisture from the earth and the plants, which looked as droopy as Allison felt. As she made her way toward the church building, she wondered if Brady and Cilla would come, or if, under the circumstances, Colt would prefer that they not spend any more time with her. When she saw them standing outside with some of the other children, she murmured a little prayer of thanksgiving. Neither of them looked very happy, but at least they were there, which said a lot.

"Good morning, children," she said, her smile and greeting intended for them all.

"'Morning, Miss Grainger," they said in unison.

"Cilla, Brady. Would you like to sit with me?"

"Yes, ma'am," they said, sounding almost grateful.

They filed inside, where Allison was inundated with people asking how she was feeling and if she'd rid herself of her headache. She and the children sat on the same row as Ellie and Bethany, Allison next to her sister.

"You don't look as if you got any rest," Ellie murmured under her breath.

"I didn't shut an eye until almost dawn," Allison replied.

"Any new conclusions?"

"Nothing really, except that if it were one obstacle or the other, I might make some concessions."

"What do you mean? One obstacle or the other?"

"If I were one-hundred-percent certain that Colt loved me, I might be willing to take a chance that he would someday forge a new relationship to God, or if he were the Christian husband I'd like him to be, I might trust that he would come to love me in time, but two big question marks is more of a chance than I'm comfortable with taking."

"Well, he is a good man," Ellie whispered. "And I do believe he'll find his way back one day, maybe through the children. Sometimes I think men are just too stubborn to admit they're wrong."

Allison shrugged.

"What would it take to prove he loved you?"

The question came out of the blue, giving Allison pause. She turned to meet her sister's curious look. "I'm not sure. It just…happened so fast that it's hard to believe it's real, especially since we were thrown together in such an unusual manner."

"Why is it so hard to believe that he fell fast when you've done the same thing? Why can't it work both ways?"

Allison's eyes widened. Ellie had a valid point. Why should it be any different? The only answer Allison could come up with was the same as it had always been: What woman in her right mind could help falling in love with Colt? She was saved from having to reply by the song leader's announcement that the first song would be "The Old Rugged Cross."

As usual, the heartfelt words brought a measure of peace and put Allison's own problems into perspective. Midway through the final song before the sermon, she became aware that there was a lot of head-turning and whispering going on. Brady, Cilla, Bethany and even Ellie turned to look toward the commotion in the back. Their triumphant smiles could mean only one thing. Colt had come to the worship service.

Her heart seemed to stumble before settling into a faster rhythm. Her gloved fingers tightened on the edges of her hymnal, and she fought the urge to turn and see for herself if he was really here.

What did it mean, after he'd turned and walked away from her the evening before? Had he had a change of heart? The song ended, and the minister stepped to the pulpit. Whatever the reason, she would have to wait until after services to find out.

Brother McAdams was perhaps fifteen minutes into his sermon when Allison heard the door at the rear of the building open. Heavy boots thudded on the wooden floor. Once again, she resisted the impulse to turn and see what was going on. Once again, the children had no such reluctance.

She heard Cilla and Brady murmuring to one another and then Cilla leaned across Ellie and whispered, "Dan's come for Pa."

Allison's heart plummeted. She had no earthly idea why Big Dan Mercer would interrupt a church service, but common sense told her that whatever it was must be important. She heard two pairs of boots headed toward the door. Moving faster than she'd ever seen him, easygoing Earl Pickens, who owned the newspaper, passed down the aisle toward the pulpit. The preacher paused midsentence, knowing he'd lost his audience, and leaned over to hear whatever it was Earl whispered into his ear.

Allison saw the alarm on his face and the way his body stiffened. Not good news.

The minister stepped aside and Earl took his place at the podium. "Sheriff Garrett wants to apologize for the interruption," he told them, "but Dan just came to tell him that Ace Allen got word that Elton Thomerson and his buddy escaped from prison sometime last night."

Loud murmuring swept through the crowd, and the only thing Allison could hear with any clarity was "Ace."

"What's Ace Allen doing delivering messages? I thought he was serving time with Elton," someone called from the other side of the room.

The preacher stepped forward. "Though it isn't common knowledge, Mr. Allen was only in prison a short time after Elton claimed Mr. Allen was his partner in the robberies that had plagued the county the last several months. That wasn't true. Sheriff Garrett arrested the guilty party, who confessed, and Mr. Allen was freed."

Conversation exploded. There were disgruntled murmurs, exclamations of disbelief, curiosity and downright anger. As usual, there were a few voices more demanding than others.

"When did this happen?"

"Why weren't we told?"

"Where's he been all these months?"

"If Allen wasn't Elton's partner, who was?"

Earl held up a hand. "Everyone please listen."

The room became silent. "The man who'd been helping Elton rob people who were coming and going from town was a guy—an Indian—from over around Murfreesboro by the name of Joseph Jones. We all know what kind of misery Elton has dealt to the people of this town, and Gabe and Sarah know firsthand."

All eyes turned to Gabe Gentry and Sarah VanSickle, both of whom had suffered Elton's brutality back in the spring. Sarah's face had taken on an ashy tint and she clung to Randolph's arm.

"Everyone knows what Meg has gone through at his hands. I see she isn't here today. The sheriff and Ace are worried that Elton will go to the farm, so that's where they're headed. That's all I can tell you right now."

The babble of voices filled the room, questions for which there were no immediate answers. "Quiet, please," the minister said. "Under the circumstances, I think we'll dismiss early. But first I think it would be appropriate to offer a prayer for the sheriff and his efforts. Earl?"

Earl began to pray. Allison closed her eyes and bowed her head. Her mind whirled with what she'd just heard, as well as the implications. This was something she'd never considered as she'd woven daydreams about life with Colt. Wolf Creek had little crime—mostly an occasional round of fisticuffs or someone indulging in a drunken binge. But there were times like today, when he was called on to deal with something or someone that was truly dangerous. Elton was one of those people, and this was one of those times.

The prayer ended and true to his word, the minister wrapped up in record time. The members were soon spilling out the door, chattering about what had happened.

"It's scary to think that Elton's on the loose, isn't it?" Ellie asked, as she and Bethany strolled along beside Allison.

"Very."

"Who's going to take care of Cilla and Brady?"

Allison glanced around. Though no one had been appointed to care for them in Colt's absence, he knew there were plenty of folks who would be happy to do so until he returned. "Me, I guess."

"Why don't you come home with us? I'm having bacon, tomato and lettuce sandwiches. There's plenty."

Reluctant to be alone with her troubling thoughts,

Allison smiled her gratitude. "That sounds lovely, thank you."

"Miss Grainger?" Brady asked, tugging on Allison's sleeve. "Is Pa gonna be okay?"

Would he? She couldn't lie to Brady, but neither could she deny him the comfort he was seeking.

"I'm sure your father has told you that his job is sometimes dangerous, Brady." Though she spoke to the boy, her gaze moved from him to Cilla. "But we also know that he is very good at what he does. So are Dan and Ace. Why, you've seen how fast and accurate Ace is with his target practice."

"Yes, ma'am," Brady said, but his eyes glittered with tears.

Allison placed a hand on his shoulder. "Here's what we're going to do. Ellie has invited us to eat with her and Bethany. After that, we'll have Cilla and Bethany play the piano for us. How does that sound?"

"Will you teach me how to pray, Miss Grainger," Brady asked, "so I can pray for my dad and the others?"

Allison's gaze met her sister's. Ellie offered her a poignant smile. Allison heard the thickness of tears in her voice when she said, "Of course I'll teach you to pray, Brady, but there's nothing to it. We just tell the Lord what's on our hearts. As soon as we get to Ellie's, we'll say another prayer for your pa and Dan and Ace to be safe and ask Him to keep us from worrying."

"Then what?"

"And then we trust that He'll grant what we ask for," she said.

Brady flung his arms around her and buried his face against her middle. "I love you, Miss Grainger."

Allison's hands cupped the back of his head, holding

him close and offering him what comfort she could. "I love you, too, Brady," she whispered.

As she spoke the words, she knew she meant them. How wonderful it would be to be a mother to this ornery, smart, incredible little boy and his sister. She didn't think she could bear to give up the time she spent with them, but how could she continue to do so and not lose her heart completely? Besides, if the truth were known, she feared it was already too late.

She glanced at Cilla. Though her back was ramrod-straight and she didn't say a word, the expression in her blue eyes was one of thanks.

Allison ruffled Brady's hair. "Come on, you two. Let's go eat, and after Cilla and Bethany play for us, I'll trounce you all at checkers."

The noontime meal was a fairly solemn affair, but as usual, Ellie's simple lunch was amazing. It escaped no one's notice that Brady stayed extra close to Allison, which only deepened her regret and sorrow.

It was midafternoon when the three of them left Ellie's and made their way home. Not a breath of air stirred anywhere; even the tree branches seemed to sag beneath the weight of the oppressive heat that rose from the parched earth in waves Allison could feel through the thin soles of her Sunday shoes.

As soon as they entered the house, she left the children in the parlor and went into the kitchen to get them all a cold glass of water.

When she got back, she found Brady sprawled on the davenport fast asleep. Poor little guy! Though he'd seemed to enjoy the time at Ellie's, the day's stress had taken its toll. She set down the tray of glasses and went over to lift his feet onto the sofa, reasoning that it wouldn't hurt just this once.

"Shall we sit on the back porch?" Allison whispered to Cilla. "That way we won't wake Brady."

Cilla nodded, and followed Allison into the kitchen. They carried two bentwood chairs to the back and placed them in the shaded area at the end.

"We need rain," Allison said, staring out across the meadow at the cloudless cerulean sky.

"Pa says if we don't get some more soon, the farmers will lose their crops."

"He's right."

After they sipped their water in silence for a while, Allison said, "I know you're as worried about your father as Brady is, but we have to keep praying and trust that God will protect him and the others."

"I know." Cilla took another swallow of water. "I don't remember a lot about my ma, but I do remember that sometimes when Pa left that she would walk the floor and cry."

"Being married to a lawman must be very hard on his family."

Cilla looked at her a moment, as if she were trying to decide something, then blurted, "Is that why you won't marry him?"

Allison knew her surprise must be obvious. One thing about the Garrett children—they were not afraid to walk where angels feared to tread. Never in her life had she experienced any children as blunt and outspoken as Brady and Priscilla Garrett.

"Well," Allison said, careful to choose words that would skirt the main part of the question, "I confess that until he was called away this morning, I'd never given any consideration to the dangers that go with his job. I mean, Wolf Creek is a pretty quiet town, and it's seldom something like the Elton Thomerson jailbreak comes up."

"But you would…miss him if something happened to him, wouldn't you?" Cilla persisted, a frown wrinkling her smooth brow.

Miss him? The very thought of something happening to him made Allison's blood run cold. She wasn't sure what she might do if he didn't come back. Like it or not, she loved him and could not imagine her world without him. She had the sudden notion that refusing his proposal was the dumbest thing she had ever done. Was it?

"I'd miss him very much."

"It's church, isn't it? You said you could never marry a man who didn't love God."

"Yes, I did tell you that."

"But Pa came this morning!" Cilla cried. "Don't you think that means he's going to try to change for you?"

"I don't want him to change for me," Allison said. "I want him to change for himself. That's the only way he'll ever find true happiness and peace, Cilla. People can *go* to services all their lives and not be a true Christian. We serve God because we want to, not because we have to, or just to make someone else happy."

Cilla stared into her water glass and thought about that while Allison's heart ached for them both.

"What if he does change? Really change? Would you marry him then?"

"Oh, Cilla!" Allison breathed, on a little chuckle. She reached out and smoothed a palm over the child's gleaming brown hair. "It isn't just about me and what I would do. In an ideal world, people marry because they love each other. And in our case there's you and Brady to consider."

"But we like you and we told him we wanted you for our ma, so that's all taken care of. The question is, do you love Pa?"

Again, Allison was amazed by the child's forthrightness. "I...care for him very much," she admitted.

"That means yes," Cilla said shrewdly. "I haven't heard him say it, but I know he loves you, too. He's been like a dog with a sore paw ever since you turned him down."

"I'm afraid that's just wishful thinking on your part."

"No, it's true!" Cilla set her glass on a small table sitting between the two chairs and leaped to her feet. She plunged her hand into her skirt pocket and pulled a folded piece of paper out. With a triumphant grin, she held it out to Allison.

"What's this?"

"Open it. You'll see."

Frowning, Allison reached out a cautious hand and took the page from Cilla. She couldn't imagine what it could be.

Cilla stood there, a wide smile on her face, her hands clasped together in anticipation. Allison unfolded the page that had been torn from a tablet. The heading leaped out at her.

PROSPECTIVE BRIDES

Elton was here, no doubt about it. Both his and Joseph Jones's horses were tied near the front of the small tumbledown house.

A woodpecker hammered away at a nearby tree, and

a squirrel chattered high above. When they'd arrived, Colt and his deputies had hunkered down behind a rotted, fallen tree in the midst of a thicket of young persimmon sprouts that provided good cover and made a respectable observation place.

Even in the shadows of the woods, the heat was oppressive. An occasional rumble of thunder sounded in the distance, threatening rain. That had happened a lot since the brief but torrential storm that canceled the ice-cream social the previous week, but so far the warnings hadn't produced a single drop of moisture.

They'd been here since before noon, and it was about half past three. He was getting thirsty, and waiting for something to happen was growing wearisome. With some silent hand signals to his friends, Colt eased through the trees toward the horses that were tied farther back in the woods, intending to fetch the canteens.

About an hour ago, they'd heard one of Elton and Meg Thomerson's babies crying and a lot of yelling back and forth between her and Elton. Ace had tensed and Colt could see the muscles in his jaw knot in fury. All had been quiet since.

After retrieving the canteens, Colt slipped back through the woods, handing one to each of his friends. He unscrewed the cap and started to take a swallow when Dan jerked his head toward the cabin and whispered, "Look there."

Elton had come out onto the porch, shoving Meg in front of him, using her as a shield. She was terrified.

Colt put the cap back and lowered the metal container to the ground by the strap, while he reached for his rifle with his free hand, peering through gaps in the drooping leaves of the scrub trees. Kneeling, Dan rested his weapon on the stump of the dead tree. Ace stood slowly, his rifle at the ready.

Meg's hair had come loose from its pins, and Elton's hand was twisted through it to hold her in place. His other hand gripped the revolver he had pressed against her side. She was cradling her left elbow against her body with her right hand. Sounds of her soft sobbing mingled with the moaning of the wind and the sounds of the woods.

Ace muttered something in either Cherokee or Celtic. Whichever it was, Colt didn't understand a word of it, but he got the gist nevertheless. A muscle knotted in Ace's lean jaw.

"Hiding behind a woman's skirts?" Ace taunted so that Elton would have no trouble hearing.

"Keep your mouth shut, breed," Elton screamed back.

He was drunk and probably still drinking. After all, he'd been deprived of his favorite pastime while he was behind bars. Elton, a country boy with more than his fair share of "blarney," as Ace might say, was once considered one of the best-looking men in the county.

Always one to have his way with the women, he'd set his sights on Meg, a pretty little thing who came from a poor family. He'd charmed her and wooed her and bought her pretty things, and when she'd come up pregnant, he'd done the right thing according to society's standards and married her. It might have been the right thing to do in the eyes of the world, but her marriage had been pure hell for Meg.

"Are the kids okay?" Colt called.

"Don't you worry about my kids," Elton said. "I'd never hurt a hair of their heads."

"Then let them come out, and Dan can take them back to town."

With the children gone, it would be two less people Colt had to worry about getting hurt in the standoff he knew was to come.

"They're fine right where they are," Elton insisted.

"You know this isn't going to end well for you, Thomerson, so why don't you give yourself up?" Dan called.

Elton laughed, an ugly sound with no kinship to joy. "Your deputy deaf, Sheriff? I ain't changed my mind in the last couple minutes."

"Then what are you doing out here?"

"Well," the outlaw drawled, "I just want you all to take a good gander at my pretty wife. She ain't hurt too bad right now, but that's easy changed if y'all don't hightail it back to town and let me leave here in peace."

To prove his point, he gave a hard yank on Meg's hair. She gave a sharp cry of pain. "I can hurt her real bad, and you know I'll do it if I have to."

"You know I can't just let you ride away from here, Elton," Colt called. "My job is to bring you in. I'd prefer to take you in alive, and it would be a lot easier for everyone if you just let her go and you and Joseph give yourselves up."

"I don't think so, Sheriff. Prison life don't agree with me. If you'da just let well enough alone, my good friend Joe woulda had time to move the loot. Then when we broke out, we'd have been long gone, and none of this would be happenin'."

Colt forced a bitter laugh. "The problem with that is you lied and sent *my* friend to the pen when he didn't belong there. The law is all about justice, Elton."

"Justice be hanged! Hey, Injun! You see this here hurt

arm of my wife's?" He reached out and took Meg's injured arm in a cruel grip that sent her to her knees and elicited a piercing scream. "It's your fault."

Gripping his rifle until his knuckles grew white, Colt fought the growing urge to shoot Elton himself. When Ace took a step forward, Colt reached out and stopped him with a warning shake of his head. "He's got the gun aimed right at her head."

Ace nodded, challenging Elton instead. "How do you figure that?"

"She says you been bringin' her food and such."

"She and the children need to eat."

"I reckon that's true, but I been wonderin' how she's paying you." His insinuation was obvious.

Ace shot Colt a dark look that said without words he'd reached the end of his patience, which Colt knew was not inconsiderable. He heard his friend push a low hissing breath through his teeth, and in one smooth motion, he lifted his rifle to his shoulder and fired a single shot into the porch boards near Thomerson's feet. There was no doubt he could have hit him if he'd wanted.

Jumping back and letting loose a string of curses worthy of the saltiest sailor, Elton grabbed Meg by her good arm, hauled her to her feet and pulled her back inside. Just before he slammed the door shut, he screamed, "You'll pay for that, Injun."

After Colt shot Ace a disgruntled look, they settled down to wait.

Every half hour or so, they repeated their calls for Elton and Joe to come out. Colt knew they were playing a waiting game. There was a chance that one of them would pass by a window, making a target of themselves. The only thing wrong with that was that Meg and the kids, an eight-month-old baby girl and a three-year-old boy, were somewhere inside. Colt had no way of knowing where, and there was a chance they could be hit by the bullet.

Fury radiated off Ace. Colt halfway expected him to rush into the house to try to save Meg and the kids, and get killed in the process. Having been the recipient of several beatings in prison, his friend didn't much like the notion of a man abusing women and children.

To distract Ace from his anger, Colt told both men he figured that Elton was biding his time for the sun to go down so he and Joseph could make a run for it. He couldn't leave now because his horses were in plain sight, and if he or Joseph came to fetch them, they'd have a bull's-eye on their backs.

Darkness was still a while away, but Colt figured they needed to have a plan and be in place long before then so that they could keep an eye on all the exits. He told Ace to circle through the woods on one side of the house and Dan to do the same on the other. Both men slipped through the trees. It always amazed Colt that as big as Dan was, he could move like a ghost when he needed to. With both his helpers on their way to new positions, Colt settled down for another wait.

Even though he knew he needed to stay sharp and focused, his sleepless night plus the heat and boredom of waiting lulled him into a state of lethargy, and he found his mind wandering back to his kids and Allison. There hadn't been time to ask her to look after Brady and Cilla while he was gone, but there was no doubt in his mind that she would do just that.

He wondered if she'd noticed that he'd gone to church and if she'd slept the night before or lain awake and thought about the things they'd said. Did she regret her answer as much as he did? He knew she might regret it, but he doubted that she'd change her mind.

God was important to her, a huge reason she was the incredible woman she was. He wouldn't have her any other way. The question was, would she have him if she believed he truly wanted to be that man?

Could he be that man?

Please, God... He wasn't even aware that a prayer was taking shape in his mind. He wanted her in his life. Wanted her as a mother for his children, both the ones he had and the ones he wanted to have with her. He wanted to come in at night and find her doing things around the house. Wanted to play croquet with her and maybe even start reading with her in the cold winter evenings. He wanted to cuddle with her as they fell asleep in each other's arms and wake up next to her warmth every morning.

That thought brought him around to the still-unanswered question of why she refused to believe that he loved her. A memory of the day they'd had breakfast at Ellie's flitted through his mind. That was the day he'd discovered her hidden insecurities. Was it possible that she'd convinced herself he couldn't love her for the same reasons he'd used to try to convince himself that she was not his type? Thank goodness he'd figured out that nothing was further from the truth! It might have taken him a couple of weeks to realize it, but she was exactly what he'd been looking for. Exactly what he needed.

Colt waved away a couple of mosquitoes. In fact, he thought, she was downright adorable. He loved her fiery hair and her freckles. And, when she didn't wear all the flounces and gathers and ruffles, she didn't look the least bit plump. The word to describe her, he'd long realized, was *curvy*.

If there was anything that might put men off, it was her intelligence, her shyness and the wall she'd put up between herself and the male populace to protect her heart: the persona adopted by the strict no-nonsense Miss Grainger. A bit haughty. Composed. Unflappable. All the things he knew she had to be to be a good teacher. More than that, she was good and kind and…

He jerked aside and smacked his neck, hoping to foil a couple of bloodsucking mosquitoes that had decided it was supper time and he was the main course. At the same time he bobbed to the side, several things happened. He seemed to register them in slow motion.

There was an earsplitting *crack* quickly followed by another. A sharp cry. The sensation of something whizzing by his head. Wood chips spewing over him. A crashing sound. He realized in a split second that someone had taken a shot at him and dived onto his belly in an instinctive gesture.

As he lay there panting for breath, he heard another two shots from the other side of the house. The thought of what had happened slammed into him. Someone had tried to kill him. Thomerson or Jones? It didn't matter. What mattered was that Dan and Ace were battling it out with the two outlaws and needed his help.

Thanking God for mosquitoes, he rose to his knees and pivoted slowly, resting his Winchester on top of the log and scanning the area in front of him. All was silent. The shot that had almost ended his life had come from his right. So had the crash. Had Ace wounded the shooter? A couple of rounds had been fired in Dan's vicinity, too. Had he gotten his man?

Without warning, Colt felt a hand on his shoulder. He whipped his head to the right and saw Ace squatting behind him. How did he do that? Colt wondered as relief washed through him.

"Thomerson is dead."

Colt nodded, taking in the implications of the grim pronouncement. A plethora of emotions assaulted him. Stark terror at the knowledge that things could have ended differently. Gratitude. Joy at being alive to go home and take care of his kids. And at being given a second chance. He'd almost been killed. Mosquitoes and Ace had saved him.

It was almost too much to deal with, so Colt focused on his job. "What happened?"

The expression on Ace's face could only be described as "bleak." His voice matched. "Thomerson must have gone far enough around me from behind that I didn't see or hear him. He didn't see me, either. Thank God I did see the movement to my left when he stood up and took a bead on you."

"Yeah," Colt murmured. "Thank God. Do you think Dan got Joseph?"

"My guess would be yes," Ace said. "We need to go inside and see about Meg and the children."

"Not until I know Jones is out of the picture."

About that time, they heard the crashing of brush as two people entered the clearing from the woods to the left. Joseph Jones, his hands tied together in the back, walked in front of Dan, who was prodding him with his rifle. Blood seeped from a wound in the outlaw's side.

Colt heaved a sigh of relief and pushed unsteadily to his feet. He met Ace's dark gaze. "Thanks."

Ace offered one of his rare, quicksilver smiles. "That's what friends are for."

Colt clasped Ace's shoulder. "Let's go see about Meg and the kids."

Chapter Thirteen

Allison stared down at the piece of paper Cilla had handed her. It took mere seconds to scan the page. What she saw sent her heart plunging right down to her toes.

PROSPECTIVE BRIDES

She pressed her fingertips to her lips to hold back a sob, but she couldn't hold back the tears that filled her eyes and slipped down her cheeks.

Colt had made a list of eligible women. Her name was at the bottom.

"What's the matter, Miss Grainger?" Cilla asked with genuine concern.

Instead of answering, Allison asked in a trembling voice, "Where did you get this, Cilla?"

The child's eyes held an expression of bewilderment, as if she had no idea what the problem was.

"Brady and I found it when we were looking for some paper to leave Pa a note on. I thought it would make you happy that he put you on his list. It shows he was interested in you for a while. Maybe even before we started spending so much time with you."

Oh, he put me on the list, all right, Allison thought. The last name on the blasted list! As an afterthought. She scanned the names once more. Interested in her? Hardly. Even though he had crossed out the other names, her name was even below Gracie's. Not that Gracie wasn't perfectly wonderful. It was just…hard to be pleased when one attained success by default. Another thought struck her. Had Colt crossed out the names, or had Cilla and Brady done it in an attempt to make her feel better?

She jumped to her feet and began to pace, something she did when she was upset or thinking something through. She was both. And fast becoming angry.

What kind of man made a list of credentials when he was looking for a wife? What kind of man was so choosy he recorded a woman's good and bad points? What kind of man had certain conditions a potential candidate must meet before she would even be considered?

The answer to her question came to her quietly and squelched her irritation.

A man who had loved his wife and probably always would. A man who was perhaps looking for a helpmeet, but not love, at least not the kind of love Allison wanted. To her, those two went hand in hand.

"Miss Grainger?"

The sound of Cilla's voice roused Allison from her thoughts. "Yes?"

"Why aren't you happy?"

The child's disappointment would have to be addressed. Allison folded the paper. She didn't have the heart to ask if the young woman had scratched off the other names. "May I keep this?"

Cilla nodded, and Allison stuffed the square into the pocket of her skirt. She squatted in front of the young girl's chair and took both her hands. "I'm unhappy because no one makes a list to find someone to marry. And you don't write down their good and bad points and mark them off as if it were a chore you've finished."

She sighed.

"It's true that people get married for many reasons, and often love has no place in their decision, but for me, love and respect and putting one another's happiness before your own is important for a marriage to succeed."

"Pa says everyone has problems."

"That's true, and maybe I'm romantic and idealistic, but it's how I feel. We know that your father didn't love any of these women. He's just written down the names of the single ladies in town, most of whom he's courted for a while and then moved on."

Cilla had the grace to look embarrassed. Both she and Allison knew the reasons some of those fledgling relationships hadn't lasted long.

"Pa says that's what courting is all about," Cilla said, leaning toward Allison, the expression in her eyes begging her to understand. "He says a man considers the single ladies and decides which one he likes, and then he courts her to see if they have common interests and if they're compatible and love could grow in time."

There was no way Allison could argue with that reasoning. She gave Cilla's hands a squeeze. "That's true, but that doesn't change our situation. He hasn't courted me, and prior to us being thrown together to help you and Brady, he didn't even know I existed."

And it hurts to be last on the list.

"I think it's best for everyone if we just leave things as they are. He will find someone one day who will love you all and be exactly what you need."

"But we want you, Miss Grainger," Cilla said, as tears pooled in her blue eyes. "We all want you."

Unable to speak for the tears clogging her own throat, Allison pulled Cilla into a close embrace. She wanted them, too. Badly.

"I know, Cilla, and I think that would be the most wonderful thing in the world, but sometimes we don't get what we want, and sometimes that turns out to be the best thing after all."

After their talk, Allison and Cilla took the checkers outside and played to fill the silence growing between them and avoid the heat of the house. The good news was that clouds were beginning to move into the area. Maybe they'd bring some much-needed rain and cooler temperatures.

Brady woke and they snacked on cookies and lemonade. They spent the rest of the time until the evening church service with Cilla working on a new piece of embroidery and Brady and Allison working on his reading.

After church, Allison, who didn't want to try to fill the silence between her and Colt's disappointed children by herself, took them back to Ellie's for a quick supper. It was beginning to look as if Colt might not make it back before bedtime, which meant the children would have to spend the night.

While Allison and Ellie cleaned up the kitchen, the kids drew pictures on brown paper. Brady had grown tired of his sister picking at him and had gone to the window to look out at the dark clouds blowing across the sky. "Pa's back," he yelled after a few moments.

Allison, who was drying her last pan, froze. She wanted to run to the window to see, but stubborn pride held her in place. Ellie smiled gently. "Go on and see if he's okay. No sense worrying yourself sick."

Without a word, Allison dropped her cloth and hurried to the upstairs window to see if the group of men who had gone in pursuit of the escaped prisoners was alive and well.

It was that rare few minutes when daylight seemed reluctant to give over to the encroaching darkness, and the fading light was soft as the world started settling down for the night. This evening was different, the gloom more intense. Thunder rumbled, and a sudden gust of wind sent dust devils twirling down the street.

Allison looked down. Colt, a child nestled in his arms, led the solemn procession. Allison sucked in a shocked breath and made a quick survey of the group, as Ellie joined her at the window. Meg's son, Teddy, sat in front of Dan, clinging to the saddle horn for dear life. Ace held Meg against his chest. Her head lolled from side to side with each step the horse took. Allison sucked in a frightened breath, wondering what had happened to her and if she was badly hurt.

"Pa's okay," Brady said, looking up at Allison with a wide smile.

"Yes," she said, her answering smile encompassing him and his sister. "It looks as if God answered our prayers, doesn't it?"

"Is Miss Meg dead?" Brady blurted.

Allison looked at her sister.

"I don't know, Brady. I hope not." Ellie was often brutally honest.

"Me, too," he said. "I like Miss Meg."

"Everyone likes Miss Meg," Cilla said.

"Is that Joseph Jones?" Ellie asked, indicating a fourth man who sat astride a horse Big Dan was leading.

"His hands are tied behind his back, and he looks Indian, so it must be," Allison said. Her troubled gaze met Ellie's. If the man still able to ride was Jones, it meant that the body draped over the saddle of the horse following Colt was Elton.

"Do you think Elton is wounded or dead?"

"From the looks of things, I'd say dead."

"Poor Meg," Allison whispered. "How will she manage now?"

"Much better than she has with Elton whipping up on her whenever he took a notion," Ellie said in a sharp tone. "She'll be fine." With that, she marched away from the window.

The line of horses wandered down the street. A flash of sheet lightning lit the gloom, quickly followed by a faraway rumble of thunder that brought Allison to her senses.

"Cilla, Brady, help Bethany pick up the mess, please. We'd better get home before the storm hits, or your father won't know where to find you."

"Do you think he'll be there soon?"

"You and Cilla would know more about that than I do. I imagine he'll have to see that his prisoners are secure and that Doc Rachel fixes up anyone who was hurt. I'm not sure how long that will take."

"Long," Cilla offered with weary resignation.

"Then I think the best thing to do is plan on the two

of you staying at my house tonight. Cilla, you can sleep with me, and Brady you can have the sofa."

They both nodded, and Ellie insisted that she and Bethany would clean up. After thanks and hugs all around, Allison and the kids ran down the stairs and across the street toward her house. Though they reached the front door in record time, they were pelted with fat drops of rain the last few yards.

They barreled into the small parlor, and Allison went to fetch a towel. When they'd blotted the dampness from their faces and arms, she said, "Let me find something for you to sleep in. I think I have some old shirtwaists that will do."

"I'm not a girl, and I'm not wearing no woman's blouse," Brady said, crossing his arms over his chest.

Rather than argue after the stressful day they'd had, Allison said, "Good point. I suppose you can sleep in your clothes. You aren't too wet, so they should be dry by bedtime. And the correct wording is 'I'm not wearing *any* women's blouse.'"

Brady rolled his eyes.

"Cilla, will a shirtwaist do for you?"

"That'll be fine, Miss Grainger."

That settled, Allison got out the Chinese checkers and they played until Brady began to yawn.

Colt still hadn't come to fetch them, and the storm had arrived in earnest. Both children seemed edgy, but unless they were really violent, storms had never bothered Allison much. She actually liked a good storm. There was something about the intensity that made her think of God's power; however, this one was about to cross the line from incredible to worrisome. In the middle of the game, it started blowing so hard that she had to shut the front door to keep the rain from coming through the screen.

After they put away the game, she settled Brady on the divan, and then she and Cilla got ready for bed, taking turns braiding each other's hair while Brady watched from his makeshift bed.

The moment was bittersweet. Allison knew the independent Priscilla could do her own hair, but sensed she needed the comfort that could only be found in the monotony of day-to-day routine.

"I remember when my mother used to braid my hair," she said.

"Me, too," Allison confided. "Those are special memories." She tied off the loose braid with a length of ribbon, and then impulsively put her arms around Cilla's neck from behind. Leaning down, she pressed her cheek to the top of the child's head.

"It's going to be all right, Cilla," she promised. "However things turn out for all of us, it will be what's meant to be."

Giving her another hug, Allison released her and went to tuck in Brady for the night. When she leaned over to give him a good-night kiss, a bolt of lightning cracked. A deafening boom of thunder followed. Brady grabbed her around the neck, holding her as if he'd never let her go.

"I'm scared, Miss Grainger," he said in a trembling voice. "I don't want to sleep in here by myself. Is it okay if I sleep with you and Cilla?"

Allison disengaged herself from his stranglehold. There were tears in his eyes, though he was working hard to keep them from falling. He'd had a trying day, worrying whether or not his father would come back alive. Now he would be sleeping in an unfamiliar place. It was pretty clear that he was terrified of the storm. Did they all bother him? If so, where did he seek comfort? He had no mother to crawl into bed with, and somehow, Allison couldn't see him climbing into bed with his pa.

Without a second thought, she stood and held out her hand. "Come on, then. It will be crowded, but we'll make do."

It was the wee hours when Colt made his way to Allison's. He knew they were all sleeping, and he didn't want to wake them. On the other hand, after the day he'd experienced and coming so close to death, he wanted to see his children, to reassure himself that everything was all right in his little corner of the world. He wanted to see Allie, too. He needed to talk to her and try to explain how he was feeling.

He walked to her place. He'd have ridden his horse, but he'd pulled off the saddle to keep it from getting drenched when they'd arrived at the jail, and he was flat-out too tired to resaddle him. Walking seemed the lesser of two evils.

The rain had stopped around midnight, and a strong wind had blown the clouds off to the northeast, thunder complaining all the way. Except for the clean smell of the rain and the cooler temperature, the storm might never have happened. The sky looked as if it were littered with diamonds. An almost full moon lit his way, its glow flowing over the still-dripping leaves like molten silver. The streets were a muddy quagmire, but at least his clothes had mostly dried out from his first dousing.

Declaring there was no way he could sleep just then,

Ace had agreed to stay with the prisoner while Colt and Dan caught a few hours of shut-eye. Colt had seen the torment in his friend's eyes and knew he was taking the killing of Elton Thomerson hard. Being the cause of a second man's death, accident or not, was bound to bring a lot of guilt and grief to a man who valued all living things as Ace did. Colt wondered just how long Ace would disappear this time before making what peace he could with his actions and deciding he was ready to come back and join the rest of the world.

Both of Meg's children were fine. Thankfully they were so young that Rachel said there was a decent chance they wouldn't remember the horrors their father had put them and their mother through.

Meg had taken her worst battering so far. As badly as she was injured, she had not shed a tear. They'd found her in the bedroom unable to move, her unseeing gaze fixed on the ceiling. Elton had broken her nose and her arm and a couple of ribs, but his worst crime, in Colt's opinion, was forcing himself on her after he'd dragged her back into the house.

They'd gleaned that information from Jones during a lengthy interrogation after Rachel patched up his wounds. Though Meg had always emerged from one of her husband's thrashings with her faith and her smile intact, Colt wondered if that would be the case this time.

Knowing he was headed back to prison for a lengthy stay, Jones had also told them where he and Elton had hidden the fruits of their robberies. Colt would check it out after he got some rest.

He stepped up onto Allison's porch and pulled his muddy boots off before opening both front doors and stepping inside. He'd never been in her house before, but the light of the moon told him it was the perfect setting for her. Neat. Clean. Feminine, without containing an overabundance of froufrou. The moonlight also showed him that the room was empty. He'd expected to find Cilla and Brady sleeping at each end of the oversize sofa.

There were two doors off the parlor. He picked one at random, eased across the wood floors and stepped inside. The moonlight told him he'd chosen right. The silvery luster pierced the frilly curtains hanging at a nearby window, splashing the lacy design of shadow and light over the occupants of an ornate iron bedstead that sat to his right.

He moved nearer.

Curled into a ball, Cilla was asleep on the side against the wall. Brady was in the middle and Allison was on the edge nearest him. Brady was snuggled against her, and her left arm lay across his middle.

A pang of love, sharp and poignant, pierced Colt's heart, bringing tears to his eyes. He wished he were an artist with the ability to capture this perfect picture of a mother and her children. Except that she wasn't their mother and wouldn't be if he couldn't figure out a way to make her believe that his feelings were real and strong.

A wave of bone-deep weariness washed over him. He was too tired to think. There would be time tomorrow to figure out what to do about Allie. A muted sigh trickled from him, and she stirred in her sleep. He waited until she settled again, then bent down and pressed a whisper-soft kiss to her temple. Then he turned and retraced his steps to the parlor.

He needed to go home, but the thought of putting his

muddy boots back on and traipsing to the other side of town was more than he thought he could handle. The camelback sofa lured him. He was so tired. Physically and emotionally. Maybe if he sat down for just a minute he could muster enough energy to make it to his own bed....

"Pa!" The sound of Brady's voice jerked Colt to sudden wakefulness. He bolted upright, just in time to catch Brady in his arms.

Colt closed his eyes and held his son close, breathing in his little-boy scent. He could almost taste Brady's relief and felt his trembling. The previous day had been hard on his kids, too.

"Pa."

He opened his eyes and saw Cilla standing in the doorway of Allison's bedroom. Colt pried Brady's arms from around his neck and shifted him to one side, holding out an arm toward his daughter, who looked to be wearing a blouse of Allison's for a nightgown. Cilla launched herself across the room, and he was soon holding them both close. He was barely aware of the quick heartfelt "thank you" that raced through his mind at the same moment he spied Allison in the doorway, a floral seersucker wrapper belted around her waist.

She looked warm and rumpled from sleep, and there was a mark down her right cheek where she'd lain on a wrinkle in the pillowcase. She wasn't wearing her spectacles, so she was squinting at him in that familiar, endearing way. He'd no longer mistake it for anger; it was just her attempt to focus better. He smiled in genuine pleasure, wishing he could hold her close, too.

"Thank you." This time he spoke the words aloud.

"You're welcome," she said, clearly knowing that he was referring to her watching the children while he was gone.

"We were worried about you, Pa," Brady said. "But we prayed, and I felt better."

"I prayed, too." The words were for Brady, but he was looking at Allison.

He saw her eyes widen.

"There's nothing like staring at death to give you a whole new perspective on life," he told her with a lop-sided grin.

"I suppose not. Did you sleep on my divan?"

He had the grace to look sheepish and ruffled his already tousled hair with a back-and-forth gesture. "I did. I'm sorry. It was the wee hours when I finished at the jail and Ace said for me and Dan to go get some rest, but all I wanted to do was see my kids."

"Miss Grainger took real good care of us," Brady said, turning in his father's embrace to look at Allison.

"I'm sure she did. I knew they were all right with you," he hastened to say, "but I just wanted to…see for myself."

"That's understandable."

He couldn't tell what she was thinking, but it sounded as if she did understand. "And then I just sat down to rest a minute before starting across town, and…" He finished the sentence with a shrug.

The little clock on the mantel chimed a melodious song, indicating that it was half past six. Colt scrubbed a hand over his day's growth of whiskers. "I need to go get cleaned up and spell Ace. He's got to be whipped."

"Elton's dead?"

"Yes." He saw in her eyes that she wanted to ask how

it had happened and who had done it, but she knew it was something not to be discussed in front of Cilla and her brother.

"Miss Meg?" This time it was Cilla who asked the question.

"She's alive." Recalling the state they'd found her in, Colt couldn't add anything more. Unless something unforeseen happened, he figured that time, as it always had, would heal her physical wounds.

Allison bit down hard on her bottom lip, and he saw tears welling up in her eyes. "I'll ask Rachel if there's anything I can do."

"I'm sure she'd appreciate that," he said, giving the kids another hard hug and standing. "The excitement is over. You two go on about your day the way we always do," he told them.

"I'll see to it that they get home after I give them breakfast."

He was already headed for the door. "Thanks, Allie," he said, turning to flash a quick, weary smile. He opened the door, pushed through the screen, stepped outside and pulled on his mud-covered boots. When he turned to give them a final goodbye, he saw one child on each side of Allison, who had an arm around each of them.

"I'll talk to you later."

The look in her eyes said without words that she knew exactly what kind of talk he was referring to. Before she could even nod, he turned and went down the steps.

Knowing that Colt was unharmed eased the tension that had gripped Allison ever since Dan had interrupted the church service the day before. She knew that he was right; they had to talk, and womanlike, she wondered what he would say and if it would make any difference to how she felt.

To keep her thoughts at bay, she fixed breakfast for Cilla and Brady and then deposited them at their front door with instructions to do whatever it was that they did when their father was gone. Brady said he had a harmonica session with Lew and Cilla said she planned to sweep and dust until it was time for her piano lesson with Hattie. When Allison asked if they would be okay, Cilla assured her with the first sign of bad temper she'd exhibited in a long time that she could take perfectly good care of her brother since she'd been caring for him for two years without supervision.

Put in her place by a twelve-year-old that Allison knew was miffed at her for her refusal to consider her father as a husband, she left satisfied they would be fine. She headed for the café, knowing it would be abuzz with details of the previous day's ordeal—some of it true, some of it exaggerated and some of it downright lies.

The day was cloudless and summertime gorgeous. The storm had broken the grip of the stifling heat that had oppressed them for so long. The grasses and flowers along the way seemed refreshed, and everything looked clean from the recent washing. They would be right back where they'd been before the storm in a few days, but at least for now things were much more pleasant.

To her surprise, she found Gracie, Big Dan and Win Granville sitting at a table near the back. Both Ellie and Bethany were bustling around taking orders and setting plates with generous helpings of eggs, grits and bacon in front of people engaged in earnest conversation, no doubt about the recent happenings. Dan was tucking away a plate of food with such gusto it looked as if he hadn't eaten for a week. Though he laughed at something Win said, Allison noticed that there was still a hint of strain around his eyes.

Allison gave her sister a wave and crossed to the table. The men rose as politeness demanded, and Gracie jumped up and enveloped her in a friendly hug.

"How are the children?" she asked.

"They're fine. I fed them breakfast and took them home."

"Have they seen Colt?" Dan asked.

"Um, yes, for a minute early this morning."

She had no intention of mentioning that he'd been asleep on her sofa. There were gossips in town besides Sarah VanSickle, and Allison had no desire to become the butt of another round of speculation, not when everyone was still mulling over their unusual association. Let them believe that he'd stopped by on his way to relieve Ace.

She took a seat next to Gracie and asked Bethany to bring her a cup of coffee.

"I'm sure there are a dozen different stories going around town about what happened, but you were there," Allison said to Dan. She wanted to hear from someone with firsthand knowledge what had happened to Colt.

Even though he'd told the story several times, Dan recounted it once more. Allison could only imagine the boredom and wretchedness of the heat as they waited for Elton to make some sort of move.

She clenched her hands in her lap as she sat. With Win feeding him direct questions, Dan painted a realistic picture of the scene with Meg on the porch. She could almost feel the younger woman's pain.

"If Ace hadn't seen Elton with a bead on Colt, and if he hadn't been swatting those dad-blasted mosquitoes, we'd a had another body slung over the saddle. There was a big ol' chunk missin' out of that stump he was leaning against," Dan said with a weary shake of his head.

Picturing the scene in her mind, Allison felt a little frisson of anxiety scamper down her spine. So Colt had been telling the truth when he'd said he'd come close to death—not that she'd doubted his word, but hearing it from a neutral party gave it extra weight. With her curiosity about Colt satisfied, she asked about Meg.

"She was bad," Dan said, but added no explanation.

"Rachel was in a bit ago," Gracie said. "Dan's right. Meg's in a bad way, but Lord willing, she'll heal."

"Thank heaven." Allison drained the last swallow of her coffee and stood. "I think I'll go over and see what I can do to help Rachel."

"I'm sure she'll be glad to see you," Gracie said.

Allison started toward the counter to pay for her coffee, but Gracie said, "Would you like to hear some good news?"

Smiling, Allison turned. "I think we could all use some good news right about now."

Gracie blushed and Dan's smile could have given the summer sunshine a run for its money. He reached out a big hamlike hand and covered hers. She glanced from Allison to Win and back again. "Dan and I are getting married."

Allison hugged and congratulated the two lovebirds and left. Gracie was getting married! Her sweet friend deserved the happiness radiating from her, but Allison couldn't help feeling a little sorry for herself. Would she ever find that kind of joy?

As promised, she went to ask Rachel about helping with Meg however was necessary. Knowing that Allison didn't deal with illness well, Rachel assured her that for the moment, she and her father had things under control and told her that Meg's children were with her family. Allison was just turning to go when Rachel said, "I have a bit of good news."

"What's that?" Allison asked, almost dreading to hear it since she was already feeling so blue about Gracie's announcement.

Rachel's face positively glowed with delight. "I'm expecting a baby."

For the span of a heartbeat, Allison wasn't certain she could summon a smile of congratulations. Then she remembered how long Rachel had been alone and how much she must have suffered through the years bringing up an illegitimate child. She deserved her newfound happiness as Mrs. Gabriel Gentry, and she deserved to have a pregnancy she could enjoy. Surely she was a better friend than to begrudge Rachel this wonderful bit of news.

Smiling in spite of her breaking heart, Allison wrapped her arms around her friend and drew her close. "That's marvelous, Rachel," she said, meaning every word of it. "I bet Gabe is ecstatic."

"On top of the world."

What must it be like to be "on top of the world," to be filled with joy that seemed to ooze from every fiber of your being? Allison wondered that evening as she sat picking the thread from the ruffles of one of her old dresses.

Plucking out the small stitches kept her mind more or less off her unhappiness. Under subtle pressure from Blythe and Libby, Allison had bowed to the inevitable. Both Granville women supported Ellie's stance about the unsuitability of Allison's wardrobe, so she had decided to revamp her older clothing into styles that the three other women claimed were more suitable.

Though she knew she was not as slim as some, after seeing herself in her new dress, she was convinced that without the furbelows she usually added, she did look much thinner. Imagine that.

It wasn't quite dusk, and she was listening to the tune of a mockingbird when she heard footsteps on the porch. Before she could set her work aside, Colt appeared on the other side of the screen door.

Her heart began to tap out an erratic rhythm.

"May I come in?"

"Of course."

He came inside and stood awkwardly in the doorway.

"Please sit," she said, setting the dress aside and indicating the wingback chair next to the sofa. "Would you like some lemonade?"

"No, thank you. I came to tell you what happened out at the Thomersons and before that."

Had something happened that no one knew about? "Dan told us this morning at Ellie's."

"Dan told his version. I need to tell you mine."

"All right."

He drew in a fortifying breath. "After we talked the other day, I started thinking that for a lot of reasons, I should try to be a better person. And then I remembered the scripture about fathers bringing up their children the way they should go."

He looked her directly in the eye. "I realized that I hadn't done that, and figured that my kids had become such messes because I'd failed to teach them the way they should behave and why. I'd already come to terms with the fact that I'd failed them in a lot of ways, but I don't think I really understood how badly until then.

"I prayed, and I think I had my first heart-to-heart talk with God in years." He smiled. "It felt good, Allie. I felt better afterward. So I decided to go to church after all. And then we got called away.

"While I was waiting for Elton to make his move, I started thinking about what you want in a husband. Like I said this morning, looking death in the eye sort of puts things into perspective. I think God sent those mosquitoes as part of the way to save me from a bullet, so I can be that man." His sincere, golden gaze held a tender expression. "I believe in time that I can be that man."

"You're doing it for me?"

"No! I thought I'd just made that clear. I'm doing it for me. I've done some things in my past that I'm not proud of, and I believed that God was punishing me by taking Patty away from me. Then while I was so miserable about you turning me down, I remembered that scripture, and it was like my eyes were open for the first time. I thought—hoped—it would make a difference to you."

Allison rose and went across the room to look out the screen door. Did she believe his claim that he wanted to change his life? Strangely enough, she did, and she was glad. She'd thought that if he made this commitment, she would be able to give him a chance, but now that she was faced with that scenario, she wasn't so sure.... Memories of her old heartache surfaced, bringing all the pain and shame. Could she take another chance with her heart?

Turning to face him, she dipped her head and looked at him over the tops of her glasses. "Are you saying that you love me?"

"Yes!" he cried, actually leaping to his feet and throwing up his hands. "Why is that so hard for you to believe?"

"Because you're...everything I'm not."

He made a slashing gesture to cut her off. She paused, clasping her fingers together at her waist to still their trembling. He looked furious. Nothing at all like a man declaring his love.

"We've been through all this." He took another deep breath, as if he were gathering himself for a major confrontation. "I know you're insecure about your looks. You as much as told me so that morning at Ellie's. What if I said that sometimes you make me more than a little insecure?"

"Me? Why on earth would I make you insecure?"

"You can deny it all you want, but deep in my heart, I think you care for me at least a little. That's scary to a guy like me. You're far better educated than I am, far more knowledgeable about a whole slew of topics I can only begin to guess at. The thought of trying to make conversation with you for the next fifty years scares me to death, but I'm willing to try."

This was something she'd never considered. She couldn't fathom anything threatening him. Could it be possible that her education was a deterrent? Still, she knew she had to get everything she was feeling out in the open. Otherwise, they wouldn't stand a chance. She began to pace the room.

"You talk about being together for fifty years, but for love to last that long, it has to be real. You don't find it by making a list."

There! She'd said it.

Colt, who was following her every step with his eyes, grew very still. "List?"

"Yes. I saw the list you made of potential brides."

The expression on his face was somehow both horrified and remorseful. She felt no satisfaction for having caught him out, only sadness.

"How?"

"Cilla and Brady found it one day looking for something to write you a note on. She showed it to me thinking it might make me feel better to know that you've been considering me. Instead it showed me that you were wooing women, and when one didn't work out, you moved on to the next."

"Guilty as charged."

He seemed to be regaining his composure, and she thought she detected a hint of irritation in his eyes.

"Again, that's how I thought it worked," he told her with a shrug. "You meet someone and try to find out if she's the one. If not, you move on. None of those women was right for me for one reason and another. Of course, what do I know?" he added in a scorn-filled voice. "I'm just an inexperienced country sheriff, not a man of the world."

"Some of those relationships ended because they were sabotaged by your children," she reminded him, letting his sarcasm pass. "Not because you ended them."

"Yes, they were. And while their conduct was way

out of line, in the long run they saved me from a lot of wasted time. None of those women was right for me."

"And I am?"

"My heart says you are."

Oh, how she wanted to believe him, but there were still so many unanswered questions! "Then why is my name at the bottom of the list?"

Colt shook his head and one side of his mouth lifted in a half smile. "You don't intend to make this easy for me, do you?"

"No, because it certainly isn't easy on me. I feel like...like—" she sniffed "—like I win by default or something."

"I see." He crossed the room to take both of her hands in his. There was no denying the determination in his eyes. "I'll try to explain, but I confess I've been knocked for six by everything myself."

He lifted her chin to force her to look at him and began. "Until I came here, I didn't think I was quite ready to marry again, but I realized I'd moved past my grief over Patrice's death, so I started consciously looking for a wife and mother for my children. When you came to me after the incident at Gabe's, I realized for the first time how out of control they'd become, and it really brought home just how much we all need a woman in our lives."

He lifted one of her hands and rubbed his cheek against her knuckles. His end-of-day whiskers felt rough and exciting.

"You made the list after our, uh, confrontation?"

"Soon after, yes. I made a list. I admit to feeling a little desperate that day, so I was determined to put down the name of every available woman in town whether she was single or widowed, young or old. I even wrote down the names of the women who'd already come and gone on the off chance that I'd missed something, but when I tried to see each of them in my life, I couldn't. I knew they wouldn't work for me or the kids, even though they had some good qualities.

"Your name was at the bottom of the list simply because I hadn't thought about you. Then Dan mentioned you and Ellie, who we know will probably never marry, so I added your name."

It was not heartening to know that she was last to enter his mind but even more disturbing that Dan knew. "Dan knows about the list?" she cried, aghast.

"I caught him looking over my shoulder. He was a little put out that I'd scratched off Gracie's name, and that's when he decided he'd better not waste any more time trying to win her hand."

"Why hadn't you thought about me?" she asked.

"Honestly?" That wry grin was back. "Before the day you stormed into my office, you weren't a woman—you were just Miss Grainger, the teacher. You've never taken part of the social scene, so for the most part, the only time I ever saw you was when you were giving me what for because of Cilla and Brady's behavior. And then you were always so stern and confident. You laid down the law and I was supposed to do as you said."

He flashed her one of the smiles that melted her heart. "That chafed. No man likes hearing the truth when it isn't pretty, and it's not pleasant to be put in your place by some pint-size female. You must know you can be a bit intimidating, Miss Grainger. When I did add you, I really couldn't see myself with the schoolteacher."

Oh, dear! According to her mama, she'd done the unspeakable. Somehow he'd taken her strong suggestions of keeping the children in line as a personal attack on his manhood. Not good for a man whose job it was to keep the populace in line.

"What really stung was that deep down I knew I wasn't doing right by them. I didn't know how to deal with them until you came along and helped me realize what the real problems were and showed me how to address them."

Well, that wasn't exactly what a woman wanted to hear. She pulled her hand free.

"How flattering," she told him in a cool tone. "You became *interested* in me when you realized I could help with your problems with the children, is that it?"

"No!" He narrowed his eyes at her in exasperation. "You're determined to misunderstand, aren't you? Or maybe you aren't as smart as I think you are."

"How…how dare you!" she gasped.

"Oh, I dare a lot more than that," he drawled, pulling her into his arms and kissing her until she was breathless.

Allison was so stunned she couldn't do anything but stand there and allow him to plunder her mouth. When he stopped, she had to cling to him, since her knees seemed determined to buckle.

"I became interested in you the day you barged into my office like a crazy woman with your hat askew and your hair straggling down, breathing fire and accusing my children of attacking you in a public place. No matter what I dished out, you refused to back down. I couldn't help admiring you for that. I've spent years perfecting my 'scary sheriff' look," he told her ruefully.

He pressed a kiss to the tip of her nose. Smiled. "And

you looked at me with an unfocused expression in your eyes, sort of like you're looking at me now."

"I couldn't see without my glasses," she squeaked, barely able to breathe, much less talk with him so close.

"Mmm." He kissed a freckle on her chin. "I know that now." His voice was husky. "And then you licked your lips and I thought you looked like someone had kissed you thoroughly. Like you do now."

Very deliberately, he set her away from him and took a step back. "It's been downhill for me from there. I don't know how it happened or when it happened or why. All I know is that I haven't been able to get you off my mind longer than ten minutes at a time since then."

Allison reached out and placed a hand on his arm to steady herself. His kiss had pretty much decimated her argument that he didn't care.

"And as far as lists go, everyone has things they want or don't want in a mate. Even you have a list, Allison Grainger."

"I've never made a prospective-husband list in my life," she denied hotly.

"You might not have written down your likes and dislikes," he told her, "but you have one, all right. You're looking for a man to love you for who you are, and you want him to be a Christian. When that bullet came inches from killing me, I knew for certain that if you'll give me a chance, I'll spend the rest of my life trying my best to be both. All I ask is that you think about what I've said, and remember…life's short, sweetheart. We may not get another chance."

Without waiting for her to comment, he strode across the room and pushed through the screen door, leaving her there, her doubts doing battle with her dreams.

* * *

She hardly slept all night. Instead, she replayed every conversation she'd ever had with Colt, looking for every nuance of how he felt, weighing every look, every word.

Common sense told her that he was an honorable man, a man who would not lie to get his way. Her fearful heart was afraid, whispering that, like Jesse, he would find someone prettier and more amiable. Someone who would not challenge him as she was bound to do from time to time. Could she trust that he would do as he promised? Could she trust that he truly loved her and was not marrying her to fulfill a hole in his life?

Finally, toward dawn, she prayed, asking for guidance and trust and for something to happen to help her make the right decision. Feeling more at peace than before, she drifted into a light sleep.

A woodpecker pounding at a tree outside her open window jolted Allison to wakefulness. She glanced at the gold-finish windup clock sitting on the small table next to the bed. Ten o'clock. What a slugabed! She'd almost slept the morning away!

Covering a wide yawn, she scrambled to her feet, reached for her wrapper and slipped her arms inside. She tied the sash around her waist as she padded barefoot toward kitchen.

An hour later, freshly bathed and wearing one of her revamped dresses, she headed toward Ellie's to see what was for lunch and maybe to ask her sister's advice on what to do about Colt.

She managed to reach the café before the big lunch rush, only to find that Ellie was no help at all. In fact, she was thrilled with the turn of events.

"Well, let's see. He claims to love you, and I don't think he's the kind of man to lie about that. He's willing to try to be what you want, and I can't see him saying that if he didn't mean it. He's employed, very good-looking and you love him. What more can you ask?" Ellie said, pulling two loaves of fresh bread from the oven.

"I'm so scared of being hurt, Ellie."

Ellie turned out the bread to cool on some clean tea towels and began to smear the crusts with butter. "Everyone who loves someone takes a chance on getting hurt, Allie," she told her. "And you do get hurt from time to time. It comes with the territory. But if you don't take that chance, you'll never experience the good times."

Leave it to Ellie to cut to the chase.

"Believe me, I wish I had a chance to find love." Ellie sighed and pushed a wisp of hair away from her eyes. "I have a good life, but it would be nice to share the ups and downs with someone and have them hold you when things get tough."

Allison's heart went out to her sister. She wondered if Ellie would ever be free of the husband who'd walked out on her the day their baby daughter was born, her features clearly announcing that she was mentally deficient. Twelve years and Ellie had no idea where he was, if he'd divorced her or was dead. All she knew was that she was not free to look for love. Not with anyone.

"Does that help?" Ellie asked with a tired smile.

"I don't know," she said with a wan smile.

"Well," her sister said, refusing to meet Allison's eyes. "I've heard something that might help you decide."

"Oh? What?"

"It's all over town that Colt spent the night at your place the night they brought Elton and Joe in."

"Sarah VanSickle!" Allison cried, her face flaming with embarrassment and anger. "I thought she'd turned over a new leaf, she—"

"Calm down," Ellie said, laughing. "It wasn't Sarah."

The gentle words left Allison with her mouth wide open.

"Who else would say something so hurtful?"

"It wasn't said to be hurtful. It was just said, and as usual, a few people couldn't wait to get the word out."

"I'm not following you," Allison said with a frown.

"Cilla and Brady were telling Gabe how glad they were to see their dad asleep on your sofa yesterday morning, and of course there were some shoppers there and the usual crew was playing checkers, and from there it spread like wildfire. Hattie heard it from Lew, and she told me, and who knows how many others? You know as well as I do that you can't keep anything a secret in Wolf Creek."

Allison was mortified. What had Colt been thinking when he stretched out on her couch? She'd never been the brunt of so much gossip in her life as she had the past couple of weeks! Her panicked gaze found Ellie's. "Homer!"

Ellie's eyes widened as she realized what Allison was getting at.

"Homer will fire me—probably Colt, too—if he hears this," Allison wailed. "Oh, Ellie, what am I going to do?"

"I'd say the first thing you should do is go and see Colt. Maybe he'll have some suggestion as to how to deal with this. He and Homer are pretty chummy."

"Yes," Allison said, already heading for the door. "Thanks, Ellie." Before she reached the jail, she'd worked up a pretty good head of steam.

Colt was leaned back in his chair, his feet propped on the top of the scarred desk, his hands folded behind his head as he stared up at the ceiling. He'd done everything he could to persuade Allison that he loved her and wanted to spend the rest of his life with her. He didn't know what else he could do to convince her that he was serious. The next move was hers.

He was savoring the memory of their kiss the night before when the door crashed against the wall. He lowered his gaze and saw the object of his daydreams storm through the open door like a miniature tornado—eyes flashing, temper obviously high. What now? he thought with a sigh of resignation that didn't quite extinguish the pleasure darting through him just seeing her and knowing they were about to embark on another round of their verbal sparring.

Uncertain what to expect, he uncrossed his arms from behind his head and drawled, "Miss Grainger. What can I do for you this fine morning?"

A feeling of déjà vu came over him as she swept across the room and placed her hands palms down on the desk.

"Marry me."

Colt froze for a second or two, unsure he'd heard right. He lowered his booted feet to the floor very carefully and stood, placing his palms on the desk and leaning toward her as he'd done on another occasion.

"I beg your pardon," he said. "Did you just propose?"

She narrowed her eyes and leaned farther forward.

"It's all over town that you spent the night before last at my place," she said in a deadly murmur. "My reputation will be ruined! Homer will run us both out of town so fast that—"

"I'm sorry," Colt interrupted, trying to keep a straight face. "While I'm very sorry about your reputation, I'm afraid that, like you, I can't marry someone who doesn't love me."

He almost laughed at the startled look on her face. It didn't seem that Miss Grainger liked having her words thrown back at her.

"But I do love you. You must know I do."

"Funny that you only realized it when the gossip started," he said with a slight shrug.

Looking a little bewildered, she said, "I knew it long before that, but I wouldn't admit it for fear of being hurt again. But when you were out there with Ace and Dan and there was a chance that you might not come back, I knew I was being foolish. You just walked out and didn't give me a chance to say it before.

"You're right. Love just happens, and life is short, and we don't have any guarantees about anything. All I know is that I'm ready to take a chance again with you." She watched him closely, uncertainty in her eyes.

Colt closed the distance between them and pressed a brief hard kiss to her lips. "Okay," he said when he drew back.

"Okay what?" she asked, staring at him in confusion.

He was grinning from ear to ear. "You proposed and I accepted. I would love to marry you, but not to save your reputation, because you love me and I certainly love you. Actually, though it's a tad unmanly to admit it, I'll take you any way I can get you, Miss Grainger."

"You…you will?"

He nodded. "I can't imagine a life without you in it."

He saw her need to believe him in her eyes. "B-but I'm not beautiful like Leticia or Ellie."

"I think you are exquisite."

"In case you haven't noticed, I'm, uh…a bit plump."

"It was recently brought to my attention that you are very…curvy."

"My hair is red, not a pretty auburn like Ellie's."

"I have noticed that," he said, straightening and rounding the desk. "And you definitely have a temper to match."

"I…have lots and lots of freckles."

He unhooked the wire frames of her spectacles from behind her ears, folded them closed and put them in his shirt pocket, even as his gaze moved over her sweet face with loving thoroughness.

"My grandmother called them 'angel kisses.'" He touched his lips to a place on her temple, then her jaw-line and her chin.

He lifted his head and looked down at her, his eyes smiling into hers. "I plan to count and kiss each and every one. Several times, probably. Even if it takes a lifetime. In fact," he said, "I plan for it to."

He kissed her again, and Allison's arms slid around his middle.

From the other side of the open doorway where they'd been listening to every word, Cilla and Brady turned to each other and grinned. Brady gave his sister a thumbs-up. He'd been skeptical about the idea proposed by Ben Gentry, who was well acquainted with how gossip could force two people into marriage, since the same thing had brought his mother and Caleb together.

Cilla had loved the notion from the start, but it had taken a lot of persuasion from her and Ben, especially since Brady maintained that they had promised their dad no more dirty tricks. Cilla had insisted that all they would be doing was telling the truth and that they would be doing it for a good reason. What could be wrong with that? Finally Brady had agreed to try the cockamamy idea. Now, watching his pa kiss Miss Grainger and hearing that they planned to get married after all, it looked as if their plotting and planning and machinations had worked exactly the way they'd hoped.

He blew out a sigh of relief and made himself a promise. This was the very last time he would let his sister talk him into anything like this. Absolutely the last time.

* * * * *

Award-winning author **Dorothy Clark** lives in rural New York. Dorothy enjoys traveling with her husband throughout the United States, doing research and gaining inspiration for future books. Dorothy believes in God, love, family and happy endings, which explains why she feels so at home writing stories for Love Inspired.

Books by Dorothy Clark

Love Inspired Historical

Stand-In Brides

His Substitute Wife
Wedded for the Baby
Mail-Order Bride Switch

Pinewood Weddings

Wooing the Schoolmarm
Courting Miss Callie
Falling for the Teacher
A Season of the Heart

An Unlikely Love
His Precious Inheritance

Visit the Author Profile page
at Harlequin.com for more titles.

WOOING THE SCHOOLMARM

Dorothy Clark

The Lord is nigh unto them that are of a broken heart;
and saveth such as be of a contrite spirit.
—*Psalms* 34:18

Books with historical settings require a great deal of time-consuming research. This book is dedicated with deep appreciation to Rhonda Shaner Pollock of the Portville Historical & Preservation Society for her gracious and unfailing help in uncovering details of a schoolmarm's daily life in a rural village in 1840. Thank you, Rhonda.

"Commit thy works unto the Lord, and thy thoughts shall be established."

Your Word is truth. Thank You, Jesus.

To You be the glory.

Chapter One

Pinewood Village, 1840

"Here we are. This is the schoolhouse." Matthew Calvert looked from the small, white, frame building to his deceased brother's children. Joshua had on his "brave" face, which meant he was really afraid, and Sally looked about to cry. *Please, Lord, don't let her cry. You know my heart turns to mush when she tears up.* "Everything is going to be fine. You'll make nice friends and have a good time learning new things."

He placed his hands on the children's backs and urged them up the steps to the small porch before they could resume their pleading to stay at home with him this first day in the new town. Their small bodies tensed, moved with reluctance.

He leaned forward and glanced in the open door. A slender woman was writing on a large slate at the far end of the room. The sunlight coming in a side window played upon the thick roll of chestnut-colored hair that coiled from one small ear across the nape of her neck to the other, and warmed the pale skin of a narrow wrist that was exposed by the movement of her sleeve cuff as she printed out a list of words. She looked neat and efficient. *Please, God, let her also be kindhearted.* He nudged his niece and nephew forward and stepped inside. "Excuse me."

The teacher turned. Her gaze met his over the top of the double rows of bench desks and his heart jolted. He stared into blue-green eyes rimmed with long, black lashes, rendered speechless by an attraction so immediate, so strong, every sensible thought in his head disappeared.

The teacher's gaze dropped to the children, then rose back to meet his. "Good morning, Reverend Calvert. Welcome to Pinewood."

The formal tone of the teacher's voice brought him to his senses. He broke off his stare and cleared his throat. "Thank you. I—" He focused his attention, gave her a questioning look. "How did you know who I am?"

Her mouth curved into a smile that made his pulse trip all over itself. She placed the book she held on her desk. "You are from the city, Reverend Calvert. You will soon learn in a village as small as Pinewood that one knows all the residents and everything that happens." She brushed her fingertips together and minuscule bits of chalk dust danced in the stream of sunlight. "I dare say I knew within ten minutes of the time you descended from your carriage and carried your bags into the parsonage that you had arrived." She gave him a wry look. "But, I confess, I did not know you were coming here this morning."

"I see." He lifted the left side of his mouth in the crooked grin his mother had called his mischief escape.

"So I have managed a 'coup' of sorts by bringing the children to school?"

She stared at him a moment, then looked away. "So it would seem. Have these children names?"

Her reversion to the formal, polite tone called him back to his purpose in coming. "Yes, of course. This is Joshua—he's six years old." He smiled down at his nephew. "And this is Sally." His niece pressed back against his legs. He placed his hands on her small, narrow shoulders and gave a reassuring squeeze. "She's five years old, and feeling a little overwhelmed at the moment."

The hem of the teacher's gown whispered over the wide plank floor as she came to stand in front of them. She looked down and gave the children a warm, welcoming smile he wished were aimed at him. "Hello, Joshua and Sally. I'm your teacher, Miss Wright. Welcome to Oak Street School."

Miss Wright. She was indeed. Matthew frowned at his burst of whimsy. Miss Wright, with her narrow, aristocratic nose and small square chin, was wreaking havoc with his normally sensible behavior. He was acting like a smitten schoolboy.

Children's voices floated in the door. Their light, quick footfalls sounded on the steps. The voices quieted as five children entered and bunched at the doorway to stare at them.

"Come in and take your seats, children. We have a lovely surprise this morning. You are going to have some new classmates." The teacher gave a graceful little gesture and the clustered children separated, casting surreptitious glances their way as they moved toward the bench desks.

Matthew drew in a breath and hid the pang of sympathy he felt for Joshua and Sally. "I'd best be going, Miss Wright." She looked up at him and that same odd jolt in his heart happened. He hurried on. "The children have slates and chalk. And also some bread and butter for dinner. I wasn't sure—"

She smiled. "That is fine."

His pulse thudded. He jerked his gaze from Miss Wright's captivating eyes and looked down at Joshua and Sally. "Be good, now—do as Miss Wright says. Joshua, you take Sally's hand and help her across the street when you come home. I'll be waiting for you." He tore his gaze from Sally's small, trembling mouth and, circling around three more children filing into the schoolroom, escaped out the open door. The children needed to adjust to their new situation. And so did he. What had happened to him in there?

"Miss Wright!"

Willa halted as Danny Brody skidded to a stop in front of her. "Miss Hall wants you." He pointed behind her, then raced off.

Willa turned, saw Ellen promenading toward her and fought to hold back a frown. She loved her lifelong friend, but sometimes the pretentious ways she had developed irritated her. Still, one couldn't blame Ellen for parading about. She was the prettiest girl in town now that Callie Conner had moved away—and one of the biggest gossips. If this was about Thomas again—

"Gracious, Willa, why were you walking at such an unseemly pace? If Danny weren't handy I never would have caught you."

"I have to fix supper, then help Mother with the ironing." She shifted the paper-wrapped package of meat she held to her other hand for emphasis. "Was there something you wanted, Ellen?"

Excitement glinted in her friend's big, blue eyes. "I wanted to tell you the latest news. Father told me that the new pastor is a *young* man. And nice-looking."

"He is." Willa gave an inward sigh and relaxed. She should have guessed Ellen had stopped her to talk about Reverend Calvert. The new church and pastor were all anyone in the village talked about these days. *Thank goodness.* She disliked discussing anything pertaining to God, but at least the church topic had replaced the gossip about her abruptly cancelled wedding.

"You've *seen* him?" Ellen leaned close, gripped her arm. "What does he look like? I didn't dare ask Father for details."

She thought back to that morning. "Well, Reverend Calvert is quite tall…with blond hair and brown eyes." She cast back for her impression of the pastor and tempered her words so Ellen would not guess she had felt a momentary attraction to the man. *That* would elicit a hundred questions from her friend. "He has a strong appearance, with a square jaw. But his smile is charming." *And his lopsided grin disarming.* She ignored the image of that grin that snapped into her head and forged on. "As is his son's. His daughter's smile is more shy in nature."

Ellen jerked back. "He has *children?*"

"Yes. Joshua and Sally. He brought them to school this morning." She tilted her head to one side and grinned up at her friend. "How did that important detail escape you?"

"I've been helping Mother with my new gown all

day." Ellen's lovely face darkened. "Father didn't mention that the reverend was *married*."

"Oh." Willa gaped at her perturbed friend. "*Ellen Hall!* Surely you weren't thinking of— Why, you haven't even seen the man!"

"Well, gracious, a girl can hope, Willa. When I heard the pastor was young and handsome I thought, perhaps at last there was a man of distinction I could marry in this *place*. I should have known it was hopeless." Ellen sighed with a little shrug. "I must go home. Mother is waiting to hem my new dress for Sunday. I'll have to tell her there's no hurry now. I certainly don't care to impress a bunch of *loggers*. Bye, Willa."

"Bye, Ellen." Willa shook her head and cut across Main Street away from the block of huddled stores before anyone else could stop her to chat. Imagine Ellen being so eager to marry a "man of distinction" she would make plans toward that end before she even *saw* Pastor Calvert.

She frowned, hurried across the Stony Creek bridge and turned onto the beaten path along Brook Street. Perhaps she should have told Ellen the truth about Thomas and why their wedding had been canceled. Perhaps she should have cautioned her about trusting a man. *Any* man. Not that it mattered. Her friend was in no danger from the attractive Reverend Calvert, and neither was she. The man was married. And that was perfect as far as she was concerned. She'd had enough of handsome men with charming smiles.

Willa tossed the soapy dishwater out the lean-to door then eyed the neat piles of clean, folded clothing that covered the long table against the wall. The sight of the fruit of her mother's dawn-to-dusk labor over hot laundry tubs and a hot iron kindled the old resentment. How could her father have simply walked away knowing his wife and child would no longer be allowed to live in the cabin the company provided for its loggers? He'd known they had no other place to go. If the company owner hadn't accepted her mother's offer to do laundry for the unmarried loggers in exchange for staying in the cabin…

Willa set her jaw, rinsed the dishpan at the pump, then walked back into the kitchen. She had struggled to find an answer for her father's behavior since she was seven years old, and now she had—thanks to Thomas. Perhaps one day she would be grateful to him for teaching her that men were selfish and faithless and their words of love were not to be believed. But it had been only three months since he'd tossed her aside to go west and her hurt and anger left little room for gratitude.

She plunked the dishpan down onto the wide boards of the sink cupboard, yanked off her apron and jammed it on its hook. Thomas's desertion didn't bear thinking on, but she couldn't seem to stop. At least the gossip had died—thanks to the new pastor's arrival. She took a breath to calm herself and stepped into the living room.

"Why did you do the ironing, Mama? I told you I would do it tonight. You work too hard."

Her mother glanced up from the shirt she was mending and gave her a tired smile. "You've got your job, and I've got mine, Willa. I'll do the ironing. But it would be good if you're of a mind to help me with the mending. It's hard for me to keep up with it. Especially the socks."

She nodded, crossed the rag rug and seated herself opposite her mother at the small table beneath the window. "I have two new students—Joshua and Sally Calvert. The new pastor brought them to school today."

"I heard he had young children. But I haven't heard about his wife." Her mother adjusted the sides of the tear in the shirt and took another neat stitch. "Is she the friendly sort or city standoffish?"

"Mrs. Calvert wasn't with them." Willa pulled the basket of darning supplies close and lifted a sock off the pile. "The pastor is friendly. Of course, given his profession, he would be. But the children are very quiet." She eyed the sock's heel and sighed. It was a large hole. "Mr. Dibble was outside the livery hitching horses to a wagon when I passed on my way home. He always asks after you, Mama." She threaded a needle, then slipped the darning egg inside the sock. "He asked to be remembered to you."

"I don't care to be talking about David Dibble or any other man, Willa."

She nodded, frowned at the bitterness in her mother's voice. Not that she blamed her after the way her father had betrayed them by walking off to make a new life for himself. "I know how you feel, Mama. Every word Thomas spoke to me of love and marriage was a lie. But I will not let his deserting me three days before we were to be wed make me bitter."

She leaned closer to the evening light coming in the window, wove the needle through the sock fabric and stretched the darning floss across the hole, then repeated the maneuver in the other direction. "I learned my lesson well, Mama. I will never trust another man. Thomas's perfidy robbed me of any desire to fall in love or marry. But I refuse to let him rob me of anything more." Her voice broke. She blinked away the tears welling into her eyes and glared down at the sock in her hand. "I shall have a good, useful life teaching children. And I will be happy."

Silence followed her proclamation.

She glanced across the table from beneath her low-ered lashes. Her mother was looking at her, a mixture of sadness and anger in her eyes, her hands idle in her lap. "You didn't deserve that sort of treatment, Willa. Thomas Hunter is a selfish man, and you're well rid of him."

She raised her head. "Like you were well rid of Papa?"

"That was different. We were married and had a child." Her mother cleared her throat, reached across the table and covered her hand. "I tried my best to make your father stay, Willa. I didn't want you hurt."

There was a mountain of love behind the quiet, strained words. She stared down at her mother's dry, work-roughened hand. How many times had its touch comforted her, taken away her childish hurts? But Thomas's treachery had pierced too deep. The wound he'd given her would remain. She took a breath and forced a smile. "Papa left thirteen years ago, Mama. The hurt is gone. All that's left is an empty spot in my heart. But it's only been three months since Thomas cast me aside. That part of my heart still hurts." She drew another deep breath and made another turn with the darning floss. "You were right about Thomas not being trustworthy, Mama. I should have listened to you."

"And I should have remembered ears do not hear when a heart is full." There was a fierceness in her mother's voice she'd never before heard. "Now, let's put this behind us and not speak of Thomas again. Time will heal the wound." Her mother drew her hand back, tied off her sewing thread, snipped it, set aside the finished shirt and picked up another off the mending pile. She laid it in her lap and looked off into the distance. "I'm so *thankful* you hadn't married Thomas and aren't doomed to spend your life alone, not knowing if you're married or a widow. One day you will find a man who truly loves you and you will be free to love him."

Willa jerked her head up and stared at her mother, stunned by her words, suddenly understanding her bitterness, her secluded lifestyle. She'd always thought of her father's leaving as a single event, as the moment he had said goodbye and walked out the door, and her wound from his leaving had scarred over with the passing years. But her mother lived with the consequences of her father's selfish act every day. Her father had stolen her mother's life.

She caught her breath, looked down and wove the needle over and under the threads she'd stretched across the hole in the sock, thankfulness rising to weave through the hurt of Thomas's desertion. At least her life was still her own. And it would remain so. She would let no man steal it from her. No man! Not ever.

Matthew gathered his courage and peeked in the bedroom door. If Sally spotted him, the crying and begging to sleep in Joshua's room would start again. He considered himself as brave and stalwart as the next man, but Sally's tears undid him.

Moonlight streamed in the windows, slanted across the bed. He huffed out a breath of relief. She was asleep, one small hand tucked beneath her chin, her long, blond curls splayed across her pillow. He stared at the spot of white fabric visible where the edge of the covers met her hand and a pang struck his heart. He didn't have to go closer to see what it was. He knew. She was clutching her mother's glove.

Lord, I don't know what to do. Will allowing Sally to have Judith's glove lessen her grief? Or does it prolong it? Should I take the glove away? I need wisdom, Lord. I need help!

He walked to the stairs and started down. He loved Joshua and Sally and willingly accepted their guardianship, but being thrust into the role of parent to two young, grieving children was daunting. He was faced with tasks and decisions he was ill-prepared to handle. That one child was a little girl made it even more difficult. And he had his own grief to contend with.

He shot a glance toward the ceiling of the small entrance hall. "I miss you, Robert. And I'm doing the best I can. But it would be a lot easier if you'd had two sons." The thought of Sally's little arms around his neck, of her small hand thrust so trustingly into his made his heart ache. "Not that I would want it different, big brother. I'll figure it out. But it would certainly help with the girl things if I had a wife."

He frowned and walked into his study to arrange his possessions that had come by freight wagon that afternoon. Why couldn't he find a woman to love and marry? He was tired of this emptiness, this yearning for someone to share his life with that he'd been carrying around the last few years. He wanted a wife and children. Having Joshua and Sally these last few weeks had only increased that desire.

He lifted a box of books to his desk, pulled out his pocketknife and cut the cord that bound it. Robert had known Judith was the one for him as soon as he met her. But he'd never felt that immediate draw to a woman, the certainty that she was the one. He'd been making it a matter of prayer for the last year or so. But God hadn't seen fit to answer those prayers. Unless...

He stared down at the book he'd pulled from the box, a vision of a lovely face with beautiful blue-green eyes framed by soft waves of chestnut-colored hair dancing against the leather cover. His pulse quickened. Was what had happened to him in the schoolhouse God's answer to his prayers? There was no denying his immediate attraction to Miss Wright. An attraction so strong that he'd lost his normal good sense and eyed her like a besotted schoolboy. That had never happened to him before. But was it the beginning of love? Or only an aberration caused by his loneliness and grief?

He slid the book onto the top shelf of the bookcase behind his desk and reached into the box for another. It had been a humbling moment when the church council had asked him to leave the pulpit of his well-established church in Albany for two years to come and establish a foundation for the church here in Pinewood. But he'd been inclined to turn them down because of his loneliness. If he couldn't find a woman to love and marry among his large congregation and abundant friends in the city, what chance had he to find one in a small, rural village nestled among the foothills of the Allegheny Mountains in western New York?

He scowled, put the book on the shelf and picked up another. Robert's death had made up his mind. He had accepted the offer, hoping that a change of scene might help the children over their grief. Two years out of his life was a price he was willing to pay for the children's healing. That was his plan.

He reached into the box for the last book, then paused. What if God had placed that yielding in his heart because *He* had a plan? One that helped the children, but also included the answer to his prayers? He blew out a breath, put the last book on the shelf and tossed the empty box to the floor. And what if he were simply letting his imagination run away with him? At least he knew the answer to that question. "Thy will be done, Lord. Thy will be done."

He picked up the box with his desk supplies, cut the cord and started putting things in the drawers.

Chapter Two

Willa spotted their gray-haired neighbor sweeping her walk next door and sighed. Mrs. Braynard was as plump as her mother was lean, and as cheerful as her mother was bitter. She was also kind and concerned and…nosy. She closed the door and walked down their short, plank walk to the leaf-strewn beaten path beside the street. "Good morning, Mrs. Braynard. How is Daniel today?"

"He's doing better. He was able to move his arm a little when I was getting him up and around. The Lord bless you for caring." Her neighbor cleared the leaves and dirt from the end of her walk, paused and looked at her over the broom handle. "I heard the new pastor brought his children to your school. His wife a pleasant woman, is she?"

Willa clenched her fingers on the handle of the small basket holding her lunch. She hated gossip. She'd been on the receiving end of too much of it. But Mrs. Braynard meant no harm. She was simply overcurious. Nonetheless, whatever she said would be all over town within an hour. She took a breath to hold her smile in place. "I haven't met Mrs. Calvert. The pastor was alone when he brought the children. I'm looking forward to meeting her at the welcome dinner after church this Sunday." She turned away, hoping…

"Are you getting on all right, Willa? I mean—"

"I know what you mean, Mrs. Braynard." The sympathy in her neighbor's voice grated on her nerves. She hated being the object of people's pity—even if it was well-meant. She smiled and gave the same answer she'd been giving since Thomas had abruptly left town. "I'm fine. Now, I'm afraid I must hurry off to school. Tell Daniel I'm pleased to hear he is mending."

"I'll tell him. And I'll keep praying for you, Willa."

As if prayer would help. She pressed her lips together, lifted her hand in farewell and hurried down the path to the corner, a choked-back reply driving her steps. Mrs. Braynard, of all people, should know God had no interest in her or her plight. The woman had been praying for her mother and her ever since the day her father had said goodbye and walked out on them, and not one thing had changed. Not one. Except that now Thomas had deserted her, as well. So much for prayer!

She wheeled right onto Main Street and onto the bridge over Stony Creek, the heels of her shoes announcing her irritation by their quick, staccato beats on the wide, thick planks. She avoided a wagon pulling into the Dibble Smithy, passed the harness shop and livery and lowered her gaze to avoid eye contact with anyone heading across the street to the row of shops that formed the village center. She was in no mood for any more friendly, but prying, questions.

She crossed Church Street, then reined in her pace and her thoughts. Her students did not deserve a sour-faced teacher. She took a long breath and lifted her gaze.

Oh, no! Her steps faltered, came to a halt. A clergyman was the last person she wanted to see.

On the walkway ahead, Reverent Calvert was squatted on his heels, his hands clasping Sally's upper arms, while he talked to her. It seemed Sally was in disagreement with him if her stiff stance and bowed head was any indication. Joshua stood off to one side, the intent expression on his face a mirror of the pastor's. The boy certainly looked like his father. He also looked unhappy.

Something was wrong. Had it to do with school? Her self-involvement dissolved in a spate of concern. Joshua must have felt her attention for he raised his gaze and caught her looking at them. His lips moved. The pastor glanced in her direction, then surged to his feet. She put on a polite smile and moved forward. "Good morning, Reverend Calvert. I see Joshua and Sally are ready for school."

A look of chagrin flitted across the pastor's face. "We were discussing that."

So there *was* a problem. Joshua and Sally did not want to go to school. She glanced down at the little girl and her heart melted at the sight of her teary-eyed unhappiness. "Well, I hope you are through with your discussion and Joshua and Sally may come with me. I am running a bit late this morning and I...could use their help." Something flickered in the pastor's eyes. Puzzlement? Doubt? It was too quickly gone for her to judge.

"I'm certain they will be happy to help you, Miss Wright. What is it you want them to do?"

What indeed? The schoolroom had been set to rights last night before she left for home. She looked at the tears now flowing down Sally's cheeks and scrambled for an idea. "Well… I am going to begin a story about a cat today. But the cat…has no name."

Sally lifted her head and looked up at her. Joshua stepped closer. Ah, a spark of interest.

"I see. And how does that require the children's help?"

She glanced up at the pastor. A look of understanding flashed between them. So he had guessed she was making this up and was trying to help her. Now what? How could she involve Joshua and Sally? "Well…each student will have a chance to suggest a name for the cat—" she felt her way, forming the idea as she spoke.

"Ah, a contest." The proclamation bore the hint of a suggestion.

A contest. An excellent idea. "Yes. The class will choose which name they like best." She shot the pastor a grateful look. He inclined his head slightly and she glanced down. Sally had inched closer, and there was a definite glint in Joshua's eyes. So the boy liked to compete. "And the student who suggests the chosen name will…win a prize." What prize? She stopped, completely out of inspiration. That still did not require the children's help.

"And you need Joshua and Sally to help you with the prize?" Reverend Calvert's deep voice was soft, encouraging.

"Yes…" Now what? She took a breath and shoved aside her dilemma. She would think of something by the time they reached the schoolhouse. She stared at the tree beside the reverend. Ah! A smile curved her lips, widened as the idea took hold. "The prize will be a basket of hickory nuts from the tree behind the school. And I need someone to gather the nuts for me." She shot the reverend a triumphant look, then glanced from Joshua to Sally. "Will you collect the nuts for me?"

The little girl looked at her brother, followed his lead and nodded.

"It sounds like an interesting day for the children, Miss Wright."

She glanced up. The reverend smiled and mouthed "Thank you." Her stomach fluttered. He really did have a charming smile. She gave him a polite nod and held her free hand out to Sally. "Come along, then. We must hurry so you children can gather the nuts before the other children come. The prize must be a *secret.*" She halted, tipped her head to the side and gave them a solemn look. "You *can* keep a secret?"

They nodded again, their brown eyes serious, their blond curls bright in the sunlight.

"Lovely!" She smiled and moved forward, Sally's small hand in hers, Joshua on her other side, and the Reverend Calvert's gaze fastened on them. The awareness of it tingled between her shoulder blades until they turned the corner onto Oak Street. A frown wrinkled her brow. Twice now she had seen the pastor with his children. Where was their mother?

"It was a pleasure meeting you, gentlemen." Matthew shook hands with the church elders and watched them file out through the small storage room at the back of the church. They seemed to be men of strong faith, eager to do all they could to make the church flourish. He was looking forward to working with them.

He scanned the interior of the small church, admired the craftsmanship in the paneled pew boxes and the white plastered walls. He moved to the pulpit, the strike of his bootheels against the wood floor echoing in the silence. The wood was satin-smooth beneath his hands. He brushed his fingers across the leather cover of the Bible that rested there, closed his eyes and quieted his thoughts. A sense of waiting, of expectation hovered in the stillness.

"Almighty God, be with me, I pray. Lead and guide me to green pastures by the paths of Your choosing that I might feed Your flock according to Thy will. Amen."

He opened his eyes and pictured the church full of people. Would Miss Wright be one of them? He frowned and stepped out from behind the pulpit. He was becoming too concerned with Miss Wright; it was time to get acquainted with the village.

He stretched out his arms and touched the end of each pew as he walked down the center aisle, then crossed the small vestibule and stepped out onto the wide stoop. Warmth from the October sun chased the chill of the closed building from him. Did someone come early on Sunday morning to open the doors and let in the warmth?

Across the street stood an impressive, three-story building with the name Sheffield House carved into a sign attached to the fascia board of the porch roof. Passengers were alighting from a long, roofed wagon at the edge of the road that bore the legend Totten's Trolley.

He exchanged a friendly nod with the driver, then jogged diagonally across the street and trotted up three steps to a wide, wooden walkway that ran in front of a block of stores standing shoulder to shoulder, like an army at attention.

He doffed his hat to a woman coming out of a millinery store, skirted around two men debating the virtues of a pair of boots in a shoemaker's window next to Barley's Grocery and entered the Cargrave Mercantile.

Smells mingled on the air and tantalized his nose, leather, coffee and molasses prominent among them. He stepped out of the doorway and blinked his eyes to adjust to the dim indoors. The hum of conversation stopped, resumed in lower tones. He glanced left, skimmed his gaze over the long wood counter adorned with various wood and tin boxes, a coffee mill and at the far end a scale and cashbox.

He gave a polite nod in answer to the frankly curious gazes of the proprietor and the customers, then swept his gaze across the wood stove and the displays of tools along the back wall. On the right side of the store was the dry goods section and the object of his search. A glass-fronted nest of pigeonhole mailboxes constituted the post office. He stepped to the narrow, waist-high opening in the center of the boxes. A stout, gray-haired man, suspenders forming an X across the back of his white shirt, sat on a stool sorting through a pile of mail on a high table with a safe beneath it.

"Excuse me—"

The man turned, squinted at him through a pair of wire-rimmed glasses perched on the end of his nose, then slid off his stool and came to stand in front of the small shelf on the other side of the window. "What can I do for you, stranger?"

Matthew smiled. "I've come to introduce myself, and see about getting a mailbox. I'm Matthew Calvert, pastor of Pinewood Church." The conversations in the store stopped. There was a soft rustling sound as people turned to look at him.

The postmaster nodded. "Heard you'd arrived. Figured you'd be along. I'm pleased to make your acquaintance, Pastor Calvert."

"And I, yours, Mr.…."

"Hubble. Zarius Hubble." The man stretched out his hand and tapped the glass of one of the small cubicles. "This is the church mailbox. Lest you have an objection, I'll put your mail in here. Save you having to rent a box."

"Thank you, Mr. Hubble. That will be fine."

The postmaster nodded, then fixed a stern gaze on him. "I can't do that for others with you who will be getting mail, mind you. Your missus or such will need their own box."

"That won't be necessary." Matthew turned and almost collided with a small group of people standing behind him. The short, thin man closest to him held out his hand.

"I'm Allan Cargrave. I own this establishment, along with my brother Henry. You met him this morning. I've been looking forward to your coming, Pastor Calvert. We all have."

Matthew took his hand in a firm clasp. "Then our goal has been the same, Mr. Cargrave. I'm pleased to meet you." He smiled and turned to the others.

Willa glanced at her lunch basket, now half-full of hickory nuts, going out the door in Trudy Hoffman's hand and smiled. The impromptu contest had proved successful in a way she had not expected. Trudy and Sally Calvert had both suggested Puffy as a name for the cat in the story and friendship had budded between the girls when the name was chosen as the favorite by the class. The friendship was firmed when Sally told Trudy she could have the basket as they shared the prize.

Her smile faded. She was quite certain there was something more than shyness bothering Sally. She'd seen tears glistening in the little girl's eyes that afternoon. She walked to the door to watch Joshua and Sally cross the town park to the parsonage. Another smile formed. If the squirrels didn't get them, the park would soon be boasting a trail of hickory nut trees started by Sally's half of the prize falling from Joshua's pockets.

She pulled the door closed and watched the children. Why weren't they running and laughing on their way home? She studied their slow steps, the slump of their small shoulders. Something was amiss. They looked… sad. Perhaps they missed their friends in Albany. It was hard for children to leave a familiar home and move to a strange town where they knew no one. She would make certain the village children included Joshua and Sally in their games at the welcome dinner Sunday. And she would speak with Mrs. Calvert about the children. Perhaps there was something more she could do to help them adjust to their new life in Pinewood. Meanwhile, she had a new lunch basket to buy. She hurried down the stairs and headed for the mercantile.

Matthew blotted his notes, closed his Bible and pushed back from his desk. Moonlight drew a lacy shadow of the denuded branches of the maple in the side yard on the ground, silvered the fallen leaves beneath it. An owl hooted. His lips slanted into a grin. Miss Wright was correct. Pinewood was very different from Albany.

His pulse sped at the memory of her walking toward

them, neat and trim in her dark red gown with a soft smile warming her lovely face. She had, again, stolen his breath when their gazes met. And the way she had solved Sally's rebellion against going to school today…

A chuckle rumbled deep in his chest. She had made up that business about a cat with no name and the contest with a prize right there on the spot.

It was obvious Miss Wright loved children. How did she feel about God?

He clenched his hands and set his jaw, shaken by a sudden awareness of the expectation in his heart of seeing her sitting in the congregation Sunday morning.

Chapter Three

"How could you be so wrong about those children? They are his *wards*."

Willa placed her platter of meat tarts on the plank table and looked up at Ellen. "Pastor Calvert brought them to school, they look like him and their last name is the same. I assumed he was their father, not their uncle. It was an understandable mistake." Tears stung her eyes. Those poor children. To lose both their mother and father at such a young age. No wonder they looked sad.

"Perhaps, but— Oh, *look* at this old gown." Ellen batted at the ruffles on her bodice. "If I had known Pastor Calvert was a bachelor I would have had Mother hem my new gown. She says the color makes my eyes look larger and bluer."

Willa squared her shoulders and gave Ellen a look permitted by their years of friendship. Her friend hadn't given a thought to the children—other than to be thankful the pastor was not their father. "You look beautiful in that gown, and you know it, Ellen. Now stop pouting.

It's wasted on me. I've watched you looking in the mirror to practice protruding your lower lip, remember?"

The offending lip was pulled back into its normal position. "Very well. I suppose I understand your error. And I forgive you. But all the same, I *am* distressed. Had I known the truth of Matthew Calvert's marital state, I could have thought of a plan to catch his attention. Look!"

The hissed words tickled her ear. She glanced in the direction Ellen indicated. Matthew Calvert was coming across the church grounds toward the tables, his progress hindered by every young, unmarried lady in his congregation *and* their mothers. "So that's where all the women are. I wondered. Usually they are hovering over the food to— Billy Karcher, you put down those cookies! They're for after the meal."

The eight-year-old looked up from beneath the dark locks dangling on his forehead and gave her a gap-tooth grin. "I'm only makin' thure I get thome."

Willa fought back a smile at his lost-tooth lisp and gave him her teacher look. "Those cookies are to share. You put that handful back and I promise to save two of them for you."

The boy heaved a sigh, dropped the cookies back onto the plate and ran off to join the children playing tag in the park. She searched the group. Where were Joshua and Sally?

"Selfish little beast."

Willa jerked her gaze back to Ellen. "Billy is a *child*, not a beast."

"They seem one and the same to me." Ellen glanced toward the church and sucked in a breath. "Pastor Calvert is coming this way. And he seems quite purposeful in his destination. I guess I caught his attention when Father introduced us after all." A smug smile curved Ellen's lovely, rosy lips. She turned her back, raised her hands and pinched her cheeks. "Are my curls in place, Willa?"

She looked at the cluster of blond curls peeking from beneath the back of Ellen's flower-bedecked hat and fought down a sudden, strong urge to yank one of them. "They're fine." She turned away from her friend's smug smile. Ellen's conceit had alienated most of their old friends, and it was putting a strain on their friendship. She sighed and moved the cookie plate to the back side of the table out of the reach of small, grasping hands. Ellen had been different before Callie Conner's family had moved away. Their raven-haired friend's astonishing beauty had kept Ellen's vanity subdued. And Callie's sweet nature—

"May I interrupt your work a moment, ladies?"

Matthew Calvert's deep voice, as warm and smooth as the maple syrup the villagers made every spring, caused a shiver to run up her spine. She frowned, snatched the stem of a bright red leaf that had fallen on a bowl of boiled potatoes and tossed it to the ground. With a voice like that, it was no wonder the man was a preacher of some renown.

Good manners dictated that she turn and smile—indignation rooted her in place. Joshua and Sally were nowhere in sight, yet Matthew Calvert had come seeking out Ellen to satisfy his own...*aims.* Well, she wanted nothing to do with a man who neglected the care of his young wards to satisfy his own selfishness. She looked at the people spreading blankets on the ground in preparation for their picnic meal and silently urged them to hurry. Beside her, Ellen made a slow turn, smiled and looked up through her long lashes. *Another* ploy perfected before the mirror. One that made men stammer and stutter.

"May I help you, Reverend Calvert?"

Willa scowled at her friend's dulcet tone and moved a small crock of pickles closer to the potatoes, focused her attention on the green vine pattern circling the rim of the large bowl. She had no desire to hear the pastor's flirtatious response to Ellen's coyness. She wanted to go home—away from them both.

"Thank you, Miss Hall, you're most kind. But it's Miss Wright I seek."

Shock zinged all the way to her toes. What could Matthew Calvert possibly want with her? Ellen evidently thought the same if the hastily erased look of surprise on her friend's face was any indication. She turned. "You wished to speak with me?"

Something flashed in the pastor's eyes. Surprise? Puzzlement? Shock at her coolness? No doubt the handsome Matthew Calvert was unaccustomed to such treatment from women.

He dipped his head. "Yes. I've come to ask if you would be so kind as to keep watch on Joshua and Sally this afternoon, Miss Wright." He glanced at the tables and a frown furrowed his forehead. "I see that you are busy, and I hate to impose, but I am at a loss as to what else to do."

His gaze lifted to meet hers and she read apparent concern in his eyes. Guilt tugged at her. Had she been wrong about him neglecting his wards?

"As this welcome dinner is in my honor, I must visit with my parishioners, and Joshua and Sally are uncomfortable among so many new people. I thought, perhaps, as the children know you and are comfortable with you…" He stopped, gave a little shrug. "I would consider it a great favor if you could help them. But, of course, I will understand if you must stay here at the tables."

So he wanted to be free of the children so he could get acquainted with his parishioners…like Ellen, no doubt. She forced a smile.

"Not at all. Ellen can help in my place." She ignored her friend's soft gasp. Let her flirt her way out of that! "Where are the children?"

"They're sitting on the front steps at the parsonage. I didn't want to force them to join us."

Of course not. That would hamper his…getting acquainted. She nodded, reached under the table and drew a plate from her basket, placed three meat tarts and three boiled eggs on it, then lifted the cookie plate in her other hand and started across the intervening ground. The pastor fell in beside her.

"Let me carry those for you, Miss Wright."

She halted, glanced up and shook her head. "I think it best if I go alone. You go and meet the *people* of Pinewood, Reverend Calvert." From the corner of her eye she saw Ellen shake out the ruffles on her long skirt and glide across the leaf-strewn ground toward them. She hurried on toward the children, but could not resist looking over her shoulder. It did not seem to bother the pastor that Ellen had left the table of food unattended. They were laughing together as they walked toward the blanket Mrs. Hall had spread on the ground. It seemed

Reverend Calvert would partake of his first church dinner in Pinewood with the prettiest girl in the village by his side.

Willa glanced toward the church. People were beginning to gather their things together. She moved to the top of the gazebo steps. "Children, the game is over. Come and get your cookies, then go join your parents. It's time to go home."

"First one to touch wood wins!" Tommy Burke shouted the challenge, then turned and sprinted toward the gazebo. Children came running from every direction. Joshua put on a burst of speed surprising in one so young.

Willa smiled and gripped the post beside her, secretly rooting for him to outrun the older boys. Joshua needed something fun and exciting to think about. So did Sally.

She glanced over her shoulder, her heart aching for the little girl curled up on the bench along the railing. It was easy to get Joshua involved in games because he was very competitive. But Sally was different. The little girl had said her stomach hurt and stayed there on the bench while the other children played. Was it shyness or grief over her parents' deaths that made her so quiet and withdrawn?

She lifted the plate of cookies she'd saved from the bench and held them ready for the racing, laughing boys and girls. Billy Karcher stretched out his hand and touched the gazebo rail, Joshua right behind him.

"I win!" Billy tripped up the steps, snatched a cookie from the plate, grinned and took his promised second one. He lisped out, "Thee you tomorrow, Joth!" and jumped to the ground. Joshua waved at his new friend, turned and grabbed a cookie.

Willa resisted the temptation to smooth back the blond curls that had fallen over his brown eyes and contented herself with a smile. "A race well run, Joshua."

He grinned, a slow, lopsided grin that lifted the left side of his mouth, and flopped down on the bench beside his sister. "I'll *beat* him next time!"

He looked so different! So happy and carefree. The way a six-year-old should look. If only Sally would have joined in the games. She sighed and turned her attention back to the children grabbing cookies and saying goodbye.

"I find no words adequate to express my appreciation for your having come to my aid this afternoon, Miss Wright." Matthew smiled at Joshua busy kicking maple leaves into a pile while Sally leaned against the tree trunk and watched. "Or for engaging Joshua in the games."

"It was easy enough. Joshua is very competitive."

His gaze veered back to fasten on her. "I suppose I should correct him for bragging about that race, but I'm too happy to see that smile on his face. And, truth be told, I feel like bragging about it myself. I saw those boys, some of them had to be two or three years older than Joshua."

There was a definite glint of pride in the pastor's eyes. It seemed the competitive spirit ran in the Calvert family. "You're right, they are." She turned to look at Joshua, smiled and shook her head. "I've no doubt I will have my hands full at recess time tomorrow. Joshua declares he will beat Billy the next time they race, and I hear the ring of a challenge in those words."

"Do you want me to speak with him about it?"

The pastor's voice was controlled, but there was an underlying reluctance in it. She glanced his way. "No, I do not, Reverend Calvert. I am accustomed to handling the exuberance of young children. And I believe a few challenges, given and taken with his new schoolmates, is exactly what Joshua needs—under the circumstances."

She bent and picked up the plate she had left on the porch after her earlier, impromptu picnic with Joshua and Sally.

"I believe today proved that to be true, Miss Wright. This is the first time since Robert and Judith's deaths that Joshua has really played as a youngster should. I think he's going to be all right. I cannot tell you how grateful I am. But I'm concerned about Sally."

There was a heaviness in his voice. She turned. He was looking at the children, his face drawn with sorrow. She drew in her breath, told herself to keep quiet and leave. But she couldn't turn away from a hurting child. "I don't mean to pry, Reverend Calvert, but it's very difficult to engage Sally's interest in playing with the others. She is very quiet and withdrawn for a young child. And, though she tries very hard to hide them, I have seen tears in her eyes. I thought it was her shyness, but perhaps it is grief?"

"She misses her mother terribly. And it's hard for me to understand about girl things. Joshua is easier—I know about boys." He scrubbed his hand over his neck, turned and looked at her. "It's difficult dealing with their grief. It's only been six weeks since my brother and his wife died in the carriage accident. It was such a shock that I am still trying to handle my own grief. But I have talked to the children, tried to explain about God's mercy, and that they will see their mother and father again…" He took another breath and looked away.

She drew breath into her own lungs, forced them to expand against the tightness in her chest. "Forgive me, I did not mean to intrude on your privacy." She started down the path to the wood walkway.

"Wait! Please."

She paused, squared her shoulders and turned.

His lips lifted in a wry smile. "Once again I must appeal to you for help, Miss Wright. I am a pastor, not a cook, and the children and I are getting tired of eating eggs for every meal. I need a housekeeper, but it must be someone who understands children and will be careful of their grief. I thought, perhaps, as you are familiar with everyone in the village, you could suggest someone I could interview?"

She drew her gaze from the sadness in his eyes and gathered her thoughts. Who was available who would also understand the special needs of the Calvert children? "I believe Bertha Franklin might suit. She's a lovely, kind woman, an excellent cook…and no stranger to sorrow. And she definitely understands children. She has raised eight of her own. If you wish, I can stop and ask her to come by and see you tomorrow. Her home is on my way."

"I would appreciate that, Miss Wright." His gaze captured hers. "And thank you again for watching the children this afternoon. And for helping Joshua remember how to play."

His soft words brought tears to her eyes. She nodded, spun about and hurried down the wood walkway toward town.

Willa dipped her fingers in the small crock, rubbed them together, then spread the cream on her face and neck. A faint fragrance of honeysuckle hovered. She replaced the lid, tied the ribbons at the neck of her cotton nightgown and reached up to free her hair from its confining roll. The chestnut-colored mass tumbled onto her shoulders and down her back. She brushed it free of snarls, gathered it at the nape of her neck with a ribbon and stepped back from the mirror.

The touch of her bare feet against the plank floor sent a shiver prickling along her flesh. She hopped back onto the small, rag rug in front of the commode stand and rubbed her upper arms. The nights were turning colder, the air taking on the bite that announced winter was on its way. Thank goodness the company loggers kept her mother well supplied with firewood. And the parents of her students provided wood for the stove at school. There was already a large pile outside the back door.

She sighed, stepped off the rug and hurried to the window to push the curtain hems against the crack along the sill to block the cold air seeping in around the frame. Tomorrow morning she would start her winter schedule. She would rise early and go to school and light a fire in the stove to chase away the night chill. And then she would make a list of boys to help her keep the woodbox full throughout the winter.

She stepped to her nightstand, cupped her hand around the chimney globe, blew out the flame then climbed into bed. Two boys working together in weeklong rotations should be sufficient. Joshua and Billy would be the first team. She gave a soft laugh, tugged the covers close and snuggled down against her pillow. Those two boys would probably race to see who could carry in the most wood in the shortest time.

An image of Joshua's happy, lopsided grin formed against the darkness. He certainly looked like his uncle. And so did Sally, in a small, feminine way. Tears burned at the back of her eyes. Those poor children, losing both of their parents so unexpectedly. She had been devastated when her father left, and she'd had her mother to comfort her. Of course, Joshua and Sally had their uncle. He had looked concerned for the children when he talked with her. But that didn't mean his concern was real. Her father had seemed concerned for her before he turned his back and walked away never to return. But why would Matthew Calvert bother to put on an act for her? The children were not her concern.

Once again I must appeal to you for help, Miss Wright.

Oh, of course. Her facial muscles drew taut. She was a teacher. The pastor must have reasoned that she cared about children and played on her emotions to enlist her aid. And it had worked. She had been so gullible. Because of the children? Or because she wanted to believe there was truth behind Matthew Calvert's quiet strength and disarming grin?

She jerked onto her side, opened the small wood box on the nightstand with her free hand and fingered through the familiar contents, felt paper and withdrew the note Thomas had left on her desk the day he deserted her. There was no need to light the lamp and read it, the words were seared into her mind. *Willa, I'm sorry I haven't time to wait and talk to you, but I must hasten to meet Jack. He sent word he has funds for us to head west, and I am going after my dream. Wish me well, dearest Willa.*

Her chest tightened, restricted her breath. Three days before their wedding and Thomas had forsaken her without so much as a word of apology or regret. A man's concern for others was conditional on his own needs.

She clenched her hand around the small, folded piece of paper, drew a long, slow breath and closed her eyes. When her father abandoned her he'd left behind nothing but a painful memory and a void in her heart. Thomas had left her tangible proof of a man's perfidy. She had only to look at the note to remind herself a man was not to be trusted. Not even a man of the cloth with a stomach-fluttering grin.

Chapter Four

"Thank you for coming by, Reverend Calvert."

"Not at all, Mrs. Karcher." Matthew inclined his head in a small, polite bow. "I find making personal calls is the best way to get acquainted with my parishioners. And it is beneficial to do so as quickly as possible." He included the Karcher daughter, who'd had the misfortune of inheriting her father's long-jawed, hawk-nosed looks, in his goodbye smile.

"Well, Agnes and I are honored to be your first call." A look of smug satisfaction settled on the woman's face, one of her plump elbows dug into her daughter's side. "Aren't we, Agnes?"

"Yes, Ma." Agnes tittered and looked up at him, her avid expression bringing an uneasy twinge to his stomach. "I'm pleased you liked my berry pie, Reverend Calvert. I'll make an apple pie the next time you come." Her bony elbow returned her mother's nudge.

The *next* time? The expectation in Agnes's tone set warning bells clanging in his head. "Indeed?" A lame reply, but there was no good answer he could make to her presumption. He looked down at his hat and brushed a bit of lint from the felt brim, then stepped closer to the door. Perhaps he could get away before—

"Agnes's pies are the best of any young woman in Pinewood. And she's a wonderful cook."

—and perhaps he couldn't. He braced himself for what he sensed was coming.

"Mayhap you can come for dinner Saturday night, Reverend? I'm thinking those wards of yours would be thankful for some of Agnes's good cooking."

And there went his chance for an uneventful leave-taking. Mrs. Karcher's invitation could not be ignored. He looked up, noted the eager, hopeful gleam in both women's eyes and held back the frown that tugged at his own features. Both mother and daughter seemed to have forgotten his visit included Mr. Karcher and decided he had come because of Agnes. He cleared his throat and set himself to the task of disabusing them of that notion without hurting their feelings and damaging the pastor-and-congregant relationship. "I appreciate your kind invitation, Mrs. Karcher, but I'm afraid I must decline. My Saturdays are spent in prayer and preparation for Sunday. As for the children, I have hired Mrs. Franklin as housekeeper and cook. She feeds us well."

Surprise flitted across their faces. They had apparently not yet heard that piece of news. He hurried on before Mrs. Karcher recovered and extended another, amended, invitation. "Please convey my regards to Mr. Karcher. I regret that I had so little time to spend visiting with him. I shall make another call on *him* when he is less busy at the grist mill."

His slight emphasis on the word *him* dulled the hopeful gleam in the women's eyes. They had understood. He dipped his head in farewell, stepped outside and blew the air from his lungs in a long, low whistle. He was accustomed to the fact that young ladies and their mothers found bachelor pastors attractive as potential husband material, but he'd never before been subjected to anything quite so…blatant.

He ran his fingers through his hair, slapped on his hat and trotted to his carriage. Thunder grumbled in the distance. He glanced up and frowned at the sight of black clouds roiling across the sky. They were coming fast. The other visit he'd planned for this afternoon would have to wait.

"Time to head for home, girl." He patted his bay mare on her shoulder, climbed to the seat and picked up the reins. Lightning flashed. Thunder crashed. The mare jerked, danced in the traces. "Whoa, Clover. It's all right. Everything's all right."

The bay tossed her head and turned her ears toward his voice, calmed. "Good girl. Let's go now." He clicked his tongue and flicked the reins, glancing up as lightning glinted along the edge of the tumbling clouds. The black, foaming mass was almost overhead now. He would never make it back to town before the storm hit, and the children…

His chest tightened. Joshua would be all right. But Sally— "Lord, please be with Sally. Please comfort her, Lord, until I can get home." He reined the mare onto the Butternut Hill Road, stole another look at the sky and eased his grip on the lines to let her stretch her stride as he headed back toward the village.

"The…hen…is on the…b-*box*."

Willa smiled and nodded encouragement as Micah

Lester shot her a questioning look. "Box is correct. Continue, please."

The boy lowered his gaze to the English Reader book in his hands and took a deep breath. "The rat ran…fr-*from*…the box."

She nodded as he again glanced her way. "And the last sentence, please."

"C-can the…hen…run?"

"Very good, Micah. You may take your seat." She stepped to his side and held out her hand for the book. Thunder grumbled. Her students straightened on their benches and looked up at her. She placed the book on her desk and went to the window. Black clouds were rolling across the sky out of the west. She turned back, looked at the expectant expressions on the children's faces and laughed. "Yes, school is over for today. A storm is coming, but if you hurry, there is time for you to reach home before it arrives. Gather your things. And remember…you're to go straight home."

She moved to the door, stepped out onto the small porch and held the door open against a rising wind. The children scurried past her and ran down the stairs still donning their coats and hats, calling out their good-byes as they scattered in every direction. "Hurry home now, or you'll be caught out in the open and get a good drenching!"

She glanced up at the dark sky. Lightning glinted against the black storm clouds. Thunder crashed. She stared at the gray curtain falling to earth from beneath the approaching clouds and frowned. She was in for a soaking. By the time she snuffed the oil lamp, adjusted the drafts on the heating stove and gathered her things it would be impossible for her to reach home before the storm hit. Those clouds were moving fast. Should she wait it out? No. If she waited it could get worse. There was no promise of clearing behind that black wall of froth. She sighed, stepped inside and closed the door.

"C'mon, Sally. We got to get home. Miss Wright said so!"

Joshua. She turned and peered through the dim light in the direction of the boy's voice. He was tugging at his sister who was huddled into a ball in the corner. "Joshua, what's wrong with Sally?" Her skirt hems skimmed her shoe tops and swirled around her ankles as she hurried toward them.

The boy jerked to his feet and spun around to look up at her. "I'm sorry, Miss Wright. I know we're supposed to go home, but Sally's scared. She won't get up."

His face was pale, his voice teetered on the edge of tears. "It's all right, Joshua." She gave him a reassuring touch on the shoulder, then knelt down. "Sally—"

White light flickered through the dark room. Thunder cracked. The little girl screamed and launched herself upright and straight into her arms with such force that she almost tumbled backward. She caught her balance and wrapped her arms around Sally's small, trembling body.

Rain pelted the roof. Lightning streaked against the darkness outside the window and lit the room with a sulfurous yellow glow. Thunder crashed and rumbled. Sally sobbed and burrowed her face hard into the curve of her neck. She placed her hand on top of the little girl's soft, blond curls and looked up at Joshua. The boy's eyes were watery with held-back tears, his lips trembling.

"Joshua, what is—" The door jerked open. She started and glanced up.

Matthew Calvert stepped into the schoolroom and swiveled his head left and right, peering into the dim interior. *"Josh? Sally?"*

"Uncle Matt!" Joshua lunged at his uncle. Sally slipped out of her arms and ran after him.

She rose, shook out her skirts then lifted her hands to smooth her hair.

Matthew Calvert dropped to his knees and drew the children close. "I was out on a call. I came as quickly as I could." The pastor tipped his head and kissed Sally's cheek, loosed his hold on Joshua and reached up to tousle the boy's hair. "You all right, Josh?"

Joshua straightened his small, narrow shoulders and nodded. "Yes, sir. But Sally's scared."

"I know. Thanks for taking care of her for me."

She noted Joshua's brave pose and the adoration in his eyes as he looked at his uncle, Sally clinging so trustingly, and turned away from the sight before she gave in to the impulse to tear the children out of his arms. She well remembered how loved and safe she had felt when her father had held her—and how devastating it had been to learn that the love and security had been a lie.

She swallowed to ease a sudden tightness in her throat and stepped to the open door. *Those children have no one else. Please don't let Joshua or Sally be hurt by their uncle.* Her face tightened. Who was she talking to? Certainly not God. He didn't care about such things.

Lightning crackled and snapped, turned the room brilliant with its brief flash of light. Thunder growled. A gust of wind spattered the rain sluicing off the porch roof against her and banged the door against the porch railing. She shivered, grabbed the door and tugged it shut. Murky darkness descended, too deep for the single overhead oil lamp she had lit.

"Forgive me, Miss Wright, I forgot about the door."

She turned and met Matthew Calvert's gaze, found something compelling there and looked away. "It's of no matter." She rubbed the drops of moisture from her hands and moved toward the heating stove, then paused. She would have to walk by him to reach it, and she did not want to get close to Matthew Calvert. Something about him stirred emotions from the past she wanted dead and buried. She busied herself brushing at the small, wet blotches on her sleeves.

"Joshua, get your coat and hat on. Sally, you must get yours on, too. It's time to go home."

She watched from under her lowered lashes as he gently loosed Sally's arms from around his neck and urged the little girl after her brother.

"Miss Wright…"

His deep voice was quiet, warm against the drumming of the rain on the roof. She lifted her head and again met his gaze. It was as quiet and warm as his voice. And dangerous. It made her want to believe him—as she had believed her father and Thomas. She clenched her hands. "Yes?"

"I need to speak with you…alone." His gaze flicked toward Joshua and Sally, then came back to rest on hers. "Would you please stop at the parsonage on your way home? I need to explain—" Another sizzling streak of lightning and sharp crack of thunder brought Sally flying back to him. Joshua was close behind her.

She swallowed back the refusal that was on her lips. She wanted no part of Matthew Calvert. The man had already used her once to free himself from his responsibility to the children so he could spend time with Ellen at the church dinner. But she was a teacher, and his wards were her students. She needed to learn whatever she could that might help the sad, frightened children. Especially if their uncle continued that sort of behavior. She well knew the pain a man's selfishness could bring others. She gave a stiff little nod and went to adjust the drafts on the stove.

"Thank you for coming, Miss Wright. Let me help you out of that wet cloak." Matthew stepped behind her, waited until she had pushed back the hood and unfastened the buttons, then lifted the garment from her shoulders.

"Thank you." She took a quick step forward, squared her shoulders and clasped her hands in front of her.

He stifled an unreasonable sense of disappointment. Willa Wright's expression, her pose, every inch of her proclaimed she was a schoolmarm here on business. Well, what had he expected? No...*hoped*. That she would come as a friend?

He hung her damp cloak on one of the pegs beside the door and gestured to the doorway on his left. "Please come into the sitting room. We can talk freely there. Sally has calmed, now that the lightning and thunder have stopped, and she and Josh are playing checkers in his room." He urged her forward, led her to the pair of padded chairs that flanked the fireplace. "We'll sit here by the fire. The rain has brought a decided chill to the air."

"Yes, and it shows no sign of abating." She cast a sidelong glance up at him. "You had best be prepared for cold weather, Mr. Calvert. It will soon be snow-storms coming our way."

Would they be colder than her voice or frostier than her demeanor? Clearly, she was perturbed over his asking her to come. "I'm no stranger to winter cold, Miss Wright. We have snowstorms in Albany." He offered her a smile of placation. Perhaps he could soothe away some of her starchiness. "In truth, I enjoy them. There's nothing as invigorating as a toboggan run down a steep hill with your friends, or as enjoyable as a ride on a moonlit night with the sleigh bells jingling and the snow falling."

"A sleigh ride with…friends?"

"Yes, with friends."

She nodded, smoothed her skirts and took a seat. "A very romantic view of winter in the city, Mr. Calvert. I'm afraid there are harsher realities to snowstorms here in the country." She folded her hands in her lap and looked up at him. "You wanted to speak with me. I assume it is about the children?"

He looked down at her, so prim and proper and…and *disapproving*. He glanced at the rain coursing down the window panes. Small wonder the woman was irritated with him. He turned and pushed a length of firewood closer to another log with the toe of his boot. What did it matter if she was upset with him? This was not about him or his confusing feelings for the aloof teacher. "Yes, it's about the children."

He looked into the entrance hall, toward the stairs that climbed to their bedrooms, then sat on the edge of the chair opposite her. "Miss Wright, as I have previously explained, I had parenthood thrust upon me a little over seven weeks ago under extremely stressful circumstances, and I—well, I'm at a loss. As I mentioned, there is much I don't understand. Especially with Sally. However, I did not go into detail."

He stole another look toward the stairs and leaned forward. "I asked to speak with you because I believe you are due an explanation of Sally's behavior during a storm. You see, the day my brother and his wife died—" The pain of loss he carried swelled, constricted his throat. He looked down at the floor, gripped his hands and waited for the wave of grief to ease.

The fire crackled and hissed in the silence. The rain tapped on the windows—just as it had that day. He lifted his head. The firelight played across Willa Wright's face, outlined each lovely feature. He looked into her eyes, no longer cool, but warm with sympathy, and let the memories pour out. "I was teaching Joshua to play chess, and that day Robert and Judith brought him to spend the afternoon with me while they went to visit friends. Sally went with them."

He pushed to his feet, shoved his hands in his pockets and stood in front of the fire. "When it grew close to the time when Robert said they would return for Josh, a severe thunderstorm, much like the one today, blew in. We were finishing our game when a bolt of lightning struck so close to the house that it rattled the windows and vibrated my chest. A horse squealed in panic out front. I jumped to my feet and hurried to the window. Josh followed me."

He stared down at the flames, but saw only the carnage of a memory he prayed to forget. "There were two overturned, broken carriages in the street. One of them was Robert's. His horse was down and thrashing, caught in the tangled harness. I told Josh to stay in the house and ran outside, but there was nothing I could do. Robert and Judith were…gone."

He hunched his shoulders, shoved his hands deeper in his pockets and cleared the lump from his throat. "Sally was standing beside her mother, tugging on her hand and begging her to get up. She was scraped and bleeding, but, thankfully, not seriously injured." His ragged breath filled the silence. That, and the sound of Sally's sobs and Joshua's running feet and sharp cry that lived in his head.

"I'm so sorry for you and the children, Reverend Calvert. I can't imagine suffering through such a terrible occurrence. And for Sally to—" there was a sharply indrawn breath "—it's no wonder she is terrified of thunderstorms."

The warm, compassionate understanding in Willa Wright's voice flowed like balm over his hurt and concern. The pressure in his chest eased. "Yes."

"And it's why Josh tries so hard to protect her and take care of her, even though he hates thunderstorms, too." He looked down into her tear-filled eyes. "He recognized his father's rig and followed me outside. He… saw…his mother and father." He shook off the despair that threatened to overwhelm him when he thought of the children standing there in the storm looking shocked and lost and made his voice matter-of-fact. "I thought you should know—so you could understand their behavior. I'm sure you have rules about such things."

She nodded and rose to her feet. "There are rules, yes. It is the custom in Pinewood to close the schools and send the village children home when a storm threatens, lest they be caught out in it." Her voice steadied. She lifted her head and met his gaze. "I'm thankful you called me here and told me what happened, Reverend Calvert. Now that I understand, should there be another thunderstorm, I will keep Sally and Joshua with me until you come for them, or should the hour grow late, I will bring them home and stay with them until your return."

"That is far beyond your duty as their teacher, Miss Wright." A frown tugged at his brows. "I appreciate your kindness, as will the children, but I assure you, I meant only to explain, not to impose upon you."

She went still, stared up at him. "Nor did you, Reverend Calvert. You did not ask—I offered." A look he could only describe as disgust flashed into her eyes. She tore her gaze from his and turned toward the door. "I must get home."

He held himself from stopping her, from demanding that she tell him what he had done to bring about that look. "Yes, of course. I did not mean to take so much of your time."

They walked out into the entrance hall and he lifted her cloak off the hook. The sound of rain drumming on the porch roof was clear in the small room. "You cannot walk home in that downpour, Miss Wright." He settled the still-damp garment on her shoulders. "If you will wait here, I will get the buggy and drive you home."

"That is not necessary, Reverend Calvert." She raised her hands and tugged the hood in place. "I'm accustomed to walking home in all sorts of weather. The children need you here."

Why must the woman be so *prickly* when he was trying to do her a kindness? The stubborn side of his nature stirred. "I insist, Miss Wright. The lightning has stopped. The children will be fine with Mrs. Franklin.

Wait here." He snatched his coat off its hook and hurried out the door before she could voice the refusal he read in her eyes.

The buggy moved along the muddy road, each rhythmic thud of the horse's hooves a step closer to her home, yet the way had never seemed so long. She had done it again! She'd allowed the man to reach her heart in spite of her resolve. Willa stared down at her hands and willed her gaze not to drift to the handsome profile of Reverend Matthew Calvert. The sense of intimacy created by the curtain of rain around the buggy did not help.

The horse's hooves struck against the planks of Stony Creek bridge and the carriage lurched slightly as the wheels rolled onto the hard surface. She grabbed for the hold strap to keep from brushing against him and held herself rigid as the buggy rumbled across the span, splashed back onto the mud of Main Street, then swayed around the corner onto her road.

"Miss Wright, may I ask your opinion about something that troubles me with Sally?" Matthew Calvert turned his head and looked at her.

She lifted her hand and adjusted her hood to avoid meeting his gaze. She was too easily swayed by the look of sincerity in his brown eyes. And she knew better, although her actions didn't reflect it. Hadn't the man just manipulated her into offering to watch his children if he was delayed, perhaps deliberately, in coming for them during a thunderstorm? What did he want of her now?

"To be fair, I must tell you it is a personal situation and has nothing to do with school. I simply don't know what to do for the best. And I thought a woman would have a better understanding of a little girl's needs than I."

If it did not pertain to school, why involve her? She opened her mouth to suggest he ask Bertha Franklin, then closed it again at the remembered feel of Sally clinging to her. "What is it?" She fixed her mind on her father's and Thomas's selfishness and brought a "no" ready to her lips.

"Sally misses her mother terribly. It seems especially difficult for her at bedtime. That first evening, when I put them to bed in the parsonage, she wanted to sleep in Joshua's bedroom. She cried so hard, I moved a trundle bed in for her." He glanced her way again. "Perhaps I should not have done so, but it…troubles…me when she cries."

She steeled her heart against the image of the grieving little girl and boy, and kept her eyes firmly fixed on the rain splashing off the horse's rump. Sympathy came too easily when she looked into Matthew Calvert's eyes.

"When we moved here, I decided permitting Sally to sleep in Joshua's room was not for the best, and, in spite of her tears, I put her in a bedroom by herself. When I went to check on her later that night, I found her asleep—with one of Judith's gloves clutched in her hand."

The poor, hurting child! Tears stung her eyes. She blinked them away and, under the cover of her cloak, rubbed at the growing tightness in her chest. "That is my cabin ahead."

The reverend nodded and drew back on the reins. The horse stopped. The drum of the rain on the buggy roof grew louder.

"Miss Wright, Sally takes comfort from Judith's

glove, but it seems she is becoming more dependent on it. It was the first thing she wanted when we came home earlier." He turned on the seat to face her. "I don't know what to do, Miss Wright. And, though I feel it is unfair of me to ask for your advice, I feel so inadequate to the situation that I find myself unable to refrain from doing so." The sincerity in his voice tugged her gaze to meet his. "In your opinion, should I let Sally keep the glove? Or should I take it away?"

She couldn't answer—couldn't *think* clearly. Her memories were too strong, her emotions too stirred. This man and his wards were a danger to her. She squared her shoulders and shook her head. "I'm afraid I have no answer for you, Reverend Calvert. However, I will consider the problem, and if a suggestion should occur to me, I will tell you." She pulled her hood farther forward and prepared to alight.

He drooped the reins over the dashboard, climbed down and hurried around to offer her his hand. She did not want his help, did not want to touch him, but there was no way around it. She placed her hand on his wet, uplifted palm and felt the warm strength of his fingers close over hers as she stepped down. The gesture was meant to steady her, but the effect was the opposite. She withdrew her hand, clasped the edges of her cloak against the driving rain and looked up at him. "Thank you for your kindness in bringing me home, Reverend Calvert."

"Not at all, Miss Wright. It was the least I could do. Watch that puddle."

His hand clasped her elbow. He guided her around the muddy water onto the wet planks that led to the stoop. Water from the soaked yard squished around his boots as he walked her to her door, released his hold and gave a polite bow of his head.

"Thank you for allowing me to unburden myself of my concerns over Sally and Joshua, Miss Wright. It was good of you to listen. Good afternoon."

She nodded, opened the door and stepped inside, but could not resist a glance over her shoulder. He was running to his buggy.

"I expected you home when the storm started, Willa. Was there something wrong? I heard a buggy. Are you all right?"

She closed the door, turned and shoved the wet hood off her head. "I'm fine, Mama. Reverend Calvert's ward, Sally, is frightened of thunderstorms and it took a bit to calm her. The reverend drove me home because of the rain."

"You were scared of thunder and lightning when you were little. Remember?"

"Yes, I remember." *Too many things. The memories keep rearing up and betraying me.* "You used to hold me and tell me stories."

Her mother smiled and nodded. "I hope the reverend's little girl gets over her fright. It's a terrible thing when a child is afraid." She narrowed her eyes, peered closely at her. "Are you certain you're all right, Willa? You look…odd."

"Well, I can't imagine why. I'm perfectly fine." She *was*. Or at least she would be, as soon as the tingly warmth of Matthew Calvert's touch left her hand.

Chapter Five

Willa wrapped her bread and butter with a napkin, placed the bundle in the small wicker basket, added an apple and slammed the lid closed. Why couldn't she stop thinking about yesterday? About the way her heart had sped at Matthew Calvert's nearness when he removed her cloak? About that carriage ride, and the way her breath had caught when he took her hand in his? Those things were mere courtesies. Yet here she was mooning about them. It was disgusting. Why wasn't she thinking about the way he had again manipulated her into offering to help with the children to free his time? Where was her self-control?

She dropped the dirty knife in the dishpan, swirled her cloak about her shoulders, grabbed her lunch basket and strode to the kitchen doorway. "I'm ready to go, Mama."

Her mother nodded, poured the iron kettle of steaming water she held into the washtub, then turned and stepped to the pump to refill it. "I figured you'd be going early to stoke up the stove. It turned right cold last night."

She pressed her lips together and nodded. She hated the tiredness that lived in her mother's voice. Hated that her mother worked from dawn to dusk every day but Sunday to keep the small cabin they called home. Most of all she hated her father for walking away and leaving her mother to find a way for them to survive without him.

She lifted the hem of her long skirt and stepped down into the lean-to wash shed.

Her mother raised her head and gave her a wry smile. "One thing about scrubbing clothes for a living—you're never cold." Her green eyes narrowed, peered at her. "What are you riled about?"

"Nothing. Except that you work too hard. Let me get that!" Willa plopped her basket on the corner of the wash bench and grabbed hold of the kettle handle. "You need to eat, Mama. I made a piece of bread and honey for you. It's on the kitchen table."

Her mother straightened and brushed a lock of curly hair off her sweat-beaded forehead. "Don't you know it's the mother who's supposed to take care of the child, Willa?" There was sorrow and regret in the soft words.

"You've been doing that all my life, Mama." She grabbed a towel and pulled the iron crane toward her, lifted the newly filled kettle onto a hook beside the one already heating and slowly pushed the crane back. The flames devouring the chunks of wood rose and licked at the large pot. The beads of water sliding down the iron sides hissed in protest. "I hope that someday I will be able to take care of you, and you will never have to do laundry again."

Her mother smiled, dumped the first pile of dirty clothes into the washtub, set the washboard in place and reached for the bar of soap. "You're a wonderful daughter to want to take care of me, Willa. But your future husband might have something to say about that."

She snatched the soap out of her mother's reach. "I told you there's not going to be a future husband for me, Mama. I am never going to marry. Thomas cured me of that desire." *And Papa.* "Now please, go and eat your bread while the rinse water is heating. I have to go."

She put the soap back in its place, hung the towel back on its nail and picked up her basket. "Please leave the ironing, Mama. I will do it tonight. And I'll stop at Brody's on my way home and get some pork chops for supper. Danny told me they were butchering pigs at their farm yesterday. Now, I've got to leave or I'll never get the schoolroom warm before my students come."

She kissed her mother's warm, moist cheek, opened the door of the lean-to and stepped out into breaking dawn of the brisk October morning. Dim, gray light guided her around the cabin to the road and filtered through the overhanging branches of trees along the path as she hurried on her way.

The stove was cold to the touch. Willa grabbed the handle of the grate, gave it a vigorous shake to get rid of the ashes that covered the live embers, then opened the drafts. The remaining coals glowed, turned red. She added a handful of kindling, stood shivering until it caught fire, then fed in a few chunks of firewood, lit a spill and closed the firebox door.

The flame on the spill fluttered. She cupped her free hand around it, stepped to the wall and unwound the narrow chain to lower the oil-lamp chandelier. The glass chimneys fogged from her warm breath as she lifted them one by one, lit the wicks, set the flame to a smoke-less, steady burn and settled them back in place. Heat smarted her fingertips. She lit the oil lamp on her desk and blew out the shortened sliver of wood.

Everything was in readiness. Almost. She grabbed the oak bucket off the short bench and headed for the back door to fetch fresh drinking water from the well.

The door latch chilled her fingers. She stared at her hand gripping the metal and a horrible, hollow feeling settled in her stomach. This would be the sum of her life. She turned and surveyed the readied classroom, then looked down at the bucket dangling from her hand. She would spend her years teaching the children of others—until her mother's strength gave out and she had to take over doing the loggers' laundry to keep their home. Her back stiffened. "Well, at least I won't have to live with a broken heart." She hurled the defiant words into the emptiness, squared her shoulders and opened the door. If she hurried there was still time for her to write her letter before the children came.

Dearest Callie,

I was so pleased to receive your latest letter. And I thank you for your kind invitation to visit, perhaps I shall, later when school closes. I do apologize for being so tardy in answering, but you know help-ing Mama with her work leaves me little time for pleasurable activities.

I must tell you about Reverend Calvert and his wards. I am certain your aunt Sophia has written you about him as there is little talk of anything else in Pinewood since his arrival. And, truly, I am grateful for that as talk of Thomas's hasty departure has ceased.

Willa frowned, tapped her lips with her fingertip and stared at the letter, then dipped her pen in the inkwell and made her confession.

You, and Sadie, and Mama are the only ones who know the truth of Thomas's desertion of me. My pride demands that others believe I told him to follow his dream and go west without me, that the choice to remain behind was mine. I could not bear to face the pity of the entire village! Sadie knows well what I mean.

Oh, Callie, the *folly* of believing a man's words of love. But I know you are aware of that danger. How my heart aches for you, my dear friend. I am so sorry your parents persist in their desire to find a wealthy husband for you, no matter his character. You write that you are praying and trusting God to undertake and bring you a man of strong faith and high morals in spite of their efforts, but I do not believe God troubles Himself with the difficulties and despairs of mere mortals. He certainly has never bestirred Himself on Mama's behalf. Or mine.

Reverend Calvert is tall, and well-proportioned, and exceedingly handsome. He possesses an abundant charm, and a very persuasive manner. A dangerous combination, as you might imagine. One must stay on one's guard around him lest

Light footfalls raced across the porch. The door

opened. Willa wiped the nib of her pen, stoppered her inkwell and blotted the unfinished letter.

"Good morning, Mith Wright." Billy Karcher shucked his jacket and hat, hung them on a peg on the wall and gave her a grin. "I'm getting a new tooth. Wanna thee?"

"Good morning, Billy. I certainly do." She folded the letter and tucked it into her lunch basket to finish later.

The second grader tipped his head up and skimmed his lips back to expose the white edge of a new front tooth.

"Thank you for the prompt service, Mr. Dibble." Matthew watched the fluid stride of his bay mare as the blacksmith led her in a tight circle. She was no longer favoring her left rear leg. "She seems fine now. What was the problem?"

"Nail was set wrong. Irritated the quick enough it got sore." The blacksmith shook his head and led the horse over to him. "It's a good thing you brought her in. Shoddy work like that can maim a horse." He handed over the halter lead. "I checked the other shoes. They're all good."

"That's good to know." He stroked the bay's neck, got a soft nicker and head bump in return. "What do I owe you?"

"Fourteen cents will take care of it."

He counted out the coins, smiled and handed them over. "Thank you again, Mr. Dibble. It's been a pleasure meeting you. I'll look forward to seeing you in church Sunday."

The man's gray eyes clouded, his hard, callused hand dropped the coins in the pocket of the leather apron that protected him. "I don't go to church, Reverend. I figure all that praying and such is a waste of time. God's never done anything for—" The livery owner's straight, dark brown brows pulled down into a frown. "I'll leave it there. Details don't matter."

"They do to the Lord. But He already knows them."

"He don't pay them no mind."

"Perhaps you've misunderstood, Mr. Dibble." He smiled to take any challenge from his words, stroked his mare's neck and framed a careful reply to the man's acrimony. "God doesn't always answer our prayers as we hope or expect He will. Or perhaps God hasn't had time—"

"I understand all right. There ain't no way to not understand. And He's had time aplenty." David Dibble gave a curt nod and strode off toward his livery stables.

He watched him disappear into the shadowed interior. "I don't know what is causing Mr. Dibble's anger and bitterness, Lord, but I pray You will answer his prayers according to Your will. And that You will save his soul. Amen." He took a firm grip on Clover's halter and started for the road.

A buggy swept into the graveled yard, rumbled to a halt beside him. He glanced up, tugged on the halter and stopped his horse. "Good afternoon, Mr. Hall." He lifted his free hand and removed his hat, dipped his head in the passenger's direction. "Miss Hall."

"Good afternoon, Reverend Calvert." Ellen Hall's full, red lips curved upward. "How fortunate that we have chanced to meet. Isn't it, Father?"

The words were almost purred. Ellen Hall looked straight into his eyes, then swept her long, dark lashes down, tipped her head and fussed with a button on her glove. A practiced maneuver if he'd ever seen one—and he'd seen plenty back in Albany. He ignored her flirting and shifted his gaze back to Conrad Hall.

"Fortuitous indeed." The man's blue eyes peered at him from beneath dark, bushy brows. "Mrs. Hall and I would like to extend you a dinner invitation, Reverend. Tomorrow night. Our home is the second house on Oak Street, opposite the village park. We eat promptly at six o'clock."

The man's tone left no room for refusal. And it was certainly impolitic to turn down an invitation to dine with one of the founders of the church, but he had no choice. He chose his words carefully. "That's very kind of you and Mrs. Hall, sir, but I'm afraid I must decline. I'm not yet fully settled in and my children—"

"Will be welcome, Reverend. We shall see you at six tomorrow night." The man glanced at his daughter, then flicked the reins and drove off.

Ellen gave him a sidelong look from beneath her lashes, lifted her gloved hand in a small wave and smiled. He dipped his head in response, then replaced his hat and tugged the bay into motion.

"Did you see that, Clover?" His growled words were punctuated by the thud of the bay's hooves as he led her across the wood walk into the road. "If I ever see you flirting with a stallion like that, I'll trade you to Mr. Totten and you can spend the rest of your days pulling his trolley."

The horse snorted and tossed her head as he turned her toward home.

"What are you *doing* in here, Willa? The children are gone. And I've been waiting…" Ellen closed the door and swept down the aisle between the bench desks.

Willa snuffed the flame of the last lamp, raised the chandelier and turned to face her friend. "I was finishing a letter to Callie. I want to post it on my way home. You wanted something?"

"I have news."

She looked at Ellen's smug expression and shook her head. "Obviously, it pleases you."

"Oh, it does."

She nodded and stepped to the stove and twisted the handles to close the drafts for a slow burn that would preserve the fire for morning.

"Don't you want to hear my news?"

"Of course." She turned and grinned up at her friend. "And you will tell me as soon as you have your little dramatic moment." She stepped to her desk and picked up her basket.

"Oh, very well." Ellen hurried up beside her and gripped her forearm. "Reverend Calvert is coming for dinner tomorrow night!"

It took her aback. There was no denying it. And there was absolutely no reason why it should. She nodded and smiled. "That's quite a 'coup,' Ellen. Every young woman in the village has been hoping to have the reverend for dinner." She started for the door. "Was the dinner your father's idea, or—"

"He thinks it was." Ellen laughed and tugged the velvet collar on her coat higher as they went out the door. "I planned it, of course—with Mother's help."

Of course. "I'm surprised he accepted." *Really?* "I know he's turned down other invitations because of the children." *But those young women don't possess Ellen's beauty.* She stifled a spurt of disgust and hurried down the porch steps and turned toward town.

"Yes, I'd heard, so I planned for that. I had father tell him the children were welcome."

She stopped and stared up at Ellen. The smug look on her friend's face made her want to shake her. "And are they welcome?"

"Of course, as long as they don't get in the way. And they won't. I've made certain of that. They will have their own meal in the breakfast room. And Isobel has been instructed to keep them there until my performance is finished." Ellen smiled and patted her curls with a gloved hand. "I'm going to recite a Psalm. I want the reverend to see my spiritual side."

"I'm certain he will be duly impressed."

"He will be when he sees my new gown." Ellen laughed and moved ahead. "Bye, Willa." She waved a gloved hand and turned onto the stone walkway to her house.

Willa released the white-knuckled grip she had on the basket handle and marched down the sidewalk. Her disgust carried her all the way to Brody's meat market. She took a deep breath, pasted a smile on her face and went inside to buy pork chops for their supper. A supper that would have *included* children at the table—if she had had any.

Chapter Six

"**W**hat's wrong with you, Willa? You've not been yourself for a couple of days now." Her mother lifted an undershirt out of the last basket of clothes she'd taken off the line, gave it a sharp snap through the air and folded it. "What's got you so nettled?"

"Nothing, Mama." Willa pressed the hot iron along the sleeve of the shirt she'd laid flat on the table, lifted it, then slammed it down on the other sleeve and shoved it along the length to remove the wrinkles.

"Well, you're certainly acting riled. If you don't calm yourself, you're gonna break that table. You have a student giving you trouble?"

She glanced up and met her mother's assessing gaze, sighed and placed the iron in its trivet, then swiped the end of the towel draped over her shoulder across her moist, heat-flushed face. "No. It's Ellen. She told me yesterday the Halls were having Reverend Calvert and his children to supper tonight. And Ellen—well, she's being *Ellen*."

She snatched the pressed shirt off the table, folded

it, then unrolled another dampened one and smoothed it out on the table with her hands.

"Flirting with the pastor, you mean?" Her mother stilled, fixed a look on her. "That bother you, does it?"

"Certainly not! I don't care about Reverend Calvert. He can flirt with whomever he pleases. But the children…" She plucked the iron off its trivet and swept it over the body of the shirt. "I've told you how they are grieving, and Ellen made plans to feed them *alone* in the breakfast room. And she has ordered Isobel to keep them there until her entertainment is over." She took another swipe at the shirt with the iron, then cast a look at her mother. "She intends to recite a Psalm for the reverend. She wants him to see her *spiritual* side." She huffed out a breath, frowned down at the shirt on the table. It was still wrinkled.

"Your iron's cold."

There was something in her mother's voice. Was she *amused?* She glanced at her, but could not see her face. She looked down and tapped the iron with her fingertip. "So it is." She marched to the fireplace, set an iron trivet over a pile of hot coals and plunked the cold iron down on it, snatched up a hot one and went back to her work. "I feel sorry for Joshua and Sally being stuck in a room by themselves in a strange house all evening, that's all."

"Hmm."

There it was again. She jerked her head up, caught the remnant of a hastily erased smile on her mother's face. "Well, isn't it right that I should be concerned about the children? They *are* my students."

"Oh, yes indeed." Her mother nodded, ducked her head and began to fold the socks in the basket.

She stared at her mother's bowed head for a long moment, then carefully lowered the iron and pressed a sleeve, concentrating on removing every wrinkle to keep from thinking about Ellen wearing her new gown for Matthew Calvert's benefit.

He shouldn't have done it. He shouldn't have walked out like that. It certainly wasn't wisdom to anger Conrad Hall or his daughter. But when their maid had rushed in apologizing because the children had *escaped* her... Matthew glanced down at Sally kneeling beside her bed while she said her prayers and his face tightened. He would do it again.

"...and bless Josh and Uncle Matt and please don't ever, ever take them away. Amen." Sally rose from her knees and climbed into bed, her mother's glove clutched in her hand.

He swallowed hard and sucked in air. He couldn't bear the fear in Sally's voice when she uttered those words to close her nightly prayers. He'd tried so hard to reassure her that he and Joshua would be all right, but that tragic carriage accident had taught her that people she loved could be taken from her life in an instant. *Please comfort Sally, Lord. Please ease her grief and take away her fear.*

He looked down into her brown eyes, bright with tears, tucked the covers close beneath her little chin and leaned down to kiss her silky, soft cheek. Her small arms slid around his neck and squeezed.

"I didn't mean to be bad, Uncle Matt." Her little voice wobbled, broke on a sob. "I was scared 'cause I couldn't find you."

"I know, Sally." He pulled her into his arms and

hugged her close. "And you're not bad. You're a very good girl."

"The lady thought I was bad." She leaned back and looked up at him. "She was mad."

Yes, Ellen had been angry when Josh had brought Sally to him, although she had tried to hide it behind a pretended concern for the children. He cleared the lump from his throat, straightened and smiled down at her. "Miss Hall didn't understand you were afraid." He wiped away her tears and covered her little hands with his. His fingers brushed against Judith's glove. "Sometimes people get angry when they don't understand. Now you go to sleep. I'll see you in the morning."

"Bertha said she'd make me and Josh pancakes. Will you eat pancakes with us?"

"I sure will." The reassurance seemed to comfort her. She sighed and closed her eyes. "Good night, Sally." He rubbed her cheek with the back of his finger, glanced at the fire to make sure it didn't need tending and walked out the door.

What was he to do about the glove? He had to decide soon. He frowned and made his way along the hall and stepped into Joshua's bedroom. "All settled in, Joshua?"

"Yes, sir." His nephew peered up at him from beneath his covers. "I brushed my teeth and said my prayers."

An ache swelled in his heart. Joshua looked so much like Robert. He acted like him, too, always trying to do the right thing. "Good man." He smiled, ruffled Joshua's blond curls, noted the unhappy look in the boy's brown eyes and sat down on the side of the bed. "Is something bothering you, Joshua?"

The boy stared up at him a moment, then nodded.

"Do we have to go and have supper at that house again? Sally was crying. She didn't like being away from you."

And neither did you. He looked down into Joshua's brown eyes, clouded with concerns and fears no little boy should have to carry, and shook his head. "Perhaps someday. But I promise you we will not go to the Halls' for supper again anytime soon." *Even if we are invited, which is doubtful after the way I walked out of there.* He leaned down close and lowered his voice. "Want to know a secret?"

Joshua's eyes widened, his curls bobbed as he nodded.

"I didn't like eating my supper away from you and Sally, either."

"You didn't?"

He gave a solemn shake of his head. "Nope."

The boy blinked, swallowed hard. "'Cause we're a family now, even if we haven't got a mama, right?"

The words squeezed his heart and constricted his throat. "Right." He pushed the word out and pulled Joshua into a close hug, fought back tears as his nephew threw his arms around his neck and buried his head against his shoulder and held on tight.

"I miss Mama and Papa."

The tears surged, smarted his eyes. Joshua tried so hard to be brave, but he was only a scared little boy. He tightened his hold and pressed his cheek against his nephew's soft, blond curls and cleared his throat. "I know you do, Josh… I know. But I promise you it will get better." *God, please help me make it better for Josh and Sally.*

Matthew poured coffee into his cup, set the pot on the cool surface at the back of the stove and crossed the kitchen to look out the window. His breath steamed the cold glass. He wiped away the fog with his palm and stared at the touch of frost on the curled edges of the dried leaves on the path to the stables.

What a failure of an evening. He frowned, leaned his shoulder against the window frame and took a swallow of the hot coffee. He never would have agreed to the dinner date had he known Ellen intended to shunt Joshua and Sally aside to spend the evening in a room by themselves. He had thought they were being entertained, until Sally had panicked and Joshua had brought her to find him.

He circled the cup in the air, watched the dark, hot brew swirl around, then took another swallow. Ellen had pretended compassion at Sally's sobs, and he'd almost believed her.

I know you have only recently become the guardian of your dear wards, Reverend Calvert, so a bit of advice from an experienced father might be in order. Father always says children need discipline, that you must keep a firm hand with them. I'm sure you agree.

His fingers tightened around his cup. Ellen's voice had been silky, her smile a sweet one meant to win his accord, but she knew Joshua and Sally had recently been orphaned, and her words had chilled him. He considered her comments insensitive and inappropriate. However, he had to admit she was right in one thing—he was inexperienced at being a father. Was he wrong in his treatment of the children? Was his sympathy for their grief only making it worse? Should he simply take Judith's glove from Sally and be done with it?

He scowled down at his cup. The coffee had lost its appeal. He crossed to the sink cupboard, tossed the rest of the brew into the bucket on the shelf below, put the cup in the dishpan and headed for his study. He needed some answers and he knew only one place to find them. He had some praying to do.

Shivers prickled her flesh. Willa brushed her hair, grabbed a ribbon off the commode stand and ran across the plank floor and climbed into bed.

Another shiver shook her. She gathered her long hair at the nape of her neck, tied it with the ribbon, then snuffed the lamp and slid beneath the covers. The air sneaking through the cracks around the window by the side of the bed touched her exposed cheek. She tugged the quilt higher, turned on her side and curled into a ball. The bed warmed. Her shivering stopped. She sighed, relaxed her taut muscles and closed her eyes.

Callie's letter. It was still in her lunch basket. She'd forgotten to mail it yesterday. She frowned and stretched out, wiggled her feet to warm their new place. That's what she got for allowing herself to be so irritated by Ellen's plans. She would mail the letter tomorrow, although the way the temperature was plummeting she didn't even want to think about morning. At least she didn't have to get up early and make that cold walk in the dark to school. Tomorrow was Saturday. She yawned, snuggled deeper beneath the covers and waited for the pleasant, drifting sensation of approaching sleep.

Had Matthew Calvert been awed by Ellen's beauty tonight? Had he enjoyed himself flirting with Ellen while his children were hidden away in the breakfast room?

She scowled, snapped her eyes open and stared into the darkness, all somnolence set to flight by her demanding thoughts. Why was she lying there thinking about the reverend and Ellen? It was the children she cared about…only the children. She yanked the quilt tighter against her back and again closed her eyes. But try as she would to concentrate on Joshua and Sally, it was images of Matthew Calvert flirting with Ellen that filled her head before sleep swept her into oblivion.

Chapter Seven

❧

Willa smiled at the wagon shop owner who had opened the door to Cargrave Mercantile and stepped back to let her pass. "Good morning, Mr. Turner." She lifted the hem of her long skirt and stepped over the threshold.

"Nippy out this morning."

"Yes, it is." She looked toward the back of the store and smiled at the elderly men seated on chairs and leaning toward the checker board on top of the large keg in front of the stove. "You're frowning, Mr. Fabrizio. Are you losing to Mr. Grant…*again?*"

The man straightened at her teasing. His bald head gleamed in the lamplight and his bushy gray eyebrows cast shadows over the dark eyes twinkling up at her. He raised one weathered hand to cover his heart, murmured something in his native Italian, winked and flashed her a grin she was sure had captured many a young woman's heart in his youth.

She had learned enough Italian to know that whatever else he had said, he'd called her beautiful. She pushed her hood off to hang down her back and shook her head. "I should know better than to tease you, Mr. Fabrizio. You are an incorrigible flirt."

She joined in the men's laughter, pulled Callie's letter from her basket and stepped to the open window in the wall of pigeonhole mailboxes. "Good morning, Mr. Hubble."

"Morning, Willa." The postmaster paused in his task of sliding mail into the small cubicles and squinted at her through his wire-rimmed glasses. "Who's the letter for this time—Callie or Sadie?"

"Callie." She placed the letter on the small shelf on the other side of the open window, watched as he wrote down the rate on the top right corner, then handed him the coins.

The door behind her opened. The attached bells announced a new customer. She glanced over her shoulder, smiled as a strikingly lovely older woman entered. "Good morning, Mrs. Sheffield."

The older woman's eyes warmed, her lips curved into an affectionate smile. "*Willa,* how lovely to see you." She peered at her from beneath the brim of her fur-trimmed coal scuttle bonnet. "I have to place an order for supplies and then I am going home. Would you have time to come and join me for a cup of tea? It's been too long since we've had a real visit."

"I would enjoy that, Mrs. Sheffield. I have to purchase some things for Mama, but then I can come along."

"Lovely. I shall see you then." The woman patted her arm, moved to the counter, laid down a list in front of Allan Cargrave, who was measuring coffee beans into a small burlap bag for another customer, then lifted her hand in farewell. The bells tinkled her departure.

Willa selected the darning supplies she'd come after and dropped them into her basket. She moved along the shelves, admired a packet of fancy pearl buttons, then ran her fingers over the end of a new bolt of bottle-green velvet. What would it be like to wear a dress of such soft, beautiful fabric trimmed with such lovely buttons? Surely such a gown would catch Matthew Calvert's eye.

She stiffened and withdrew her hand. No doubt Ellen would soon find out. Mrs. Hall was certain to purchase the new fabric and buttons for her dressmaker's shop, and Ellen was as certain to cajole her mother into making her a dress out of them. She would look beautiful in the velvet.

A twinge of envy shot through her. She frowned and headed for the counter. What was wrong with her? She had never before been envious of any of her friends' good fortune.

The scent of coffee lingered in the air. She set her opened basket on the counter, took a sniff and smiled. "That coffee smells good, Mr. Cargrave. I'll take a bag of 'Old Java.' And I need indigo and baking soda for Mama, please."

Willa followed the path that led around the Sheffield house and climbed the back stairs to the porch that stretched the length of the large building.

She crossed to the settle benches standing guard at both sides of the kitchen door and paused, overcome by a sudden rush of sentiment. How many times had she visited this house with Callie through the years? Sophia Sheffield had always welcomed her niece's friends. Memories flowed, tugged her lips into a grin.

She glanced at the far end of the porch, then hurried to

peer over the railing at the vertical boards that enclosed the space beneath. The third board from the corner had been loose and she and Callie used to crawl inside and share their childhood hurts and dreams. It was their secret place. Theirs and Sadie's. Sadie had been invited in, but no one else. Callie had been firm about that, and because it was her aunt's house, she had the say. They had all been unhappy at excluding their friend Ellen, but she had liked to gossip even then, and Callie warned that Ellen would tell. They had all stuck to their rule.

Her grin widened. Gracious, she hadn't thought about their hiding place in years. She would have to mention it the next time she wrote Callie. Was the board still loose? She looked closely but couldn't tell. Still, it was not likely. It must have been discovered and repaired by now. Her smile faded. She had shed a lot of tears under this porch after her father deserted her and her mother. And said a lot of prayers, as well. God had chosen not to answer them—if He had bothered to listen.

She turned and walked back to the kitchen door and rapped lightly.

"Come in!"

The door creaked as it always had. The delicious aroma of meat roasting on a spit in the fireplace scented the air. She turned and placed her basket on the table where she had shared many a cookie with Callie, pushed back her hood and removed her cloak. Warmth from the cooking fire chased the chill from her face and hands as she hung it on a peg beside the door. "It always smells wonderful in here."

"I guess that's because, with a hotel full of guests, we're always cooking or baking something."

She turned and looked down the length of the large kitchen. "Mrs. Sheffield! Where is Rose?"

Sophia Sheffield laid the spoon she was using to baste the meat back into the pan on the hearth that was catching the juices and straightened. "The poor woman has badly strained her back. She's in her room resting."

She nodded and eyed the puffy brown rounds cooling on the long work table that occupied the center of the space between the huge stone fireplace and the iron cook stove on the opposite wall. "Are those molasses cookies? They were Sadie's favorites."

"Callie's, too." Sophia nodded, lifted the steaming teakettle from the stove and poured hot water into the china teapot sitting on a tray beside the cookies. "You favored the 'white ones.'"

Hearing her childhood name for sugar cookies tugged her lips into another grin. "I still do." She stepped forward and carried the tea tray to the small table while Sophia put the kettle back on the stove. There were two cups and saucers on the table—china ones with blue vines circling the rims. It used to be three tin cups of milk. She sighed and took her seat. "Wouldn't it be lovely if Callie and Sadie were here, Mrs. Sheffield?"

"It would indeed, Willa. You pour, dear." The older woman set a plate of cookies on the table and sat down opposite her. "After what Sadie endured at Payne Aylward's hands, I doubt she will ever return to Pinewood, but I'm hoping Callie will come for a visit soon. It's been almost a year since I've seen her. And I'm quite sure she is unhappy in Buffalo. It doesn't seem possible it's been four years since Barbara and Michael moved away." A frown creased her high forehead. "Has Callie written you about coming home?"

"Nothing certain." She poured tea into their cups, set the teapot back on the tray and reached for the cream. I hate my life here in the city, Willa. *Don't tell Aunt Sophie because she will be concerned for me, but Mother and Father parade me in front of the wealthy, elite men of this place in hope of arranging a "favorable" marriage that will increase their wealth and improve their social status. I so wish we had never moved from Pinewood.*

"I saw Ellen the other day. She told me they were having the new preacher and his wards for supper. Ellen seems quite taken with the man."

Sophia's voice drew her thoughts from Callie, replaced them with an image of Ellen wearing her new gown and reciting a Psalm for Matthew Calvert. "Yes, she does." It came out much sharper than she intended. She glanced at Sophia's raised eyebrows, the questioning look in her violet-blue eyes and hastened to change the subject. "The pastor's wards are my students. They are lovely, well-behaved children. It's so sad that they lost their parents so tragically."

The door leading to the Sheffield House dining room opened and one of Sophia's maids stepped in. "Excuse me, Mrs. Sheffield, but there's a man come to stay. He's waiting in your office."

"Thank you, Katie." Sophia sighed and rose. "I'll only be a minute, Willa. And then we'll continue our visit." A smile creased her lovely face. "Meanwhile, have a cookie—even if they aren't 'white ones.'"

The sun had burned through the overcast sky while she was visiting with Sophia. Willa walked down the porch steps and pushed her hood off her head to let the warmth of the golden rays touch her face. The ripple of water brushing against weed-covered banks drew her gaze toward the river that flowed behind the stable. It was tame now, but in the spring the Allegheny would overflow its banks and flood the surrounding field. That area had been forbidden them as children, but they had often played in the stable.

She turned onto the path, caught movement out of the corner of her eye and turned back. A yellow kitten, chased by a small, black-and-white, barking dog, darted beneath a denuded bush growing at the corner of the stable.

"Shoo! Leave that kitten alone!" She set her basket on the steps and hurried down the path, waving her arms to distract the young dog from its prey. It barked, then turned tail and ran into the stable. The kitten crouched into a ball and stared up at her.

"Well, hello." She reached behind the bush. The kitten darted toward the open stable door. She quickly shifted her position so her long skirts blocked its way. She scooped it up, lifted it level with her face and smiled at its frightened mews.

"You have nothing to be afraid of. The puppy is gone and I'll not hurt you." She cuddled the trembling kitten close, stroked between its tiny ears and looked around for its mother, or more of the litter. There were no others in sight. She looked at the kitten, its tiny front paws now pushing against her cloak, its mouth searching for a source of sustenance, and frowned. It seemed awfully thin. She lifted it up to examine it more closely. "Are you an orphan?"

Sally. The name popped into her head, jolted her. Sally… Perhaps… She stared at the kitten, then again cuddled it close and hurried back down the path to talk with Sophia.

* * *

"Excuse me for interrupting your work, Reverend, but Willa—I mean Miss Wright—is outside. Says she'd like to talk with you."

Willa Wright wanted to see him? Matthew frowned and squelched the spurt of pleasure that shot through him. Of one thing he was certain—her call was not prompted by a desire to be in his company. "Please show her into the sitting room, Bertha. I'll be right along." He wiped the nib of his pen and blotted his notes for tomorrow's sermon.

"She doesn't want to come in. She asked particular that you come outside."

He stared at his housekeeper, then grabbed his suit jacket off the back of the chair and shrugged it on as he followed her to the kitchen.

"She's out there." Bertha Franklin nodded toward the door that led to the side porch and turned to the stove.

He straightened his cravat, smoothed the sides of his hair with the heels of his hands and stepped outside. She was standing at the end of the porch. Their gazes met. His heart lurched. "You wanted to speak with me, Miss Wright?"

"Yes. Thank you for coming outside." Her cool tone settled his pulse back to its normal beat. She stepped toward him. "I realize it's a most unusual request, but I didn't want the children to know I'm here. In case you don't—" She stopped, drew a breath. "Let me explain."

He nodded, forced himself to concentrate on her words instead of her.

"The other night during the carriage ride—" She paused, gave him a questioning look. "You do remember taking me home the night of the storm?"

"Quite well, yes." He should, it had cost him an hour or so of tossing and turning before he got to sleep. She evidently didn't like his answer for her chin raised and her shoulders squared beneath her cloak.

"Then you will recall telling me about Sally sleeping with her mother's glove, and asking for my advice."

Her voice softened when she spoke of Sally, her gaze turned warm and earnest. He lost his focus.

"I had no answer for you then, but I promised if one occurred to me I would tell you. I've come today because I believe I may have found one. If it meets with your approval of course. A kitten."

It was a moment before it sank in. "A *kitten*." What sort of an answer was that? He must have missed something. He frowned, mustered his senses.

She nodded and rushed into speech. "I know it seems odd, Reverend Calvert. I thought so, too. But then I realized— The only thing I have seen Sally truly interested in was the kitten story and contest. So, when I saw the kitten, I thought if Sally had a kitten to love and care for, it would take her mind off of her grief, at least part of the time. And—"

"Whoa. Wait a moment, Miss Wright."

She shot him a look of consternation.

He smiled and shook his head. "I'm not disagreeing, I simply need to catch up. What kitten?"

"I went to visit Sophia Sheffield earlier and discovered, quite by accident, that one of the stable cats had kittens. You see, a dog was chasing the kitten and—"

"Mrs. Sheffield's dog."

"No." She shook her head. "The dog—well, little more than a puppy really—is a stray hanging around her stable. Anyway, the dog was chasing the kitten and that's why I discovered it. And then I thought of Sally, and of how loving and caring for a kitten might help her over her grief."

"Yes, I see…" He gazed down into her incredible blue-green eyes, warm with compassion, earnest in her hope for Sally's healing. "And Mrs. Sheffield is willing to let Sally have the kitten?"

"*A* kitten, yes. She gets to choose. Unless you want Sally to have all three of them."

"Three?" Her eyes flashed with amusement. Her lips twitched, curved in a smile that made his pulse race. "I believe one will be sufficient." He turned toward the door. "I'll get Sally and Joshua, and you can take us to the kittens."

"There's one more thing."

She sounded hesitant. He turned back. "And that is?"

"I thought, perhaps, if you would allow Sally to take the kitten into her bed at night so she could cuddle it." She took a breath. "She can't do that while she is holding her mother's glove."

"Stop that barking! Get out of here!"

A stone came flying from the depths of the stable and hit the dog in the doorway. It yelped and ran off, crawled behind a clump of brush.

The stable hand stepped into view. "Way's clear now." He looked in the direction the dog ran, then walked back inside, muttering. "I'm gonna have to do somethin' about that cur. Can't have him barkin' at Mrs. Sheffield's guests when they come to the stable. Spookin' the horses all day…"

"Why did that man pitch a stone at the dog, Uncle Matt?"

He looked down at Joshua's face, noted the offended look in his eyes and squatted down to his level. "Mrs. Sheffield runs a hotel. She has a lot of guests and some of them keep their horses here in her stable. They have to be able to come in and out. And some of their horses are frightened by the dog's barking. It makes them restive. Do you understand?"

"Yes, sir. The dog shouldn't be round the stable."

He squeezed Joshua's shoulder, rose and took Sally's hand. "Lead on, Miss Wright."

She nodded and moved ahead. "This way."

"Why are we going in the barn, Uncle Matt?"

"You'll see, Sally."

Sunlight slanted in through the open door, lit their way across the plank floor strewn with bits of hay and seed. A ball of orange-and-yellow fur darted out of the shadowed area behind a grain box in the corner and attacked another ball of black-and-white fur that was swatting at a string dangling from a burlap bag draped over the wall of a stall.

"Kitties!" Sally pulled her hand free and ran forward. The black-and-white kitten darted between two boards in the stall and disappeared. The orange-and-yellow one ducked back behind the grain box. Sally wedged the toe of her boot into a crack in the wall and scrambled on top of the chest, peered behind it. He'd never seen her so lively. "I can't reach them, Joshua!"

There was no answer. No brother running to Sally's rescue. He gave a quick glance around. Where did Joshua go? He frowned, stepped to the grain chest. "I'll get them, Sally." He reached for the orange-and-yellow kitten, got scratched for his effort. "A fighter, are you?"

He captured the kitten, pulled it up and handed it to Sally. It jumped free of her grasp and ran into the stall.

"The kitty doesn't like me."

Sally's eyes teared up. Her little lower lip trembled. He vowed to stay there until he had caught one of the elusive felines and headed for the stall door.

"Look what I've found."

He turned back, watched Willa Wright reach behind a barrel, then straighten with a mewing, yellow kitten in her hands. She cooed to it, stroked it between its tiny pointed ears and carried it over to Sally. He couldn't take his gaze from Willa's face, the softness in her eyes, the gentle look of her mouth.

"Hold it gently and speak softly, Sally. It's only a baby and is frightened. If you hold it close, it will feel safe."

Sally nodded and cuddled the kitten against her velvet cloak. "Don't be afraid, kitty. I like you." The kitten stretched up and licked her chin. She giggled and looked up at it, her brown eyes shining with happiness. "The kitty likes me."

He nodded and cleared his throat, saw Willa Wright turn her back and raise her hand to wipe her cheeks. She moved in the direction of the door. He gritted his teeth and stayed rooted in place. He had no right to go to her—to keep her close.

"Can I have the kitty, Uncle Matt?"

He drew his thoughts back from the path they had started down and squatted in front of Sally. "A baby kitten needs a lot of love and care, Sally. You would have to give it food to eat and milk to drink every day. And take it outside and play with it after school. Can you do that?"

She gave a solemn nod.

"All right, then. You may have the kitten." He leaned forward and kissed her cheek, then glanced around. "You stay right here, Sally. I have to find Joshua."

"He's outside."

Willa Wright sounded odd—a little choked. He rose and hurried to her side. "Where?"

She glanced up at him, then looked away. "Beside the brush pile."

He looked where she had indicated. Joshua was on his back on the ground, laughing and squirming as the dog on his chest licked his face.

He sucked in a breath and looked down at her, fixed his face in a mock scowl to cover his feelings. "A stray dog, Miss Wright?" Her gaze skittered away from his, but not before he'd caught the flash of satisfaction in her teary eyes.

"*Was* a stray dog, Reverend Calvert. I believe that puppy has found his owner." She lifted her chin and stepped over the log sill onto the gravel wagon way.

He stared after her. So prim and proper. So beautiful and loving toward the children. *Glory,* but he wanted that woman in his arms!

Chapter Eight

Willa skimmed her gaze from the deep, rich lace on the gown's round neck that left Ellen's shoulders bare, down the fitted bodice, to the long, full skirt that cascaded from the pointed waist in a series of folds caught up at intervals with satin knots. "It's a beautiful dress, Ellen. And you look especially beautiful in it."

Ellen laughed and did a slow pirouette. "Reverend Calvert thought so. He kept stealing glances at me during dinner."

"I'm sure he did." A twinge of irritation trickled through her. She should have made an excuse and continued on home when Ellen asked her to come see her new dress. She was losing patience with Ellen's vanity.

"Do you like my headdress, Willa? Mother copied it from a picture in *Godey's Lady's Book*." Ellen leaned over her dresser and looked in her mirror, touched one of the flowers that adorned the broad ribbon encircling her blond curls.

"It's lovely. Your mother makes wonderful flowers. I've always admired her skill." She stared at the deep lace that had fallen back to expose Ellen's wrist when she lifted her hand to the headdress. How many times had Ellen used that ploy to draw Matthew Calvert's attention to her beauty? She looked down at her own high-necked, dark blue wool dress, its only adornment a narrow blue ribbon at her small waist. It was not a garment to draw a man's eye—not that she wanted to. She'd learned her lesson when Thomas deserted her. All those proclamations of undying love…

She thrust away thoughts of Thomas, caught Ellen's gaze in the mirror and smiled. "Your mother was right. The blue of that Turkish satin does make your eyes look larger and more blue than usual—especially with the matching ribbon."

She turned away from Ellen's prideful smile and noticed her friend's Bible on the bedside table. "How was your recitation of the Psalm? Was the reverend suitably impressed?"

"He was, until those *wards* of his escaped Isobel."

"Escaped?" She glanced over her shoulder. Ellen was still admiring herself in the mirror. "That's an odd word to use."

"Oh, I assure you the word is appropriate. I told you Isobel was to keep them in the morning room until I had finished my entertainment." Ellen spun from the mirror to face her. "That girl started crying because Isobel told her she couldn't go to Matthew, and the naughty thing ran from the room! The boy stepped in front of Isobel when she tried to grab the girl, then ran to his sister and brought her, whining and crying, into the living room right in the middle of my recitation! They quite stole Reverend Calvert's attention from me. I was furious—until it occurred to me that I could turn the situation to my profit."

"In what way?" What did it matter? It shouldn't matter. So why was she holding her breath?

"Why, to increase the reverend's interest in me as his future bride. His glances told me he finds me attractive, but of course, a man in his position must consider his wards, so I acted concerned for them. And then I suggested that he, being a new guardian, might profit by following Father's admonition that children must be disciplined with a firm hand." Ellen's lips curled.

She stared at her friend's smug smile. Ellen hadn't always been so callous and self-serving. Perhaps she didn't truly understand the situation. "Those children have suffered a great loss, Ellen. And they are in a new town, among people who are strangers to them. How could you suggest they needed discipline for wanting to be with their uncle?"

Ellen's gaze sharpened. "It so happened the reverend agreed with me, Willa. He took his wards off that very moment to put them abed." The smug smile returned. "I believe he was quite impressed by my maternal skills."

A heavy, sick feeling hit the pit of her stomach. Matthew Calvert had punished Sally and Joshua for interrupting his evening of flirtation with Ellen after the loss they had suffered? How could that be after the way he had so readily embraced her idea this morning and allowed them to have the kitten and the dog? Of course, if the pets helped the children heal from their grief and they were no longer so dependent on him, he would have more time for his other…pursuits. Anger chilled her. No wonder Matthew Calvert had appealed to her sympathy and asked for her advice.

"And, of course, Mother told him I had planned the entire evening—that I had chosen the menu, arranged for his wards to have their meal apart from the adults, and planned my recitation for his entertainment, so he is also aware of my homemaking and hostessing abilities. It's very important a pastor's wife possess such talents."

"Wife?" She snapped her gaping mouth closed. "You barely know Reverend Calvert, Ellen. What are you thinking? What of love?"

"Oh, I love him, Willa. Why would I not? He is exceedingly handsome and charming, and, most important, he holds a position of respect in the community. He is the perfect husband for me." Ellen smiled and did another slow pirouette in front of the mirror. "I've already told Father to accept when Matthew asks permission to court me."

Matthew? Ellen was calling him by his first name? He must have been *very* attentive last night. She closed her mind to the unwelcome images the thought conjured. "And what about Joshua and Sally?"

"Joshua and— Oh, his wards." Ellen shrugged her bare shoulders. "They won't be a problem. I'll manage them, just as I did last night. Only, when Matthew and I are married, they will soon learn they will be punished if they disobey."

"I see." She turned toward the door to hide her face. There was no telling what her expression would betray. "I must be going, Ellen. Mama is waiting for her indigo."

"Very well, Willa. I shall see you in church tomorrow."

The satin of Ellen's dress rustled. She glanced back over her shoulder and clenched her hands on the basket handle. She needn't have worried about betraying her anger. Ellen was already back before her mirror practicing her coquettish smiles.

Willa scowled at the toes of her boots rapidly flashing into view, one after the other, from beneath her skirt hems. How could she have let herself be deceived by that—that *manipulator?* How could she have believed for one instant that Matthew Calvert's requests for her help were based in an unselfish concern for Joshua and Sally's well-being? He had shown his true colors last night at the Halls', punishing those children for their need to feel cared about and safe. Well, he needn't think that she—

"Oh!" She bumped against a hard body. Strong hands clasped her shoulders, held firm when she tried to step back from the close contact. "Unhand me, sir!" She raised her free hand and shoved against the plaid jacket covering the man's chest.

"You don't mean that, Willa."

Thomas! Shock froze her. She lifted her head, gazed into the twinkling blue eyes that had so mesmerized her and came roaring back to life. "Let go of me, Thomas."

"Never, Willa. I came back to claim you for my own, and—"

"I'm not interested in your *lies,* Thomas. *Let me go!*" She dropped her basket and pushed at his arms.

Footsteps thudded against the ground, large, callused hands flashed into her view, clamped on Thomas's shoulders and pulled him away from her. David Dibble stepped in front of her, blocked Thomas from her with his body. "Be on your way, Hunter. Miss Willa doesn't want to talk to you."

Willa caught her breath at the menace in David Dibble's voice. She stared at the blue shirt stretched across his broad shoulders, at the hint of curl in the gray-brown hair that covered his nape and brushed his collar. She could swear it was bristling. Surely he wouldn't fight Thomas on her account? Tears sprang to her eyes.

"I'll go, but I'm not giving up. I'll see you again, Willa."

She drew a breath of relief, closed her eyes and listened to Thomas's retreating footsteps. Boots scuffed against the ground. She opened her eyes and looked up at David Dibble. There was anger in his gray eyes...and concern. Genuine concern. For her?

"You all right, Miss Willa?"

The concern was in his voice, too. She blinked away the tears and nodded.

He crouched down onto his heels, picked up the packet of buttons and bag of coffee off the ground, put them back in her basket, rose and held it out to her. "If Hunter bothers you again, you let me know. I'll put a stop to it."

Tears clogged her throat. She swallowed hard and took hold of the basket handle. "Thank you, Mr. Dibble."

The anger in his eyes softened. He gave a curt nod and touched the rolled brim of his knitted hat. "Remember me to your mama."

"I shall." She watched him stride back to his livery, then hurried to the bridge, rushed across and turned onto Brook Street.

She scanned the area for any sign of Thomas, and finding none, hastened down the beaten path to their cabin. The door hinges creaked their welcome. She dashed inside, closed the door and leaned back against it to catch her breath.

"What took you so long, Willa? I've been waiting for— What's wrong? What's happened?" Her mother threw down the towel she held and started toward her.

She straightened and shook her head. "I hurried and ran out of breath."

Her mother stopped, fixed a look on her. "You might as well tell me the rest of it, Willa Jean. I'll hear soon enough anyway."

Her bravado crumpled. Her desire to spare her mother the stressful news was swept away by a strong, almost overwhelming need to be comforted. "Oh, Mama, Thomas is back. He stopped me by the bridge and wouldn't let me go. I tried to push him away, but—" The tears she'd been fighting back spilled over. She went into her mother's open arms and laid her head on her thin shoulder. So many times she had cried away her hurts and her confusion in her mother's arms. "Mr. Dibble saw my struggle and came and pulled Thomas away from me. He made him leave. And he told me if Thomas bothered me again I was to come and tell him. That he would make him stop."

She sniffed and drew back. Her mother's eyes were bright with unshed tears. "Why would he do that, Mama?"

"Because that's the kind of man David Dibble is, Willa. He's a fine, fine man. Now, you go wash your face and rest a bit lest your head start to pain you. I have work to do."

Her mother touched her cheek, took the basket from her and walked into the kitchen. She stared after her. There had been something in her mother's voice when she spoke of David Dibble. It had been quickly covered, but it had been there. And it was something she'd never heard before.

A fine, fine man. She shook her head and headed for her room. There was no such thing in her experience.

Matthew started up the stairs, heard muffled giggles, smiled and went back to his study. The bedtime prayers could wait, he would give them a few more minutes to play with their pets. He shot a glance toward the ceiling. Did Robert and Judith know? Did they hear their children laughing?

He strolled over to his desk. What a blessing to hear the children's clandestine laughter instead of the dreaded, bedtime silence filled with their quiet sobs. "Thank You, Lord. Thank You that Joshua and Sally are laughing again."

What a debt he owed to Willa Wright for her suggestion about the kitten and puppy. There had been mild mayhem around the parsonage all afternoon and evening, what with Joshua and Sally darting in and out of rooms chasing after their exploring pets, and then laughing and racing around the yard trying to catch them when they took them outside.

He glanced down at his Bible and chuckled. An odd thing to be thankful for…mayhem. And Mrs. Franklin. Another blessing brought into their lives by Willa Wright. The housekeeper was stern in appearance, but she had a heart for the children—and they knew it. They hadn't even hesitated about running to the kitchen and showing her their pets and begging dishes of food and milk for them.

A log burned through, broke into pieces and sent a

shower of sparks up the chimney. He walked over and added another chunk of wood to the fire. The housekeeper was a blessing all right. She'd glanced his way, caught his nod and complied, but she'd told Joshua and Sally they would be responsible for keeping their pets' dishes clean, that she had enough work to do. And then she'd told them the kitten and puppy would need a place to stay while they were in school and she'd put an old towel on the floor behind the stove where it was always warm. "Lord, I pray You will bless Mrs. Franklin for her kind heart."

He glanced up at the wall clock. He could wait no longer to settle the children and hear their prayers or they would be tired for church tomorrow. He left his study and climbed the stairs into the silence, paused. There was something different. The quiet felt…peaceful.

He tiptoed down the hall and quietly opened Joshua's bedroom door. The boy was sound asleep, a smile on his face, one skinny arm draped over the puppy sprawled across his small chest. So much for the dog bed they'd made out of a blanket and placed on the floor in the corner. He grinned, crossed to the nightstand and snuffed the lamp, tiptoed back out into the hall, closed the door and walked to Sally's room.

"Please, Lord…" He held his breath and opened the door. Sally was curled up on her side, her eyes closed, her small, pink lips slighted parted in sleep. One of her long curls was caught in the tiny paws of the kitten cuddled beneath her chin. He expelled the breath to ease the sudden pressure in his chest and crossed to the night table. Judith's glove was lying at the base of the lamp. The pressure swelled, his throat tightened. *Thank You,*

Lord. Thank You. He snuffed the lamp, crept from the room and quietly closed the door.

Light from the lamp on the wall sconce threw a golden circle on the floor. He stood there staring at the pattern in the carpet runner for a long moment, then cleared the lump from his throat, shook his head and started down the stairs. Whoever would have thought he would rejoice that his niece and nephew had fallen asleep without saying their nightly prayers?

Willa stared into the darkness willing sleep to come, but the uncomfortable, tight feel of her body defeated her. She stretched and turned onto her side and tried to restrain her tumbling thoughts. They refused to obey her bidding.

Why had Thomas come back? What had happened to his dream of going west? *Something* had happened. She didn't, for one moment, believe he had come home because he loved her.

I came back to claim you for my own.

Hah! She huffed a breath and flopped onto her other side. As if she would believe that lie! A man who loves you and wants you for his own doesn't walk out on you three days before you're to be wed.

What was she to do? The news of Thomas's return would have spread through the village like the flood waters of the Allegheny River in the spring—even faster. And tomorrow was Sunday. She couldn't even stay home and hide for a day while she thought about what to do. Everyone would be waiting and watching to see what she—

Oh, no! She bolted upright, her heart pounding. Everyone thought Thomas had left with her blessing. They would expect her to joyously welcome him back.

A pang of guilt struck. So did the cold, damp night air.

She shivered, flopped back onto her pillow and tugged the quilt up to her chin. Talk about being hoist by your own petard. She should have told the truth and faced the shame of Thomas's desertion. Still… Thomas would never cast himself in a bad light. He would not tell anyone about his foul treatment of her. She had only to wait a few days and then simply refuse his suit. There would be no stigma raised if she changed her mind. Everything would work out fine.

She yawned, turned on her side and closed her eyes. Everything would turn out fine.…

Chapter Nine

"It's only until church is over, pup." Matthew scratched behind the whining dog's ears, opened the lid of the kitten's basket he'd set on top of the grain chest, closed the stable door and walked back to the house. Childish chatter and the calm responses of the housekeeper floated out of the kitchen. His heart swelled with thankfulness. Those pets had changed the entire atmosphere of the house. He picked up his sermon notes from his study and strode to the kitchen doorway. "I'm going to the church now, Mrs. Franklin."

The older woman nodded, put another piece of jam-slathered bread in front of Joshua. "We'll be coming as soon as these poke-alongs finish their breakfast and I get them fit out in their Sunday best."

Joshua shoved a spoonful of oatmeal into his mouth and lifted his head. "I'm not a poke-along, Uncle Matt. I'm just hungry."

He grinned at his tousle-haired nephew. "If you lick that elderberry jam off your cheek it should help ease that hunger problem."

Sally giggled.

"You, too, princess." He tapped a spot above the corner of his mouth, winked at her and stepped back into the entrance hall to check his own appearance.

The face that stared back at him from the mirror was nice-looking enough in a woman's eyes, he supposed. At least there were no major flaws he could see. He frowned and smoothed the hair at his temples *again,* straightened the folds on his cravat *again,* looked himself in the eye and shook his head. He'd never before had this hunger for a woman's approval. This gnawing eagerness, this *need* to have one look on him with favor. Willa Wright, and her cool demeanor, had changed all of that.

He turned from the mirror, walked to the door and stepped out into the cold morning air. The mere thought of seeing the woman had his stomach taut with anticipation. Willa Wright was not as distant as she acted, and he couldn't wait to look into her beautiful blue-green eyes and watch the warmth come into them as he shared with her the amazing change in the children her suggestion regarding the pets had wrought.

A cloud of warm breath formed in front of his face as he trotted down the steps to the frost-covered ground and strode toward the church. Why did she affect such a cool remoteness? He had never before experienced the sense of shared purpose, of *oneness* he'd felt when he talked with her about the children the other day. And he wanted to see that warmth in her eyes because of *him.* He wanted Willa Wright to look on him with— more than favor.

He puffed out another cloud and entered the church through the back room. The chill was gone. He laid his notes on the altar, moved to the stove and added more wood to the fire he'd started earlier. A wisp of concern he didn't want to acknowledge drifted into his mind. Where did Willa stand in her relationship with God? It was something he'd wondered about. She came to church, but people attended church for many different reasons, and he'd been a preacher long enough to know that some of those reasons had nothing to do with the Lord.

A small twist adjusted the stove dampers for a slower burn. He leaned against the nearest box pew and cast back through his memory. He couldn't recall any conversation in which Willa had mentioned her faith or spoken of the Lord. His calling, *and* his heart, required that the woman he married be possessed of a strong faith. Before his…regard…for Willa Wright grew any deeper, he had to know the answer to that question.

He shook off his sense of unease, set aside his personal concerns, and went and knelt before the altar to pray for God's blessing on the church and on the message he was about to share.

Thank goodness the wool hood hid her face. Willa tugged it farther forward and hurried up the steps. Her nose was probably as red as a beet—her cheeks, too. For sure they felt frozen. Well, what did she expect, sneaking across town and hiding in the unheated schoolhouse, like a craven coward, watching for Thomas while waiting for church to begin? But she'd had no choice. She did not want to be taken off-guard again. Thomas's unexpected appearance yesterday still had her unsettled and shaken.

It wasn't that she lacked fortitude. It was simply that she wanted to speak with him privately lest he make his claim of her in front of everyone. His *claim*. It made her sound like a piece of property. Well, she had no intention of becoming his possession. His desertion had broken their betrothal and released her from any responsibility of fidelity. Of course, the townspeople didn't know that. That's why she had to speak to him. Oh, why hadn't she simply swallowed her pride and been honest?

The door opened with a soft whisper. She slipped inside and eased the door closed. Henry Cargrave was offering the opening prayer. She stepped to the open pew on the left, spotted Sophia Sheffield motioning her to come and tiptoed down the aisle and joined her in her private box. Thankfully, the door was well oiled. She acknowledged her kindness with a nod and a smile and bowed her head. The aggravating thing was her plan to speak with Thomas alone had failed. He had not appeared. All her shivering and shaking had been in vain. And now, she had to worry about him waiting for her after the service. He knew she would be here. In Pinewood, teachers were expected to attend church.

"I take my text this morning from the book of Revelations…"

Matthew Calvert's deep, rich voice drew her from her thoughts. She pushed her hood back slightly, lifted her head and looked forward. His gaze shifted, met hers, lingered. Her fingers fumbled, froze. His gaze moved on. She let out a breath and lowered her hands to her lap.

Sophia leaned her way. She pushed her hood away from her ear and inclined her head.

"Matthew Calvert is too handsome for words. And a much better catch than Thomas Hunter."

Sophia's whispered words tickled her ear and stiffened her body. She cast a quick glance at those closest to them to make sure they hadn't overheard, then looked at the older woman. Why had she made such an outrageous statement? The answer lay in the violet-colored eyes twinkling at her from beneath the feather-trimmed brim of Sophia's green velvet bonnet. The woman had heard Thomas was back and was teasing her.

She settled back against the pew and cast another covert glance around. No one was paying them any mind. Thank goodness no one had overheard! There would be gossip enough sweeping through the village over Thomas's return—she didn't need another rumor, about her refusing his hand and setting her cap for the preacher. She would tell Sophia of Ellen's feelings for Matthew Calvert directly after church and that would be the end of it.

"Thank you for your kind invitation, Mrs. Townsend. I accept." Matthew smiled at the plump, elderly woman and shook her husband's hand. "I'll see you at tea Tuesday afternoon, Manning." He watched the tall, gray-haired man take hold of his wife's elbow and start down the steps, then turned to the next person in line.

"Excellent sermon, Reverend Calvert. Made a lot of sense. I'll be thinking on it this week while I'm milking an' caring for the cows an' such."

He met the dairy farmer's strong grip and nodded. "I'm pleased to hear that, sir."

"My heart, also, was stirred to response, Reverend. I intend to make a stronger effort to draw closer to the Lord, to know Him as my personal Savior in the way you described."

His heart swelled with thanksgiving. He flexed his squeezed hand and smiled at the farmer's wife. "Nothing would please the Lord more. He longs for fellowship with His children, and—"

"'Behold, I stand, at the door, and knock: If any man hear my voice, and open the door, I will come in to him, and will sup with him, and he with me.'"

Ellen Hall. He held back the frown that started at her interruption.

The farmer glanced over his shoulder. "Hello, Mrs. Hall… Mr. Hall. You quote Scripture very well, Ellen." The man's gaze came back to rest on him. "We'll move on. Goodbye, Reverend Calvert." He took hold of his wife's arm and started down the porch steps.

He made a mental note to pay a visit to the man's farm during the coming week, and turned to bid farewell to the Halls.

"You preached a wonderful message today, Reverend Calvert."

He ignored Ellen's flattering tone and inclined his head. "I see you remembered the Scripture I took as my text, Miss Hall."

The feather trim on her blue velvet bonnet quivered as she tilted her head. She looked up through her long eyelashes and gave him a small smile. "It brings to my mind our dining together the other night."

"Indeed?" Must the woman turn everything—even the quotation of Holy Scripture—into an occasion for flirting? He shifted his gaze to her parents. "And that reminds me that I must thank you again for the lovely dinner, and again, apologize for my hasty leave-taking."

"We were sorry you left us early, Reverend." Conrad Hall shook his offered hand. "Ellen's recitation of Psalm eighty-four was excellent."

"I'm sure it was, sir."

"Father, please, Reverend Calvert was simply following your admonition to strong discipline for children. My small entertainment was of little importance compared to that."

His gaze was drawn by the movement of Ellen's hand. She tucked the collar of her velvet cape closer around her chin and protruded her bottom lip in a small pout. "I'm certain your adorable, young wards profited from your firmness, Reverend." The pout morphed into another smile.

He held his silence, dipped his head in response. How often did she practice those coy through-her-lashes looks? He couldn't imagine Willa Wright doing such a thing. But he did, there and then. And the image conjured of the prim-and-proper schoolmarm indulging in such an activity made his lips curve into a smile and his hunger to see her grow.

He skimmed his gaze over the people climbing into carriages, strolling home on the walkway or visiting with each other in the yard, but did not see her neat, trim figure among them. He'd missed her. She must have left before he reached the door. His smile died.

From the corner of his eye he saw Simon Pritchard step through the church door, pause and lean heavily on his cane. He made the Halls a polite bow. "Excuse me, please."

He stepped to the elderly man's side. "Mr. Pritchard, it's good to see you well again, sir. May I help you down the steps?"

The silk of Ellen Hall's long skirt rustled. He cast a sidelong glance her way. The young woman *was* pretty, very pretty, as the admiring glances of the men gazing up at her from the yard testified.

"Thank you, Reverend, but John's brung the carriage. He'll fetch me."

"Very well, Mr. Pritchard." He smiled and placed his hand on the elderly man's bony shoulder. "Perhaps one of these Sundays John will come inside."

"I ain't 'spectin' that to happen anytime soon." The old man snorted, shook his head and shuffled toward the steps.

He turned and went inside and swept his glance over the empty pews. "Thank You, Lord, for the privilege of ministering to Your people. Settle Your message of truth in their hearts and spirits that it may bear fruit for Thee, I pray. Amen."

He picked up his notes from the pulpit, closed the Bible and headed for the back door, his footsteps echoing in the empty church, the disappointment of not seeing Willa after the service, of not being able to share with her the news of the change in the children clouding his otherwise satisfying morning.

"Have you given your kitten a name?" Willa stood at the base of the steps of the side porch, reached toward the kitten curled up in Sally's lap and stroked between its small pointed ears with her fingertip. It was the only spot available. The rest of the purring ball of fur was covered by Sally's little hands.

Sally's nod set her blond curls bouncing. "I named him Tickles, 'cause his fur tickles my face when he sleeps under my chin."

"I see." She stared at Sally's beaming face and blinked back the tears that smarted her eyes. She could hardly believe the change in the little girl. "I think that's a wonderful name, and an excellent reason for choosing it." Perhaps Matthew Calvert had allowed Sally to have the kitten in her bed? And if so, had she given up her mother's glove?

"I could have named him Scratchy, 'cause that's how his tongue feels when he kisses me."

Sally giggled, a sound so joyous that it brought her own laughter bubbling up.

"Watch this, Miss Wright!"

She turned and looked at Joshua. He drew back his arm and threw a small piece of branch.

"Fetch it, boy! Fetch the stick!"

The puppy beside him barked, ran around in circles, then raced back to plant his front paws against Joshua's knees. The boy leaned down and petted his dog, looked up and gave her a sheepish grin. "I guess he hasn't learned the trick yet, but he will. He's a real smart dog." His brown eyes were alight with pride and love for his dog.

Her heart swelled. "I'm sure he is, Joshua." She squatted, drew her cloak over her long skirts that ballooned around her, and rubbed behind the dog's ears before she gave in to the urge to hug the young boy. "Does this fellow have a name yet?"

"Yes, ma'am. I call him Happy, because that's how he makes me feel."

Oh dear. She blinked. Blinked again.

"Well! What's going on here?"

She jerked her head up and looked straight into Matthew Calvert's brown eyes. Her breath caught in her throat, warmth flowed across her cheeks. She yanked her gaze away from his, let go of the dog and started to rise.

"Allow me."

She stared at his outstretched hand, remembered the tingling warmth of his touch when he'd helped her from his buggy and wished she had never yielded to the children's pleas for her to come see their pets. Irritation spurted through her. What was he doing home so soon anyway? The way he had been smiling at Ellen, she'd assumed she would have plenty of time to see the pets and leave.

She placed her hand on his palm, ignored the strength, the feel of his hand holding hers and rose.

The kitchen door squeaked open. "Joshua and Sally, you catch up those animals and come inside now. Dinner's ready." Bertha Franklin stepped to the edge of the porch and squinted down at her. "Why, Willa, I didn't know you were here. Did you want—" The older woman's gaze dropped, her eyes widened.

She jerked her hand from Matthew Calvert's grasp. "The children asked me to come and see their pets. They— You see, I found them, the pets I mean, and—" she took a breath, pulled herself together "—and I have a proprietary interest in them." Bertha was staring at her. Were her cheeks red? They felt on fire. She leaned down and picked up the kitten's basket.

"Bye, Miss Wright!"

"Goodbye, children."

She fussed with the lid of the basket. Joshua and the puppy scrambled up the steps and followed Sally and her kitten inside. Bertha's footsteps crossed the porch.

"Remember me to your mama, Willa."

"I will, Bertha."

The door closed. She heaved a sigh, placed the basket on the porch and turned. Matthew Calvert had a definite, amused glint in his eyes, and something more.

Something that brought that heat back to her cheeks. She looked down.

"I'm glad you came when the children asked, Miss Wright. I wanted to speak with you, and I thought I had missed you after church."

When you were talking with Ellen? The thought steadied her, fortified her against the oh-so-charming reverend. She stiffened her spine.

"I wanted to tell you that your suggestion about the kitten worked. Sally cuddled it all night. Her mother's glove stayed on her nightstand."

Tears welled. She took a breath to control them. "I'm so pleased for Sally's sake." She brushed at a bit of dried leaf clinging to her cloak, groped for the resistance his soft words had undermined. Think of how he behaves apart from the children. She lifted her chin and met his gaze full on. "Thank you for telling me, Reverend Calvert. Good afternoon."

He didn't move out of her path. She stumbled to a stop. So did her heart. Mindless things, hearts. She took a step back.

"I also wanted to tell you that I have discussed plans with the church elders to begin a Sunday school class for the young children." He smiled.

She stared at that oh-so-warm and sincere smile and her racing pulse slowed. Thomas smiled like that. Suspicion reared.

"They decided to have the class meet in the schoolhouse as it is close by and will be convenient for those who live outside the village and must drive to church. Of course, we need someone to teach the children."

Of course. He'd wanted to talk to her because he needed yet another favor. Would she never learn?

"The elders suggested I ask you. And I wholeheartedly agreed. You are wonderful with children, Miss Wright." His gaze captured hers. "Will you accept?"

His smile and his compliment left her cold. She shook her head, drew breath to explain that she could not teach children about a God she did not believe in, then clamped her lips shut. If the elders found out about her lack of faith, they would dismiss her and hire another to teach in her place. She was trapped into accepting. Unless…

She drew back her shoulders and lifted her chin. "Please thank the elders for considering me for the position, Reverend Calvert, but I feel there is someone better suited than I to teach the Sunday school class. A person with whom you share a mutual belief in 'firm discipline' for children. I suggest you ask Miss Hall to teach the class. I'm quite certain she will be eager to do so. Good day."

She swept by him and hurried down the stone walk toward the road. *Thomas.* She jerked to a halt. Thomas smiled and came toward her. She glanced back over her shoulder. Reverend Calvert was still standing by the porch steps watching her. Trapped again. She took a deep breath and moved forward.

Chapter Ten

Everyone they walked past stared and smiled. Willa threw a sidelong look at Thomas waving and calling out greetings, and tugged her hood forward. She forced yet another smile and waved at another couple, the carriage rumbling by.

"Must you be so…exuberant, Thomas?" She breathed a sigh of relief as they stepped off the Stony Creek bridge and turned onto Brook Street. It wasn't far now.

"How can I be otherwise when I have my promised bride walking at my side, Willa?"

"I am not your promised bride." She gave him a cool look. "We have been discussing how you walked out on our wedding, remember?"

"Tom!"

She glanced across the road at the hail.

Thomas turned slightly and waved to the man slouching against the hitching post in front of Nate Turner's Wagon Shop. "Good afternoon, Arnie."

"For sure it is you, Tom!" The wheelwright grinned and waggled his eyebrows. "Meet me later. I'll be at Jack's." The young man straightened, swept off his hat and made her a deep bow. "Good afternoon, Miss Wright."

Mocker! He knew she did not appreciate his flirtatious teasing. Arnold Dixon had a very unsavory reputation. She lifted her chin, turned her head away and quickened her pace. Tom? Arnie? She hadn't known Thomas was friends with Arnold Dixon. And had Mr. Dixon been speaking of Johnny Taylor, another man of low repute, when he asked Thomas to join him?

"Whoa, slow down, Willa, honey. I want—"

"Do not call me 'Willa honey,' Thomas." She put a chill in her voice. "Nor 'your bride' nor any other such—" the word *endearment* stuck in her throat "—such…*thing*. You have no right. You forfeited that privilege when you de— When you left. I am Miss Wright to you."

He smiled and took hold of her elbow. "Now, Willa—"

"*Miss Wright*. And don't speak to me in that condescending tone." She pulled her elbow from his grasp and slipped her arm inside her cape where he could not reach it.

His features tightened.

"I know you're angry about my leaving the way I did, but I don't think you want to be acting that way, Willa. After all, you said everyone thinks you told me to go west after my dream. That being the way of it, they will all expect us to take up our plans to be wed again now that I'm back. You can tell that from their smiles."

"Then they shall be sorely disappointed." She caught her breath at her slip of tongue and started back down the path. Hopefully, he hadn't noticed.

"Is that what you're going to tell that nosy neighbor of yours? And suppose you tell *me* what that means."

He gave her a speculative glance. "You agreed to accept my suit again."

She stopped and lifted her head. Mrs. Braynard was on her stoop, looking their way. She looked up at Thomas, took a breath and told him the truth. "It means I agreed to again accept your court, but I do not care for your presumption that my willingness to do so means our relationship is as before." She lifted her chin and confessed her plan. "I shall, of course, honor my word—for a few days—but then I shall tell Mrs. Braynard, and everyone else, that I have discovered I do not esteem you highly enough to marry you."

He rubbed his chin, then slowly nodded. "I see. Well, I guess I understand that." He narrowed his eyes, focused on hers.

She wanted to turn away, to avoid the intensity of his gaze, but held her ground.

"You don't want everyone to know I up and left you like I did."

She sucked in a breath at his bald statement, fought back tears at the cruelty of his words.

His expression changed into one she was quite certain was meant to show contrition, but it fell short of the mark.

"I made a bad mistake, Willa. I admit that. But what I did isn't the same as your pa deserting you and your ma."

She stiffened, clenched her hands. How dare he bring up her father! She never should have told him about him.

"Now don't get riled." He smiled down at her. "All I want is another chance to prove how much I love you, Willa, honey. I guess a few days is long enough to do that, then we'll go ahead with that wedding we had planned."

"No, Thomas. I—"

"Will most likely change your mind." His hand pressed against the small of her back, urged her forward on the path. "How is your mama, Willa?"

She glanced up at his abrupt change of topic, stared at the hard edge on his smile, at the dark glint in his eyes. What had happened to his charming ways? She didn't know this man. Unease settled like a stone in her stomach.

"Hello, Willa, dear." Mrs. Braynard beamed at them. "How nice to see you back, Mr. Hunter."

"Thank you, Mrs. Braynard. It's good to be back." Thomas made the elderly woman an exaggerated bow. "May I say you put this lovely October day to shame?"

"Well, aren't you silver-tongued, young man. As if you had eyes for any except your betrothed." Mrs. Braynard laughed. Her pudgy hands smoothed her full skirt over her thick girth.

Silver-tongued? Or a glib liar? Either way, she had been duped by Thomas into thinking he was something he was not. She wanted nothing more to do with him. She paused on the stoop of her cabin and turned toward him, drew breath to speak.

"Careful, Willa. The old busybody is still watching." Thomas grabbed her hand, held it firm and bowed. "I'll see you tomorrow. Give my regards to your mama."

There it was again, that slight change in his voice when he mentioned her mother. She kept silent, stared at him, her unease growing.

He smiled, opened the door for her and walked back to the path, whistling.

There was something unsettling about him. How could she ever have thought herself in love with such a man? She took a deep breath and glanced next door. She would tell Mrs. Braynard the truth right now and face the shame. At least she would be done with Thomas.

"Willa?"

She spun around.

Her mother wiped her hands on her apron and smoothed back a lock of hair. "Why are you standing there with the door open? The house will cool down. Come and eat your dinner. I fixed chicken."

She looked into her mother's eyes and read the love there. *How is your mama, Willa?* Nausea swirled. So that was why Thomas was so certain she would overlook his desertion and marry him.

Her fierce, protective love for her mother rose. Her hands clenched in helpless fury. She could not subject her mother to the furor of resurrected gossip about her father's abandonment that would flood the village if the truth about Thomas's desertion of her became known. She couldn't put her mother through that again. Her stomach churned. She stepped inside and pushed against the door until it clicked shut.

"I'm coming, Mama." She unfastened her cloak and hung it on a peg, forced a cheerful tone into her voice. "I was hoping you'd fix chicken."

"I know. It's your favorite." Her mother smiled and stepped back into the kitchen.

She took a deep breath, pressed her hand to her roiling stomach and followed. She'd find some way to swallow the food.

A game of chess could not compete with a puppy. Matthew looked at the abandoned game board on the table beside the window in the sitting room and smiled.

He picked up a captured knight and absently fingered it. Who was that man? Did Willa Wright have a brother? He'd not heard of one. Of course, he'd been here only a few weeks. Still, Willa was right when she'd told him a small village has few secrets. News here traveled at a head-swirling pace. There was nothing malicious about it, though. It was simply how the villagers kept up with news of one another. Anyway, it seemed as though if she had a brother, he would have heard by now.

He set the knight back on the table and jammed his hands in his pockets. Whoever the man was, she knew him. She'd paused for a moment, glanced back at him, then walked on to meet the man. What had that quick glance at him meant? Probably nothing. To assign a motive to it would be pure conjecture, not to mention wishful thinking.

The man was a good-looking fellow. Fit, too. Looked to be a logger or a sawmill worker, judging by his clothes. Probably a sawyer. He plopped down onto the settee, leaned his head against the padded curved back and stretched out his legs. He'd been told loggers worked out of their camps in the hills and seldom showed up in town this time of year. He frowned down at his toes. Of course, the man might be a jobber. The foremen of the various camps lived in cabins in town and sometimes came home at weeks' end. That could explain why he hadn't seen him before.

Shouts and laughter from outside pulled him off the settee to see what was going on. He stepped to the window and looked out. The dog was chasing Joshua and Sally around the base of the huge maple tree that dominated the front yard. Sally tripped and fell headlong to the leaf-strewn ground.

He tensed, spun to go outside, heard her laughter and turned back. The puppy was licking her face and wagging his tail so furiously that he almost tipped himself over.

He grinned, leaned his shoulder against the frame and watched. Sally giggled and tried to push the puppy away, but she was no match for the wiggling, squirming dog who obviously enjoyed the game. He evaded her small hands, barked and attacked with new vigor, his tongue licking as fast as his tail wagged. Sally giggled harder and covered her face with her small arms.

"Joshua, help me!"

Her call to her brother came, muted but distinct, through the window.

Joshua jumped from behind the tree. "C'mon, Happy, c'mon, boy!" He slapped his small hands against his thighs, turned and ran. The dog left off his licking and raced after his master, barking and quickly gaining ground. Sally scrambled to her feet and ran after them.

His heart swelled so much it hurt. "Are you watching, Robert? Do you see your children laughing and playing, Judith? I sure hope so. I believe you do. Somehow, someway, I think you two know Josh and Sally are going to be all right. And that we have Willa Wright to thank for it."

Willa. He liked the name. It was sort of strong, yet soft. And it fit her. That little chin of hers raised like a flag of warning when she was feeling...what? Threatened in some way? But the truth of her nature was found in the softness and warmth of her eyes when her emotions overcame her... He frowned. The word that came to mind was...defenses.

He went back and collapsed onto the settee, stretched

out his legs, clasped his hands behind the back of his neck and stared up at the plaster ceiling. Why would Willa feel threatened and defensive around him? He cast around in his memory for a reason but came up empty. He'd figure it out, though. Willa Wright was an enigma…a challenge. And he never backed away from—

"Uncle Matt! Uncle Matt!" The front door slammed against the wall.

He bolted upright and ran to the doorway, almost lost his balance and toppled backward when Sally hurled herself against his legs.

"C'mon!" She grabbed his hand and tugged him toward the open front door. "Happy chased Tickles up the tree and she's crying and she won't come down and it's getting dark and she's scared and—" She stopped tugging on his hand and looked up at him. Her little lip trembled, her eyes overflowed with tears. "I w-want my k-kitty. I don't want m-my kitty to be g-gone."

"Shh, Sally, don't cry." He bent, scooped her into his arms and wiped the tears from her soft little cheeks. "Tickles isn't going anywhere. I'll get him out of the tree."

She leaned back and looked into his eyes. "P-promise?"

He gave an emphatic nod and closed the door behind them. "I promise."

Willa shifted the bowl of potato peelings and chicken scraps from her mother's preparation of their dinner, leaned over the fence and dumped it into the trough for the Braynards' pigs. Most of the food from her plate was included in the slop. She hadn't been able to force it down after all.

The two sows lunged upright, snorting and grunting, and stuck their snouts into the wood basin. "Enjoy your meal, pigs. I couldn't eat mine."

"You ailing, Willa?"

"Oh!" The bowl slipped from her hands. She spun around, her hand pressed to her chest. "Daniel! It's good to see you out and around again… I think." She blew out a breath. "You startled me."

"I can tell." He grinned with the ease of a lifelong friend, stepped to her side, leaned over the fence and smacked the largest sow on the shoulder with his good hand. "Give over now!" He snatched her bowl out of the pigpen, squatted and wiped it on the grass.

"You're using your arm. Oh, Daniel, I'm so glad you're getting better." She smiled down at him.

"I've a ways to go, but I should be going back to camp soon. I'll help out with the cooking and stuff until I can get back to logging."

Her smile faded. "Do you think you should? Go back to logging, I mean. You were badly injured, Daniel." Would Thomas go to work logging? Hope stirred. That would give her time to think of what to do.

"You sound like Ma." Daniel rose and handed her the bowl. "If I don't go back we'd have to give up the cabin. I'd get along, but Ma wouldn't have a place to live."

Yes. She knew about that. So did Thomas. *But what I did isn't the same as your pa deserting you and your ma.* Had he always been so cruel? Why had she not noticed?

"Besides, that accident never should have happened—wouldn't have if that new hick on the crew had called out a warning like he should have." Daniel frowned and shook his head. "By the time I heard the snapping and cracking of that tree falling it was too late to get out of the way." He rubbed at his left shoulder. "I'm hoping the jobber might let me work as a teamster from now on. I've always been good with horses."

A teamster. Is that how Thomas earned his living? How could she not know? It seemed that in the rush of his courtship she'd made a lot of assumptions. "That would be wonderful. I'm sure your mother would be relieved."

He nodded, squinted down at her. "So what's ailing you?"

She shook her head. "Nothing serious. My stomach is…upset."

"That all?" He leaned back against the fence and studied her face. "You look kind of…unsettled, 'special when I came up on you."

She noted the concern in his eyes, sighed and leaned against the fence beside him. "Thomas is back."

"I heard. And that you didn't want to talk with him." He frowned. "He bothering you, is he? I thought David Dibble warned him off."

Her stomach knotted afresh. News spread so quickly. People must be wondering about her actions. "He did, but Thomas came and walked home with me after church." She looked down at the bowl she held against her apron so he couldn't read the turmoil in her eyes. "He says he wants to—" She caught her breath. She couldn't tell him *that,* he would know Thomas had deserted her. "He wants us to get married."

"That what you want? 'Cause if it's not, and he pesters you, I'll take care of it."

Tears threatened. If only she could tell him the truth. She blinked, looked over at Daniel and forced a teasing note into her voice. "With your bad arm?"

His jaw jutted. "I'd manage."

And hurt your arm again in the doing. No, my friend, this is my problem. "Thank you, Daniel. I'm certain you would, but it's not necessary. I simply have to decide what I want to do."

She pushed away from the fence. "I have to get back to the house. I have the lamps to clean." She took a few steps, slowed and glanced over her shoulder at him. "Don't leave for the camp without saying goodbye."

"I won't."

She nodded and picked up her pace.

"Willa?"

She stopped and turned. "Yes?"

"It's all right if you tell Thomas no. You won't be the first woman to change your mind about marrying a man. And it wouldn't be as if you didn't have a good reason."

Her breath snagged. What did that mean? Was he talking about Thomas's leaving? Did he know he had deserted her? No. There was no way anyone could know that. If they did, it would have been all over town when he left. She nodded and forced a smile. "Thank you, Daniel. I'll keep that in mind."

"Ain't you kind of old to be shinnyin' up and down trees?" Bertha ducked her head and washed another dish.

"I saw that smile, Mrs. Franklin." Matthew poured a cup of coffee and set the pot on a back stove plate to keep warm. "But to answer your question, yes, I suppose I am. Still, I did quite well until that dead limb broke." He sat at the table and took a swallow of the dark brew.

Bertha snorted and pulled her hands out of the sudsy water. "I suppose you did all right for a city-raised man. For sure no country-raised boy would grab hold of a dead branch while he's climbing—lest it was to break it out his way."

She dried her hands on her apron and came to stand in front of him. "Let me see that wound."

It was like being a ten-year-old boy again. He gave her a sheepish grin and pulled up his shirt sleeve. A deep, ragged gouge ran from a few inches above his wrist over the back of his hand to the base of his fingers.

The housekeeper peered at it from all angles. "Looks like it bled well."

"I'll say. It ruined my shirt. Well, that and the tear."

She squinted down at him. "You wash it out good?"

"Yes." He had the sudden dread of a young boy that she was going to start scrubbing away at the gouge. A chuckle started in his gut and climbed into his throat. He took another swallow of his coffee and drowned the laughter before it broke free. There was no point in fueling a fire.

Bertha nodded, pulled his shirt sleeve down and straightened. "It needs salve and a bandage. You go to Cargrave's and tell Allan I said you need some of that green Indian salve and a bandage roll. He'll open the store and get you some." She moved back to the cupboard, rubbed the soap over the washrag and lifted another dish out from the water. "You ought to have salve and bandages in the house anyway with these youngsters running around willy-nilly. You never know when one of them will get banged up."

"That's true." He took another swallow.

Bertha turned and looked at him.

He put his cup down and jumped to his feet. "I'll leave as soon as I get my coat."

She nodded and went back to washing the dish. "I'll bandage that up when you get back."

The bells on the door of the mercantile tinkled clear and crisp on the cool air. Matthew stepped out of the store and looked up at the rim of pink and gold outlining the banks of clouds above the dark hills that surrounded Pinewood. Days were growing shorter. Winter would soon be upon them.

There was a click as the door was locked. He turned and held out his hand. "Thank you again for opening the store for me, Mr. Cargrave. I surely appreciate it."

The man shoved the skeleton key in his waistcoat pocket, gave him a wry smile and shook his offered hand. "I wouldn't dare defy Bertha Franklin, Reverend. Good evening."

He watched the storekeeper cross the wide wood walkway, walk down the three steps to the road and turn toward his home. He glanced down at the items in his hand and smiled. There were definite benefits to living in a small village. And to having Bertha Franklin for his housekeeper.

He moved to leave the small alcove that protected the doorway, heard footsteps coming and stepped back to wait for the people to pass.

"…marry her?"

"…gotta…somewhere…live. An'…'nough money… stake me…"

The thud of bootheels on the planks of the walkway blocked out stretches of the slurred, indistinct speech. Even so, he didn't care to hear more of the men's drunken conversation. He stepped out into the deepening dusk and turned for home.

"But…marry…"

"No one…gonna…where… I'm goin'. I'm…not tellin' ladies…for sure."

The two men in the darker area between storefronts laughed uproariously, came closer. The one nearest to him lifted his hat and made a small bow in his direction as they passed.

"Good evening…sir."

His companion grabbed him as he toppled forward and yanked him erect. They laughed and thumped toward the steps.

He turned and stared after them. Was that… The men stumbled down the three steps into the open roadway and he got a better look. His brows knit in a deep frown. It was. That was the man who had come for Willa.

Chapter Eleven

"I'm *talking* to you, Willa."

Ellen's petulant tone penetrated her troubling thoughts. Willa stopped walking and looked over at her friend. "I'm sorry, Ellen. You were saying..." She let her voice trail off in invitation.

Ellen tossed her head, pulled her hems away from some thorny weeds and moved toward the slight rise ahead. "You asked me to come along with you, and I have. The least you can do is pay attention to me." She cast a pouty glance at her from beneath the quilted brim of her Neapolitan bonnet. "What's wrong with you anyway, Willa? You've been acting as vague as fog over the river all week long."

Oh dear. If Ellen had noticed her distraction, it was certain others had. She would have to do better. "There's nothing wrong with me. I've merely been preoccupied with a problem." She snagged her lower lip with her teeth. That bit of truth should not have been spoken. If Ellen connected that with Thomas— She took a breath and added a bit of obfuscation. "Teachers sometimes have problems, you know."

"Yes, problems called *children*." Ellen tossed another glance her way. "That is part of what I was trying to tell you before, Willa. I shall soon be a teacher."

She stopped dead in her tracks. "A teacher! *You*, Ellen?" She hurried to walk alongside her again.

"I know it's surprising, given the way I feel about the noisy, unkempt little beasts, but I have a reason."

She nodded and stepped round a pile of deer droppings. "You always do."

"Hi, Miss Wright… Miss Hall." Danny Brody raced by, backpedaled, waved, then turned and charged up the slope. "Hey, Billy, Tommy, wait for me!"

She lifted her hand to return the boy's wave, then instead smiled and waved at his older sister and her friends, who were hurrying by at a slower pace. Danny had already forgotten them.

"As I was *saying*..."

She turned her attention back to Ellen. "Yes?"

"Reverend Calvert is forming a Sunday school class for the young children of church members, and he has asked *me* to be the instructor."

Memory flashed. With her trouble with Thomas, she had forgotten about that. "And you accepted?"

"Of course. I'm certain he chose me because he was impressed by my handling of his wards the night Mother and Father invited him to dinner." A smug smile curved Ellen's lips. "I *knew* that inviting his wards would make him see me in a favorable light as a future mate."

Something inside her went still. "Why do you say that? Has Reverend Calvert asked permission to court you?"

"Not yet, but he will. That's why I accepted the position." Ellen laughed and started climbing the sloped ground. "I think of questions about teaching the 'dear, little children' and use them to engage him in conversation whenever we 'chance' to meet about town, which has been several times this week." Ellen gave another little laugh. "Living close to the church and parsonage has made it easy for me to see when he goes out, and it's a simple thing to have chores to do in the same stores." Ellen's delicate brows lifted in an arched, satisfied look. "He has already warmed considerably in his…response…to me."

"Been widening those big blue eyes and looking at the reverend through your long lashes, have you?"

Daniel. Willa squelched a smile.

Ellen gasped and whirled about. "How dare you sneak up on us and listen to our private conversation, Daniel Braynard!"

Their childhood friend spread his hands in a gesture of innocence. "I can't help it if the ground is soft and the grass doesn't make noise when it's stepped on."

Ellen's eyes glinted. "You could have warned us you were there."

Willa lowered her head and bit down on her lower lip to stop her urge to laugh. The way Ellen spat out the words reminded her of Sally's kitten. But then, Ellen and Daniel had always scrapped like a cat and a dog whenever they were together. He loved to tease, and Ellen always took his bait.

"Now that would have been downright rude. Mama always taught me not to interrupt when other people were speaking." Daniel grinned.

"And you think *eavesdropping* is good manners?" Ellen gave a disdainful snort—definitely a throwback response from their childhood—spun back around and flounced off up the hill.

She shook her head and hurried to catch Ellen, then looked back at Daniel. He dipped his head, but he was too late. She had seen his eyes. She froze on the spot, shock rooting her feet to the ground. "Daniel…"

He lifted his head at her whisper, met her gaze and his long legs ate up the short distance between them. "Don't tell her, Willa."

She stared at him, uncertain and tentative. They had shared secrets and confidences since early childhood, but it seemed there was one very important secret Daniel hadn't shared with her. "When?"

He didn't even try to pretend he misunderstood her. "Remember that day when we were walking across that log over Stony Creek and she fell in and I had to pull her out?"

She nodded, the image of twelve-year-old Daniel diving off the log into the swollen, swift-running flood waters beneath clear in her head.

"That was it for me." He shoved his hands in his jacket pockets and gave her a rueful grin that broke her heart. "You all thought I was shivering from that icy water. I wasn't." He turned his head and looked after Ellen stalking up the hill with anger in every line of her body. "I was shaking because when I pulled Ellen out of that water, looking so still and white, I realized she could have died and, right then, I knew I didn't want to live my life without her in it."

"But…" She stared at him, at his compressed lips, his square jaw, his hazel eyes dark with emotion, a Daniel she didn't recognize. She looked down at the ground and began climbing the hill after Ellen.

He fell into step beside her. "But what, Willa?"

She blinked, swallowed hard and shook her head.

He leaned close and nudged her with the elbow of his good arm. "You might as well ask before it worries you to the point you can't stand it anymore." He grinned down at her. "I don't want you coming knocking on my window in the middle of the night because you can't sleep."

This was the Daniel she knew. But now she knew it was a Daniel who hid a hurting heart behind teasing and laugher. She blinked again and forced a laugh. "That happened only once."

"And I had to find that baby bird, climb that tree and put it back in its nest while you held the lantern safe below. I thought that mama bird was going to peck my eyes out." He fell silent.

She stopped, placed her hand on his arm and looked full into his eyes. "You saved Ellen ten years ago, Daniel. Why haven't you told her?"

He stared down at her hand. She could hear the hum of people talking amidst bursts of laughter beyond the rise. She wished he would speak and ease the ache in her heart for him.

"Well, at first we were too young." His voice was full of memories. "And then—" His shoulders hunched, his voice hardened. "You see what's under your hand, Willa?"

She looked down, glanced back up. "Your coat?"

He nodded.

"I don't understand, Daniel."

His face tightened. "That's a plain old plaid wool jacket, Willa. The same as every other logger and teamster and sawmill worker wears. Ellen's got her sights set on something far above that. She wants the arm she rests her hand on to be wearing a fancy suit. And she wants all that goes along with that suit. She wants an easy life and prestige. I might be fool enough to love her, but I'm not fool enough to let her know." He looked up. "Sometimes, when a man loses his heart, all he's got left is his pride, Willa. He's got to protect that."

She gazed into his eyes and wished she hadn't asked, wished more that he hadn't answered.

"Are you *coming,* Willa?"

She raised her head and looked at Ellen standing on the crest of the rise. She drew breath. Daniel's good arm looped over her shoulders, and she lost it again.

"She's coming, Ellen." He moved forward, the strength of his arm carrying her along with him. "We were talking about that day you fell in Stony Creek and I pulled you out looking like a drowned muskrat." He chuckled and shook his head as they came up to her. "You sure were a sorry sight. You look some better today."

"Oh!" It was more huffed-out breath than a word.

Daniel laughed, then touched the rolled-up brim of his knit hat to them both. "Enjoy yourself, ladies. I see some of my crew over across the way, and I want to talk with them."

He strolled off, leaving her with an ache in her heart, a lump in her throat and an intense desire to grab Ellen Hall by the shoulders and give her a good shake.

"Here comes Reverend Calvert, Willa. I *told* you he was becoming interested in me."

"So you did." And why you're interested in him. Daniel was right. Willa looked the direction of Ellen's gaze. Matthew Calvert was indeed wending his way through the assembled people and heading in their general direction. Where were Joshua and Sally?

"Don't stare, Willa. And stop frowning!"

She drew her gaze back, watched Ellen pinch color into her cheeks and fluff the bow of her wide satin bonnet strings. Hurt for Daniel squeezed her heart. She looked across the field to where he stood with his logger crewmates beside the towering pile of stumps farmers and land owners had grubbed from their fields. They were lighting the fire. He was looking their way.

"Good afternoon, Miss Hall... Miss Wright."

She glanced over her shoulder. Matthew Calvert stood beside Ellen, his charming smile on his face. He was so handsome standing there in his *suit* that she could have slapped him.

"Good afternoon, Reverend. I see you've come out to enjoy the stump burning."

Ellen's purring tone made her feel like retching. She looked again toward Daniel. He had turned his back. She clenched her hands and dug her fingernails into her palms to keep the tears from her eyes.

"I'm sure I shall, Miss Hall. It will be a new experience for me. Good afternoon, Miss Wright."

She turned to face him. "Good afternoon, Reverend Calvert." She gave a quick glance around the area, pretended surprise. "Where are your children, Reverend?" She ignored the irritated look Ellen sent her way. "Did they not want to attend the stump burning?" Her cool tone didn't seem to put him off. He turned that charming smile on her.

"Oh, indeed they did. But I'm afraid they've deserted me." He gestured toward the children scattered over the field, playing games and running races. "They are somewhere in that melee, playing with their friends."

The gaze he had fastened on hers warmed, his smile turned into a lopsided grin. Her heart faltered, then bounded along like a deer leaping logs, much to her fury. Where was her loyalty? Her common sense? What sort of spineless fool was she to let his charm so easily sway her?

"How delightful, Reverend. You shall not have to hurry off."

That purr again! She jerked her gaze to Ellen, watched her widen her big blue eyes and look at Matthew Calvert through her long lashes. Her fingers twitched to yank the Neapolitan bonnet down over her friend's face.

She darted another glance across the field toward Daniel, but the fire had caught hold and billowing smoke hid him from her view. A small flash beneath the trees at the edge of the clearing drew her attention. Thomas, Arnold Dixon and Johnny Taylor stood in the shadows, light from the flames of the soaring fire glinting off the flask they passed to one another. Her stomach knotted. So they *were* friends. *Drinking* friends. What else did she not know about Thomas? What if he saw her and came over?

The knots twisted tighter. She bowed her head, pressed her hand against her stomach and turned her back.

"You're very pale. Are you feeling ill, Miss Wright?"

She raised her head and looked straight into Matthew Calvert's brown eyes. Concern darkened them. She took a deep breath. "No, I— Excuse me." She whipped around. "I have to go, Ellen."

"You do look peaked, Willa. I'll come—"

"No, I'll be fine. You stay. Agnes will be looking for us." She pulled her hood forward, hurried to the top of the rise and started down the other side, her steps keeping pace with her rushing thoughts. What had she gotten herself into? How could she marry Thomas? She didn't even know this man he had become, or had kept hidden from her. But her mother—

"Wait, Miss Wright."

She spun about, startled to find the reverend still with her. In two long strides he was by her side.

"You shouldn't be alone while you're ill. Please allow me to escort you home."

His deep voice, calm and quiet, both soothed her jangled nerves and made her want to burst into tears. She shook her head. "You mustn't leave your children. I—"

"I asked Miss Hall to watch over Joshua and Sally until I return."

Ellen? Watching his children? Inappropriate laughter bubbled up. Her mouth twitched. She bit down on her lip…hard. Her thoughts raced, but she could think of no other reasonable excuse to refuse his polite offer. She took a breath to gain control. Her nerves were taut as bow strings. She had to get home before she came totally undone.

She nodded and turned onto the path leading to town, with Matthew Calvert's presence beside her unreasonably comforting. She had neither the strength nor the will to figure out why.

The sounds of the late afternoon settled like a blanket around them. She blocked out all thought and concentrated on the whisper of her long skirts and the soft thump of his boots against the ground, timed her breathing to match them. The tension in her body eased.

"You make a habit o' poaching on 'nother man's property, Reverend?"

Thomas! She jolted to a stop, jerked her head up. He stood in the center of the path, his eyes glassy from drink, narrow with anger. Her stomach contracted and bile surged into her throat.

"You have the advantage of me…sir."

She flicked her gaze to Matthew Calvert. His voice was calm and controlled, but there was nothing of the tranquil gentleness she had come to associate with him in his face. A tiny muscle along his jaw twitched; his brown eyes were dark, wary.

"Thomas Hunter. I'm Willa's b—betrothed."

No. Oh, please no. Tears stung her eyes.

Matthew Calvert's jaw tightened, the tiny muscle leaped. "I see." His gaze shifted, bored down into hers. "Is that true, Miss Wright?"

Words clogged in her throat.

Thomas fisted his hands, took a step toward them. "'s true all right. You qu-questionin' my—"

"Yes." Thomas's belligerence pushed the answer from her. *Please, please understand that I don't want it to be so.* She closed her eyes and clamped her lips together lest she blurt the truth.

Silence descended, scraped along her strained nerves. She held her breath. *Please, Reverend Calvert, please go before—*

"You have no reason for anger, Mr. Hunter. There is no impropriety here. I was escorting Miss Wright home because she felt unwell. I leave her in your hands."

His voice was different, controlled and cold. Dismay

gripped her. Matthew Calvert's footsteps trailed away. She heard movement and opened her eyes. Thomas pushed his face close to hers, his hand gripped her wrist.

"Don't e'er do that again, Willa. Don't e'er go walkin' out with the reverend or any other man, 'cause if you do, the gossip that flies 'round this town won't be 'bout your pa desertin' your ma an' you." He smiled. The pressure on her wrist increased. "You're mine. See you remember it."

She stared into the eyes mere inches from her own. A ruffian's eyes. Thomas was no different from the occasional bully she had dealt with among the children. Strength flowed into her. She lifted her chin, forced every ounce of "teacher" authority she possessed into her voice. "Unhand me."

Shock flashed into his eyes. His grip slackened.

She pulled her hand from his grasp before he had the chance to recover. Her wrist throbbed. She refused to rub it, or to step back. To do so would encourage his bullying. "What do you want, Thomas?" She held her voice steady, allowed no trace of fear to color it. "And do not insult me with your answer. It's obvious you have no regard for me."

He studied her a long moment, then shrugged. "Jack and I lost our stake in a game of chance, so we come back to get more. I figure about six months of your teacher's pay should be enough to stake me again. Meanwhile, I'll live cozy and warm with you in that cabin of your ma." His eyes flashed. "That is, lest you want gossip about your loose virtue spread around town."

What a vile man! How had she ever thought him handsome or charming? She clenched her hands until they hurt to stop a shudder then drew back her shoulders and adjusted her hood. He had unwittingly given her the answer she had been searching for. "You have made a serious error in your plans, Mr. Hunter."

His face darkened, his eyes clouded with suspicion. "What's that?"

"Were you to marry me, I would lose my position. There would be no pay. Married women are not permitted to teach school."

Chapter Twelve

Willa's steps lagged. She might be free of Thomas, but she was quite certain he would take revenge and start the gossip he threatened. How was she to tell her mother? How was she to face her friends and neighbors?

She took a deep breath and opened the door to the cabin.

"Willa!" Her mother stopped sewing. A frown drew a small, vertical line between her arched brows. "Why aren't you at the stump burning?"

"I decided to come home and help you with the mending. You have a lot to do tonight." She hung her cloak on a peg and crossed to the table by the window, sat so that the lamplight would not fall on her face.

"How are Ellen and Agnes?" Her mother had not gone back to her sewing, and the look in her eyes made her want to fidget the way she had as a child.

"Ellen is fine. She's going to be teaching a Sunday school class for the young children." She lifted a shirt off the pile at her mother's side and examined the rent in the sleeve. "I didn't see Agnes. I left before—" She sighed, let the shirt sleeve fall into her lap. "I saw

Thomas, Mama. He was with Arnold Dixon and Johnny Taylor. They were imbibing."

Her mother stilled, fixed a look on her. "Those two are no good, Willa, but what has it do with you if Thomas—" The look in her mother's eyes sharpened. "Dora said Thomas walked you home from church last Sunday. And that he had waited for you and spoken with you after school a few times, but— Oh, Willa! You haven't accepted his court again?"

She shook her head. "Not really, Mama. It was only for a few days until I could think of what to do about—"

"About what?"

She blew out a breath and folded her hands in her lap. "He threatened to tell everyone the truth about his running off and deserting me. And he hinted that he would resurrect the gossip about Papa abandoning us. I couldn't face that. I couldn't put you through that again, Mama, so—"

"So you let Thomas court you to protect me from *gossip?*" Her mother's voice was hushed, horrified. "Oh, Willa…" Tears slid down her mother's cheeks.

She pushed out of the chair, went to her knees and grasped her mother's hands. "Not you alone, Mama. I *hate* gossip. That's why I pretended I told Thomas to go west before. I don't want people's scorn, or their pity. And I don't want them to hurt you again. But—" her mother squeezed her hands "—there's no way—" another squeeze "—to avoid it now." She stopped her rush of words. "What, Mama?"

"Willa, I have done you a disservice." Her mother, her eyes bright with tears, gazed down at her. "You were so young when your papa left I didn't realize you even noticed the talk about the village." Her mother's hands squeezed hers again, gave them a little shake. "*Talk,* Willa, not gossip. The people in this village are our friends. They care about us—about you. They were angry and concerned when your papa deserted us, and so they talked about it."

"Yes. And they hurt you, Mama." She rose and went back to her chair. "I heard you crying at night. And I hated Papa for leaving and them for gossiping about us and hurting you."

"You're *wrong,* Willa. I didn't cry because of gossip. I cried because I didn't know how I was going to care for you. We were about to lose our home and I had nowhere to go, no way to earn a living. It was our friends, talking together, who came up with the idea of my doing laundry in exchange for living in our cabin. I will be eternally grateful to them for that."

"I didn't know… I thought you were the one…"

Her mother shook her head and wiped moisture from her cheeks. "No. I was too devastated when your papa walked out on us to think clearly. All I could see was the trouble and want ahead. It was the women of the village who figured out the answer. Now… What did you mean by 'there's no way to avoid it now'?"

She studied her mother's face, took a deep breath and let the words flow. "When I saw Thomas tonight, I hurried away. I was shocked by his drinking and did not want him to approach me. Reverend Calvert, who was chatting with Ellen, thought I was ill. He followed and offered to escort me home."

The memory of his concern for her stole the strength from her voice. She leaned down and picked up the shirt that had fallen to the floor earlier and smoothed it out on her lap. "Thomas stopped us on the path and ac-

cused Reverend Calvert of 'poaching on his property.'
He told him we were betrothed." *The look on his face!
What must he think of her...* She blinked, swallowed
back a rush of tears. "When the reverend left, Thomas
reminded me I was 'his,' and warned me not to 'walk
out' with another man again. He said if I did, he would
spread gossip about my 'loose virtue.'"

Her mother jerked erect. "I wish David Dibble *had*
beaten him!"

She'd never seen her mother so angry. She grabbed
hold of her nearest fisted, work-roughened hand. "It's
all right. Sit down, Mama."

"It certainly is *not* all right!" Her mother pulled her
hand away and paced around the room, stopped by the
door. "I've a good mind to go and speak to David right
now."

"David?" She stared at her mother, shocked by her
use of the given name, even more by the color that
climbed into her mother's cheeks.

"I mean, *Mr. Dibble,* of course. I misspoke in my
anger."

She nodded, watched her mother rub her hands on
her skirt, smooth back her hair, then come back and
take her seat. She was *nervous!*

"Why do you say it's all right, Willa?"

The question brought the memory of her confrontation with Thomas flooding back. "Because the strangest
thing happened. I was frightened of the way Thomas
was acting, and then I suddenly realized he was a bully,
like some children are, and I was no longer frightened."
She folded the shirt and set it aside. "I demanded to
know what he wanted as it was obvious he had no re-

gard for me. And he told me." She stopped, still amazed at the way things had changed.

"What did he say?"

"That he had lost his stake to go west in a game of chance and come back to Pinewood to get another. That he figured about six months of my teaching pay would be enough."

His note! *Willa, I'm sorry I haven't time to wait and talk to you, but I must hasten to meet Jack. He sent word he has funds for us to head west, and I am going after my dream.* It all made sense now.

"Willa…"

She jerked her thoughts back. "I just realized he *never* wanted me, Mama, not even before when he wooed me. He only wanted to marry me for my pay, and this time, when I refused, he threatened me to make me agree."

"But, Willa, if—"

"Yes." She looked at her mother and nodded. "I told him his plan was flawed, that married women were not allowed to teach and, therefore, there would be no pay if he wed me." Laughter surged. She shook her head. "Isn't it *odd,* Mama, that the very thing that made Thomas pursue me is the thing that set me free of him!"

The urge to laugh died. Her breath caught. "I could be *married* to him, Mama. Thank goodness he left that first time."

"Yes, thank goodness!" Her mother leaned forward and gripped her hands. "I'm so glad you're rid of him, Willa."

"Yes, but he was very angry, and I'm certain he will seek revenge. I'm afraid the gossip will start tomorrow, and that I might be dismissed from my teaching position because of it. A teacher must have no hint of a taint on her reputation." Her throat constricted, tears stung her eyes. "I'm sorry, Mama. I don't know what we'll do without my earnings."

Her mother rose and came to her. "Hush, Willa." She yielded to her mother's comforting arms, rested her head against her breast. "There's no reason to cry. Trust our friends, dear. No one in this village will believe such a vicious tale about you." Her mother cupped her chin and tilted her head up to meet her gaze. "I promise you, Willa Jean, if Thomas Hunter spreads that rumor, all he will do is make it impossible for him to stay in Pinewood."

Moonlight flowed from the sky, endowed the landscape with silver splendor and created shadows and dimensions that played tricks on the eye. Cold from off the small window panes touched Matthew's face. He frowned, wished for something pressing to do. He had heard Joshua and Sally's bedtime prayers, and now there was nothing but the empty night stretching out before him.

Willa was betrothed. The knowledge brought an inner emptiness, a hollowness. He would no longer be able to seek her out, to try to win her…favor. He yanked his hands from his pockets, scrubbed the back of his neck and paced to the other side of his study. He sat at his desk, closed his eyes to pray, saw an image of Willa's face, the stricken look in her eyes as she had acknowledged her betrothal, and opened them again.

Something was wrong. She had seemed…what? He couldn't put a name to it. It was simply something he'd sensed. Or was it something he wished? How could she marry a man like that? There was something about Thomas Hunter, something beyond the drinking and the belligerence, something in his eyes…

The muscles in his face drew taut. It had taken all of his inner strength to walk away and leave Willa standing there alone on the path to town with that two-bit drunk. And then he'd had to go back and pretend to enjoy the stump burning for Joshua's and Sally's sakes. It had been a miserable afternoon.

It was time for some coffee. He yanked his thoughts from the memory and headed for the kitchen. It would give him something to do. He raised the wick on the oil lamp to give more light, quietly fitted it into the slot on the stove plate and set it aside even though his hands itched to slam it down. He'd wanted to slam and bang things ever since he'd refrained from punching Thomas Hunter's sneering face. If only the man had thrown a punch with those fisted hands and given him a reason, he would have put all that sparring he and Robert had done when they were young to good use.

He curved his lips in a grim smile, cleared away the ashes, placed wood on the smoldering embers, then replaced the plate and opened the draft. The lingering smell of the beef stew Bertha had cooked for dinner made his stomach turn over. It was good, and Bertha was an excellent cook, but he'd only been able to choke down a few bites for the children's sakes.

Being a parent was more difficult than he'd expected. He shook his head and ladled water into the coffeepot. He hadn't thought about all the little ordinary things you had to do, like smiling and pretending you were having a good time, or eating when your stomach was tied in knots. But Joshua and Sally were worth it.

He snatched up the bag of "Old Java" and grabbed a spoon. He'd always wanted a family, a wife and children of his own, and lately he'd been thinking—

A knock jolted him out of his thoughts. He spun around and hurried to the door. People coming at this time of night meant an emergency. He paused and closed his eyes. "Give me grace to answer the need, Lord. Amen." He opened the door, peered out into the night. "Yes?"

Thomas Hunter stepped out of the shadows into the moonlight and looked up at him. "C'mon outside, Reverend. You an' me got to talk."

Something decidedly unspiritual rushed through him. *I'll handle this one on my own, Lord.*

The thought went winging on its way before he had even closed the door. His second thought, as he crossed the porch, was that he'd have to repent for the first one later. He found he didn't mind. He walked down the steps and stopped. "You have something to say to me, Mr. Hunter?"

"I want money."

Was the man asking alms of the church? That was doubtful, judging from the look on his face. "Would you care to explain that request?"

"I need money to head west. See, I planned to marry Willa, figured about six months or so of her teacher's pay would stake me, and meanwhile, I'd have it nice and cozy living with her in her ma's cabin."

He sucked in a breath, stepped forward. *Wait, let him strike the first blow.* He stopped, took another breath.

"Don't like that idea, do you, Reverend?"

What he would like was to wipe the sneering smile right off Thomas Hunter's face.

"Well, don't fret about it. I found out tonight married women can't teach school, an' if I married Willa she wouldn't have any pay."

Thank You, Lord!

"That's why I come here."

The *gall* of the man! "To ask alms of the church?"

Thomas stepped closer, narrowed his eyes. "I ain't askin' nothin' of any church." His lips curled into that contemptuous smile again. "I seen the way you looked at Willa today, an' your bein' a preacher an' all, I figure you wouldn't want any sort of gossip 'bout that gettin' round."

Let him strike the first blow. He flexed his hands, left them open. "And you want me to give you money to keep those rumors from starting. That, Mr. Hunter, is blackmail."

"I don't care what you call it, just give me the money. I figure a hundred dollars will do."

He shook his head. "I'm afraid not. I'm not frightened by your threatened rumors, Mr. Hunter, and I do not pay blackmail. 'Treasures of wickedness profit nothing, but righteousness delivereth from death.' I suggest you give up your scheme, repent and go to work to earn your money."

"I ain't interested in your suggestions, Preacher!" Thomas's eyes darkened, glittered. Moonlight outlined his jutted chin. "Maybe you don't care if rumors 'bout you travel 'round town, but how 'bout Willa? How would you feel if rumors of Willa's loose virtue—"

His left fist jabbed forward in a blur, connected with Thomas's jaw with a satisfying thud, his right followed in an uppercut to that perfectly outlined jutting jaw that landed with all the force of his shoulder behind it.

Thomas Hunter's head snapped back and he dropped like a stone at his feet.

"'Violence covereth the mouth of the wicked.' But you sure took your sweet time about it, Reverend."

He pivoted. Bertha stood in the dark shadow on the porch. He frowned. "How long have you been there, Bertha?"

"I followed you out the door."

"Then you heard—"

"Not a thing worth repeating." She stepped to the edge of the porch and looked down at him. "You needn't fear of anything that plug-ugly said going any further than us, Reverend. I love Willa, too."

Too. His heart jolted. Were his feelings for Willa that plain to see? Probably so because he'd just knocked a man unconscious for threatening to besmirch her reputation. He grinned and rubbed his stinging knuckles. "I trust that information also will go no further than the two of us."

Bertha grinned right back. "I let a man do his own courting, Reverend. Now, you'd best stop feeling proud of yourself and think about what comes next." She dipped her head toward Thomas, who was beginning to stir. "What're you going to do with him?"

"Why, I'm going to give him his heart's desire and help him on his way west." His grin died. "Thankfully, no one will pay any attention to my leaving in my buggy this time of night. Pastors get emergency calls at all hours." He leaned down, grabbed hold of the back of Thomas Hunter's jacket collar and started dragging him toward the stable. "But I have to say, this one is going to befuddle those who see my buggy and try to figure out what the emergency was and who came for me."

"For sure it'll give people something to talk about." Bertha chuckled and turned to go inside. "I'll get your coat."

The buggy jolted and swayed. Thomas Hunter gave a groan and lifted his head. "What happened?"

Matthew watched as the trussed man slumped in the corner tried to shove himself erect by placing his shoulder against the roof frame. "A wheel hit a deep rut. Go back to sleep."

Hunter swore and gave up the struggle. "Whyn't you untie my hands now? My jaw hurts an' I want to rub it."

"I'll untie you when we get to the depot and it's time for you to board the stage, not before." An animal broke from the woods and dashed across the road in front of them. He tightened his grip on the reins as the mare snorted and tossed her head. "Easy, girl, easy. It's only a fox."

"I can always come back you know."

He glanced at Hunter. Must be the alcohol and the fogginess from being knocked unconscious had worn off—the man's belligerent attitude was back. "I wouldn't advise it. You're not the only one who can start gossip, and if you ever show up in Pinewood again I will personally see to it that you are not welcomed by anyone. Including your drinking pals. How will Johnny Taylor…excuse me… I mean, *Jack,* feel when he finds out you had money for the stage ride and headed west without him? He did share his stake with you the last time, did he not?"

"How did you find out about that?"

He turned his head and gave the two-bit bully a wide smile. "You talk in your sleep. It's very enlightening."

Hunter glared. "I ain't afraid of your threats. You're a preacher an' preachers don't do things like startin' rumors."

"I'll bet you didn't think preachers knew how to throw a knockout punch, either." He gave him another smile.

A surly growl was his only answer. A few minutes later snores came from the other corner. He drove on, thankful for the bright moonlight.

Matthew glanced up at the sky. Dawn was but a lighter gray promise in the east. It was a long trip to the depot in Dunkirk, especially through the night, but worth the time. He didn't want anyone to find out about this. Thankfully, he had Bertha to care for Joshua and Sally until he got home. He frowned, glanced at the sky again. He ought to reach home by dusk, he'd make better time in the daylight.

He tightened his grip on Hunter's arm and hurried him to the stage. "I've paid your fare to Buffalo." He stepped behind him and untied the rope that bound his hands. "This time, when you get to Buffalo, you will have to get a job on a boat and work your way west from there."

Hunter scowled and rubbed his wrists. "I'll need some money for food and such, 'til I get that job."

He coiled the rope and shook his head. "Sorry, but paying your stage fare is as much as I will do."

"Then I'll have to take the money!"

Hunter's fist punched through the air toward him. He jerked his head to the side, rammed his fist into the bully's exposed gut, then caught his chin with an uppercut when he bent over.

"Ugh!" Hunter's eyes widened, then closed. He collapsed in a heap beside the stage.

He opened the door, picked Hunter up by the collar and the seat of the pants, heaved him inside and closed the door. He handed a half eagle up to the driver. "That's for putting him on a boat headed west."

The driver nodded, tucked the coin in his leather vest and grinned down at him. "That's quite an uppercut you've got there."

He rubbed his swollen knuckles and returned the grin. "Thanks. I learned it from my brother."

"You a boxer or somethin'?"

His grin widened. "No, I'm a preacher."

Chapter Thirteen

"**V**ery good, Eli." Willa took the stick of chalk the boy handed her and turned to the class. "Chloe, please come and work the next problem."

Someone coughed. She sighed. It was that time of year. There would be coughs and sniffles among the children all winter. She made a mental note to bring in camphor and keep thyme and peppermint tea on hand and gave Chloe the chalk.

The sun's golden rays streamed through the small glass panes from a blue, cloudless sky. It was a welcome break after the cold weather they had been experiencing. But there was a dark cloud hanging over her. This afternoon it would be two days since Thomas had made his threats. Nothing had happened yesterday. When would the gossip start? Would she have to face it when she left school today? Her already-sour stomach roiled. She dreaded having her name besmirched, even if, as her mother said, no one in the village would believe the lies.

"I'm done, Miss Wright."

"Oh. Yes. Very good, Chloe. You may take your

seat." She focused her thoughts and moved over to stand by the slate board. "Now that the examples are completed, I want you first graders to copy the last four problems on your slates and write the answers. Be sure to keep your numbers in a straight line and make your plus signs clear."

She raised the piece of chalk and wrote the five vowels in upper and lower cases. "Kindergartners, write these letters on your slates, and form them carefully. I shall come around to check them and to help you. Second graders—" She brushed the chalk dust from her fingers and lifted her gaze to the last bench where the oldest children in her class were seated. Mary Burton was bent forward, her forehead resting on her crossed arms on the bench desk. That did not bode well. Mary was a very painstaking scholar.

"Mary?" She hurried to the young girl, placed her hand on her small back and leaned over her. "What's wrong, Mary?"

"I don't f-feel good." The muffled words ended with a cough.

"Look at me, Mary."

The eight-year-old lifted her head and looked up at her through squinted eyes.

"Have you a headache?" She noted Mary's glassy eyes and red cheeks and placed her hand on her forehead. Too warm.

"Yes, Miss Wright." Mary coughed and winced. "My stomach feels sick, too."

"All right. You rest, dear."

Mary's friend and seatmate raised her hand.

"Yes, Susan?"

"Mary didn't eat her potato at dinnertime, Miss Wright. And she's been coughing all day."

"Thank you, Susan." That was true. She'd noticed the cough, but only as a distraction. One or the other of the children were always coughing and, given the cold weather they'd been having until a few days ago, she'd placed little importance on it. Now, with the headache, fever and stomach upset taken in conjunction with the cough…

She shifted her gaze to the second row. "Jeffery…" The boy stood and turned to face her. "I want you to run home and tell your mother that I said Mary is ill and she should bring the wagon to take her home."

"Ma's not home, Miss Wright. Pa took the wagon to Olville to get some supplies, and Ma went along to see Aunt Beth's new baby. Cissy's the only one at home."

"I see. All right, Jeffery. Take your seat." She looked down at Mary, brushed a lock of hair off the child's hot, dry temple. Now what? She could keep her here until her parents came home, but that might not be until late tonight. That wouldn't do.

She lifted her head and scanned the class. The children had twisted around on the benches to watch. "Continue your assigned work, please."

There was a rustle as the young scholars turned back to face the front, then silence, broken only by the ticking of the pendulum clock on the wall. She glanced up at its round face. It was almost time for dismissal. Perhaps she could walk Mary home. No, that wouldn't do, either. Mary was too ill to walk that distance.

She sighed and drew her gaze back. It snared on Joshua's golden-blond curls. She straightened, stared at the boy as he bent over his slate working the problems, fought a battle with herself and won. "Joshua, come here please."

The boy stood and hurried to her. "Yes, Miss Wright?"

"I have a very important task for you, so listen carefully." She held his gaze with hers. "I want you to go home, and if your uncle is there I want you to tell him Miss Wright says Mary Burton is ill and asks if he will please take her home in his buggy. Then I want you to come back and tell me what he says. Do you understand?"

"Yes, Miss Wright."

"All right, then. Go, and please hurry."

She moved to the front of the room as Joshua rushed out the door. "Children, it's time to go home. Leave your work. We will continue it tomorrow. For now, quietly gather your things and leave. Sally and Jeffery, you wait here until Joshua returns."

She opened a desk drawer, lifted the top rag off the pile she kept there to wipe the slate board clean, crossed to the short bench, doused the rag in the bucket and squeezed out the excess water. She turned, glanced at the children silently filing out the door, then looked at the two still seated and smiled reassurance. "Joshua will be back soon, Sally. Jeffery, you may gather your things now—and Mary's also. I want you to be ready to go if the pastor comes."

The boy scurried to obey.

The clock ticked. Her long skirts whispered across the plank floor as she hurried back to her sick scholar. "I have a cold cloth, Mary. It should help you feel better. Lift your head a bit." She folded the rag to fit Mary's small forehead, slipped it in place, then sat on the bench beside her and rubbed her back to comfort her and ease her coughing. She looked up at the sound of tiptoeing footsteps. Sally climbed onto her knees on the bench.

"I'll hold your hand, Mary. It made me feel better when Mama held my hand." Sally's small hand clasped Mary's larger one.

Willa blinked and swallowed past the lump Sally's concern for her schoolmate brought to her throat. She couldn't resist touching Sally's cheek, then smiling her approval when Sally glanced at her. The little girl's face lit with a return smile so sweet it made her catch her breath.

"He's coming!" Joshua burst into the schoolroom, bent over, grasped his knees and gasped for air. "Uncle Matt is…hitching up the buggy. He says to tell you… he'll be…right along."

"That's wonderful. Thank you, Joshua. You've been very helpful." *The poor boy, he must have run the entire way.* She rose, placed her hand on his shoulder and led him to the bench. "Sit down and catch your breath, then gather your things and take Sally home."

She touched the rag on Mary's forehead. It was already warm. The little girl coughed again, a raspy, dry cough. Worry squiggled through her. She removed the rag, carried it to the bucket, squeezed it out in the cold water and hurried back.

Joshua and Sally were going out the door. She waved goodbye, replaced the rag then sat on the bench, rubbed Mary's back and tried to recall the signs of the various childhood illnesses the children in previous classes had suffered. It didn't work. The embarrassment crept in. How was she to face Matthew Calvert after the insulting accusations Thomas had hurled at him? She had hoped at least a few days would pass before—

She jolted at the click of the door opening. Her stomach knotted.

"I understand there is a sick young lady here who needs a ride home."

She rose, watched Matthew Calvert close the distance between them in two long strides and lifted her chin. "Yes, and her brother also. Thank you for coming, Reverend Calvert. I wouldn't have sent for you, but Mary's mother and father are in Olville, and I could not think of any other way." She took a deep breath, pressed her lips together to stop her nervous prattling and bent over Mary. It was easier not to look at him.

"I'm happy to be of service, Miss Wright."

His deep voice was calm and pleasant, without a trace of accusation or disgust. She glanced sideways, watched him bend down and scoop the young girl into his arms. Her tension eased. He would be gone in a few moments.

"We'll have you home soon, Mary. Come along, son." He stepped to the door. Jeffery, his hands full of his and Mary's things, walked at his side. The reverend stopped at the door and turned his head. The expectant look in his eyes brought the word he'd used crashing into her consciousness.

We'll. She opened her mouth to explain she would not be going with them, then closed it. Mary needed her to hold her to protect her from the buggy's jouncing. Avoiding embarrassment was a petty and selfish aim in the face of the child's misery. And the fear that someone might see her riding in the buggy with the pastor and add that tidbit to the gossip that must by now be circulating throughout the village was not to be considered. She hurried to open the door.

* * *

The buggy dipped and swayed over the rutted, weed-covered wagon path that stretched from the Burton farmhouse. Willa gripped the hold strap and held herself erect as Matthew Calvert reined the horse back out onto the road.

"Mary seemed relieved to get home. She looked quite ill to me, Miss Wright—and you look concerned. Is there something seriously wrong with the girl?"

She turned her head and met his troubled gaze, noted the frown that creased his forehead. "I don't know, Reverend. I've seen these symptoms before, and I think she may be coming down with measles or, perhaps, chicken pox or whooping cough." She let her breath out in a long sigh. "If I'm right, it's likely that, whatever the disease, it will spread through the entire class."

His frown deepened. "Then Joshua and Sally could become ill?"

There was worry in his voice. For the children or himself? "We'll know in a few days. Whatever is wrong with Mary will be apparent by then." She stared ahead at the horse's rump, wished for more speed. Being alone with Matthew Calvert was disquieting.

The reins snapped. The horse picked up its pace.

A wry smile touched her lips. Perhaps he was as eager to be out of her company.

"Whenever I think I have this parenting thing figured out, something else comes along." Frustration laced through his ordinarily calm tone. "There's only one thing I know for sure."

She couldn't resist. "And that is?"

"Raising children is no easy task."

"Indeed." She glanced over at him. He sounded so

sincere. But where was his concern and worry over the children's welfare the night of the Halls' dinner when he had put them abed early as punishment for needing to be with him? It seemed as if—like her father's—Matthew Calvert's concern for his children rose only when their welfare did not interfere with his own pleasures. It would no doubt give out quickly in the face of the time and attention demanded of a parent by a sick child. She turned her head back to face forward, dipped it when wagons passed and wished for her cloak to hide behind.

The buggy wheels whispered a gritty accompaniment to the thud of the horse's hooves as they rolled along the hardpacked dirt road. The silence grew tense. She cast a sidelong look at Matthew Calvert, caught his gaze on her and clenched her jaw. Why was he looking at her like that? She smoothed a fold from the skirt of her red wool dress and frowned. It was such a plain, serviceable gown. Certainly nothing like the satin confections Ellen wore.

Something tickled her cheek. She reached up to brush the irritation away and froze. Hair! No wonder he'd been staring. She stole another glance at him. He was looking at her hand. Warmth rushed along her cheekbones. "Forgive my appearance, Reverend Calvert. I didn't realize, in the hustle of getting Mary out to the buggy, I'd forgotten my bonnet." *More fodder for gossip if they were seen.* She would warn him when she apologized.

"The Bible says a woman's hair is her glory, Miss Wright. I find nothing wrong with your appearance. It is both modest and pleasing."

Her pulse skittered and sped. She whipped her head back around, stared into his warm, quiet gaze and irritation surged. The man was doing it again. He always managed to undermine her strongest intentions to stay aloof.

The buggy jolted, jarred her back to her senses. She jerked her gaze forward, tucked the errant wisp of hair behind her ear, tugged the rolled hem of her dress sleeve down in place and clasped her hands in her lap. The buggy swayed around the corner onto Oak Street. Relief relaxed her grip. The school was just ahead.

"Shall I stop at the schoolhouse so you can fetch your bonnet and other things?"

Stop so— Surely he didn't think she expected that he would take her home? "Yes. Please stop."

He pulled back on the reins, the horse stopped and the buggy swayed to a halt.

She burst into speech before he could climb down to assist her. "Before I leave you, I want to, again, thank you for taking Mary home. It was very kind of you."

"Leave?" He draped the reins over the dashboard and turned on the seat to face her.

She ignored the measuring look he fixed on her and rushed on. "And also, I wish to apologize for Thomas Hunter's uncivil behavior the other day."

His eyes darkened. "There's no need for you to apologize, Miss Wright. You did nothing wrong."

"Yes, Mr. Calvert, I did." She looked into his frowning face and lifted her chin. "Were I not so cowardly, you would not have been placed in such an embarrassing position. You see, Thomas and I were betrothed a few months ago, but then he…left town. When he returned recently, he wanted to continue with our plans to wed. I refused him, but he did not accept my answer." She took a breath and looked down. "He was angry when he confronted us, and, well, I was frightened, and so did not deny his false statement." Why was he rubbing his knuckles? They looked bruised. His hands stilled.

She lifted her gaze, found it ensnared by his. Everything in her went quiet. His eyes darkened, amber flames burned in their depths.

"I would never have allowed him to harm you, Miss Wright."

His soft, quiet words settled over her like a warm blanket.

"Willa! *There* you are."

She snapped her gaze to the road. Ellen was coming down the path toward the buggy. *Ellen.* She gathered her wits and looked back at Matthew. He was looking at Ellen—of course. What a weak-willed fool she was. She rose, grabbed hold of the roof brace and turned to back out of the buggy. "Thank you again for your help, Reverend Calvert."

"Wait, I'll help—"

"No, I'll manage." Satisfaction shot through her. Her voice was as cool as the metal brace she clutched—he would never guess these last minutes had brought her to the brink of tears. She lowered herself to the ground, stiffened her spine and headed down the path to meet Ellen.

Chapter Fourteen

The last person she wanted to see at the moment was Ellen. But Ellen was also the person she most needed to see—fancy gown and all. Willa squared her shoulders.

The clop of a horse's hooves sounded behind her. Wheels started to roll. She clenched her hands. Would he stop? She couldn't bear the thought of Matthew Calvert flirting with Ellen. Not after…what? The caring she had felt from him. Or had she misread him? Was he only being polite in saying he would have protected her from Thomas? She could have misunderstood that. But his eyes…

She thrust the image of Matthew Calvert's dark, intent gaze from her mind and pasted a smile on her face. "You were looking for me, Ellen?" The hooves sounded beside her. *Please don't stop. Please go home.*

"Yes, I wanted to tell you—" Ellen stopped, turned toward the street and smiled.

She clenched her hands tighter and held her breath. From the corner of her eye she saw Matthew Calvert smile and doff his hat in greeting. Her breath escaped in a gust when he drove on. She braced herself and studied Ellen's face. Had the gossip about her started? Is that what she was going to tell her?

Ellen frowned and stared after the buggy. "I guess Matthew is in a hurry."

Matthew. Ellen's use of his given name stabbed deep. She'd forgotten they were on a first-name basis in private. Should she warn Ellen that he was a Lothario? No. She could be wrong. "What did you want, Ellen?"

Her friend turned back, gasped, her eyes widened. "Willa, for goodness' sakes! Where is your bonnet?" Her eyes narrowed. "And why were you riding in Matthew's carriage?"

"Mary Burton is ill, and Reverend Calvert was kind enough to help me take her home. In the rush, I forgot my bonnet." *That's all it was. He was being kind. It was a mistake to read anything more into those last few minutes.* "Now tell me what you wanted, so I can get my things and go home."

"Well, you needn't be huffish! What's wrong with you?"

What indeed? "I'm sorry, Ellen. I'm concerned about Mary and her illness. I suspect it is either measles or chicken pox or—"

"Chicken pox!" Ellen gasped the word and stepped back. "You know I haven't had chicken pox, Willa. I was visiting Grandma Stanton when you all caught them."

She frowned and hurried to cover her slip of the tongue. If she weren't so upset she never would have mentioned the disease. "I don't *know* if Mary has chicken pox. It will be a few days before we will find out what is causing her illness. Now—"

"Nonetheless, you know how I feel about being around illness."

Memory rose and overcame her irritation. "Yes, I do." Her voice softened. "I remember when Walker died. He was my friend."

"And he was my only brother. And the measles took him from me. I suppose it's well that I've been warned, but I don't want to talk about it." Ellen tossed her head. "I chanced to meet Mrs. Sheffield at *Evans's Millinery,* and she requested that I ask you to stop and see her on your way home."

Ellen's head toss, and her emphasis on the store's name, drew her attention to the bonnet that framed Ellen's beautiful face. A dark blue chip cottage bonnet with flowers adorning the quilted brim. "Your new bonnet is lovely."

Her friend smiled, lifted her hand and touched the bow of wide satin ribbon beneath her chin. "Mrs. Evans finished it today." Ellen glanced in the direction Matthew's buggy had gone and her lower lip pouted out. "I so wanted Matthew to see it. He's so attentive and—" She gasped. Her hand pressed against her chest. "Oh, Willa! You don't think Matthew will get ill? I couldn't bear to lose him."

Horror whispered through Ellen's voice. Guilt shook her. "I'm sure he will be fine, Ellen. And it may well be that Mary only has a very bad cold." She smiled reassurance and changed the subject. The less she thought about Matthew Calvert the better. "Do you want to come with me while I fetch my things?"

Ellen's gaze darted to the schoolhouse. A shudder shook her. "I'll not step foot in that building again until we know it's safe."

She stood and watched her friend hurry away. Ellen *was* afraid. She wasn't gliding now. She was walking the way she had before her vanity had taken over. She sighed and started up the stone walk to the schoolhouse. There was nothing she could do to relieve Ellen's fear. Only time could do that.

She climbed the steps, crossed the small porch to the door and stopped. Ellen hadn't mentioned any gossip. And Ellen had been to town. She would surely know. But then, there was Sophia's request that she come to see her.…

She sighed and entered the schoolhouse to gather her things.

Willa skirted the settle, stepped to the door and knocked. Her fingers tightened on her basket's handle. Why had Sophia asked her to come by?

"Come in!"

Sophia's voice, not Rose's. She took a deep breath, put her worries aside and opened the door. If anyone in the village would reject tales of her having "loose morals" it would be Sophia. The smell of stewing chicken permeated the air. She stepped inside, set her basket on the table and sniffed. "Mmm, I remember that smell. Your guests will enjoy their supper tonight."

"Some of them will."

"What do you mean, 'some of them'?" She crossed to the long work table, picked up a piece of diced carrot and popped it in her mouth.

Sophia looked up. "Gracious, that's like old times, except that Callie is not here begging for a piece of chicken." A smile warmed the older woman's violet eyes. "I'd give you a hug, Willa, dear, but my hands are a mess." She wiggled her fingers in the air, then went back to pulling chicken meat off the bones. "I meant that two of my guests are feeling poorly. I'm making chicken soup for them, but I'm not sure Mr. Arthur will be able to eat."

"Have you given him some of your red pepper and sumac leaf tea?" She pulled a face and gave an exaggerated shudder.

Sophia laughed and picked up the platter of chicken pieces. "I have. And it has helped Mr. Wingate. But I fear Mr. Arthur's illness is too advanced to benefit from it." She headed for the fireplace. "Bring along those carrots and onions please, Willa."

She grabbed the large, crockery bowl and followed. Chicken broth, with ripples of clear, rich fat floating on top, simmered in two large iron pots hanging from the crane. Her mouth watered at the delicious smell. "It reminds me of when I was a child to see you cooking. Is Rose still suffering with her back?"

"Yes, poor dear. If she's not better soon, I'll have to find a new cook. It's most inconvenient being without one." Sophia divided the pieces of meat between the pots, set the platter down and turned to her. "Hold on tight." She scooped her hands into the bowl, cupped them and added the captured diced carrots and onions to one of the pots, then reached for more. "I had a letter from Carrie this week."

The vegetables plopped into the broth, sank beneath the liquid, then floated to the top. Another double handful followed them.

"I hope she's well."

"Yes, but she seems unhappy. She mentions lots of beaus, but she seems to have little regard for the lot of them. I'm getting a mite concerned. I don't suppose she's told you anything?"

Don't tell Aunt Sophie. She shook her head. "Only the same. That she doesn't really care for any of her suitors." *And that her parents keep insisting she choose the wealthiest and most prominent socially among them.*

"Well, I don't like what I'm feeling when I read her letters. I'm going to write and insist she come for a visit soon." The older woman frowned and picked up the empty platter. "Dump the rest of those vegetables into the other pot, Willa. And mind your skirts with the fire. Have you time for tea?"

"I'm afraid not today." She added the carrots and onions to the soup broth and carried the bowl back to the work table. "Mary Burton took sick just before school let out, and I'm already late getting home."

Sophia slipped the platter into the dishpan and reached for the bowl. "Mary's mother and father went to Olville this morning. How did you get the poor child home?" The bowl joined the platter in the dishpan.

"Reverend Calvert was good enough to take her home in his buggy." She held her breath. The mention of Matthew Calvert would give Sophia the opportunity to bring up any gossip Thomas may have started.

Sophia nodded, scooped the chicken and vegetable leavings into the waste bucket, scrubbed her hands together in the dishwater and wiped them on her apron. "I would expect that of him. From what I've seen and heard of the reverend, he has a kind heart."

"Yes." *Though a wayward one.*

"Did you know he leaves a lamp burning all night? Bertha says he does it so people won't feel bad if they have to call on him for an emergency. And he always answers a call for help, no matter the hour. Like the other night." A frown creased Sophia's lovely face. "No, *two* nights ago, it was. I was straightening up a bit in the sitting room after the guests had retired, and I saw him heading toward Olville in his buggy." Her frown deepened. "No one seems to know where he went or what the emergency was."

And I don't want to gossip. Especially about Matthew Calvert and his pursuits. "No. I didn't know." She forced a smile. "I don't mean to press you, but if you could tell me why you wanted me to call? Mama will be wondering where I am."

"Mercy! I forgot all about that in the pleasure of your company. Wait here."

"Of course." She walked to the table and picked up her basket.

Sophia hurried to the door that led to her private quarters. Her voice floated back out the door. "I saw your mother when I was buying groceries at Barley's this morning, and she mentioned she needed to buy some fabric to make new aprons." The older woman emerged carrying a small bundle of cloth. "I told her I had some pieces left from the last time I had bed and table linens made that I thought would suit, and that I would send them home with you."

"Oh, how kind and thoughtful of you." She took the bundle into her arms, leaned forward and kissed Sophia's cheek. "I'm sure Mama will be most appreciative of these. Thank you. Now, I must get home."

"Of course, dear. And I must go check on my guests." Sophia patted her cheek and stepped in front of her. "Let me get the door for you."

Dusk had fallen. Willa hurried off the porch and around Sheffield House to Main Street. Oil lamps on the storefronts lit her way to the bridge over Stony Creek. She shifted the bundle in her arms to a more comfortable position and quickened her steps onto Brook Street.

Ahead, a shadow detached from a tree trunk, morphed into a man. *Thomas?* It was too dark to tell. She lifted her chin and, heart pounding, walked forward. No, not Thomas. The man was too short. He stepped out onto the path in front of her.

"Evening, Miss Wright."

Arnold Dixon. The smell of alcohol wafted toward her. Apprehension tingled along her nerves. He'd always been flirtatious, but he'd never been this bold before. She stopped, took a breath to steady her voice. "Let me pass, Mr. Dixon."

"Not yet." Johnny Taylor stepped from behind the tree and came over to them. "We want to talk to you."

Her mouth went dry. A tremor started in her knees and spread into her legs. She hiked her chin a notch higher. "I'm not interested in anything you have to say. Now, let me pass." She started around them.

They moved to block her.

Her heart lurched. She inched the bundle upward in front of her chest, took comfort in the barrier it presented between her and the men.

"Where's Thomas?"

"Thomas?" She stared at Johnny Taylor, confused by his tone. "I don't know where he is. I haven't seen him."

"Neither have we. Not since the stump burning. We thought maybe you two had gone off and got married."

"Certainly not." She itched to slap the leer off Arnold Dixon's face, but dared not make a move toward him. She shifted her gaze to Johnny Taylor and pushed authority into her voice. "I refused Thomas's suit that evening. We will not be wed. And it is certain he will no longer call on me. I would think he would come and see you, however. You *are* his friends, are you not?" *Where was Thomas?* She took a breath and tried again. "Now, please step out of my way."

"He figured to get the money from you to stake our trip west. Did you give him the money?"

Our trip? Johnny Taylor's tone sent shivers slithering up and down her spine, anger stiffened it. "I did not. I have no money to give anyone, Mr. Taylor. Now, good evening." She stepped straight ahead and looked up at him.

He scowled, nodded at Arnold Dixon and stepped aside.

She walked between the two men, fastened her gaze on her cabin and kept her shaking legs moving. *We haven't seen him since the stump burning.* Had Thomas left town again? Is that why there had been no gossip thus far? If only it could be so!

Two terse sentences and a scripture reference. Not much to show for two hours of work—or rather non-work.

Matthew shoved back from his desk, scrubbed his hand over the nape of his neck and frowned. He needed a haircut. Come to think of it, so did Joshua. The boy's hair was getting so long his blond curls flopped into his eyes. He would take him with him to Rizzo's barbershop tomorrow.

Why had she turned cool and aloof?

The thought hovered in his head. He rose and paced the room. No matter what he thought about, no matter what he did, or more accurately, *tried* to do, his thoughts circled back to Willa, to the way she had looked at him in the carriage this afternoon. There had been such warmth, such softness, such...trust...in her eyes in those last moments. And then, in an instant, it was gone. What had he done to make her withdraw like that?

His frown deepened, drew his brows down and creased his forehead. He'd never felt like this in his life. The woman had him completely flummoxed. He was elated and hopeful one moment, deflated and despairing the next. A wry smile tugged at his lips. Was this love? Was this what Robert and Judith had shared that had made them so blissfully happy? It was making him miserable.

He turned, grabbed his suit coat off the back of his chair and snuffed the lamp. He climbed the stairs by the dim light of the lamp in the entrance hall.

All was quiet. He opened the door and peeked in at Sally. She was sound asleep, the kitten curled on the cover beside her small hand. Her empty hand. She had put Judith's glove in the drawer of her nightstand a few days after she got the kitten, and there it had stayed. But she still wanted the lamp burning.

He stepped inside and lowered the wick. The kitten opened its eyes, yawned and closed them again. He stared down at the curled-up ball of fur. The day they had gone to pick out the kitten had been the first time he suspected his feelings for Willa Wright were growing beyond a strong attraction. He *had* wanted to kiss her that day. And that want was getting stronger every time he saw her. This afternoon, in the buggy, he'd had all he could do to keep from taking her in his arms.

He closed Sally's door, moved down the hall and peeked in at Joshua. The boy was sprawled out on his stomach, one arm hanging down over the side of the bed, the dog's head resting on his other shoulder. He grinned. That dog purely wore the boy out.

A feeling of lack spread through him, a hunger to share these quiet, private moments with a wife. And the wife he wanted to share them with was Willa.

He picked up the lamp from the hall table and walked to his bedroom. Light moved in a golden circle over the carpet as he crossed the room. He set the lamp on his nightstand, threw back the covers, slipped out of his shirt, shoes and pants and flopped down against the pillows.

He'd begun seriously praying about a wife and family of his own about a year ago, but he'd met no woman who had drawn his heart. And then Robert and Judith had died and he'd brought their children here to Pinewood to heal and met Willa.

Nothing in his life had ever prepared him for the immediate, strong attraction he'd felt the moment he looked into Willa's eyes. Nor for the way that attraction continued to grow, to deepen every time he saw her. He snuffed the lamp, pulled the covers up to his chest and laced his hands behind his head. Was she the mate God had for him?

He let out a frustrated growl, flopped onto his side and yanked his pillow into place. "The woman has me going in circles, Lord. My head can't figure out what is going on, and I don't dare trust my heart. Make Your will clear to me, oh, Lord. Tell me, what is Your will?"

Willa bolted upright and stared into the darkness. Something kept taunting her—floating just out of reach at the edge of her dream. What *was* it?

She frowned and propped her pillow against the headboard. Whatever nagged at her, she would get no sleep until she figured it out. Her day had certainly been an unsettling one. Beginning with Mary's illness and that unnerving buggy ride alone with Matthew Calvert on the way back to the schoolhouse. What was wrong with her, responding to him that way? Ellen loved him, and believed that he cared for her. That they would be wed.

She tugged the quilt up around her shoulders and thought about those last few minutes. He had seemed so sincere, so...caring, sitting there rubbing his knuckles and listening to her apology. And the way he had looked at her when he'd said "I would never have let him hurt you, Miss Wright" had stolen her breath. The thing gnawing at her slipped closer. She grasped for the thought, and it skittered away.

Was that it? Had it to do with her apology? She had been honest. Perhaps not precise, but honest. Nothing came to her. She sighed and skimmed over her conversation with Ellen, found nothing enlightening there, and moved on to her call on Sophia. There was nothing of note there, either. She had helped with the soup...they had spoken about Callie and about Mary's illness and Matthew Calvert taking her home. Sophia had commented on Matthew's kindness, and shared a bit about how she had seen him driving his buggy toward Olville two nights ago to—

She stiffened, went still. There it was again! She tried to capture the thought, but it disappeared like a wisp of smoke. Was it the gossip? How could it be? What had Matthew Calvert's driving his buggy to Olville to do with her?

Two nights ago.

She gasped, jerked forward and clasped her hands over her mouth. *We haven't seen him since the stump burning.* That was two nights ago. And Matthew Calvert's knuckles were bruised. Had he… Oh, that was ridiculous! Why would he fight with Thomas and then take him out of town? The man was a *preacher.* It was all a mere coincidence. Still…where was Thomas?

I would never have let him hurt you, Miss Wright.

She frowned, lowered her pillow, slipped beneath the quilt and closed her eyes. Matthew Calvert was courting Ellen—or soon would be. And he was a gentleman. What he had said meant nothing beyond mere politeness. A gentleman was expected to protect a lady, and of course, he would profess to do that. Yet, his remembered words enfolded her like a warm, soft blanket.

Chapter Fifteen

"I'm home, Mama." Willa set her basket on the lamp table, shoved off her hood, unfastened her cloak and hung it on a peg beside the door. "Mama?"

Silence.

She frowned and walked into the kitchen, skirted around the table and glanced into the lean-to wash shed. Water steamed in the large iron pots hanging from the crane in the fireplace. Clothes soaked in the wash and rinse tubs.

She crossed to the back door and stepped outside into the chill November air. "Mama?"

The yard was empty. An uneasy feeling hit the pit of her stomach. Her mother was always home. She whirled and went back inside, headed for her mother's bedroom.

"Oh!"

"Mama!" She jolted to a stop, pressed her hand to her chest and stared at her mother who had jerked to a halt in the kitchen doorway.

"Gracious!" Her mother huffed out a breath. "You startled me, Willa."

"And you, me." She laughed and patted her chest. "I was looking for you."

"Are you ill?" Her mother's long skirts swished as she hurried toward her with a purposeful stride.

"No, Mama. I'm fine."

"Then why are you home this time of day?"

Her mother stopped in front of her and scanned her face, touched her cheek with the backs of her fingers. How often that touch had soothed her as a child, especially when she was ill. There would likely be a lot of such concerned, yet comforting, touches going on around the village soon.

"I'm home because school is closed. Mary broke out with chicken pox last night. And so did Jeffery. I'm sorry if I worried you." She leaned forward and kissed her mother's cheek. It was smooth and soft, unlike the dry, work-roughened hand that had pressed against her face. "Mr. Townsend came by early this morning and told me the board had decided to close the school in hope that it will stop the spread of the disease. When the children arrived, I sent them home."

"That's different. It sounds like a good idea."

"Perhaps, but I fear it is already too late. Mary was very sick the other day, and Jeffery was coughing a bit, too. In my experience—from past years—it's likely that some of the other children may have already caught chicken pox from them."

"I suppose. Seems like it doesn't take much."

She followed her mother into the lean-to and watched her remove her old, threadbare wool cape and hang it by the back door. A frown wrinkled her brow. She'd been saving every penny she could to buy fabric and sew her mother a new cloak. One with a collar. And Mrs. Hall had promised to help her make a matching bonnet. Now, with the school closed, and no pay… She shook off the gloomy thought. "Anyway, until school opens again, I will have more time to help you."

She lifted an apron off a peg on the wall, slipped it on, grabbed the ties and made a bow at the small of her back. "I don't recall your mentioning going to town. I would have been happy to pick up whatever you needed on my way home."

"I didn't go to town. I was next door at Dora's." Her mother lifted a shirt out of the water, soaped it, then bunched it in her hands and rubbed it up and down on the washboard. "I went out to hang— Oh, I forgot about the clothes! They're still outside in the basket. When I saw Dora looking so sick, I left them and went to help her." Her mother dropped the shirt back in the water and rinsed her hands free of clinging soapsuds.

"I'll go hang the clothes, Mama." She took the old cape down and swirled it around her shoulders. "What's wrong with Mrs. Braynard?"

"She thinks she's got the grippe. Ina and Paul were sick with it when they came home from their visit to Luke, and Dora helped nurse them. I guess they told her the grippe is rife in Syracuse. It's awful when your children are sick." Her mother shook her head and went back to scrubbing the shirt. "It took Dora awful fast. I saw her carrying water to the hogs when I carried the laundry outside. By the time I hung a couple of shirts up to dry, she was leaning against the fence and holding her head in her hands. I hustled over to see if she was all right and ended up helping her to the cabin and putting her to bed. She's some fevered. I told her I'd look in on her this afternoon."

"I could make her some chicken soup. It might make her feel better." Memory flashed. She frowned and absently fastened the ties down the front of the cape. "There were two men staying at Sheffield House the other day when I went to pick up the apron fabric. Mrs. Sheffield said they were quite ill—so much so she thought one of them would not be able to eat the soup she was making for them. Perhaps the men were from Syracuse."

She shrugged off the speculation and pulled her attention back to the work at hand. One way or the other, those men had nothing to do with her. Unless Sophia Sheffield took sick. The thought was unsettling. She was very fond of Callie's aunt. "Where are the clothes pegs, Mama?"

"In the basket. On top of the clothes."

She nodded and opened the door. "As soon as I finish hanging the clothes, I'm going to town and call on Mrs. Sheffield. I'll stop by Brody's and get a chicken, then come home and start the soup."

She closed the door and walked through the dead leaves and dying grasses to the wicker basket holding the laundry. The chill in the air was more pronounced. She glanced up at the overcast sky and sighed. It looked and felt like snow was on the way. She shook out a pair of pants, folded the edge of the waist over the thin rope loggers that stretched from tree to tree around the yard, then slipped a peg over the fabric, moved a few inches along the waist and slipped on another.

A sudden, sharp gust of wind set the pant legs flapping. She shivered, the threadbare wool of the cape little protection. Her determination firmed. She would find a way to earn money to buy the fabric for a cloak. Her mother was not going to suffer another winter shivering from the cold.

She bent down and picked up a shirt, snapped it through the air to shake out some of the wrinkles and cast another look at the sky. Hopefully, the snow would hold off until the clothes were dry.

Matthew climbed the stairs to the second floor of Sheffield House, the doctor's words weighting his steps. *There's no hope. His heart's weakened. At best, he won't last more than an hour or so.*

No hope. A fallacy. There was always hope in God. He squared his shoulders and walked down the hall, grateful for these few minutes he would have alone with Mr. Arthur before the doctor returned. He glanced at the numbers on the doors he passed. Number eight. The fourth door on the left. That was it.

He stopped before the paneled portal, bowed his head and closed his eyes. "Almighty God, I humbly beseech Thee to give unto me the right words to speak that this man's need of comfort may be met, and he will peacefully enter into Your rest. Amen."

He lifted his hand and gently rapped his knuckles against the polished wood. No summons to enter came. He took a breath and opened the door, crossed the room.

Raspy, shallow and uneven breaths issued from the man in the bed. He gazed down at the gaunt, pale, yet fever-flushed features and released another silent prayer for guidance. "Mr. Arthur..."

The man's eyelids fluttered, opened.

He looked into watery, glassy blue eyes filled with fear. His heart swelled with compassion. He rested his hand on the covers over the man's shoulder and hoped

Mr. Arthur would sense God's love flowing through him. "I'm Reverend Calvert, Mr. Arthur. You asked to speak with me?"

The man gasped, struggled to form words. "Need… pray…for me."

He nodded, leaned closer to better hear the man's weak, halting voice. "Do you enjoy salvation, Mr. Arthur? Are you assured in your relationship with the Lord?"

The man's eyes flooded with dread. "Never…seen much…need…" He gasped, struggled for air.

"It's never too late for God's salvation, Mr. Arthur." He spoke slowly, deliberately, willing the man to hear him, praying he would accept the truth and live long enough to proclaim it. "Do you believe Jesus is the Son of God?"

"Yes…" The word wheezed out. Mr. Arthur's eyes closed.

He jerked the covers aside, grabbed the man's hand and squeezed. The closed eyelids fluttered. "Mr. Arthur!" He squeezed harder.

The man sucked in a ragged breath, opened his eyes and fixed his gaze on him.

Thank You, Lord. "Mr. Arthur, do you ask Jesus into your heart and proclaim Him to be Your Lord and Savior?"

"Yes…" The man stared at him. He watched, rejoicing, as the fear drained from Mr. Arthur's eyes and peace washed over the gaunt face. "Thank…you…"

Joy flooded him. He smiled. "You are now a child of God, Mr. Arthur. Welcome to His Kingdom, where you shall abide forever more."

The man's trembling lips parted to struggle for air,

relaxed, then lifted in a small smile. The fingers on the thin hand gripped in his tightened slightly, then released. A soft sigh escaped the previously straining lungs and Mr. Arthur closed his eyes.

He stood for a moment, his head bowed and his heart lifted in prayer, then gently drew the covers back over Mr. Arthur's arm and shoulder.

The door opened. The doctor entered and strode to the bedside, looked a question at him.

He shook his head and left the room to find Sophia Sheffield and inquire if Mr. Arthur had left any requests or instructions to be carried out on his demise.

Willa shifted the large, paper-wrapped bundle of cotton sheeting she'd picked up for Mrs. Braynard to one arm, lifted her free hand and knocked.

"Come in."

She opened Sophia's door, stepped inside and bumped the door shut with her hip, turned to put her burden on the table and looked straight at Matthew Calvert. "Oh."

Shock streaked through her, slackened her grip and her jaw. The bundle slid. She snapped her gaping mouth closed and grabbed for it, caught the edge of the basket dangling from her arm instead. The package slipped to the floor. She dropped to a stoop to pick it up, saw Matthew Calvert rise from his chair, and bowed her head to hide her face. What was *he* doing here?

"Slippery paper, Willa, dear?"

She glanced up and met Sophia's knowing, amused gaze. If Sophia had guessed her reaction was due to Matthew Calvert's being there, then perhaps he had also. Heat rushed to her cheeks. "The package is awkward to carry."

"Hmm."

Black boots appeared at the edge of her vision. *No!* She grabbed the package and rose before Matthew Calvert could offer her his hand and she came completely undone. She certainly didn't need *that* happening with Sophia watching. The older woman was obviously misreading her surprise at seeing Matthew Calvert seated at the table in her kitchen for something else entirely.

He stepped closer. "Allow me to relieve you of your burden, Miss Wright."

His presence, so near to her, set her already-taut nerves atingle. She shook her head. "Thank you, but no, Reverend. I can't stay." *Not with you here.*

"Are you sure, Willa, dear? It must be getting colder out—your cheeks are quite rosy."

She shot a stop-teasing-me look at Sophia.

The older woman's violet eyes twinkled, her lips curved in a sweet smile. "Surely, you can stay long enough to join us for a nice warming cup of tea?"

She swept her gaze to the tea set on the tray in front of Sophia, slid her gaze to the half-empty cup across the table in front of a pushed-back chair. "No, truly." She turned slightly, used the movement to gain a little space between herself and Matthew Calvert. "I have to get home. Mrs. Braynard has taken ill, and I'm going to make her some chicken soup."

The amused look in Sophia's eyes died. "What's wrong with Dora?"

She relaxed and launched into the safe subject. "She has the grippe. Ina and Paul took sick with it when they were visiting Luke in Syracuse. They said it has spread all through the city." She stepped closer to Sophia. "That's why I came. I remembered about the two men you said were so ill and I wondered if they were from Syracuse. I wanted to make certain you were all right."

Sophia reached up and patted her arm. "I'm fine, Willa."

"I'm so glad." She smiled and took a firmer hold on the bundle. "I really must go. I have to stop at Brody's and get a chicken."

"Nonsense. Dora is my friend, too. And I ordered a stewing chicken this morning that I...no longer need." Sophia took a swallow of tea and rose. "Bring your basket and come with me to the buttery."

Sophia's tone left no room for discussion on the matter. She placed her bundle on a chair and followed her out the door to the small, stone building a few feet from the porch.

Hams and thick slabs of bacon hung from hooks in the ceiling. Crocks of various sizes, some with lids, some covered with cloth, sat on the floor or on a bench along the wall. Eggs were piled in a bowl. Her lips curved. She and Callie and Sadie used to come in here and sneak cream from the top of the milk.

"Here we are." Sophia pulled a piece of cheesecloth off a deep bowl, lifted out a plucked chicken, wrapped it in the piece of cheesecloth and put it in her basket. "Now, let's get back to my nice warm kitchen."

She followed her outside and stopped. Matthew Calvert, wearing his hat and holding her bundle tucked under his arm, stood at the bottom of the porch steps. He smiled and doffed his hat at Sophia. "Thank you for the tea and the pleasure of your company, Mrs. Sheffield." His gaze shifted to her. "Are you ready to go, Miss Wright?"

"Yes, but—"

"Then let me carry that." He stepped forward and took hold of the basket.

She stood frozen in place and stared at her things in his hands, unsure of whether to be grateful for his gentlemanly kindness, or offended at his high-handed tactics.

Sophia turned and, eyes twinkling, kissed her cheek. "Goodbye, Willa, dear." She leaned closer. "Oh, yes, a much, *much* better catch than Thomas Hunter."

She stiffened at the whispered words, darted a glance at Matthew Calvert. Had he heard Sophia? It didn't appear so.

"Goodbye, Reverend. Come and have tea with me again sometime—under better circumstances." Sophia climbed the steps and entered the house.

They were alone. Something close to panic gripped her. Why did this man so unnerve her? How could he both attract and repel her? She knew him for the flirt he was, and he was not to be trusted.

"Shall we go?"

She nodded, reached up and pulled her hood forward, squared her shoulders and started down the path to the gravel carriageway that led out to Main Street.

Matthew glanced at Willa's set face and frowned. She had changed the minute Sophia Sheffield had left them. Why? *Lord, if she is the one you have for me, please help me reach her heart.*

They stopped where the Sheffield House carriageway met Main Street and waited for a wagon loaded with cabbages to pass. "Mind the ruts, they've gotten deeper with the recent rains." He shifted the basket into his other hand and took her elbow to cross, felt her stiffen and let go immediately when they reached the other side. "Until you mentioned it, I didn't know Mrs. Sheffield had two ill guests. Dr. Palmer did not mention a second man."

"Dr. Palmer?"

Ah, he had gotten her to break her silence. "Yes. He summoned me to the hotel at Mr. Arthur's request." He stopped as she paused and looked up at him, worry clouding her beautiful blue-green eyes.

"I wasn't aware Mr. Arthur's illness was severe enough to require a doctor's attendance." She sighed, and started walking again. "I hope he improves quickly and leaves the hotel. And the other man as well. I'm concerned about Mrs. Sheffield's health."

He hated to tell her, but there was no help for it. "Mr. Arthur passed away this morning, Miss Wright. Mrs. Sheffield and I were discussing his last wishes when you came."

She stopped and stared at him. The cloud of worry in her eyes darkened. "What was Mr. Arthur's illness? Was it the grippe?"

He shook his head, wished he could tell her no and take the worry from her. "I don't know. I was called at the last to pray with Mr. Arthur."

"Clearly, prayer didn't help."

Such bitterness in her voice! He looked down and shifted the package he carried to hide his shock, then took a breath and addressed her comment. "But it did, Miss Wright. The prayer of salvation alleviated Mr. Arthur's fear, and he entered into God's rest peacefully."

"It was kind of you to comfort him in his last moments."

She thought he prayed only as a means to comfort Mr. Arthur? The thought chilled his heart, settled like a rock in his gut and raised a question he didn't want to face. But he must. "You do not believe in prayer, Miss Wright?"

She stopped and looked up at him. "As a source of comfort for those who believe in it, yes."

Lord, please... "But *you* do not believe in prayer?" Hurt flashed in her eyes, hovered there like a shadow. It was all he could do not to drop her things and take her in his arms right there on Main Street.

"If you are asking if I believe that God hears our pleas and answers them, then my answer, sir, in truth, is no, I do not." Her chin lifted. "I'm sure that is disturbing to a man of faith, such as yourself, but I learned very early in my childhood not to depend on a benevolent, loving God who watches over us. He has never bothered to demonstrate any such care toward me or my mother. I do, however, as behooves a teacher, keep such thoughts to myself." She turned and headed down the walkway toward the Stony Creek bridge, the heels of her shoes clicking against the planks.

He fell into step at her side, his thoughts churning, his heart sick with fear. He *did* believe in prayer. Was this God's answer to his cry to show him His will? Was the one woman he had ever been attracted to, the woman he was in love with, to be denied him?

"I wish I knew if Mr. Arthur was from Syracuse."

He dragged his attention from the sickening fear in his heart to address hers. "Because of the grippe your sick friend said is prevalent there?"

"Yes. If Mr. Arthur brought the grippe from there… And if he died of it, then Mrs. Sheffield and Mrs. Braynard are both in danger."

"There is no need to be concerned about that, Miss Wright."

She lifted her chin. Her pained gaze fastened on his. "Because of prayer, Reverend Calvert?"

He set his personal need aside and let her challenge pass. He was her pastor, and it was too soon to confront her hurt. He needed first to seek God's wisdom. "Because Mrs. Sheffield told me Mr. Arthur was from Schenectady. It was his wish that she write his family there."

Chapter Sixteen

Matthew scowled, pushed back from his desk and headed for the kitchen. It was hard to separate his personal feelings from his pastoral ones where Willa was concerned, but one way or the other, he needed information. He couldn't help her find her way to God if he didn't know the problem. And whether he ever held her as his wife, he wanted her safe in God's arms.

He stepped into the kitchen, caught a flash of Joshua going outside, heard his footsteps pound across the porch and an anguished plea from Sally for Joshua to hurry before the door slammed shut. "What's that about?"

Bertha looked up from the dough she was kneading. "Cat's up the tree again." She grinned and punched the dough. "Sally calls Joshua now. *He* scales that tree like a country boy—doesn't hurt himself grabbing on to dead branches."

Matthew snorted, lifted the coffeepot Bertha kept filled for him off the stove and poured some of the steaming brew into a cup.

Bertha's brow furrowed. "What're you looking so sour about?"

"I didn't know I was." He blew across the surface of the coffee and took a tentative sip, followed it with a bigger swallow. "Bertha, you've lived in Pinewood a long time, haven't you?"

"Since it was only a lumbering camp with a few cabins amongst all the trees. It didn't even have a name back then." She stopped kneading and glanced up at him. "I've been around you long enough now to know you don't ask questions for no reason. What's on your mind?"

"Do you remember Willa as a child?" He took another swallow of his coffee and indulged himself thinking about how good her name felt on his tongue. So did not having to hide his love for her. He'd been honest about that with Bertha ever since the night he'd escorted Thomas Hunter out of town.

"'Course, I do." Her gaze sharpened. "Why?"

He looked down into his cup, swirled the coffee up close to the rim and chose his words. Bertha was not one to take part in idle gossip. "She said something a few days ago that made me think someone had hurt her badly when she was small."

"Seven years old, she was."

He swallowed, lowered the cup from his mouth and looked at her.

"Her papa up and walked away." Anger glinted in Bertha's hazel eyes. "Left Helen alone with little Willa and nowhere to live and no way to provide for her."

Willa had been only a little older than Joshua. The muscles in his jaw twitched. He set his cup on the table, leaned against the wall and crossed his arms over his chest. "What happened to them?"

"The women in the camp took a hand." Bertha shoved the heels of her hands against the pile of dough, turned it and shoved again. "The cabins on Brook Street belong to Manning Townsend. If you don't work for Manning, you can't live in the cabins. So, when George Wright left, it meant Helen had to get out—and she had no folks to go to. We women got together and reasoned out if Helen worked for Manning, she and Willa could still have the use of the cabin. We lit on the idea of her doing wash for the bachelor loggers."

"And Mr. Townsend agreed?"

Bertha's lips twitched. "Willa and Sadie Spencer—she's the Townsends' granddaughter—were best friends, and Rachel Townsend wouldn't have any part of putting Willa and Helen out of that cabin. Manning wasn't given a choice."

An image of sweet-natured, plump and gray-haired Rachel Townsend popped into his head. The woman must have more starch to her spine than it appeared. He'd never heard of their granddaughter. And he didn't know Mrs. Wright. "I've never met Willa's mother. She doesn't come to church." He frowned, stared at the floor and searched his memory. "I don't believe I've ever seen her about town. Of course, I can't put a name to everyone I've seen."

"It's not likely you've laid eyes on her. Helen works at doing wash from break of day to full dark, and pretty much keeps to herself otherwise. Doesn't come into town very often. Willa picks up what they need at the store."

He nodded, thought about how hard it all must have

been, especially for a young child. "What happened to Willa's father?"

"Never heard and don't care to." Bertha clamped her lips closed, flopped the kneaded dough into a bowl, greased the top and covered it with a cloth. "You'd best check on those youngsters. I've work enough to do without having to care for a broken leg or something."

He summoned a grin. "I thought you said Joshua scaled that tree like a real country boy."

She looked at him.

"I'm going." He pushed away from the wall, picked up his cup, refilled it and headed for the kitchen door. Whatever happened to a man being the king of his castle? He smiled and shook his head. One thing was sure, whoever that king was, he didn't have a woman like Bertha Franklin for his housekeeper. And was the poorer for it.

A knock on the front door interrupted his musings. He reversed directions, set the cup down on the table and hurried to the entrance hall to open the front door. "Why, hello, Billy." He glanced through lazily drifting snowflakes at the barebacked horse tied to the hitching post by a halter. "Did you want Joshua?"

The boy shook his head and sent the lock of black hair on his forehead flopping from side to side. "No, sir. Ma sent me to fetch you." The boy's eyes teared up, he swallowed hard. "Grandma's took sick and is doing poorly. Doc Palmer said you best come."

"As soon as I hitch up the buggy." He rested a comforting hand on the boy's shoulder. "We'll tether your horse to the back, and you can ride home in the buggy with me. Meanwhile, Joshua is in the side yard. Why don't you go see him while I'm in the stable? He's rescuing Sally's cat from the tree."

The boy nodded and trotted down the steps.

He stepped back to shut the door, paused as a buggy stopped out front. A young man climbed from the carriage, tethered his horse and hurried toward the house.

He studied the man's face, tried to place him and failed. "May I help you, sir?"

The man stopped at the base of the steps and looked up at him. Fear shadowed his blue eyes. "I was told Bertha Franklin is here. May I speak to her please?"

"Of course, come in Mr...."

"Danvers. Charles Danvers." The man trotted up the stairs and across the porch, stepped into the entrance hall. "I'm Bertha's son-in-law. If you'll—"

"You'll find Bertha in the kitchen. It's through that door." He gestured toward the kitchen, frowned as the man spun on his heel and hurried that direction. Should he follow? No, Bertha was quite capable of handling Mr. Danvers and whatever was upsetting him on her own. He slapped his hat on his head, grabbed his coat and headed for the stables.

"Billy, it's time to go. Take your horse around to the stables and tie him to the back of the buggy. I'll be right along."

"Yes, sir." Billy ran for his horse.

Matthew smiled at Joshua, safe now on the ground, and Sally holding her beloved kitten. "It's getting colder. You two had best come inside for a while." He gestured the two of them up the porch steps ahead of him and grinned down at the dog who stood looking up at him, his tail wagging furiously. "You, too."

The dog raced up the steps ahead of him. "Mind you wipe your feet." Too late. Children and animals were already through the door. He lunged, caught the door before it slammed closed, and stepped inside. "Bertha, I'm leav— What's wrong?"

"Take these to the buggy. I'll come in a minute."

He glanced at the tied bundle of clothes Bertha handed her son-in-law, then raised his gaze to her face, drew in a sharp breath at her grim expression.

"My daughter and her baby are dreadful sick with the grippe, Reverend. I have to go tend them. I'm sorry to leave you with no supper prepared, but—" Her eyes narrowed, clouded. "You going somewhere?"

"Yes, Billy Karcher came for me. His grandmother is ill and not doing well." He stepped toward her. "I'm sorry about your daughter and her baby, Bertha. If I can help in any way, please let me know."

She nodded, then looked up at him, her brow furrowed. "The youngsters—"

"Will be all right, Bertha. I'll find someone to—"

"Isobel!" Bertha grabbed her cloak off a chair, threw it around her thin shoulders and headed for the door. "You go comfort Grandma Karcher, Reverend. I'll run across the street and get the Halls' maid to come stay with the children 'til you come home."

Willa stomped the snow from her boots and opened the door of the apothecary shop. The bells on the door tinkled merrily when she closed it again. She blinked and walked into the warm interior.

"Hello, Willa. Looks like winter has arrived."

"Yes, and with a vengeance." She smiled at Steven Roberts and set her basket on the counter. "There is already three inches of snow on the ground, and it shows no sign of stopping."

"At that rate, we'll have six inches or more by closing time." The proprietor's lips lifted into a wry grin. "I guess I'd better hunt up my shovel. Meantime, what can I do for you?"

She opened her basket and consulted the list she'd tucked inside. "I'd like one pint of medicinal spirits, one-half ounce each of snakeroot, golden seal and wormwood please. Oh, and some ginger root."

"This for you?" The store owner turned and began lifting containers down from a shelf.

"Only the ginger root. The rest goes on Mrs. Braynard's account."

"Mrs. Braynard is still not feeling well?" Steven Roberts started measuring out the requested amounts of the dried herbs.

She shook her head, pulled off her gloves and warmed her hands over the round heating stove. "She still has a cough and is very easily fatigued."

"It's good of you and your mother to care for her, Willa." He placed her order in her basket, drew his account book toward him and dipped his pen in the inkwell.

"She would do the same for us." She tugged her gloves on, grasped the basket and headed for the door.

"Be careful, Willa. The grippe is spreading, and it seems to hang on for a good long while."

"That's what the ginger root is for. Mama won't let me tend to anyone unless I keep a piece of it in my mouth." She smiled, opened the door to the accompaniment of the tinkling bells, and hurried out so she didn't chill off the store.

"Willa! Wait!"

She turned and squinted through the rapidly falling snow in the direction of the call.

Ellen waved at her from the other side of the street, then lifted her hems and started across.

She stopped and waited, waved as Mr. Totten drove his trolley past, the horses' heads bobbing in time to the thud of their hooves against the snow-covered road.

"I'm so glad I saw you, Willa." Ellen stepped up onto the wood walkway and shook her cloak of blue wool into place over her long skirts. "I'm so excited to tell you what has happened!"

She looked into Ellen's shining blue eyes and smiled. "It must be good news."

"Oh, it is." Ellen tucked her hands into her fur muff and stepped closer. "Bertha Franklin's son-in-law came for her late this morning. Her daughter is very ill with the grippe, and other members of her family are sick as well. Bertha has gone to Bentford to care for them."

She stared through the falling snow at Ellen's sparkling blue eyes. "Forgive me, but I do not see how that is cause for elation."

Ellen leaned close. "Oh, but it is! You see, Matthew was gone out on a call, and, of course, Bertha's son-in-law was worried about leaving his wife alone and wanted to start the trip back to Bentford immediately. Bertha came to ask if Isobel could stay with Matthew's wards until he came home, and I immediately realized that with Bertha gone Matthew would be without anyone to watch over his wards when he is called away, or to act as his housekeeper. I asked Mother and Father if I could do so, and they agreed it would be proper as long as Matthew's wards are there."

She gaped. "But Ellen…you don't like children."

"What has *that* to do with it? I love Matthew." Ellen tugged her hand from her muff and gripped her forearm. "Don't you see, Willa? Matthew has been increasingly warm to me since I began teaching the Sunday school class, and he was most grateful to find me watching over his wards when he came home a short while ago. I am certain that when he sees me caring for them and his home every day, during Bertha's absence, he will ask for my hand in marriage."

"Oh, Ellen…"

"What?" Her friend's lower lip pouted. "I thought you would be happy for me, Willa."

She gazed at her lifelong friend's lovely, crestfallen face and forced a smile to her lips and conviction into her voice. "I am, Ellen. I simply think it's a little premature for celebrating your betrothal." The possibility of that truly happening struck her with unexpected dismaying force. She firmly closed her mind to the thoughts being conjured, ignored the sudden, sick feeling in the pit of her stomach and widened her smile. "That usually comes after your beau asks you to be his bride."

"Is that what concerns you?" Ellen laughed and tucked her hand back into her muff. "Don't fret yourself, Willa. That shall happen very soon. And I am going to have Mother make me a new gown for when we make the announcement." Ellen's eyes widened and her lovely lips parted in a small gasp. "I just thought—I shall have Matthew make the announcement in church! Oh, how exciting! That will be perfect. I have to go tell Mother. But first, I have to pick up some buttons for her at Cargrave's. Bye, Willa."

She stood and watched Ellen glide down the street, her long skirts brushing a wide swath through the snow. *I am certain that when he sees me caring for his wards and his home he will ask for my hand in marriage.* She pressed her free hand against her stomach and took a deep breath. The queasy feeling stayed. And why wouldn't it? She was concerned for Sally and Joshua. That's all it was. She was concerned for the children. Ellen didn't even call them by name.

Matthew prowled through the house, his hands stuffed in his pockets and his brows drawn into a deep scowl. Nothing was working out as he had hoped.

He'd been too long paying his comfort visit to Mrs. Karcher to have time to speak to Willa today. And Bertha had left to care for her ill family members. And Ellen Hall was going to come and spend the days so he would have someone to watch over Joshua and Sally when he was called away.

He flopped onto the settee in the sitting room and stared up at the ceiling. He should be grateful for Miss Hall's thoughtfulness in realizing his need and offering her services, but the truth was, the woman made him uncomfortable with her constant flirting. And Joshua and Sally were not happy that Miss Hall was coming.

He yanked his hands from his pockets and laced them behind his head. It wasn't as if he had a choice. Dr. Palmer had told him the grippe was spreading rapidly, and so was chicken pox. Little Trudy Hoffman had come down with the pox today, and the Brody boy had them, also. He frowned and blew out a long breath. As the sicknesses spread there would be an increased demand for him to make comfort calls and pray for the sick. When would he find time to speak with Willa? Was he being selfish? No. If she should become ill before—

He shoved the thought away, lunged to his feet and crossed to look out the window. Snow was piled in the corners of the grids that held the small panes and more was falling. If this weather kept up, he would have to start using the cutter to get around.

What if Joshua or Sally got sick? The thought set him hurrying up the stairs to check on them.

The other thought, the one hovering in the deep recesses of his mind, he wasn't ready to face. But it would not be denied. *Was God using these obstacles that kept him from being with Willa to show him His will?*

Chapter Seventeen

There! The last piece for her mother's new hood was cut out. Willa added it to the pile of other pieces on her bed and picked up the remnants of green wool. She would quilt some of the linen material Sophia had given her mother for a lining.

She sighed, folded the pieces, wrapped them in half of a worn-out blanket she'd saved to make a rag rug and hid them under her bed. She had so wanted to make her mother a new cloak, but it would have to wait until school opened again and she could save more money from her earnings. And the hood would be warmer than her mother's old bonnet. And lovely.

A shiver shook her. She rubbed her cold hands together and pictured just how she would make the hood. She would gather it at the nape, to ensure enough fullness to fit easily over her mother's pulled-back hair, and she'd buy some of that dark gold satin ribbon she'd seen at Cargrave's for ties. And flowers. Yes! She smiled, the image clear in her mind. She would have Mrs. Hall make two flowers out of the wide ribbon, and then she would attach the ties with them. Oh, her mother would look so pretty with her green eyes shining above the gold satin bow!

Another shiver shook her. She whirled around, picked up the scissors and hurried out to the sitting room to put them back in the mending basket before her mother returned from next door.

The flames in the fireplace beckoned. The wood crackled a welcome. She stepped close and held out her hands to warm them. Another shiver passed through her. How was she ever going to keep the hood a secret until it was finished? It was too cold to sew in her bedroom, and— Thread! She had forgotten to buy thread. She couldn't use her mother's; she would know it was missing. She would have to pick some up at Cargrave's later, when she went to Brody's to buy meat for supper.

The door creaked open. A draft of cold air hit her back, made the flames of the fire leap and dance.

"Mercy, it's getting cold out there!"

She turned, stepped to the side and smiled. "The fire's nice and warm, Mama. Come join me."

"For a minute." Her mother hung her cape on a peg and came to stand beside her. "Edda stopped to visit with Dora. She said the grippe has spread into the logging camps now. As sick as Dora's been, she's some worried about Daniel."

An image of Daniel's grinning face popped into her head. "I hope he's spared. I hate to think of him being sick out in the camp with no one to care for him." She lifted a piece of wood out of the woodbox beside the hearth and added it to the fire. "Who will care for the loggers who become seriously ill, Mama? Dr. Palmer is already overburdened caring for the villagers."

"That's true, 'specially with chicken pox spreading

around on top of the grippe. But, I'm thinking, he'll hold up to the load well enough now he's got Reverend Calvert helping him." Her mother pulled a chair close to the hearth, picked up a shirt she was mending, drew the needle out of the fabric and resumed stitching a torn sleeve.

He's got Reverend Calvert helping him. Her mind seized on the thought. Would Matthew know about chewing on a piece of ginger root to keep the grippe from taking hold of you? Did he know he should carry spirits of alcohol and clean his hands with it when he left a sick person's bedside? What if he didn't wear a wool scarf to keep his chest warm? Or drink birch bark and cherry stone tea when he came home?

Silence.

She looked down. Her mother was staring at her. "I'm sorry, Mama. You were saying…"

"The Karcher boy and Susan Lund are down with chicken pox now." Her mother's head tilted, her eyes narrowed. "Is something troubling you, Willa?"

She shook her head and turned toward the fire, away from her mother's penetrating gaze. Why? What was she afraid her mother would see? She had nothing to hide. "No. It's only… There's so much sickness…" Did Ellen know all of those things? Would she think to tell him?

A deep breath helped calm her. "I think I'll go to town now, Mama. I have to go to Brody's and get stew meat. And we're out of molasses and saleratus, and I want to make a pudding for supper."

Her long skirt whispered against the rug as she hurried to the door. She swirled her cloak around her shoulders and pulled the hood up in place. "I may call on

Ellen to see how she's faring, so don't worry if I'm not home directly."

She opened the door and stepped outside.

"You forgot your basket."

There was a speculative look in her mother's eyes. She stepped back inside, grabbed her shopping basket off the lamp table and hurried out the door.

"How lovely that you are home in time for dinner, Reverend Calvert. You must be hungry and tired after your long morning."

Matthew ignored the way Ellen Hall was looking up at him through her long lashes and shook his head. "Thank you for your concern, Miss Hall. But I haven't time to wait for dinner. I merely stopped to see how you were getting on with…things." Why was the house so quiet? "I am very appreciative of your generous offer to watch over Joshua and Sally, and I don't want you to be overburdened by their care."

"Not at all, Reverend. But please, can't you spare time from your calls to eat? Everything is in readiness for you."

For *him?* What about Joshua and Sally? Had they already eaten? Where were they? And why didn't Happy come to greet him? He held back a frown and placed his hat on the tree in the corner beside the door. He wasn't leaving until he found out what was going on. "Very well. It's most kind of you to think of me."

He shrugged out of his chesterfield, hung the coat on a peg and followed her down the entrance hall.

"If you will be seated, Reverend, I will bring in the stew."

Matthew paused in the dining room doorway and

looked at the table. A vase of colored tissue paper flowers sat in the center of a linen cloth with two place settings of good china on either end. His thoughts flashed back to the night of the Halls' dinner party. He took a breath. "Where are Joshua's and Sally's places, Miss Hall?"

Ellen turned at the kitchen door and her lips lifted in a winsome smile. "Your wards will be eating at the table here in the kitchen. I'm sure you agree they are too young to be included at an adults' meal. At their tender ages, their manners are still unformed and their minds are not equal to educated conversation."

"Nor will they ever be if they are not exposed to it, Miss Hall." He kept his voice pleasant and his expression bland. "The table looks lovely, and I thank you for your consideration in preparing it, but I will be eating in the kitchen with my children."

Annoyance flashed in Ellen Hall's blue eyes, but was quickly erased by another smile. "Of course, Reverend, if that is your wish. I'll set places at the table immediately. Perhaps you would be so kind as to call your wards from their rooms." The long skirts of her fancy gown billowed out as she whirled into the kitchen.

He strode to the stairs and trotted up them. Muffled voices came from Joshua's room. He opened the door and looked in. Sally was sitting on the bed beside her brother, her kitten in her arms. Josh was holding a picture book. They looked…resigned.

The dog jumped from his sprawled position across Joshua's extended legs and ran to greet him. Sally's face lit. Joshua grinned. "Uncle Matt!" They chorused his name, scrambled off the bed and rushed toward him.

"What are you two doing here in your room, Joshua?

Why aren't you downstairs playing checkers, or drawing pictures or something?"

"We'd rather stay up here with Happy and Tickles."

Sally gave an emphatic nod. "We don't want them to have to stay outside. Tickles might go up the tree and get gone!"

"I see." Indeed he did. "I'm sorry I didn't tell Miss Hall your pets are to be allowed to stay in the house. Let's all go down to dinner, and I'll explain it to her."

Joshua grinned and rubbed his stomach. "Good, I'm hungry! I haven't had any cookies or *anything* since breakfast!"

"Me neither!" Sally tucked Tickles under her arm and slipped her free hand into his. "When is Bertha coming back, Uncle Matt?"

"I don't know, Sally. And I'm sorry I have to be gone so often, but the people who are sick need my help. We'll all just have to do the best we can meanwhile." He smiled and guided the whole entourage toward the kitchen. "I saw Billy today, Joshua."

"Is his grandma better?"

"She's still ill." He glossed over the subject. The elderly woman was not doing well, and he didn't want to discuss her with them unless needed. "And Billy has chicken pox. Susan Lund has them, too."

Joshua's shoulders slumped. "I guess we won't be going back to school, then."

"Not for a while."

Sally's lower lip quivered. "I want to see Miss Wright."

So do I. "Hopefully, the chicken pox won't spread any further and school will be open again soon." He smiled and tweaked her little nose. "Now, let's have dinner. I know there are some of Bertha's molasses cookies left that we can have for dessert."

Willa hurried down Main Street, her head ducked against the wind-blown snow, the toes of her boots flashing in and out from beneath the hems of her long skirts. Dread dogged her steps.

Please don't let him be there. Her face tightened. Who was she talking to? *God*—who cared nothing about her? She set her jaw. It didn't really matter anyway. She would have to get used to seeing Ellen with Matthew and the children in his home. That sick feeling hit her stomach again. She took a deep breath, broke into a coughing fit when the cold air hit her lungs.

"Willa, are you ill?"

She lifted her head and looked toward Cargrave's entrance, blinked as snow blew against her face. The tension in her stomach eased. She wouldn't have to go to the parsonage after all. "What are you doing here, Ellen? Aren't you supposed to be watching over Joshua and Sally?"

"Isobel is with them." Ellen's narrow nose wrinkled. "Those animals are smelly creatures, and all their running around has given me a headache. I came outside for some fresh air."

"Are you speaking of Happy and Tickles?"

Ellen's face went blank.

"The children's pets."

"Oh. Yes."

It didn't sound as if things were going well for the children. She held back a frown and followed Ellen into the warmth of the store's interior.

"Good day, ladies."

"Good day, Mr. Cargrave."

She smiled at the proprietor and stepped closer to Ellen to better hear her lowered voice.

"…told his wards they must confine them to their rooms, but when Matthew came home, he insisted the dirty beasts run free throughout the house."

"He's home?" Thank goodness she hadn't had to go there. She moved over to the dry goods section and picked up the dark gold satin ribbon.

"Of course not, or I would be there. Oh, that's a pretty color, Willa." Ellen pulled her hand from her muff and touched the ribbon, moved on and ran her hand over a bolt of plaid foulard on the shelf. "I asked him to stay at home for a while this afternoon, but he insisted he had to make more calls."

She looked at the perplexed expression on Ellen's face. It seemed dangerously close to becoming a pout. "He's comforting the sick, Ellen. It's part of his calling."

"I suppose. Still, I thought once I was in his home, he would devote more of his time to me."

"I'm sure he will once the grippe and chicken pox have passed, and he's not so busy making calls and helping Dr. Palmer." The sick feeling in her stomach struck again. Perhaps, despite her precautions, she was coming down with the grippe. She moved to the notions shelf and picked up the thread she needed. "Do you know if he carries ginger root to chew on? Or spirits of alcohol to cleanse his hands once he leaves the sick?"

Ellen dropped a packet back into the button basket and stared at her. "I hadn't thought… He might bring the grippe or chicken pox home, and I— Oh dear! I have to go to the apothecary and get those things immediately."

"Ellen, wait, he may already—"

"No, I must protect myself!"

Herself—not Matthew. She watched Ellen rush out the door to the accompaniment of the tinkling bells, sighed and carried her selections to the counter. She would think no more about it. She had done the best she could.

Matthew scrubbed a towel over his still-damp hair, then tossed it over the side of the emptied bathtub and eyed the growing pile of dirty clothes in the corner. What should he do with them? Bertha had taken care of their laundry, but somehow, he couldn't picture Ellen Hall washing clothes. He'd have to think of something. He would soon be out of clean socks, shirts and cravats. Perhaps he could hire Isobel to do the wash.

He fastened the waist on his long underwear, pulled his clean undershirt over his head, tucked it in and buttoned it. Weariness weighted his movements. He lifted the oil lamp from the washstand, trudged up the stairs, threw back the covers, snuffed the lamp and flopped into bed.

The dark silence enveloped him. He yawned and closed his eyes, yielded to its caressing arms. At last. It had seemed as if Ellen Hall would never stop her flirting and go home. Sleep fled with the thought.

He scowled and jammed his fist beneath his pillow to better support his head. This situation could not go on. Her actions today had made it clear Ellen Hall had matrimony on her mind, and that was not going to be. So what was he to do? He had no wish to encourage the woman's hopes by allowing her to come and care for his children and his home. But how was he to get out of the situation? He didn't want to hurt Miss Hall, and he needed someone to stay with Joshua and Sally. And with so many sick or tending to the ill in their families, choice was limited.

He struggled to find a solution, but his tired mind refused to cope with the problem. He yawned and yielded to the weariness enticing him to close his eyes and let sleep come.

"Almighty God, I don't know…what to do. Please have… Your way…"

Willa carried her writing materials through the dark silence of the sitting room to the kitchen table, removed a front stove plate, touched a spill to the smoldering coals and lit the oil lamp. She added a few pieces of wood to the fire, opened the draft to make them burn and scooted a chair closer to the warmth. If she wrote down some of her churning thoughts, perhaps she would be able to sleep. She pursed her lips and unstopped the inkwell. How much should she tell?

Dearest Sadie,
It has been long since my last letter and much has happened. I hope this finds you well.
There has been a serious outbreak of illness here in Pinewood. Chicken pox came to the village when Mary and Jeffery Burton's cousin came for a visit. Ina and Paul Johnson brought the grippe home to the village from Syracuse, and two of the guests at Sheffield House were ill with the grippe when they arrived. The disease strikes fast and seems to be of long duration.
I write you of the presence of the grippe in our area lest you should hear from another source

and it causes you to worry. I hasten to assure you your grandparents remain healthy. As does Sophia Sheffield. Mama and I are well also.

The new preacher, Reverend Calvert (I wrote you of him in my last letter), is helping Dr. Palmer tend the sick as the disease has spread even to the logging camps. Ellen is watching over his children.

She stopped and frowned down at what she had written. Matthew Calvert kept doing things that surprised and unsettled her. He could have taken the children home to Albany until the diseases had run their courses. Instead, he had stayed to care for his flock and help Dr. Palmer.

She braced her elbow on the table, rested her chin in her palm and stared off into the distance. Her father and Thomas would never have done that. Thomas. She hadn't thought of him in days. Matthew was so different from Thomas. He was unselfish and dependable and—

She jerked erect. And he was Ellen's intended. She had no business thinking about him. She set her jaw, dipped her pen in the ink and leaned over the paper.

I must tell you, in closing, that Ellen is smitten with Reverend Calvert. She feels he is the perfect mate for her and plans to marry him. Perhaps they will be wed this summer. I know you will not attend their wedding, Sadie, and, of course, I understand why. But, oh, how I wish you would. I miss you, my dear friend.

My fondest love always,
Willa

That sick feeling had returned to her stomach. She blotted the letter, folded and sealed it, put her writing materials back in the basket and took a deep breath. Perhaps some ginger tea…

She rose and pulled the teapot to the front of the stove over the fire. Maybe after a soothing cup of tea, she would be able to sleep. If she could quiet her thoughts.

Chapter Eighteen

"**W**illa!"

The back door of the house slammed. She stopped and looked over her shoulder, frowned at the sight of her mother hurrying across the yard toward her. "What is it, Mama?"

"Ellen says she needs you. She's sent her father to fetch you. He's waiting out front in his sleigh."

Matthew or the children? Her stomach flopped, coiled into a hard knot. Her mind spun out dire scenarios.

"Give me the slop bucket, dear—I'll feed the pigs." Her mother took hold of the bucket's handle and shoved the basket she held in her other hand toward her. "I put everything in here I thought you might need."

She closed her fingers over the braided wicker handle. "Thank you, Mama."

Her mother touched her cheek. "It will be all right, Willa."

She nodded, blinked back a rush of tears and ran for the street.

"Don't forget to chew the ginger, Willa!"

"I won't, Mama!" She rounded the corner of the cabin and hurried to the sleigh sitting in the road at the end of their plank walk.

"Good afternoon, Willa." Mr. Hall stepped forward, took her basket, handed her in, then returned it to her and walked around the horse to climb in. He slapped the reins against the horse's rump and the sleigh slipped forward.

Willa gripped the basket handle with both hands and glanced over at Ellen's father. "Do you know why Ellen has sent for me, Mr. Hall?"

"No, I don't, Willa. All I know is she came to the house, told me she needed you and asked me to come and fetch you right away, then hurried back to the parsonage."

She nodded, faced forward and reassured herself she was being foolish to imagine dire things. With Ellen, it could be anything. Perhaps she was having trouble getting along with the children and simply wanted her advice.

She held on to that thought as they turned the corner, glided over the Stony Creek bridge and traveled down Main Street toward the parsonage at a brisk pace. But it was not enough to keep her in her seat when the sleigh halted.

"Thank you, Mr. Hall."

"Wait, Willa, I'll help you—"

"There's no need. I can manage." She gripped the edge of the frame with her free hand, kicked the hems of her long skirts out of the way and climbed down. She took the basket Mr. Hall handed down to her and turned to start up the walkway to the parsonage.

"Ellen!" She broke into a run toward where Ellen stood on the stoop. "What's wrong?"

"I don't know, Willa. The girl was crying when I went to the stairs to call them for dinner." Ellen shuddered, wrapped her arms about herself. "I sent Father for you right away. I think the girl may be sick."

"Oh, *Ellen!* You haven't left her *alone* all this time, have you? She may be hurt!" She brushed past Ellen and yanked open the door.

"The boy is with her. I couldn't—"

She let the door slam shut on Ellen's words and ran up the stairs, followed the sound of muted voices to a room on the right and opened the door. Joshua was sitting on the edge of the bed leaning over his sister with a cup in his hand.

"C'mon, try to drink some water, Sally. It might make you feel better."

The poor boy sounded frightened to death. And well he might. Sally's face was flushed with fever. She pasted a smile on her face and swept into the room. "Well, what is going on in here?"

Joshua leaped from the bed and spun toward the door, his young face dark with anger. The water in the cup sloshed over the brim onto the floor.

"Miss Wright!"

Relief swept the anger from Joshua's face. He took a step toward her, stopped, looked at his sister, then back at her and squared his shoulders. "I think Sally's sick, and I couldn't find Miss Hall. I— I didn't know what to do." His voice wavered.

How brave he was, trying to care for his sister. Her heart ached to comfort him. "Why don't I have a look?"

He swallowed hard and nodded.

She moved forward, allowed herself to touch his blond curls, then brush his smooth cheek with her fingertips as she withdrew her hand and took his place on the side of the bed.

She set her basket on the floor and placed the backs of her fingers against Sally's flushed cheek, just as her mother had touched her so many times.

Sally's eyes opened—glassy and watery with fever and tears. Her lip quivered.

"I don't…f-feel good."

"I know, sweetie." She placed her palm against Sally's fevered forehead, brushed back a clinging curl. "Does your head hurt?"

"Yes…" Tears overflowed Sally's eyes, rolled down her temples onto her pillow. "And my throat…and…and…"

"Your stomach?"

"Y-yes…" Sally sobbed the word, pushed up from the bed and threw herself into her arms. "I w-want Uncle M-Matt."

"Shh, sweetie, shh. I'm sure he'll be here soon." She held the little girl close, pressed her cheek against the damp blond curls and rubbed her small back. "Try not to cry, Sally, it will make your head feel worse. Can you do that?"

Sally's head nodded against her shoulder. The sobbing lessened, stopped.

"That's better." She kissed Sally's cheek and eased her back down onto her bed. "Now, I want you to close your eyes and rest while I go downstairs and fix you a cup of tea that will make your stomach and throat feel better."

"Can I have my k-kitty?" Tears flooded Sally's eyes.

Her heart sank. Where was the kitten? If Ellen had put it outside— She cast a tentative look at Joshua.

"He's in my room with Happy. I didn't want—"

The boy pressed his lips together and set his jaw, obviously holding back the words he'd been about to speak. She nodded and rose. "Would you please bring Tickles to Sally, Joshua? And then I think it would be good if you took Happy outside for a romp in the snow."

She saw the protective look flash in Joshua's eyes and spoke before he could voice a protest. The boy needed to go outside and play with his dog the way little boys were supposed to do. "It only need be for a short time. I'll be here to watch over Sally. Dress warmly, Joshua. It's cold outside."

He nodded and ran from the room.

She leaned over the bed and tucked Sally's small too-warm hand beneath the covers. "Try to sleep, Sally. I'll be back as soon as I've made your tea."

Willa hurried down the stairs and peeked out the front door. There was no sign of Ellen. Had she gone home? Well, she would have to worry about Ellen later. Right now she had tea to make—as soon as she found the kitchen.

She turned and looked down the length of the entrance hall. The door on her right opened into the sitting room. A memory of that rainy day when Matthew had asked her to come to the house flashed into her head. She pushed it away and peeked into the door on her left, swept her gaze over a desk and bookshelf, a suit coat hanging over the back of the desk chair.

Her gaze fell on his open Bible and the notes written in a strong, bold script that rested beside it. Matthew's personal things. A flush crawled into her cheeks. She hurried past the stairs and peered into a second door on her left. The dining room. Colored tissue paper flowers filled a vase on the table. Her stomach tensed. Ellen made flowers like those.

She spun from the doorway and hurried to a door straight ahead, stepped into a large, well-appointed kitchen. She set her basket on the work table, lifted out the spirits of alcohol her mother had included, poured a bit into her cupped palm and then scrubbed her hands together. There was no heat radiating from the stove. She touched the edge of the cooking surface with her fingertips. It was barely warm. She lifted the cold lid of an iron pot and peered inside. Stew.

Footsteps and the padding of paws drew her gaze to the door. Joshua stood there in his coat and hat, Happy beside him. "Have you eaten dinner, Joshua?"

He shook his head.

"Well the stew is cold and the fire in the stove is out." She looked around the kitchen. "Do you know where Bertha keeps the bread and jam?"

"In there." Joshua pointed to a large cupboard.

She opened the tin-paneled doors, peeked into various small covered crocks, found butter and jam and set it on the table along with a cloth-covered loaf of bread.

"The knife's in there."

She opened the drawer of the step-back cupboard Joshua indicated, pulled out the knife, stepped to the table and cut a thick slice of bread, then spread it liberally with butter and jam. "This will have to do for now, Joshua."

She took a plate off the open shelves of the cupboard,

put the bread on it, set it on the table and smiled. "Come here and hold out your hands."

Joshua gave her a suspicious look but did as she bid.

She poured some of the spirits into her palm, rubbed her hands together and scrubbed them over his small ones.

"What's that for?"

She laughed at his wrinkled nose. "It helps to keep sickness from spreading. Now, sit down and eat, while I get the fire going."

He sat, removed his hat and bowed his head. "Thank You, Lord, for this food. Thank you that Miss Wright has come to help us. And please make Sally better. Amen."

The prayer spoken in his sincere young voice brought a lump to her throat. She turned to put the bread away.

Woof!

She looked down. Happy stood at her feet, looking up at her.

A smile tugged at her lips. "So you're hungry, too. Is that it?"

Woof! The dog's tail swept back and forth.

Joshua slipped off his chair, reached behind the stove and pulled out a chipped bowl. He gave her a hesitant look. "Bertha let me feed him here by the stove, if that's all right?"

What had Ellen done to make him look so worried? She smiled reassurance. "Of course it is. Hold on tight." She tore a piece of bread into the bowl and ladled some cold stew onto it. His smile melted her heart.

Joshua put the bowl down for Happy, slipped back onto his chair and took a bite out of his bread. Jam clung to the corners of his mouth.

She grinned, opened the door of the firebox on the stove, grabbed the handle and shook off the gray ashes. A few small, live coals remained. She opened the draft and added small pieces of kindling to coax the fire. Tongues of flame flickered, then licked hungrily at the new fuel. She added larger pieces of kindling, and finally, a few small chunks of firewood and closed the door.

A cast-iron teakettle sat on the back of the stove. She checked it for water, then pulled it forward to the front stove plate, turned to the work table and lifted the lid from the wicker basket. A blend of pungent and sweet scents rose.

"What's that?" Joshua came to her side and stretched up to try and look in the basket.

Her heart warmed at his exhibition of a boy's curiosity. "Herbs and spices that help people get better when they're sick."

"Oh." He grabbed his hat off the table, tugged it on and opened the door to the back porch. "C'mon, Happy."

She grinned as boy and dog trotted out onto the porch and down the steps. The door slammed shut behind them.

The stove pipe crackled. She turned and closed down the draft for a slow, steady burn, checked the teakettle, then hurried to the bottom of the stairs. There was no crying coming from above. Hopefully, Sally had fallen asleep.

A knock on the door made her jump. She hurried to open it before the knocking woke Sally. "Ellen!" She gathered her startled wits and stepped back. "Come in."

"No. I only stopped to leave a message for Matthew."

Stopped? She looked beyond Ellen to the sleigh at the end of the stone walk.

"Please tell him, as he has little time to spend with me at present, I am going to Buffalo to stay with Aunt Berdena. I will return when the chicken pox and grippe are gone from Pinewood."

"You're leaving town?" She took a breath to control the spurt of anger that rushed through her. "And what of your promise to take care of his children?"

Ellen shook her head. "You know I can't care for anyone who is ill, Willa. The school is closed—you do it. Now, I must hurry. Goodbye, Willa."

Shock held her mute.

Ellen swept down the steps and hurried to her father's sleigh.

"*Will* you take care of us, Miss Wright?"

She jerked her gaze sideways. Joshua stood at the base of a tree looking at her, fear and defiance in his brown eyes. Had he heard the whole exchange? How she longed to reassure him.

"I can't say, Joshua. That will be up to your uncle Matthew to decide. He will do what he feels is best for you and Sally." She smiled at him. "If he does decide he wants me to care for you, then I shall be happy to do so."

Joshua nodded and grinned. A slow, lopsided grin like his uncle's that went straight to her heart. "That's all right, then. Uncle Matt likes you. I can tell. C'mon, Happy! C'mon, boy." He slapped his legs and took off at a dead run for the back of the house, Happy chasing after him.

She watched the pair out of sight. She knew Joshua

meant Matthew Calvert trusted her as a teacher, but for a moment she'd thought—

She shook her head at her foolishness, closed the door and hurried to the kitchen to make Sally's tea.

Chapter Nineteen

Only three pieces of wood remained in the box. She would have to go out and get more soon. Willa placed another log on the fire, then went back to the chair she'd pulled close to Sally's bed and took the girl's small hand in hers. It seemed to quiet her.

Joshua left the chair by the hearth and came to stand beside her, an open book held in his hands. "Look at this bear, Miss Wright. He's a great big one."

His whisper tickled her ear. She glanced at the picture and nodded. "That's a polar bear. They live where it's very cold."

Joshua's eyes widened. "It's getting colder outside. Maybe I'll see one."

"I'm afraid not. Polar bears don't live around here. They live in the Arctic so they can eat the fish and smaller animals that live in the Arctic Ocean."

"Oh."

He looked crestfallen. She hastened to restore his hope. "We do have black bears that live in the forests on the hills. But they don't like the cold weather. When winter comes they go to sleep in caves and sheltered spots and don't wake up until spring."

His eyes darkened as he pondered that. "Don't they get hungry?"

The teacher in her tweaked his curiosity. "How would they know? Do you know you're hungry if you're sleeping?"

He frowned and shook his head. "I don't know anything when I'm sleeping. But I know I'm hungry when I wake up." He grinned at her.

Gracious! She was going to have to be careful. The boy was charming his way right into her heart.

Woof! Woof!

She jerked her head around at the soft bark, saw a streak of black-and-white fur race out the bedroom door.

"Uncle Matt's home! Wait until I tell him what's happened!"

"What? Joshua, wait!" She bolted erect.

The book he had dropped in her lap thudded against the floor.

Sally burst into tears.

Joshua's footfalls faded away.

A door opened and closed downstairs.

Oh dear. She turned and leaned over the bed to calm Sally.

"And Sally got sick. And I couldn't find Miss Hall and—"

"Sally's *sick?* And you're alone?"

Matthew whipped around and pounded up the stairs, rushed into Sally's bedroom and stopped dead in his tracks. "Willa!"

She jerked around toward the door, rose from her position on the side of the bed. "Good even—"

"Uncle Matt!"

Sally sobbed out his name and burst into tears.

He rushed to the bed and kissed her flushed cheek, brushed her damp hair back with his hand. His anger surged at the feel of her hot skin. He took a tight hold on his choler and smiled down at her. "Josh told me you were sick, princess. I'm so sorry I wasn't here to take care of you." He looked up at Willa. "Will it hurt her if I pick her up?"

She stepped back and shook her head. "It will do her nothing but good, Reverend. She's been waiting for you to come home."

He nodded, threw back the covers, scooped Sally into his arms and cuddled her close. "Shh, don't cry, Sally. Don't cry."

"She'll stop in a moment, Reverend." Willa's hand appeared before his eyes, touched Sally's curls. "She's crying because you're here and she finally feels safe."

He glanced up and their gazes met. "Thank you. I didn't realize…"

"Fathers never do." She smiled—the saddest smile he'd ever seen—then turned, lifted a blanket from the bed and draped it around Sally. "She needs to stay warm." Her gaze touched his again, skittered away. "I'm no longer needed here. I'll just go downstairs and set the stew over the fire to warm for your supper." She turned toward the door.

Would she leave? No. Not as long as Sally needed her. "I'll be down in a few minutes to talk with you about Sally."

She paused, then nodded and walked from the room.

Joshua rushed over and stood in front of him. "You're gonna ask her to stay and take care of us, aren't you, Uncle Matt? She said she would, and Sally and me want her to and—"

"Whoa, Josh." He studied his nephew's face. The boy looked worried. He smiled and touched his shoulder. "Let me talk to Miss Wright. I'm not sure what's going on here and—" He stopped, looked at the tears flooding the boy's eyes. "What is it, Josh?"

"I *told* you, Uncle Matt. Sally got sick and Miss Hall went outside and left Sally and me alone."

"Yes, I know, but—"

"And then Miss Wright come upstairs and hugged Sally and she made Sally tea to make her feel better and she made me dinner and she fed Happy, too!" Josh sniffed, swiped his sleeve across his eyes and gulped in air.

He kept quiet, waited.

"And then Miss Hall come back and said she was going away 'cause she doesn't like to be around sick people, and Miss Wright scolded her for not taking care of us, and she told Miss Wright to take care of us, and then I asked her would she and she said she would if you said so." He stopped, gulped and wiped tears from his cheeks with the heels of his hands. "So will you? Please?"

He blinked, shot out his arm and pulled Josh close, cleared the lump from his throat. "I sure will, Josh. You don't have to worry about it anymore."

The anger simmered, felt like it was bubbling beneath his skin. Matthew flexed his hands and rotated his shoulders, took a deep breath and stepped into the kitchen. Willa was at the work table, doing something with a wicker basket.

"I am in your debt, Miss Wright...again."

She lifted her head. Light from the overhead oil lamp cast a golden glow on her dark auburn hair, shadowed her eyes. "There is no debt, Reverend. I am only thankful I was able to help."

"As am I. *Very* thankful." The muscle along his jaw twitched. He took a breath and moved toward her. "I don't know how anyone could leave a sick child alone like that. And to put the burden for that child's care on a six-year-old!" He took another breath. "Forgive my anger, Miss Wright—I know you are Miss Hall's friend. But when I think— What if you hadn't been able to come?"

"But I did come." She lifted her chin. "And had I not, I'm certain Ellen would have seen to Sally's care."

"From the front porch?"

She sucked in a breath. "How much did Joshua tell you?"

He stepped closer so he could see her eyes. "I think most everything." The muscle in his jaw twitched again. "Once he started talking, the words poured out of him like water over a dam. The boy was terrified."

"Yes, I know. I tried—" She shook her head and turned away, took something out of the basket. "Ellen had an older brother. Walker died of the measles when Ellen was Sally's age. Ellen's been terrified of becoming ill ever since. She cannot bring herself to enter a sick room."

"You're very loyal to defend your friend, Miss Wright. But there is no acceptable reason to leave a sick five-year-old without care or comfort."

She turned back to face him, her shoulders squared, her chin lifted. "Ellen did the best she could. She ran home to send her father for me and then came back here to wait on the porch where she would be close by until I arrived. She knew I would come and care for Sally and Joshua."

"And then she told you to continue to care for Joshua and Sally and left town!"

"I— Yes."

At last he could see her eyes. He looked into their beautiful blue-green depths and the words he'd been about to utter died. His breath caught. Had he been letting his anger blind him to what could become the biggest blessing of his and the children's lives? *Forgive me, Lord.* His anger drained away.

He rested back against the work table and looked at her.

She dropped her gaze, lifted her hand to brush back a tendril of hair, wiped her palms on her apron.

"And will you continue to care for Sally and Joshua, Miss Wright?"

She took a breath. "If that is your wish."

"It is." He locked his gaze on hers. "I will, of course, compensate you."

She shook her head. "In Pinewood we help each other. You are caring for the sick in the village. The least I can do is to help you until Bertha returns. I will accept no pay."

"But—"

"Those are my terms." She spun toward the stove, stirred whatever was cooking. "The stew is hot. If you will take your seat, I'll— No. Wait."

She turned back and grabbed the bottle she'd taken from the basket. "Hold out your hands."

He looked at the bottle, straightened and held his hands out in front of him. "What's this?"

"Spirits of alcohol. Turn your palms up please."

His fingers brushed against her hand. He looked into her eyes, dropped his gaze to her mouth. So close…

Pink spread across her cheekbones. She took a quick little breath, splashed a bit of the liquid into his cupped palms.

He looked down. The bottle was shaking.

She stepped back. "Now scrub your hands together. The alcohol will help prevent the spread of illness. You should carry some with you and use it each time you leave a sick person. And ginger. You should carry slices of ginger root with you and chew on it while you make your calls. It helps to keep you from taking the disease."

Her words were a little rushed, her voice a bit breathless. He glanced up. She was nibbling at the corner of her lower lip. He gripped his hands together to keep from reaching for her.

Her gaze rose and met his. She whipped around and put the bottle back in the basket.

His brows lifted. Was the prim and proper, cool and collected Miss Willa Wright nervous because of him? A grin started way down at his toes. He stifled it before it reached his lips and stepped to the table and took a seat before he betrayed himself.

"Here is some bread. The butter is in the crock on the table. And here is your stew. *Ellen* made it this morning."

He glanced up, but she turned away.

"I hope you don't mind, but I fed Joshua and Sally

earlier. Joshua had little for dinner and was hungry. And Sally needs nourishment."

"The number of those taken sick is growing. There may be many days when I return too late for their supper." He rose and pulled out a chair. "Won't you join me, Miss Wright?"

She shook her head and took a step toward the door. "I need to get home. Mama will be wondering where I am."

He stepped to her side. "You can't walk home by yourself. It's full dark outside. I'll—" He stopped, stared at her.

"You cannot leave the children, Reverend Calvert. Please don't trouble yourself over the matter. I am accustomed to walking home alone."

"I don't like it." He sounded surly, even to himself.

"You have no choice." She glanced around the room. "I think that's all. Oh! Sally's tea." Her gaze came back to meet his. "The china teapot is full of ginger tea. If Sally wakes, it would be good if she took some tea through the night. Sweeten it with a bit of honey. It will help her throat and her stomach. And keep her warm. I believe she is coming down with chicken pox and it would not do for her to become chilled."

He lifted her cloak off the peg and held it for her. She turned around, and he draped it over her shoulders.

She took a quick step forward and pulled up her hood. "Good evening, Reverend Calvert."

"Good evening, Miss Wright." He opened the door and stepped out onto the porch.

"Your stew will get cold, Rev— Oh dear." She turned back, a look of consternation on her face.

"What's the matter?"

"I forgot to add wood and trim the drafts on the stove."

"I will tend to the stove."

She nodded and started down the walk to the street.

He stood on the porch and watched her out of sight, then turned and went in the house. She was right. He had no choice.

It *was* dark. Willa hurried along Main Street, crossed Church Street and continued on, the click of her heels loud against the wood walkway in the quiet of the night.

She glanced around and quickened her pace. She had never been nervous, but since the night Arnold Dixon and Johnny Taylor had accosted her— "Oh!"

She jerked to a halt, stared at the tall, lean figure that rose from the bench outside of Dibble's Livery and strode toward her. "Gracious, Mr. Dibble, you startled me."

"I'm sorry, Willa. I didn't think about that. I guess the next time I'll have to whistle or something."

"The next time?"

He nodded and gestured her forward, fell into step alongside of her. "Word has it you're going to be caring for the preacher's boy and girl while he's out making calls on the sick. So I figured I'd just keep a watch and walk you home at night."

Something warm slipped into her heart. Her mother was right. The news that flew from mouth to mouth about town was not meant to harm but to benefit one another. She stopped and tilted her head back to look up at him. "Why?"

He shook his head and took her arm. "Mind your step. The edge of the bridge gets icy on cold nights."

He released her arm and shortened his long strides. "You know what's wrong with schoolmarms, Willa?"

Where did *that* come from? She gave him a sidelong glance. "I didn't know there was anything wrong with schoolmarms."

"Well, I might be speaking too general there. But the one I know is too curious by half. She's always wanting to know the whats and whys of something instead of just taking a thing for what it is."

His words took her aback. She looked from the kindness in his eyes to the surrounding darkness, listened to the comforting sound of his boots thudding on the bridge planks in concert with her own softer steps. "I think you may be right, Mr. Dibble." He switched sides when they turned onto Brook Street, placing himself between her and Turner's Wagon Shop where Arnold Dixon worked. The warmth in her heart grew. "I'll simply relax and enjoy our evening stroll." She smiled up at him. "And look forward to those promised."

He returned her smile, guided her around an icy spot on the path and stopped at the end of her walk.

She paused and looked at him. "It's a cold night, Mr. Dibble. Won't you come in for a cup of tea?"

He glanced at the cabin, looked back at her and shook his head. "It's a kind offer, but no thank you, Willa. Remember me to your mama."

He sounded…sad. She opened her mouth to speak— *She's always wanting to know the whats and whys of something instead of just taking a thing for what it is*— then closed it again. "I will, Mr. Dibble. Good evening." She walked up the path and opened the door, heard him start back up the path and waved.

"Well, you've had quite a day."

She stepped inside and closed the door. "I have, Mama. I think Sally Calvert is coming down with chicken pox, but she's very sick. I'm concerned about her." She shoved off her hood and unfastened her cloak.

"How's the boy?"

"Joshua is fine." A smile curved her lips. "He's a delightful little boy, Mama. Perhaps someday you'll meet him."

"Perhaps."

What did that tone mean? She studied her mother a moment, then shrugged and hung her cloak on a peg and smoothed back her hair. "Have you had supper?"

"No. There's potatoes baking in the oven." Her mother set aside the sock she was darning, rose and started for the kitchen.

"Take a small pouch of oatmeal along in the morning. If it's the pox she'll likely break out sometime tomorrow. When she commences itching, steep the bag in hot water a few minutes, squeeze it so it don't drip and dab the pox with it. That should help. Saleratus water helps, too."

She nodded, grabbed a towel and took the potatoes from the oven. "You heard about Ellen leaving, then?"

"I heard." Her mother put plates, flatware and a crock of butter on the table.

"Have you also heard that she's going to marry Reverend Calvert?"

"Wishing don't put food on the table, Willa."

"What does that mean?" She frowned, cut her potato and spread it with butter. She must be hungrier than she knew, her stomach had that sick feeling again.

"It means...we'll see."

There was that odd tone again. She stopped with a

bite of potato halfway to her mouth and looked across the table. Her mother smiled, looked down and shook salt over her plate. She stared at that small smile, then shrugged and ate the bite of potato.

"I almost forgot, Mama. Mr. Dibble asked to be remembered to you. He waited for me at the livery and walked me home. He said he'll walk me home every night." She took another bite of potato, glanced at her mother and straightened. "Are you crying, Mama?"

"Don't be foolish. I bit into a big piece of black pepper. It stings my tongue." Her mother blinked and took a swallow of water.

"Why do you think Mr. Dibble would do that, Mama?"

"I don't know, Willa. I suppose because he's a kind man."

She lifted her head and stared. Her mother never spoke with that sharp edge in her voice.

Her mother looked down, stabbed her fork into her potato, broke off a piece of the buttered flesh, then lifted her head and gestured across the table toward her. "You'd best eat before your potato gets cold."

Everything was ready. The pieces of the hood she'd cut out were tucked into her basket and covered with an apron she'd been hemming. She would take it along to work tomorrow.

Tomorrow.

Willa snuffed the lamp and climbed into bed, curled into a ball to get warm. It would be all right. The uneasiness she'd experienced around Matthew today was because everything had been so unexpected. Tomorrow she would be prepared.

He certainly loved those children. She couldn't deny it now. The look on his face when he'd seen Sally had removed all doubt. And the way he had held and comforted the child… Her papa had held her like that once. *Please don't let Matthew ever turn away from those children.*

She swallowed and blinked away the sting of tears, turned onto her side and burrowed deeper beneath the covers. He had been very angry with Ellen. How strange it was to defend Ellen's behavior to her intended. But she had succeeded. Matthew had stopped being angry and then…

Why had he looked at her that way? It was…unsettling to the point of her trembling. But when she had spoken of Ellen making the stew, the queer quivering in her stomach had stopped.

She sighed, pulled the quilt close around her face and closed her eyes. Yes, tomorrow everything would be all right. She had only to remember Ellen.

And to forget the way Matthew had looked when he rushed into Sally's room and saw her sitting there and the way his voice had sounded when he called out her name.

Chapter Twenty

Big, fluffy snowflakes fell so thickly, so rapidly that they blocked out the sky. Willa fisted her gloved hand and knocked on the door, tipped her head back and smiled.

She put her basket down and scooped up a handful of the white flakes, pressed them between her cupped hands and nodded. Yes, it was good packing snow. Perhaps Joshua would make a snowman this afternoon, or snowballs for Happy to chase after—like the perfectly good one in her hand.

Her lips twitched. She'd had quite good aim once. Of course that was years ago....

A quick glance showed no one was around. She shoved her hood back out of her way with her free hand, eyed the trunk of the tree in the side yard, imagined Daniel hiding behind it and let the snowball fly. It hit with a satisfying splat. She looked at the white blotch on the rough bark and grinned, slapped and brushed her hands together to rid her gloves of the snow.

The door opened.

She blinked the clinging snowflakes from her lashes

and stared at a disheveled-looking Matthew Calvert. Something in his eyes sent heat rushing into her cold cheeks. "I'm not too early?"

"Not at all." He huffed out a cloud of warm air, grabbed her basket, brushed the snow from its cover and stepped back. "Come in, Miss Wright."

The invitation brought an odd nervousness. She stared at him, suddenly uncertain of the wisdom of being there. And how foolish was that? Sally and Joshua needed her. She brushed off the strange feeling, shook the clinging snow from her cloak and skirt hem, walked through the door he held open for her and stopped to remove her cloak. He put down the basket and stepped behind her.

"If you'll permit me— You don't want this melting."

His hands moved across the roll of hair at her nape. His warm fingertips brushed against her cold skin, sent a shiver down her spine and froze the breath in her lungs.

"That's better." He threw a handful of snow outside and closed the door.

They were shut away from the world. Her nerves tingled. It was too...*close* in the small entrance hall, though it hadn't seemed so before. What was wrong with her this morning? The memory of yesterday?

She averted her gaze from Matthew's broad shoulders and the open vest over his white shirt, removed her gloves and unfastened her cloak.

He glanced down, gave her a rueful smile and buttoned his vest. "Please forgive my appearance. I've been trying to ready myself to make morning calls, but Sally's still restless. She's been asking for you." His gaze lifted, fastened on hers.

She dropped her gaze to the floor. "I'll go to her right away." She reached up to remove her cloak, went still when he stepped close. He lifted the cloak from her shoulders, turned and hung it on a peg.

She snatched up her basket and hurried to the stairs, lifted the hems of her long skirts to begin her climb and paused. The basket was heavy, and she had no free hand with which to grip the banister. His footsteps sounded behind her.

"Allow me."

His hand brushed against hers on the basket handle. She jerked hers away, willed her quivering knees to support her and climbed, trying not to hear his footfalls on the stairs behind her. What was *wrong* with her, allowing this situation to so unnerve her? Was she so lacking in willpower that she would fall apart because of being alone with a man? *Not a man—Matthew.* Her face went taut. That was pure foolishness! Matthew was all but betrothed to Ellen.

The thought steadied her, but the idea of them wed brought the sick feeling in her stomach again. Well, why wouldn't she sicken at the thought of Ellen and Matthew married? What would happen to these children? She took a breath and wished for some ginger to chew on.

Her skirts whispered against the hall floor, blended with the soft tap of her boots. She entered Sally's bedroom and tiptoed to the bed.

The little girl's eyes opened.

She smiled and touched the child's cheeks with the backs of her fingers. Still hot. "Did you want me, Sally?"

The girl's fever-bright brown eyes filled with tears. "I don't feel good. Will you h-hold my hand?"

I'll hold your hand, Mary. It made me feel better when Mama held my hand.

Her heart squeezed. She cleared her throat. "Of course I will." She brushed back the blond curls clinging to Sally's fevered brow. There was no sign of chicken pox. Was she wrong? Was this sickness something else? She clasped Sally's small hand in hers and sat in the chair beside the bed.

Matthew left his place by the door, came and set the basket on the floor beside the chair.

She glanced up and their gazes met. Her pulse leaped at the look in his eyes. She jerked her gaze back to Sally, chided herself for her failing.

"I have to finish preparing for the day. I'll be in my bedroom down the hall should you need me."

His deep, rich voice, so vibrant and resonant in church, was little more than a whisper. She nodded, settled her mind on practical matters and glanced up at him. "Have you and Joshua had breakfast? Did Sally eat?"

He shook his head, ran his fingers through his already-tousled hair. "We've had nothing yet. I've been here with Sally, and Joshua is in his bedroom still. I think yesterday wore him out." He leaned down and kissed Sally's forehead. "I'll be back in a few minutes, princess."

He left the room and she drew her first easy breath since coming in the house. She looked at Sally. Her eyes were closed and she was resting more quietly. "Are you hungry, Sally?"

"I don't w-want to eat. My throat hurts."

"I know, but you have to take nourishment to get better. Will you try and go to sleep while I go downstairs and fix you a nice gruel that won't hurt your throat?"

The fever-bright eyes opened. "Will you come b-back and hold my h-hand?"

"Yes, I will. I promise."

Sally's little lips trembled into a smile. "I promise, too." She sighed and closed her eyes.

It took only a moment to coax the coals in the stove into a hot fire. Willa trimmed the dampers, lifted the top off the coffeepot and wrinkled her nose. That explained the abundant coals and the sour odor that hovered in the air. Matthew had made coffee sometime during the night and forgotten to set the pot back off the fire.

She carried it to the sink cupboard, gripped the pump handle and splashed water into it, then left it there to soften the burned-on grounds while she hunted for oatmeal. The small amount in the pouch she'd brought was not sufficient.

She rooted through the tin cupboard, found coffee, oatmeal and maple syrup, set them and the crock of butter and a crust of bread on the work table and went searching for pans. She located them in the bottom of the step-back cupboard and carried one to the pump.

How lovely to have water right in the kitchen! She filled the pan and set it on the stove, scrubbed the coffeepot, dumped the rinse water into the slop bucket on the bottom shelf of the sink cupboard, tossed a palmful of the ground coffee in the clean pot and pumped in water.

"Do I smell coffee?"

She jerked and the pot slipped. She tightened her grip and turned.

"I'm sorry, I didn't mean to startle you."

"I thought you were upstairs." She almost dropped the pot again at the sight of Matthew with his suit coat on and his hair freshly combed. The man was too handsome by half.

"Sally is asleep. And Josh and Happy are awake and stirring about."

She managed to return his smile. "I'm only just putting the coffee on to boil. I made it strong, but I can add more water if you like."

"Strong and black is perfect."

She nodded, marched to the stove and set the pot down then turned to the work table. Matthew was standing in front of the step-back cupboard watching her. Her taut nerves stretched a bit tighter. "It will take a few minutes for the coffee to brew properly. I'm sure you have work to do, Reverend Calvert. I can call you when the coffee is ready."

"I'll wait." He smiled, rested back against the cupboard and crossed one ankle over the other.

"Very well." She dropped a small lump of butter into the boiling water, then ladled a small amount of the water into a bowl of oatmeal and stirred the thickened mixture into the water on the stove.

He hadn't moved. She blew out a breath, rubbed her hands down the front of her apron and turned to face him across the table. "Do you have a buttery for keeping perishables?"

"Yes indeed. It's through that door." He nodded toward a narrow door to the left of the stove.

She escaped into a large stone closet lit by the dim light filtering in through the snow-flecked glass of a small window. Cold air chilled the exposed flesh of her face and hands.

"Did you find what you need?"

Matthew's deep voice filled the buttery, made the chill bumps on her flesh tingle. "Yes." She whipped the cover off a crock, grabbed a tin cup and scooped it full of milk, then snatched up a bowl of eggs and turned. He was in the doorway. Her breath snagged in her lungs.

"Excuse me." She took a step, and he moved aside.

She put the eggs on the work table, picked up the spoon and stirred the cup of milk into the thickening gruel, wished he would go sit down at the table.

"The coffee smells good."

"It will be ready soon." She moved the boiling brew to the back of the stove to let the grounds settle, wiped her hands down her apron and turned to dice the crust of bread.

He moved past her to the window on the other side of the stove. "All of this snow reminds me of my fondest wish as a child—a toboggan my brother, Robert, and I could fly down the hills on." He glanced her way and smiled. "I prayed long and fervently for that toboggan. I finally got it for Christmas when I was eight years old. It was that answered prayer that set me on the path to becoming a minister." He leaned a shoulder against the window frame and fastened his gaze on her. "What was your most fervent childhood prayer, Miss Wright?"

"That my father, who had abandoned us, would return. He never did." The hurt of all those years of unanswered prayers brought a bitter taste to her mouth. She scooped the diced crust into her hands and dropped it into the gruel, set her jaw to keep from saying more, but the anger she'd carried so long drove the words from her. "However, all of those prayers I prayed were not wasted. They taught me a valuable lesson."

"And that is?"

She stirred the softening bread into the gruel and threw a quick glance his direction. "Forgive me, Reverend, but the lesson I learned was that the God preachers, such as yourself, speak of as a 'loving father' who cares for us and watches over us does not exist. And, as I told you before, I learned it was a waste of time to pray."

He straightened and stepped toward her. "God gave man a free will, Miss Wright. He allows man to choose his own path." His voice, warm with compassion, flowed over her. "God would never *force* your father to do something against his will—that would go against His Word. But that does not negate the fact that God truly is a loving Father who cares for us and watches over us. And He does hear and answer prayer."

Woof!

She started and glanced over her shoulder. Happy trotted into the kitchen. Joshua, dressed in his hat and coat and holding the kitten in his arms, trailed behind. His brown eyes were overbright. Her heart sank.

"If you give me a moment to get my coat, Joshua, I'll go out with you to help keep Tickles corralled and out of that tree." Matthew started toward the kitchen door.

"I think you will have to take the animals out by yourself, Reverend." She shoved the pot of gruel back off the fire, hurried to Joshua and sank to her knees to touch his flushed cheek. "Joshua has a fever."

"I'll stop by again tomorrow to see your grandmother, Miss Karcher. Good afternoon." Matthew stepped outside, slapped his winter felt on his head, tugged the collar of his chesterfield up around the nape of his neck and strode through the snow toward his cutter.

He frowned and slowed his steps before he caused the mid-calf-high snow to fly over the top of his boots and dampen his pants. He always felt as if he were escaping when he left the Karcher home. Agnes was clearly not giving up on her matrimonial ambitions, and these daily visits to her grandmother were encouraging her pursuit.

He shot a glance toward the sky—or where the sky would be if it could be seen through the thick snowfall—pulled the small flask from his coat pocket, splashed alcohol onto his palm, then held the flask against his body with his elbow and scrubbed his hands together. He still had two calls to make for Dr. Palmer before he could go home and ease his worry. "Lord, please watch over Sally and Joshua. Please touch Sally with Your healing power, and make her well. And please touch Willa's heart, oh, God. Please make her aware of Your love and care for her, and draw her heart to You. I ask it in Your holy name, Lord. Amen."

Clover whickered and tossed her head, pulled his thoughts back to his present problem. "I know, girl. If this snow doesn't stop it's going to be hard going for you." He pulled on his gloves and shoved the flask back into his pocket. "I'll bet you wish you were back in the stable, don't you?"

He shook the mare's mane free of snow, then swiped his arm over her back to clear the piled flakes off her protective winter blanket. The bells attached to the blanket's hem tinkled merrily as his body brushed against them.

He paused at the sound, looked again at the falling

snow and imagined trotting down the country road with Willa close beside him in the small cutter, snowflakes clinging to her long lashes, and her blue-green eyes glowing with fun while a smile of pure pleasure curved her soft, full lips. The way she'd looked this morning when he opened the door.

Glory, but he'd wanted to take her in his arms and feel her cold lips warm beneath his, to taste of their sweetness...

He huffed a cloud of warm air, leaned into the cutter and scooped the snow off the floor, lifted the lap robe he'd used to cover the seat and dumped off the snow, then paused and eyed the narrow space. There would be room enough for all of them to take a ride, Willa beside him on the seat holding Sally on her lap, and Josh sitting on his and learning to handle the horse. And Happy and Tickles on the floor.

If God granted his prayer, next year he'd have to buy a sleigh to accommodate a growing family. But he'd keep the cutter for special rides alone with his bride. "Grant it, Lord! Grant it, I pray."

He tossed the lap robe back over the passenger side of the tufted leather seat, put his foot on the metal step, climbed in and picked up the reins. "Let's go, Clover. Let's get these calls made so I can go home and see if I can help make that prayer come true."

There were at least seventeen or eighteen inches of snow on the church roof. If it didn't stop snowing soon they would have close to two feet by morning.

Willa moved to the top of the porch steps and clapped her hands. "Come here, Happy. Let's go see Joshua."

The dog spun around toward her and came bounding

through the deep snow. He raced up the all-but-invisible steps, stopped beside her and shook, sending snow flying in every direction.

"Oh, Happy! Now see what you've done." She laughed, swiped the snow from her apron and opened the door. The dog dashed through the kitchen and thundered up the stairs.

She gave the potato soup she was keeping warm on the back of the stove a quick stir to make sure it wasn't sticking to the bottom of the pan and followed him.

The dog had curled up on the floor with his head resting on the pallet Matthew had made for Joshua in Sally's room, his soulful black eyes fastened on his sleeping master.

"Good boy, Happy." She leaned down and placed her hand on Joshua's forehead. He was still flushed and fevered the same as earlier, but his skin wasn't hot like Sally's.

She sighed and brushed a curl back off his forehead, touched a tiny bump with her fingertip. She pulled the oil lamp on the nightstand closer, went to her knees and used both hands to brush back all of his curls. There were small, pink bumps scattered along his hairline.

His eyes blinked, opened. He stared up at her. "Whatcha doing?"

There was no sense in evading the truth. He would know soon enough. She sat back on her heels and smiled. "I was looking at your chicken pox."

His eyes widened. "I got *chicken pox?* Really?"

"Really."

"I'm gonna have Uncle Matt tell Billy!"

She laughed and brushed his hair back into place. "It isn't a contest, Joshua."

"I know, but still—" He stopped, and that slow, lop-sided grin so like his uncle's slanted his rosy lips. "I guess that smelly stuff doesn't work after all."

"I guess not, Joshua."

There wasn't enough willpower in the world to stop her—not with him looking at her with that mischievous grin on his adorable face. She leaned forward and pulled him into her arms for a big hug.

"You need to drink some water, Sally."

The little girl's eyelids fluttered, stilled.

Willa slipped her arm beneath the child's small shoulders, lifted her to a sitting position and gave her a little shake. "Wake up, sweetie!"

Sally's eyes opened.

"Good girl. Now drink the water." She lifted her a little straighter and touched the cup to her fevered lips, coaxed a few swallows into her before she lowered her back to her pillow and let her sleep again.

A log on the fire hissed and snapped. She checked to make sure no cinder had popped out into the room, then wandered over to the window. It was getting late. Where was Matthew? Did he have lamps on his cutter? And what was she doing worrying about Ellen's intended? Though it was probably natural enough under the circumstances. And she should stop thinking of him as Matthew. It wasn't decent.

She frowned and returned to the bedside chair, sat and picked up her sewing. Her mother's hood had come together quickly. Quilting the lining had been painstaking work, but with so much idle time spent watching the children sleep, she'd finished it by suppertime. As soon as she finished the front edging on the hood she would be ready to add the ties.

Sally whimpered, turned onto her side and curled into a tight ball.

She studied the little girl's flushed face a moment, then resumed her sewing. She had done all she knew to do—all her mother had suggested. Why didn't Sally get better? Why hadn't she broken out with chicken pox as Joshua had? Was her sickness something else?

She thrust her sewing into the basket and rose to touch Sally's cheek. It was so hot! If only she could *help* her.

He truly is a loving Father.... He does hear and answer prayer....

Matthew's words slipped into her thoughts. She closed her mind to them. God didn't hear *her* prayers. *Please, God in heaven. Please make my papa come home so Mama will stop crying.* Over and over she had prayed that prayer. And her father had never returned.

But her mother had stopped crying.

She froze, astounded by the thought. Her mother had stopped crying. Why had she never thought of that before?

I cried because I didn't know how I was going to care for you. We were about to lose our home and I had nowhere to go, no way to earn a living.

The memory of her mother's words brought a new understanding. She had not known why her mother was crying, but God had. And He had answered her prayer. The certainty of that settled deep into her heart and spirit. Somehow, in a way she couldn't explain, she knew it was true.

And what Matthew had said about God not forcing

a man to do something against that man's own will—was that true also? Had she been wrong all these years in blaming God for what her father chose to do? And for what Thomas did?

She walked to the window and stared out into the darkness. She was a teacher. She had trained herself to look for solutions to problems, and she had absorbed enough biblical knowledge sitting in church to know that God had given man a free will. Preachers preached on it all the time. Choose! Choose! Choose!

Her heartbeat sped, yet everything inside her felt still…poised and waiting.

She wrapped her arms about her torso, closed her eyes and let the truth come. It wasn't only about choosing salvation. Freedom of will, of choice, applied to a person's every action. And her father had *chosen* to walk away.

"Forgive me, Almighty God. I've been wrong to blame You for what my papa chose to do of his own free will. Please forgive me. And thank You, Almighty God, for answering my prayer."

How clean, how *light* she felt after her whispered words. She smiled, walked to Sally's bed, sank to her knees, folded her hands and closed her eyes.

Chapter Twenty-One

Willa swirled her cloak around her shoulders and hurried toward the lean-to washroom, came to a dead halt at the sight of her mother sitting at the kitchen table. Dread squeezed her heart. "Are you taking sick, Mama?"

Her mother jerked up her head and rose from her chair. "No, I'm fine, Willa. I have something to tell you."

Something that would stop her mother from starting the laundry first thing in the morning? She couldn't imagine… She stopped fastening her cloak and stepped closer. "What is it?"

"I went to Cargrave's for laundry supplies yesterday and Mr. Hubble gave me a letter."

"A letter? For you, Mama?" Her mother never got letters. She stared at the folded sheet of paper her mother had drawn out of her apron pocket. *For any member of George Wright's family.* The boldly slanted words carried a sense of foreboding.

She took the offered missive in her hands and unfolded it, scanned the brief message.

I hereby testify that George Wright died of pneumonia caused by the grippe on October eighteenth, in the year of our lord, 1840. By my hand, Doctor Harold Tremont, Binghamton, New York.

Her papa was never coming home.

The finality of it crushed the little girl's hope she hadn't realized was still a part of her—a hope that had been buried under years of anger. She pushed away the sorrow for all that would never be, squared her shoulders and handed the letter back to her mother. "Well, now we know what has happened to Papa." She lifted her hands and fastened her cloak.

"Yes…" Her mother's hands covered hers. "Are you all right, Willa?"

She forced a smile. "I'm fine, Mama. Are you?" She studied her mother's face, found a sort of relieved peace in her green eyes.

"Yes, Willa. I am."

"I'm glad." She leaned forward and kissed her mother's cheek. "I have to hurry, Mama. I'm worried about Sally." She yanked up her hood and headed for the door.

"I've been praying for the little girl. The Lord will undertake."

She whipped around, stared agape. "You *pray,* Mama?"

"Well, of course, Willa. God is the only reason I've managed all of these years."

"My face itches."

"Mine, too."

What beautiful words. And what a beautiful sight. Willa looked from the small bumps and blisters on Joshua's forehead to the pink bumps on Sally's face and clenched her hands, fought to keep from turning into Matthew's arms and crying out her relief against his strong shoulder.

Joshua lifted his hands and scratched at his scalp.

"Oh, no! You mustn't scratch at the itch, Joshua. It will make it worse, and perhaps leave a scar."

A chuckle rumbled from Matthew.

She lifted her gaze up, met his. The look in his eyes mesmerized her. She stood immobile as he clasped his hands behind his back and leaned toward her.

"That is no way to stop Joshua from scratching, Miss Wright. Little boys look on scars as badges of honor. They wear them proudly."

His whispered words filled her mind. Everything in her wanted to be in his arms. She closed her eyes lest her emotion show in them. When had she fallen in love with Matthew Calvert?

She leaned down and snatched the small pouch of oatmeal. "I'll go downstairs and make you a poultice that will help the itching, Joshua. I'll make you one also, Sally. Please don't scratch. I'll be right back."

She sailed out the door and hurried down the stairs, tears stinging her eyes. *Stop feeling sorry for yourself! You knew Matthew and Ellen are about to announce their betrothal. How could you be so disloyal to your friend as to fall in love with her intended!*

She marched into the buttery, snatched up a piece of cheesecloth and hurried back to the work table.

The clack of bootheels against the hall floor warned her Matthew was headed for the kitchen.

She grabbed the oatmeal out of the tin cupboard and rushed to make the poultice. She did *not* want a repeat of the time they had spent alone in the kitchen yesterday. She folded the cheesecloth double, spooned oatmeal onto it then twisted the edges of the cheesecloth closed and wound the twine around the narrow neck. Her trembling fingers botched the tie. The twist loosened.

"Having trouble?"

Please don't help—

"You twist it tight and hold it. I'll tie it for you."

Don't tremble! She glared at her hands, held her breath as his fingers touched hers.

"I was relieved to learn Mr. Dibble is escorting you home at night." He crossed the ends of twine one over the other, pulled them taut. "I was concerned about your walking home alone."

She felt his gaze on her as if it were a touch. *Don't look at him.*

"Did you want a bow?"

She swallowed to ease the tightness in her throat. "A knot is fine."

"Mr. Dibble is a wonderful example of how God ministers to his children by using us as His hands and feet. As are you, by caring for my children."

She had to stop him—to make him leave before she broke down. "And you, Reverend? Did God use your hands to save me from Thomas?" It had the desired effect. His hands stilled, dropped away. She took a relieved breath.

"How did you know?"

"Sophia Sheffield mentioned that she saw you driving your buggy toward Olville the night Thomas disappeared and that no one could discover where you went, or what emergency had called you out that time of night. And when we took Mary home from school, I noticed your knuckles were bruised."

"I see."

She dropped the two pouches into a bowl, grabbed the teakettle from the back of the stove, poured warm water over them and put the teakettle back.

"I told you I would never let him hurt you."

His voice! So quiet. So...*caring.* And why wouldn't it be? He was a pastor. It was his job to care. She blinked the tears from her eyes and lifted her chin. "Yes, you did, but I didn't understand then. Thank you for...whatever you did that convinced Thomas to leave Pinewood."

She gathered her courage and looked at him. "And thank you for what you said yesterday. I realized later that you were right. God *had* answered my childhood prayer—my mother had stopped crying." She took a deep breath. "And you were also right about God giving man free will. All these years I've blamed God for my father abandoning us—until yesterday. I know now I was wrong. It was my father who *chose* to forsake us. And today I learned he will never return."

The tears came back, pooled in her eyes and overflowed. She wiped them from her cheeks. "Mama got a letter. My father is dead."

His eyes darkened and tiny gold flames sprang to life in their depths. "Willa..." He started around the table.

Her heart lurched, yearned to go into his arms. Foolish heart, wanting his pastoral desire to comfort her to be something more, longing for a man beloved by a friend. She shook her head.

Someone banged on the front door.

He stopped, his chest heaved as he drew in and blew out a breath. The person banged again—louder. He clenched his hands, turned and strode out of the kitchen.

She sagged against the table and swallowed hard to keep the tears from flowing.

Matthew's footsteps thudded against the hall floor. She straightened and faced the door.

He stepped back into the kitchen wearing his hat and coat, his face taut, unreadable. His gaze sought and held hers. "Grandmother Karcher has taken a turn for the worse. I have to go."

She nodded. "I'll tell Joshua and Sally. Please give my sympathies to the Karchers."

His mouth parted as if to speak, then closed. He nodded and left the room.

She listened to his footsteps fade, squeezed the excess water from the pouches and carried them upstairs.

"I'm home, Mama!"

Willa set down the basket, removed her cloak, hung it on its peg and turned. "Mr. Dibble!" Shock colored her voice.

She shifted her gaze to her mother. Gracious! What had happened to her mother? Her hair was in soft waves around her face instead of pulled straight back into a bun, and she was wearing her best dress with no apron. And Mr. Dibble's large, callused hands were resting on her narrow shoulders! "Mama…"

"I have news, Willa." Her mother fixed her gaze on her. "Mr. Dibble and I just returned from Olville. We're married."

"Mama!" She closed her gaping mouth, tried to make sense of her mother's words. "You're *married?*"

"I know it seems quick-like, Willa, but it's not."

"I've loved your mama since we were young."

David Dibble's words brought color rushing into her mother's cheeks. She'd never seen her mother blush.

"It's my fault we weren't married way back then, Willa. We planned to. Then David had to go help his granny settle up on the farm and all when his grandpa died, and your papa came to town." Her mother took a deep breath. "He favored me over the other girls and that turned me proud and wrongheaded and I married him."

Her mother held out her hands and stepped toward her. "I'll never be sorry 'cause I got you, Willa. And you're the best thing that ever happened to me. But my foolishness cost David and me all these years of being alone." Her mother's chin raised. "He's stayed faithful to his promise to me all these years, Willa. So I went this morning and told him about the letter and that I wasn't a married woman anymore. And he…" The color swept back into her mother's cheeks—she looked young and beautiful. Willa blinked away the tears that sprang to her eyes. "Well, after a bit, he said, 'I'll get the buggy hitched' and we drove to Olville and got married."

She rushed forward, hugged her mother and finally found her voice. "I'm happy for you, Mama, truly happy." She looked up at the man she'd known as a friend all of her life and smiled. "I guess I know now why you've been escorting me home, Mr. Dibble."

He grinned down at her. "Just take a thing for what it is, Willa."

She laughed and shook her head. "I shall, as soon as I get used to all of this news."

Her mother stepped back and looked up at her. "I been so full of my news, I didn't think to ask…why are you home early, Willa? Is the little girl better?"

"Yes, she is, Mama." She forced a brightness she was far from feeling into her voice. "And Bertha is back. I won't be tending Reverend Calvert's children any longer."

"I see." Her mother fixed a look on her, then nodded. "Well, we need to start gathering up things. I told Mr. Townsend I won't be doing laundry for the loggers and we'll be taking our things to David's house tonight."

Her whole life had turned upside down. Willa sat on the edge of the stripped bed, looked around the room she had called her own all of her years, and tried to think of what to do. She did not want to intrude on her mother's newfound happiness with Mr. Dibble. And how could she bear to watch Matthew and Ellen marry? How could she bear to teach Joshua and Sally when—

She got to her feet, went to the bedside table and opened her wooden box. Mr. Dibble would take care of her mother now. She could use the money she had been saving to make her mother a new cloak to go away. It would pay her stage fare to Buffalo, and once there she would get a job and build a new life.

She took the money from the box, placed it in her reticule, then checked to make sure she hadn't missed any coins. There was a folded piece of paper in the bottom of the box. Thomas's note.

Tears filmed her eyes and blurred the words. How could she ever have thought Thomas and Matthew were the same? How had she let her anger at her father's abandonment blind her to the truth of Matthew's goodness? Not that it would have mattered. Matthew loved Ellen.

She blinked, laid the note on the nightstand, snatched the curtain tie off the window and tied it around the large wicker basket that held her other dress and personal grooming items to hold the top on. She was ready.

She snatched up Thomas's note, looked around the empty room, grabbed the basket handle and walked into the sitting room.

"All done, Willa?"

"Yes. There's nothing left." She threw Thomas's note in the fire, watched it burst into flame, turn black and curl, then turn into ash. "But I'm not going to Mr. Dibble's with you tonight, Mama. Bertha is back, school is still closed and I'm free now. I'm going to Buffalo to see Callie. She's been asking me to come for a visit."

"But Willa—"

"I haven't time to talk about it, Mama." She leaned forward and kissed her mother's cheek. "If I hurry I can catch the trolley to Olville."

Chapter Twenty-Two

Matthew trudged up the stairs, weary to his bones. He'd spent a long day conducting Grandmother Karcher's funeral and interment, then sitting with Simon Pritchard who remained seriously ill.

He frowned and walked down the hall. The weariness came not from any physical exertion, but rather from the frustration and heaviness in his heart. Still, Dr. Palmer no longer needed his help, and the comfort calls to pray with the sick were coming to an end. The people living in Pinewood were hardy, it seemed. And those who were going to catch the grippe already had. The spread of the disease through the village had halted. He would soon be able to put an end to the frustration one way or the other.

He opened the door and stepped to Sally's bedside, gazed down at the small pock mark at her temple and felt again the rush of thankfulness for her healing and for Willa's loving care of his children.

Willa. His frustration. Her presence lingered in the house, and the need to go after her, to find out what had gone wrong and to make amends gnawed at him.

Every time he entered Sally's bedroom or the kitchen, memories of her assailed him and made his heart ache. He would never forget the way she had looked standing right here beside him the day Sally's chicken pox had erupted and her high fever had broken. They had shared the thankfulness, the joy of that moment when their gazes met, and he'd had to clasp his hands behind his back to keep from taking her in his arms.

How he wished he'd had the right, and that she were here with him now as his wife. "'Hope deferred maketh the heart sick: but *when* the desire cometh, *it is* a tree of life.' That's Your Word, Lord, and I stand on that promise. You have drawn Willa into Your arms, now draw her into mine, I pray."

Tickles's ears twitched his way at his whisper, one eye slitted open. He soothed the curled-up cat with a few strokes of its yellow fur, stepped to the fireplace, added wood and left the room.

The hall echoed with the tap of Willa's shoes and the brush of her long skirts against the floor. He frowned and stepped to Joshua's door. He'd been so certain that day that she returned his love. He'd seen it in her eyes and felt it in the tremble of her hands at his touch. And he *knew* she loved Joshua and Sally. So what had gone wrong? Why had she left town?

He stepped into Joshua's room. Happy jumped off the bed and came to him, tail wagging. He petted the dog and glanced at the fireplace. Red coals shimmered against the darkness. Tiny flames flickered around a blackened chunk of wood. He went to the woodbox, picked up an oak log with a thick burl that would burn until morning and added it to the fire.

The bed rustled. He turned, smiled at Joshua. "I thought you were asleep."

"I been praying." The boy's earnest gaze met his. "When will Miss Wright come back, Uncle Matt? Sally and me like Bertha an' all, but…well, Miss Wright sorta felt like a mama. Could she be our mama, Uncle Matt?"

He'd never known how a child's hurt could rend your heart in pieces, but he was learning fast. He sat on the edge of the bed. "I don't know, Josh. But God knows." He brushed his hand over the boy's curls and touched his cheek. "You keep praying. And I promise you, with God's help, I will do my very best to bring Miss Wright back."

Willa brushed snow from her cloak, opened the door of the Connors' brick home and stepped into the spacious entrance hall.

"Oh!" She glanced at Callie and the gentleman dressed in a gray double-breasted coat and holding a black felt top hat. He looked familiar, but Callie had so many beaus seeking to court her that it was hard to remember them. "Forgive me, I didn't mean to intrude."

"Not at all, Willa." Callie shot her a look. "I'm sure you remember Mr. Washington? He was just leaving."

She returned the man's polite nod and turned her back to give them privacy while she removed her cloak. She fussed and fumbled with the fastenings and ignored the words murmured in the man's low voice—the look Callie had given her meant Callie did not want her to leave them alone. At last the door opened and closed. She turned around at the click of the latch.

"Thank you, Willa." Callie sighed and led the way

into the family sitting room. "I thought he would *never* leave."

"And who could blame him?" She smiled at her friend. "You are simply stunning with those black curls and violet eyes, Callie Connor. I've known you all of my life, and I still find your beauty arresting."

"Please don't say such things, Willa. I get weary of hearing them." Callie slapped at the rows of flounces on her long silk skirt. "*And* of wearing these ridiculous fancy gowns. What I wouldn't give to wear a simple wool dress, don an apron and make some molasses ginger cookies. The kind Aunt Sophie makes."

"I'll loan you mine if you give me one of the cookies."

Callie laughed. "I would accept your kind offer if your gown would fit. But, alas, you're more slender than I."

"A bit, perhaps." She shook out her own plain skirt and sat on the settee in front of the fire, smiled as Callie floated onto the seat beside her—an accurate description given the amount of yardage in all those flounces.

"I'm so glad you came to visit, Willa. It's like having a bit of Pinewood here."

Callie's wistful tone sparked a longing in her for home. She closed off the thoughts before they could reach her hurting heart. She dare not think of Matthew and Joshua and Sally.

"Tell me what happened at your meeting with the school board." Callie's beautiful eyes were alight with interest.

She drew her thoughts from Pinewood to her new life.

"I believe it went well." She brushed a piece of lint off her wool skirt, fingered a spot that was thinning.

She had best find gainful employment soon. "The board members seemed satisfied with the answers I gave to their questions. And—" she looked at Callie and smiled "—I have an interview with the principal of the Swan Street school on Thursday."

"Willa, that's wonderful! Oh, I wish Mother and Father would let me do something besides parade around for the benefit of wealthy men!"

There was a rustle of sound at the doorway. She rose to leave, paused when Callie stood and gripped her arm.

"Good afternoon, Callie, I— Willa!" Surprise flitted across Ellen's face. "I didn't know you were in Buffalo." She rushed forward.

Ellen looked prettier than ever. Willa's heart sank, her stomach knotted. She wasn't ready to face Ellen, to talk about Matthew.

"What fun to have you here, Willa. It would be like old times if only Sadie were here also." Ellen gave her a quick hug, thrust her lower lip out in a pout. "I'm so sorry I haven't time to visit, but Mr. Boyd is calling on me this evening."

Mr. Boyd? A friend?

Ellen's blue eyes gleamed with excitement. "Callie, I simply had to come and thank you for gaining me an invitation to the Halseys' soiree. I'm so *thrilled* to be attending. I know if you want to be accepted into *the* social circuit, you simply *must* be included." Ellen smiled, glanced in the mirror over the mantel and fluffed her curls. "Mr. Boyd has already asked if he might be my dinner partner. Of course, I delayed answering in hope that Mr. Lodge will ask me." Ellen glanced her way. "Harold Lodge is the heir to the Lodge Shipping Line."

Mr. Boyd? Mr. Lodge? "And what of Reverend Calvert, Ellen?"

"Reverend Calvert?"

"Yes, the man you love." How those words hurt.

"Oh, poof!" Ellen made a pretty little moue. "Matthew is fine for Pinewood, Willa. He holds a position of honor in the village, and he is *exceedingly* handsome, but his calling as a pastor is too demanding. And his wards and those animals—"

"So, because of his *children* and their pets, you are not being faithful to him?" Her disgust leaked into her voice. "What of his love for you?" A band of pain tightened around her chest at the thought.

"The way Matthew loves is not good enough for me." Ellen's lower lip pouted out again. "Why, he wouldn't even stay home with me when I asked him. And after all the trouble I went to cooking his dinner and caring for his wards!"

She stared, caught a ragged breath. "You told me you were to be *betrothed*. That you would soon be *wed*."

Ellen's face flushed. "Well, I changed my mind. What good is a husband who is so concerned with others?" Ellen's smooth brow creased into a frown. "What's wrong with you, Willa? Why are you looking at me that way?"

She clenched her hands, lifted her chin, looked straight into Ellen's big, beautiful blue eyes and forced words out of her constricted throat. "Because your vanity and your selfishness have ruined my life."

Ellen's mouth gaped.

She turned her back and walked from the room.

"Whoa, Clover." Matthew draped the reins over the dashboard and climbed from the cutter. He grabbed the top lap robe from the pile on the passenger side of the seat, tossed it over his own place and snatched the tether weight off the floor.

The three men in the yard in front of Dibble's Livery looked his way, stood watching. He waved a hand in recognition, snubbed the tether rope to Clover's bridle and strode up the shoveled path to David Dibble's house, rehearsing the reasons why Willa's mother should tell him where she had gone. There was a horseshoe for a knocker. He banged it against the metal plate embedded in the door, rocked back on his heels and waited.

The men watched.

The door opened.

He gazed down at the slender woman looking up at him with eyes amazingly like Willa's, only green, and whipped off his hat. "Mrs. Dibble?"

"Yes?"

"I'm Reverend Calvert. I've come to inquire about Willa."

Her gaze locked on his, her head tilted and her lips pursed. "About time, I'd say."

He blinked, taken aback by her unexpected remark, then smiled and met her gaze full on.

Her lips curved into an answering smile. "Well, I can see why my daughter fell in love with you."

His breath gusted out in a gray cloud.

She laughed, stepped back and pulled the door open wider. "No need to stand out in the cold, Reverend. Come in where it's warm so we can talk."

"Willa, you have to go back to Pinewood." Callie gave her an earnest look. "It's the only sensible thing to do. If Reverend Calvert is half as wonderful as you say he is, he'll understand."

She shook her head and moved closer to the fire seeking warmth. She hadn't stopped shivering since Ellen's visit, and she was terribly afraid her inner cold was caused by her anger with her friend.

"And what do I say to him, Callie? I'm sorry, Reverend. I abandoned your children and ran like a coward because I'm in love with you?" She caught her breath at her spoken admission.

"It would probably work."

Her lips twitched at Callie's wry tone. She smiled, gulped and burst into tears. "Oh, Callie! He'd probably think me *mad*." She sank into a nearby chair and covered her face with her hands. "I don't know how Matthew feels about me. Just because Ellen lied about his feelings for her doesn't mean he cares for me. I— I thought perhaps— I mean, the way he looked at me and spoke my name was— Oh, I'm being pathetic!"

She lifted her head and wiped the moisture from her cheeks. "What I saw in Matthew Calvert's eyes was most likely nothing more than gratitude for my care of his children. I must stop this foolishness and concentrate on building my new life here in Buffalo."

Matthew took the reins in one hand, lifted the other arm and blew warm air into the cuff of his leather glove to warm his fingers. He wiggled his toes and clacked his feet together beneath the lap robe that covered them, relaxed his hunched shoulders and drew his head into the robe draped around his shoulders to protect his ears from the biting cold.

The tinkle of bells sounded clear on the night air. He glanced over his shoulder at the large sleigh drawing close behind him, turned and snapped the reins to urge Clover to pick up her pace.

It wasn't far now. He'd soon be in Dunkirk where Clover could feast on some grain and have a well-deserved rest in the stables at the hotel while he slept away what remained of the night.

Tomorrow.

The word jolted through him. Tomorrow he was going to see Willa. And, somehow, in spite of Ellen's lies about his intentions, he was going to convince her of his love and bring her home as his bride.

He glanced up at the moonlit sky and sent the prayer winging. *"'Hope deferred maketh the heart sick: but when the desire cometh, it is a tree of life.' Grant this my hope and prayer, oh Lord. Grant it, and turn it into a blessed new life for all of us, I pray. Amen."*

Chapter Twenty-Three

Willa sighed, set aside the book she was pretending to read and rose. She really wasn't in the mood to rescue Callie from another of her gentleman callers, but she would answer her friend's summons and go and intrude on their privacy and stay until the man got disgusted and left. Hopefully, this time it wouldn't take long.

She shook her head and hurried down the hall from the library to the formal sitting room where Callie received her suitors. How ill-mannered these wealthy city men must find Callie's poor country friend. Well, so be it.

She paused outside the door to catch her breath, then pasted a smile on her face and swept into the sitting room. "Callie, dear, I simply must—"

Her heart lurched, stopped. "Matthew!" She stared, her senses reeling. "What—" The blood drained from her face. She pressed her hand to her chest to stop her heart's sudden wild pounding. "Sally…"

"No, Willa! Sally is fine and so is Joshua." He moved toward her. "I'm sorry if I frightened you."

She nodded, closed her eyes and took a calming

breath. "I'm only glad—" She stopped, opened her eyes and stared at him. "How did you find me?"

"Your mother told me where you were." He took another step toward her.

"My *mother?*" She slipped behind an upholstered chair. She felt safer with something solid between them. "I don't understand. You don't know Mama. How— I mean, why—" She clamped her lips together, tried to order her jumbled thoughts.

"I heard you had left town and I called on your mother to ask where you were." He took another step, locked his gaze on hers.

His eyes! Her heart started its wild pounding again.

"You see, I wanted to tell you that until the day I walked into the Oak Street schoolhouse with Joshua and Sally, I had never met a woman who drew my heart."

He came around the chair. Her mouth went dry.

"But there you were, so neat and trim and prim and proper. And when I looked into your eyes—"

He lifted his hand, cupped the side of her face and brushed his thumb along her cheekbone. Her knees went weak.

"Your beautiful, blue-green eyes..."

He lowered his head and his breath touched her cheek. She held hers...waited.

"I fell in love with you."

His lips touched hers, soft...gentle...questing... She slipped her arms around his neck, went on tiptoe and pressed her parted lips against his in answer. His arms tightened, his lips parted and he claimed her mouth fully. Time and place fell away.

At last Matthew lifted his head, drew in a ragged breath. She laid her head against his chest, her breathing unsteady, her heart stumbling to find its rhythm. His heart thudded beneath her ear. Joy flooded her eyes with tears.

His finger slid beneath her chin, tilted her head up until their gazes met...held.

"I love you, Willa. I'm not a rich man, but I have wealth enough to ensure you comfort and freedom from want. And I have two adorable children who want you for their mother almost as much as I want you for my wife. Will you marry us?" His voice, rich and deep and warm, flowed over her like a caress, saying the words she'd so longed to hear.

She blinked away the tears, touched his cheek with her hand. "I don't care about wealth, Matthew. All I need to make me secure is your love. I love you. And I love Joshua and Sally." Warmth spread along her cheek-bones. "I want very much to be your wife and to be their mother."

He sucked in another ragged breath and claimed her lips in a kiss that promised forever.

"See, Sally. I told you she's our mama now. That's what Papa used to do to Mama."

Joshua?

Joshua! And *Sally.* She stiffened, jerked back as far as Matthew's arms would allow.

"Does that mean we can call you gramma and grampa now?"

"It surely does, Sally."

"Mama!" She twisted around in Matthew's arms, stared at her mother and David Dibble and Joshua and Sally—and Callie beside them, laughing. "What—How—"

Matthew chuckled and drew her back against him.

"David brought them along in his sleigh to attend our wedding—" his mouth slanted in that lopsided grin that made her heart stop and her stomach flutter "—just in case you said yes."

Her mother smiled, came to her and touched her cheek. "And after you're wed, David and I will take our new grandchildren home and care for them while you and Matthew spend a few days here in Buffalo."

"And Happy."

"And Tickles."

David Dibble chuckled. "Looks like we're gonna have a lively house for a few days."

Her mother laughed and shook her head. "It does indeed." She walked back, corralled Joshua and Sally with a hand on each of their small backs and started out the door. "Come along now, you two. We need to get your coats and hats on for the ride to the church."

"The church?" She looked at Matthew, got another lopsided, stomach-fluttering grin.

"I wanted everything to be ready—just in case. So I talked with a preacher on my way here. He's waiting to perform the ceremony that will join us forever." He gave her another lingering kiss, then took a deep breath and tucked her hand in his arm. "Let's go get married, Miss Wright."

* * * * *

WE HOPE YOU ENJOYED
THIS BOOK FROM

LOVE INSPIRED
INSPIRATIONAL ROMANCE

Uplifting stories of faith, forgiveness and hope.

Fall in love with stories where faith helps
guide you through life's challenges, and discover
the promise of a new beginning.

6 NEW BOOKS AVAILABLE EVERY MONTH!

"I am so sorry," Daisy told Joe as they walked down the sidewalk together.

The sun had come out and it was warm. The kind of day that made her long for spring.

"I don't know that I need an apology," Joe told her. "But an explanation would be a good start."

She shook her head. "I saw you sitting with your family, and I knew how I'd feel. Ambushed."

"I could have handled it. Now I'm engaged." He tossed her a dimpled grin. "What am I supposed to tell them when I don't have a wedding?"

"I got tired of your smug attitude and left you at the altar?" she asked, half teasing. "Where are we walking to?"

"I'm not sure. I guess the park."

"The park it is," she told him.

Daisy smiled down at the stroller. Myra and Miriam belonged with their mother, Lindsey. Daisy got to love them for a short time and hoped that she'd made a difference.

"It'll be hard to let them go," Joe said.

"It will be," Daisy admitted. "I think they'll go home after New Year's."

"That's pretty soon."

"It is. We have a court date next week."

"I'm sorry," Joe said, reaching for her hand and giving it a light squeeze.

"None of that has anything to do with what I've done to your life. I've complicated things. I'm sorry. You can tell your parents I lost my mind for a few minutes. Tell them I have a horrible sense of humor and that we aren't even friends. Tell them I wanted to make your life difficult."

"Which one is true?" he asked.

"Maybe a combination," she answered. "I *do* have a horrible sense of humor. I *did* want to mess with you."

"And the part about us not being friends?"

"Honestly, I don't know what we are."

"I'll take friendship," he told her. "Don't worry, Daisy, I'm not holding you to this proposal."

She laughed and so did he.

"Good thing. The last thing I want is a real fiancé."

"I know I'm not the most handsome guy, but I'm a decent catch," he said.

She ignored the comment about his looks. The last thing she wanted to admit was that when he smiled, she forgot herself just a little.

Don't miss
The Rancher's Holiday Arrangement *by Brenda Minton,*
available November 2020 wherever
Love Inspired books and ebooks are sold.

LoveInspired.com

LIEXP1120

LOVE INSPIRED

INSPIRATIONAL ROMANCE

UPLIFTING STORIES OF FAITH, FORGIVENESS AND HOPE.

———————————

Join our social communities to connect with other readers who share your love!

Sign up for the Love Inspired newsletter at **LoveInspired.com** to be the first to find out about upcoming titles, special promotions and exclusive content.

———————————

CONNECT WITH US AT:

f Facebook.com/LoveInspiredBooks

🐦 Twitter.com/LoveInspiredBks

Facebook.com/groups/HarlequinConnection

HARLEQUIN

Heartfelt or suspenseful, inspiring or passionate, Harlequin has your happily-ever-after.

With new books published every month, you are sure to find the satisfying escape you know you deserve.